I0652488

GROWN WISE

LIMINAL MYSTERIES
BOOK ONE

CELIA LAKE

Copyright © 2025 by Celia Lake

All rights reserved.

No part of this book may be reproduced in any form or by any electronic or mechanical means, including information storage and retrieval systems, without written permission from the author, except for the use of brief quotations in a book review.

Cover design by <u>Augusta Scarlett</u>.

Human-made (no generative AI used in writing, editing, or cover design). Without in any way limiting the author's exclusive rights under copyright, any use of this publication to "train" generative artificial intelligence (AI) technologies to generate text is expressly prohibited. The author reserves all rights to license uses of this work for generative AI training and development of machine learning language models

 Formatted with Vellum

CHAPTER I

JUNE 18TH AT ARUNDEL, WEST SUSSEX

"Ursula, do you have that list handy?" Uncle Garin didn't look over at her. He was busy running one finger down the notes in front of him.

"Of course, Uncle." Naturally, every single piece of paper she'd brought with her for this meeting was properly indexed. A moment's murmur of a charm let her find the proper one by touch. Mum had taught her the indexing charms early— when Ursula was about ten— and these days, it was entirely second nature. She glanced at it once to confirm, then added, "Updated last Thursday. You said you had some further details for us, Lambert?"

It was the monthly meeting about the estate, the tenants, and the various larger scale household needs. Ursula had begun sitting in on them last winter, once she'd settled into her current life properly. Less than a year ago, she'd moved to Arundel, the family estate and the heart of West Sussex's land magic. Uncle Garin had formally named her as his Heir much earlier than expected, only a month later.

Then there was the beginning of her own apprenticeship in Incantation, and the various other events of a life. Now, though, she no longer found Lambert Knox quite so intimidating. And he'd confided, that spring, that having her at the meetings helped them go better.

Lambert had praised her knack for organisation and having the right file at hand. It was not a knack, not really. It was practice and repetition. Dad had taught her how to return to a proper resting place, and Mum had taught her that filing never got easier if left for later. Both of them had taught her a great deal more than that, naturally, but right now, the filing and piles of records were the relevant part.

For all the meetings had become more comfortable, this one had some new considerations. There were traditions for summer solstice, gifts for the tenants and the farms that had a particular connection to the estate. Ursula had pored over the older records for the past six weeks. She knew what the usual range was, allowing for changes in what money actually bought in a given year. Sometimes they weren't money, not directly, but charmwork or bringing in someone to make sure all the chimneys drew perfectly. Or maybe it involved a particular connection for the breeding of sheep, pigs, or cows. Sometimes also for hounds, but apparently not since well before the war for some reason.

Lambert cleared his throat. "Yes. It looks as if the Agriculture Act will move forward, likely in the next fortnight. Ursula, you're familiar with it?"

Uncle Garin's mouth twitched. Ursula caught that, because he'd tried the same thing on her just after their last meeting with Lambert a month ago. He didn't say a word, just waited.

"Of course. I do make a point of keeping up with the papers and the current discussion of matters that might affect the estate." It was a tricky matter to balance. The land they were on anchored the land magic for West Sussex, and they had their own duties and obligations and delights as a result. Those were due to Albion's own government or the Council, depending on the specifics. But the exact same land was also covered by the United Kingdom's laws, set for those without magic, which meant the Agriculture Act would also be in play.

In practice, keeping up meant that Ursula set aside an hour every day to read two papers, the morning edition of the Trellech Moon and the Times of London. She had also added a number of items to a list that Mum kept with a clipping service in Trellech. The clipping service also helpfully passed along various relevant comments from other sources.

Now she smiled. "In brief, based on discussion in various of the agricultural committees to date— you don't need the citations, do you?" Lambert shook his head, and Ursula sailed on. "The proposal would guarantee minimum prices, reduce fluctuations and, one hopes, allow for greater stability in the agricultural industries. The goal is to move away from the need for rationing and support more sustainable production of food, agricultural goods, and related materials."

Lambert had not quite heard her do that before

and he blinked. Before he could say anything further, she added, "I passed this along to Uncle Garin last week. I gather there is also discussion in the Courts of Equity and the Ministry of Materia to propose something similar for those plants grown for alchemical and other magical purposes. There's a working list being circulated now for comment from the usual suppliers. Uncle Garin's nearly— pardon, has finished with his notes on that." She caught the slight shift of her uncle's face at the last sentence and made an obvious but prompt course correction.

Uncle Garin snorted once, sliding a piece of paper over to Lambert. "To be fair, Ursula, I only finished it this morning. The formal response went through the portal at noon. A copy for your records, Lambert."

Lambert seemed amused now. "Thank you, Lord Fortier. The other part, Ursula, if you don't mind? I'm curious how you put this one, and whether there's any phrasing I can borrow for discussion with others."

"Surely you can find more adept framing elsewhere." Ursula was good for her age. But she was not quite twenty, and she knew knew plenty of people who were vastly better. Uncle Garin, for one, and Uncle Alexander, and honestly, Mum would probably do great at this. Or her cousin Aspen, who had come back from being a Land Girl with speeches stored up about this sort of problem, and who made them both emphatically and thoroughly.

"The second goal of the act is to provide security of tenure to tenant farmers, extending for life. Again, Albion has some considerations about continuing that to sons or daughters who have an ongoing connection with the land. Born, raised, living, working the land in some form, as I heard it put." Ursula glanced at the file in front of Uncle Garin. "All our tenants have been in place since before the war. There are no objections here. Reading back through some of the older records, back a couple of generations, I see that's been a priority."

"I gather Lord Vauquelin had quite a lot of comment about that, actually. Stability of the land being anchored by having the same people working it, when possible. He had quite a few theories that it made some of the ritual work sing. And of course, families have their own traditions, larger and smaller, that flourish in repetition." Lambert said it, then glanced at Uncle Garin, as if not sure if he'd overstepped.

Uncle Garin waved a hand, in a more agreeable mood than Ursula had expected of this meeting. "Grand-père was very thorough about that, I gather, though I never had the opportunity to hear it myself." Lord Vauquelin, Ursula's great-grandfather, had died when Uncle Garin was only about four. "No, I agree. It seems worthwhile on a number of fronts. I had a few specific points to raise in response, but nothing that would turn me against the measure, either in London or in Trellech."

"Very well. I'll keep you both informed, shall I, as I hear more? I expect progress to be fairly brisk at this point." Lambert tapped one sheet of paper back into the stack. "That brings us to the usual solstice gifts to the tenants and others connected to the estate directly."

Here, Ursula got in before Uncle Garin could say

anything. "I was wondering if we might be a tad more generous this year than usual. Given the likely passing of the Agriculture Act, the ongoing demands of rationing, and a truly awful spring. Our investments have done well, but I know a number of the farms have been struggling." The winter and spring had been full of water coming down, and then floods, destroying much of the grain crop in the fields. Magic had been some help with that, but not nearly enough.

Uncle Garin opened his mouth, closed it, and then shifted slightly to peer at her. "Did you have an amount in mind?"

"Of course, uncle. The chart here, based on your records from the last decade, with considerations for those supporting older relatives, veterans unable to work or work as fully as they did before the war, and so on." Turning someone's life into a number was entirely cruel, but Ursula had set the base deliberately, and Uncle Garin would know she'd done it, too.

Uncle Garin took the sheet, scanning it, then he just nodded once. "I was going to make a similar proposal, actually, though your maths lay it out more clearly. Lambert, can you make that happen in the next day or two? The funds are on account with the Scali already."

Lambert looked startled, then he got the look on his face that meant he was recalculating several things. "Yes, I can rearrange tomorrow morning, and of course I'd expected we'd be making at least the usual rounds. Ah. You've marked the ones you wish to visit yourself. Excellent. I know the coming fortnight will be busy."

"The Council rites on Sunday, and then the Midsummer Faire. We'll have the usual booth, of course. That's all been scheduled for months. I've taken a tent by the pavo field this year." Uncle Garin inclined his head once. "Given that Leo will be playing."

Ursula's younger brother had made a fine showing in his first pavo match earlier in the month. Ursula hadn't known that Uncle Garin had taken the tent, though, and she wondered how he had managed it. The field took up quite a lot of space at the Faire, but the spots around its perimeter were quite in demand so that people could easily watch the games, with their galloping horses and clever puzzles. Uncle Garin would not descend to a bribe, of course, but several layers of favour trading were entirely possible.

Ursula said cheerfully, "I have a number of plans for both the Council rites and the Faire, of course. But they definitely include watching Leo and his friends play." Her shoulder twitched. "Uncle Garin has said it's fine to have Leo out here for a couple of nights, so we can catch up. He's had an eventful spring, and I've heard about it, but not nearly all the details I want to."

Lambert nodded, and turned his attention to the account book in front of him, leaving Ursula and Garin to wait for him to check through the figures. Uncle Garin pulled out an article he was reading. Ursula would have to ask him about it at their usual supper tomorrow, and then figure out what it meant.

Normally, Ursula would make a note to ask Uncle Jehan about it at their usual monthly chat. That was, for one part, cramming enough alchemical knowledge into Ursula's head to keep up with Uncle Garin's research. The other part was keeping up with the various social battles of Fox House, where Uncle Jehan was Head. But Schola was on hols. Whatever time she might spend chatting with Uncle Jehan at the Faire would be against a background of a dozen other things to do or see or say.

Maybe he'd be willing to come round for supper here at Arundel during hols. He'd be interested in the gardens, of course, and the greenhouses. Both had a number of plants much in demand for alchemical work. Uncle Garin rarely bothered with anything purely decorative.

The silence left Ursula time to go through her current plans for the coming weeks again in her head. Most importantly, she wanted to hear a great deal more about Leo's adventures and his induction into one of Schola's secret societies. She had not, or not yet, told him about her own affiliations, but she planned to do that as soon as she and Leo had reasonable time alone to talk about it. After the Midsummer Faire. She didn't want to unsettle Leo before the big pavo match.

Uncle Garin didn't know. She'd tell Mum and Dad after Leo, though she was sure they had guesses. Mum and Dad were many things, but they'd both been teaching at Schola for more than two decades, and Ursula knew not much got past them anymore. Especially when it involved their children.

But before she got to a chat with Leo, she had two more days of her apprenticeship work, then the fortnight's break for solstice and the Faire. There was the

Faire itself. She wanted to spend time with a number of her friends while everyone had a bit more leisure.

Uncle Garin was certainly going to press her a bit more about having an eye to marriage. Ursula had no desire to become Lady of the land anytime soon, but she understood that she'd need to find someone to marry in. Uncle Garin had his eye on a number of second sons of current Lords, none of whom appealed to her. The trick would be getting Uncle Garin to agree, and then finding someone she did like, at least in potential.

On the happier end of matchmaking, she'd promised to have supper during the Faire with Olive and Neville. She'd nudged them together that spring. Matters seemed to be going swimmingly for both of them. If they wanted to gush about their mutual delight at Ursula over a good meal, that was a lovely thing.

And of course, circling back to Leo and his friends, she'd heard more than a handful of bits of gossip about various others who had just finished at Schola or who were older students. Ursula fancied herself a touch of a largely benevolent figure of power, blessing some and reminding others why manners and kindness were sensible aspirations. Kindness mattered more.

She knew of several people who'd been cruel and without reason, and if she had a chance to make a point to them, oh, she intended to. Lowenna Ritt, for one, Xenophon Anders-Whyte, possibly Uther Farrell. She'd heard more than enough from Susanna to want to give Cyrene Hall a little to think about.

Beyond that, it was the expected business of

strengthening her own connections among other Heirs and likely Heirs in her generation, and establishing herself as someone distinct from Uncle Garin. He cast a long shadow, and working her way into her own orbit was going to take a bit of steady, careful work. That was fine.

Most of those plans were more on the scale of the next decade. She could and would be patient. As she would be now. Next time she'd remember to bring some of her own reading. When Lambert was done, Uncle Garin would walk him out, and Ursula could have her own supper and dive into her reading and preparation for tomorrow's learning.

CHAPTER 2
JUNE 22ND AT THE COUNCIL KEEP

Edmund steered Ursula deftly between two other sets of dancers. The current song was faster and more energetic than most dances at the Council rites, but not nearly as much as it could be. Decorum prevailed, certainly no form of dance younger than three decades was permitted or approved of. Edmund did venture to let her spin, as they got away from others, and Ursula let herself fall into the pleasure of the movement. Her skirt twirled out, then settled back against her legs. She was glad Mum had let her remake this dress. The silk was scrumptious.

As they came back together again and the song began to wind down, he spoke in her ear. "The password for the Hewitts is grimble."

Ursula blinked at him. Oh, he'd told her last winter, that there was a summer tradition. At winter solstice, far too many people had vigil traditions. No one was up for a party after the formal rites. And there were many other formal gatherings between solstice and New Year's.

But in the summer, everyone took a bit of a holiday and the primary competition on the schedule was the Midsummer Faire. The younger set of Lords and Heirs and the various women of their age— and the occasional Lady in her own right— got together somewhere. Someone would host a more free-spirited party than their elders entirely approved of. "You're the one arranging it?"

"Mmhmm." Edmund grinned, looking very pleased. He was young to have that sort of responsibility, she thought; he was almost twenty-one, to her nineteen and a half. On the other hand, he'd done due and proper war service before going up to Oxford last autumn, and he'd been Heir to Lord Carillon since he'd turned twelve. She rather thought the Hewitts had good sense to pick him. "And if you want an escort to keep people off you, I'm glad to volunteer. Usual terms. Though there are a number of others coming who'll amuse. Helios Thanet. Olive and Neville, of course, but you likely knew that."

That made her smile more broadly. Uncle Garin and Edmund's father studiously avoided being anywhere near each other if they could help it. That, and he was Heir in his own right, and loved his land, and wouldn't marry into Arundel. It made Edmund quite safe to dance with. She was, apparently, equally safe for him. "Anyone you need a shield from?"

"The curse of being eligible." Edmund sighed, and Ursula considered the people she could see, taking in the people who were watching them from a distance with various expressions of desire or annoyance.

"Oh, I'd love a chance to frustrate Lowenna Ritt." That young woman looked very displeased Edmund was paying attention to Ursula. "Did Ros tell you why?" She'd heard the story from Leo, eventually, and she expected Edmund's youngest sister might have passed that tidbit along too. Lowenna had been nasty to one of Leo and Ros's friends, son of the stable head at Ytene. The Carillons took care of their people. Quietly, but indisputably, as well as they tended their horses. It was one of the first things anyone sensible noticed about them.

Edmund's smile turned sharper. "I'll leave that in your hands, then, shall I? Or rather, hold myself in reserve, in case she's one of those people who needs more than one lesson."

"Oh, I'm sure she is. Well down at the bottom of the class on average," Ursula said. "She's not invited, though? The Hewitts didn't, I mean?"

"They asked my advice on the invitation list. Lystra Hewitt's looking forward to getting to know you better, to let you prepare. She's quite curious about your matrimonial pairings thus far. Especially Olive. She's sure they'll announce a betrothal before the end of the summer." Edmund sent Ursula into one more spin. Then the music ended, and they linked arms to walk back and fetch a drink. "Meet at the portal at one, shall we?"

"Excellent." Ursula took in the range of people who were watching, then kissed Edmund on the cheek, just once, the way she'd kiss Leo. Except Edmund took it in stride, as laying out a pattern for other people to snare themselves in. Leo wouldn't have.

It took her a dance to find her brother. He'd been hanging around the edge of the dancing, watching people with his friends. Ros and Avigail had been with him for a bit, but they'd both disappeared, leaving him on his own. Avigail was dancing with her older brother, and Ros with her father. As Ursula offered her hand to Leo, she said quietly, "You may let Ros and Avigail know, if you like, that Edmund and I have discussed Lowenna Ritt."

Leo was quick on the uptake, and she just got a grin back. He'd ask what they'd done after it was over. She knew that. Leo did better with rules and structure, but he understood she had an unconventional relationship with such things. They moved into an easier dance, a waltz, but she was pleasantly surprised by his skill this time round. He'd improved quite a lot since the winter. As the music ended, she said, "Tell Dad your dancing's improved, if I don't get a chance? You're more agile than you were."

It got her brother flushing with pleasure, and she watched him go back to his friends while casting around for her next partner. This time it was Tiberius Warren, mostly to get him away from his grand-mother for a little. He'd grown another two inches since she'd last seen him close up, which made the height difference less awkward.

Silvia Warren was Head of the Council and had been since last year. Ursula felt the pressure it put on Tiberius was unkind. It was also unkind to Uncle Claudio, his father and Ursula's uncle by courtesy, but Ursula could do less about that. Tiberius was actually a little more relaxed than she'd expected, though she wasn't sure what to say about it. She could tease Leo. Tiberius would worry he'd done something wrong.

"Xenophon Anders-White is looking right at you." The comment came quietly, just as he swung her around so she could get a look for herself. "What is your pleasure, please?"

"Do let's end up on the other side of the room. Would near your father be a problem? I want a word with him at some point tonight." She would absolutely take the opportunity to see Tiberius's reaction to that. She'd had an interesting conversation with Uncle Claudio in March, and she hoped it was bearing fruit.

Tiberius's hand tightened on her back for a moment, then relaxed. "I moved into rooms at Auctoritas last week. He said you'd suggested it, when we were having a walk in the garden. My having my own space, I mean."

Ursula snorted. "So it's going well enough he's admitting a thing or two to you. How do you feel about that?" She saw the shift in his expression before he made any words happen, and quickly added. "I'm glad you're trying it. It has to be hard figuring that out."

Ursula knew many people whose families had been shaped in odd ways by the war, but she thought the space between Tiberius and Uncle Claudio was one of the hardest. Uncle Claudio and his wife were distant from each other, for all Uncle Claudio had wanted to spend time with his children. Then the war had made that harder— Uncle Claudio had been posted in places that allowed little leave, whatever he'd been doing. He'd been doing complicated magical work on the Continent as the war finished. And a whole new apprenticeship, to boot, which wasn't at all usual for someone in his late thirties.

Tiberius nodded, but then he guided them close enough to where he could pause, escort her to Uncle Claudio, and present her with a slight bow. Whatever else anyone said about the Warrens, they had excellent manners, all of them, with attention to each small detail. Ursula beamed at her uncle and chatted about a few minor things - the flowers, the decorative charms, and such - until she was sure Tiberius had disappeared into the crowd. "Uncle Claudio, Tiberius said you told him. It's going all right?"

"For only having had a week, yes. We're going out to visit Fairlight for a few days together after the Faire. A few plans during. The sort where we will have something to talk about, in case we can't think of anything on our own." He looked off after Tiberius. "I suppose you're going off after this to other parties. It's not so long since I was invited to some of those."

"You are not yet old and decrepit, Uncle Claudio. I leave that to people older than Uncle Garin." The way she put it, primly and with an utterly straight face, made him splutter. She counted that as a point to her for the evening. Then she said, quickly, "There's Mum and Mabyn. I wanted a word with her. Do you mind terribly?"

"Imp." Uncle Claudio waved her off. "I'll see you at the Faire. I'll be at the pavo matches for Leo, of course, whatever else happens." She laughed and spun off towards Mum, who was easy to spot in a crowd of people mostly not wearing her emerald green. Or the familial emerald necklace that went well with it. Mabyn, beside her, was glancing around at the assembled people. Ursula brought herself to a stop. "Mum, Magistra Teague."

"You needn't, Ursula." Mabyn Teague waved it off. She'd retired from the Council last year, but the challenge to fill her seat had been unsuccessful, and Ursula knew that was a worry. "You look lovely, and as if you have a dance card filled with precisely who you choose."

"Was it obvious? I'll have to see to that," Ursula shot right back. "Actually, Mabyn, I wanted to warn you that there's a movement to get you to do something for the Albion Inheritance. Cyrene Hall's mother, we think, several others of that set. The sort of tedious drudgery where other people get all the pleasant bits and will argue with every choice you make."

"I have more than put in my time with that sort of problem, thank you very much." Mabyn gestured at the head of the hall, where the Council presided in formal circumstances. "Do I need to invent a terribly obscure research project to avoid it, or do you think there's some other option?"

Mum spoke before Ursula could, "You needn't invent, surely. By my count, you've got at least three on tap."

"True. It's which ones I'm willing to talk about that's a trick." Mabyn shook her head. "Thank you for the warning, Ursula, it's kind."

"That, and I like you. But also it's much easier on everyone else, including me, if I give you advance notice," Ursula said cheerfully. "Fox House principle." Their shared Schola House was pragmatic about the trade of favours and alliances. While Mabyn had never made a show of it, Ursula knew the level of her skill there. She'd been on the Council for decades, and dealt with Uncle Garin and Aunt Livia's frequent arguments in the process. Along with all the rest of it. Mabyn had more than earned her retirement.

Before anyone could say anything further, there was a movement behind her, and Ursula wheeled around, skirt flaring, to find Dad there. "May I have this dance with my remarkably grown-up looking daughter?" He offered his hand. "I'd say tell me if anyone bothers you, but I suspect you have that in hand."

"Also, Dad, very few of them are worth bothering you with." She took his hand and let him escort her back to the dance floor. They slid into the movement of the music for a little. Dad was a duellist, by preference, but the skills crossed over rather nicely, as she'd noticed earlier with Leo. Dad was enjoying himself, she could tell by the way he was moving, just delighting in the physicality of it. She let him swing her out, spiralled back, then added, "Make you sure you dance with Mum. She likes you in this mood."

He laughed. "We've had two already. She wanted to catch her breath. Don't you worry about that." He glanced around. "Are you deliberately irritating Garin by only dancing with people who obviously aren't suitable marital prospects for you?"

"Have I been unsubtle, Dad? Surely not. I danced with Tiberius. And Uther Farrell was interested in a dance later. I've nothing against him. Not the sort of family I want to marry into, though." His father descended from the Teagues on one side. That was Mabyn's family by marriage, and Ursula knew enough she didn't want to marry into that. On the other side, he was descended from the Altons. She certainly didn't want Lady Alton as grandmother-in-law.

Dad snorted. "You know what you're doing. Garin's keeping count, but you knew he would." When the music ended, he kissed her cheek. "We'll see you at the Faire if you're busy the rest of the night." Then someone was tapping on his shoulder, asking a question— a parent of one of his particular duelling students— and Ursula let him focus on that. She set off on a circuit of the hall, looking for her next target. Uncle Garin had agreed to host a late summer garden party at Arundel, and she was considering the best guest list.

CHAPTER 3
JULY 1ST AT A FARM IN SUSSEX

"There you go, Jim." Little Fred put a mug down in front of him, a pint of strong beer. He'd more than earned it today. Jim had got through fifty-five sheep, an excellent day's work. He'd been lucky to get in with Captain Will's sheep shearing gang.

The rest of the men on it knew their work. There was plenty of friendly competition; Jim had lost out to their best man again today. But there was no shame in that. Tom the Brown had done a full three score, an excellent count. They'd run out of sheep, in fact, or both totals might be a tad higher.

"Ta." He nodded, waiting for the rest of them to settle down. They were up in Wilcox's barn for one more night. They'd finished up too close to the end of the day to move on. Wilcox hadn't grudged them the food, either, though of course they'd all turned in the relevant bits of their ration cards.

Now, the others all took their seats on hay bales or a bit of straw and a wool blanket on the floor. No smoking in here, of course. Magic could help stop a blaze, but none of them wanted to put in the effort. And, Jim thought, they were all being a bit thoughtful about what might give Jim nightmares.

Well, that was to their own good. Jim could keep a good enough hold on his reactions when he was awake, but sleeping was another matter. He could do the charms so him waking with a shout didn't bother anyone too much, but then he'd move, and that would get a couple of the others waking. Most all the men here had been too old to serve, or needed for the agriculture, or they'd been in the Home Guard. All except the tarboy, who tended whatever nicks and cuts happened in the shearing with a charm and a bit of salve. Small Ed was only sixteen. Jim was the next youngest, at twenty-three, a month ago. The rest were in their forties, at least.

Yeah, he'd been lucky to get in with them. That was Luke's doing. This was the gang that Luke hired for the family farm. Luke's sheep were doing well, the whole herd of them. He'd been able to swear Jim had a knack for livestock, which he did. And that he knew his way around the shears, which was also true. Thankfully, he'd not lost his touch while he was in the Army. Or recovering from what the Army had done to him, either.

Now Big Fred settled down with a mug on the bale next to him. Both of them were now half full at best. "M'be three days, for the last. Depends how fast it goes." Big Fred looked him up and down. "You looking for work after that?"

They'd begun at the start of June, though all of them had taken the ten days of the Midsummer Faire for other work. The Faire was good money. Several of this gang had other work— leather work, black-smithing, Sam made barrels. Jim had nothing like that, he'd hired on to haul people's crates and luggage around, whatever was needed that could use a strong back.

His lungs had held up, though, which was both good for the coin in his pocket and reassuring about the state of his battered lungs. Now he nodded, lifting his pint and taking a long pull. "Yeah. Not sure what. M'brother's got his people, and I'll not put anyone there out of a job. But I've got a little put by, enough I don't need to scramble right away."

He did, too, between the Faire, and the tips he'd got, from people who realised they were carting around way too many cases and crates. Big Fred snorted. "And some of that work's here. No, it's good, we're making better time. And you shear clean. Like the sheep just fall asleep, let you put them wherever."

That was a knack he'd discovered in his first year of Snap. He didn't have the Horseman's Word, though he knew a few people who did. But he was near as good with any other sort of livestock. Sheep, cattle, oxen, pigs, it didn't matter much. Mistress White had said he had an eye for what would ease them, and then she'd taught him a score of charms to help that along. Nothing that hurt them, that wouldn't do at all. More like they'd trust he'd under-stand what was needed and wanted.

And most livestock, their needs and wants were simple enough. Good food, good water, shelter some-times, no one fussing them in ways they didn't like. Shearing, it was all about making it clear that if they held still just a bit longer, all that heavy hot weight would be off their backs. Wouldn't that feel grand? The way the sheep bounded off when he was done, kicking up their heels, made their feelings clear enough.

Now, Jim just shrugged. "Always been good with livestock. All of it, though plenty of people are better with horses."

"Been generous with the charms, too." Now Big Fred's voice got a bit more cautious, and Jim was suddenly sure that he was being sounded out on purpose about something. Big Fred was the lieutenant here, Will's second.

That was another way Jim had been lucky to get in here. Will ran a tight gang. He'd only had space for Jim because Long Tim had gone and broken his ankle at the beginning of May. There were ten shearers, Old Mike, who stacked the fleeces, and Small Ed. Everyone did their part. They did it generously enough that Jim wondered why Big Fred was making a point of it. "Have it to share, makes everyone's work easier."

He shrugged, the right sort of shrug, he hoped. Jim was out of practice with this, and he'd only got more so since he'd been demobbed. He'd had three years of sharing the load being the best chance for staying alive, and then a year and a quarter of keeping his civilised face on for Mark and his girl and her family.

"We see it." Big Fred shrugged, and now his mouth twitched up. "Come have a walk, if you're done with the beer?"

Jim nearly was, so he drained the last bit of it, and

23

handed the mug back to Small Ed who was going by with the other empties. "Sure."

Everyone else seemed to expect this conversation. No one joked or made a move to stop them as they climbed down from the hayloft. It wasn't until they were outside, a good twenty feet from the barn, that Big Fred spoke up again. "T'morrow, we're at Greatham. Fortier land, though not the demesne farm."

"Oh?" Jim raised an eyebrow. He wasn't sure why Big Fred was bringing it up.

"Their steward might be looking for a man or two. Depends. Not right away, mayhap."

Luke had scores of stories about the Fortiers. He'd done a year on one of their farms, the estate's farms, not just a tenant, and then another two on one of the tenant farms. Now, Jim just shrugged. "It'd depend, wouldn't it?"

Big Fred clapped him on the shoulder, then rummaged in his vest to pull out his pipe and tobacco. "Master Lambert will want to know what you've been doing. What should I tell him, then?"

Ah, that was an interesting question. The thing of it was, Jim wasn't sure about the Fortiers three ways round. Luke had said Lord Fortier'd gone quieter. Also, that they'd always paid fair, which wasn't a thing you could count on everywhere. But he'd got more fiddly about understanding the farm details during the war. That made sense with the push for farming to make up for the losses of imports. Ease the rationing. All of that. But that didn't mean a man who'd spent his life in alchemy had much sense of a farm.

The second problem was that Jim didn't actually know what he wanted to do with himself. He had ideas, sure, but all of them felt like one of his old shirts, the shoulders too tight, the cuffs a little short. He'd put on the last of his growth once he went into the Army, despite the lousy food.

The other problem, Big Fred might know something about. "Heard his niece is living there now. That changed anything?"

"Nah, not much. Master Lambert mentioned she's sitting in their meetings sometimes. Named Heir, all formal like, he's made a fuss about that, and she's right young. Just out of Schola last year, moved in right away."

"Huh." Jim had known that, too, but not through routes he'd admit to Big Fred. He liked the man. He wanted a good character for whatever he decided to do next. But that didn't mean sharing secrets. "Might be interested. Depends on the work, the pay, if it's steady. Glad to pick up something for a bit, if there's shorter work going until I find something longer."

"That's fair. So what do I say?" Big Fred got his pipe lit, and the scent of it made Jim inhale, then cough once. Not the horrible racking cough at least, but any little irritation still could do that.

"I went to Snap, solidly good marks, even better in the practical. I've the certificates and all. A knack for charms, like you've seen, keeping livestock steady. Less worry they'll get hurt, less worry we'll get hurt. Everyone's better off." Jim offered it evenly enough. That wasn't the tricky bit.

"And the war?" Big Fred said this a bit more cautiously.

"Enlisted soon as I left school. Got assigned to the 70th Independent Infantry Brigade. They were at Dunkirk, then Iceland, before my time. By the time I got to them, they were training up for Normandy. Not the first. We went over six days after." It put him in an odd position. None of the glory, slightly less of the death, but plenty of fighting his way across France in what had seemed like endless terror for months. "Right at the end, August of '45, I got pneumonia. Bad. I was in hospital for a couple of months, and had a friend, hurt worse than me. He fell for one of our nurses, a nice American girl, Betty." He shrugged. "She had family, an aunt and uncle, in the Southwest of America. Good for the lungs, the dry air."

And he hadn't wanted to come home, not feeling like he had. It had been bad enough two months ago, to see all the damage from the bombing. The way cities were hollowed out and battered to dust hurt, and what that had done to all the innocent land that just had trees or sheep or fields. It had broken his heart. Still did, whenever he looked around some places for too long. "I stayed out there for a year and a bit. Got better. Did some construction work, doing what they told me, nothing fancy, when I got enough better. Saw Mark and Betty married, that was good. And then I missed having any bloody water in the air."

That last part made Big Fred snort. "Got plenty of that. This year..." His shoulder twitched. "The flooding's been right bad, you know that. The Fortiers have been sensible about it. Gather they were generous with the solstice gifts, too. More than the usual."

26

"Huh." Jim nodded once. "Let me see what I think while we do the work. That Master Lambert going to come around?"

"Aye. Day after t'morrow, like. I'll introduce you. Give him what you told me. See what comes of it. If you want the work, we'll be glad to have you back next summer."

"Ta." Jim nodded. "Been good to be working with you all. Captain runs a tight gang. You all work well together."

"You've fit right in. Not easy, that, for a lot of men. We'll be telling Luke as much."

Jim grunted, but made sure it was the pleased sound. "Glad of that, too. What sort of sheep does Greatham have?"

That got them onto a much more comfortable sort of topic, about the Southdowns. Jim approved. That was the traditional sheep of the region, and it suggested no one had tried to get too clever about their breed choices. Southdowns were good all-purpose, nice quality wool, and they were a fair bit smaller on average than the Suffolks they'd been shearing. That'd be a fair bit easier on his back and shoulders to finish up.

CHAPTER 4
JULY 5TH AT THE PULLAN FARM NEAR PULBOROUGH

"Come along, then?"

Jim, fortunately for everyone, heard whoever it was coming well before the question. Two years after the war, and he still jumped if surprised.

It had been a rough morning, and he'd taken himself out of the kitchen soon as he'd had a bite of food and a cuppa. Last night had been good at the time, but he was regretting it now. They'd finished up the last of the shearing yesterday afternoon, and that meant Black Ram Night, the celebration for the end of the season. The tradition was a drink a song, paid for out of the money from their fines. There'd been plenty of fines, and thus plenty of singing and drinking.

Luke more or less understood. Alice, Luke's wife, was a lot less kind about her husband's brother staggering into the kitchen near enough midday with a headache while she was trying to feed four children. Least he could do was get out of her way. He'd come out to the bench at the back of the garden, looking out over the fields. Jim hadn't expected anyone would bother him. Luke had been out since first light, Alice had the children, and everyone else had work to be doing. Any other day, Jim would have been out helping Luke, but that was for tomorrow or the days after, until he found something else.

Now he took a breath. "Paul."

"Jim. Come along? Ramble for the day? Pint at the White Horse?" That was one of the Pulborough pubs, but also Paul being pointed. They'd not caught up since Jim got back, just notes, catch as catch can, in the magical journals.

"You paying?" Jim pushed up. He was well aware that the little hoard of coins up in the tiny attic room that was his for the moment had to last him for a good while. Or might have to, anyway.

"Today, aye. Come along. Need a stick?"

They'd be cutting across fields on the walking paths, so yes, he probably did. It'd be four miles there and back, near enough, a good walk. Jim nodded and went off to tell Alice he'd be out for a bit with Paul. She shooed him off, but with less irritation than earlier. He grabbed his walking stick, a satchel with his journal and a notebook, and his hat, before meeting Paul at the door.

It was a good ten minutes before Paul said anything. Jim certainly wasn't inclined to start talking. He was enjoying being on the land. They circled around the Coombelands Farm, not wanting to disturb the cows. Eventually, Paul said, "You need a drink to do the talking?"

"You know most of it, yeah? Even the..." Jim

gestured, spreading his hand flat, palm down, one sign of the White Horse.

"Bet I know some things you don't yet," Paul said, amiably. "Where do you want to start? You need to find what's next. The glow of being home's rubbed off a bit." Paul had been old enough, and established enough as a farmer, that he'd been kept on doing that, rather than enlisting. The decade between them mattered a lot sometimes, and not at all at others, and this was one time it did.

"Tell me something I don't know." Jim hung his head. "Sorry. I'm in a snit."

"Right." Paul considered as the two of them walked along for a bit, steps punctuated by their walking sticks. A minute or two later, he said, "Tell me about what you think of the hedges."

The question wasn't really a surprise. A hedge said a lot about the state of the land and the magic. "Saw they'd taken down the ones near us. For larger farms, Luke said. Not the Fortier farm, though." He'd noticed that those had been the same size he'd expected. Each field bounded off into a manageable size, good for rotation.

"Fortiers don't have to worry about anyone without magic noticing." Paul said, his voice the sort of painful neutrality that meant he had opinions and he wasn't getting into them now. Jim likely had the same ones, and no sense in both of them getting angry about something they couldn't change. "And?"

"This, here." Jim paused, turning to peer. "There's some elder, flowering nicely. Didn't expect to see that out here." It was a sign the magic was tended sensibly. "Wasn't before," he added. "This has been trimmed right, recently enough. Though on the other side of the road, not so much."

"Old Garrick's son didn't come home. He's looking to sell." Paul said it softly. Ed Garrick had been the age of Michael, Jim's middle brother, and not inclined to have tagalongs in whatever they got up to. He'd not had magic, so that had cut across whatever other connection there might be. Not that it did Jim any good right now, there was no way he could get together the money to buy that much land. Maybe when it was sold, they'd need hands.

"Ah. I'd heard when it happened, slipped out of my head." There were far too many deaths, and that one had been years ago. "Dunkirk?"

Paul nodded, just once. Jim glanced away, looking at the base of the hedge. "Hedgehogs. Maybe badger, too."

"Aye." Paul began walking again. "And the rest of it?"

Doing this while walking wasn't fair, and Jim knew it was a test. He'd spent three years learning not to hear the pain of the ground under his feet, because there was no other way to be. Jim had been able to get some of that back in Arizona, but that was a very different land, and it had confused him as much as reassured him. He'd only been back in England— or Albion— under a month. Barely enough time to get a sense of it.

"How many bombs near here?" Jim kept walking, but he was thinking.

"A dozen or so. You can see the damage, closer to

Pulborough. Not so many were out on the farmland for a wonder. The rest of it?"

"You assigned to see if I'm fit?" Jim asked, still not answering the question.

Paul's grin got wider. "Said you had lost none of your wits. But yeah, people trying to figure what you're fit for. Not whether, what." Then he gestured. "Bit of wall there, have a sit? No one nearby."

Jim nodded. Better to talk this out here, where there was plenty of warning of anyone coming along than closer to the pub. Certainly better to get it over with. "When's the next gathering? Lammas?"

"Aye." The Society of the White Horse had its traditions, and being agriculturally minded, people were plenty busy in the growing season going into the harvest. But they could and would take a night to celebrate and keep the customs together. "Some things you should know. And some things to ask you, in case anyone comes across something you're looking for."

"That's the thing." They'd come to a bit of stone wall, this bit with a flat stone across the top, meant for a bench. Paul claimed half of it, Jim took the other, and they stared off at the hedge on the other side of the road. "I don't know. I don't know what's on offer, or if I want it, or ..." Jim gestured. "The war messed with my land sense. Same as the stories we hear of people in the trenches. Not exactly the same, I think, but enough like."

"Ah." Paul considered. "You want to do some exercises about that, then. See what comes back. There's a list. I'll get you a copy. Spare you having to hunt up the right people."

A war damaging the land sense was at least something the White Horse folks had ideas about solving. It wasn't any neater or tidier than healing anything else was, but Jim knew it'd probably help. Or rather, some of it would help, and where he got stuck would be informative. When he told Paul, or any of the seniors, he'd have to double check who had point on that right now, that information would filter to others, and he'd get more help.

It was a relief, but it was also an obligation. He wasn't in any position to shoulder his own bit of the work, other than the bluntly physical. Not that the physical wouldn't be helpful. The Society of the White Horse had its own farms, well-tended, to grow their own materia and for some of the more involved rites. Mostly, those were late in the autumn, after the harvest was in, or over the long winter. The others dotted through the other half the year were about drawing power to keep everything going.

"What about the rains and the flooding?"

"Not so much the Arun, thank the gods, but north of here, and the Thames? People, homes, crops." Paul twisted his head and spat, his fingers automatically making one of the charms against evil magic. "You might spend some time on the Arun, aye? See if the water's different from the land for you."

"Certainly different from Arizona," Jim said.

"What was that like, then? Tucson, it's a city."

"Four times the size of Trellech, maybe? Eighty thousand, give or take. Grew a lot during the war, from sixty something." Betty's aunt had told him all about it. "Different way of being on the land, for one thing."

33

"Oh?" Paul asked it idly, or at least on the surface, but Jim knew this was more of Paul's duties.

"Settlement there— um. Settler folk, I mean. It's so new compared to us. We've had the land here, one way or another, for centuries. There, it's not even been part of the United States for half a century yet. Most folks, if they didn't move there, it was their parents. Fair number with bad lungs who stayed, though. Betty's family has a house more into the hills, the property next to them's a sanitarium. TB."

"So good air, then." Paul considered. "You doing better with that?"

"Put in the same day's work as everyone else, shearing. Couple of times smoke got to me, or something in the hay where we were, but not bad. Nothing I couldn't clear with a charm." That, at least, he felt a good bit more sure about now than he had at the beginning of the shearing.

Down in his heart of hearts, he'd worried that he'd lost any chance of that sort of work forever. Whatever he did, he wanted his hands in it. He wanted the feel of grit under his fingers and lanolin on his skin, dirt under his feet, the spills of water from tending livestock. Even the smell of it. He'd missed that no end in the war. Manure was honest. Manure was generative, as Mistress Pipp had said at Snap. The smoke and tang and metal of the war weren't.

"Good." That much was entirely honest. He could hear it in Paul's voice. "I was worried."

"Dumb luck that the war didn't get me and the after did." The thing of it was, if he'd got that sick during the war, he'd probably not have made it. He'd been lucky enough that by the time the pneumonia got bad, they were in a city, there were nurses, and even a Healer or two doing rounds. He'd been able to clear enough out of Jim's lungs his body could do the rest. If it had been the middle of war, the man would have been saving bodies torn apart by munitions or bombs or whatever else, no time to spare for a slower death coming. Then he glanced at his friend. "I know you worried. When I didn't write for weeks."

"Aye." They'd kept up a good enough correspondence in the journals, though Jim had only been able to reply intermittently, the days he got a little time alone or with other magical folk who knew what the thing was. All his oaths about operational secrecy had meant he couldn't say much about where he was or what he was doing. But he'd been able to let Paul and his family and a few other friends know he was alive. Mostly, he and Paul had talked about odd bits of folklore. If any censor had actually seen it, they'd have been sure it was a code of some kind. "And Luke's said your Da's doing well, and your Mum."

"Yeah. Glad Dad recovered well enough." He'd had a bad fall in the blackout, right at the end of the war, and everyone, Mum especially, had said he ought to give up farming. "Michael's glad enough to have them." They'd set up in Michael's house in Worthing, where Michael sorted out people's shipping and how to get things from one place to another. Dad had gone full in for making beer, which quite good. "Shall we keep going?"

"Aye." Paul pushed himself upright. "I can give a

good report of you, and the rest will sort itself out. Let me catch you up on all the gossip as we go by places, and we'll see if any of it takes your fancy."

It seemed as good a way to start figuring out the rest of his life as any. It wasn't like Jim had a better idea.

CHAPTER 5
JULY 6TH NEAR THE GREATHAM BRIDGE

Ursula had enjoyed her day thus far. She'd ended up with a free afternoon, with no particular demands on her schedule from anyone else. It was Sunday, of course, which meant no apprenticeship. Mum and Leo were on a necessary seasonal visit to some of Mum's more difficult aunts. None of the interesting cousins had been on offer for this round, so Ursula had bowed out. With Mum and Dad's blessing, because one of the ways those aunts were difficult was that they had an entirely wrong idea of what being Heir involved. They thought her role was simply to marry well and have children, rather than accounting for the fact that someday, the land magic for Arundel, and all the actual related physical land, would be hers to take care of. Not that the children weren't a consideration in terms of the long-term plan, but first things first.

And Uncle Garin had been deep in his lab since after supper on Thursday. Technically speaking, during supper, since he'd had an idea and flung himself downstairs before his fork came to a rest on his plate, over something Ursula had asked about. He'd finished his meal, so she'd cleared the plates and brought the tray along to the kitchen before going back to her own work. Based on her current knowledge, he'd probably emerge on Tuesday or so. She'd made sure Mrs Borrowsmith was making up meals easy enough to eat quickly and with one hand while he turned pages with the other.

It left her slightly at loose ends. She'd not had enough warning to set up a ride with someone, or an afternoon in Trellech. And so she'd decided to go for a pleasant walk. The weather was cooperative— a partly cloudy sky, delightfully balmy for July, and there hadn't been too much recent rain to make the roads mud rather than solid surface.

Last year, she'd been round to the excavations of the Roman villa at Bignor, and she was curious to see if they'd made any more progress. She'd been invited to have a look in, anyway, and even with going up to the Greatham bridge, it was a pleasant four miles each way. A delightful afternoon by her current standards, especially with something of a picnic luncheon for a pause in the middle.

The villa had been as pleasant as she'd remembered. There'd been no one around particularly, but she'd admired the bits of pavement still visible under the protective shed, and communed a little with the history of the place. Also, she filed it mentally for part of the ongoing rounds of visiting several of the other demesne estates.

Veritas had once been a Roman villa, large, like this one, before its later forms. The manor at Arundel was much more recent, not only post-Conquest, but well after the need for a fortified castle. A beautiful house in many ways, but only late 15th century. It was a positive child compared to some of the other estates, certainly compared to Schola keep where Ursula had grown up.

She'd found a pleasant bit on the west bank of the Arun to pause for a snack and some of her flask of tea. She was coming across the Greatham bridge when she saw someone riding in the other direction. Automatically, Ursula took in the man. Older than she was, that wasn't hard. But in his twenties, she thought, not thirties.

He had sandy brown hair under a peaked cap. He was riding casually but a little awkwardly, as if it had been a while since he'd been on a horse. Then, as she sent out a little wisp of magic, she determined he was magical as well. Dad had taught her that trick, and it came in handy here, when she might meet all sorts of people on the road. The horse was a well-turned out chestnut, nothing fancy but sturdy and well-mannered.

Ursula nodded pleasantly at him. "Good day." He was walking his horse, not being very purposeful, and there was no call for being rude. He brought the horse to a halt, off on the side of the road, out of the way of any passing automobile or cart. Then he was staring at her, though only briefly. As if he were startled to see her there.

"Ma'am."

"Good day!" Ursula kept her voice bright and pleasant. Incantation was such a help here, giving her a foundation to make that feel rooted and solid, even if she was a trifle confused. "Is something the matter?"

"Oh. Oh, no." He tipped his hat. There was an odd silence, as if he were working through several things he might say and discarding all of them.

"Were you in need of directions? I don't know everyone in the area yet, but I make a good try of those." She let her voice trail off, then reached to touch the pendant at her neck, the properly set circle of silver around a purple sapphire. It looked like an ordinary pendant to the non-magical, but someone who was magical themselves would likely correctly identify her as having gone to Schola, and been in Fox House.

"Ah." The man swung his leg over the horse's rump, dismounting evenly enough. She knew how to watch for a bad knee or ankle or whatever else, and he showed no immediate sign of those. "Would you have a moment for a word, then?"

Ursula considered. They were on a public road. She certainly knew a wide range of protective charms and such. Ursula might not be a duellist like Dad, but she was his daughter and learning a range of tools was just good sense. She was suitably dressed to take off at a run if she had to, and duck in along the Arun where a horse would have trouble following. Or she could turn and bolt back to the village, there were people around there. Most of all, Ursula didn't think the man meant her harm. She was curious. "May I ask who I'm speaking with?"

"Jim Pullan. I live up past Pulborough." He gestured to the north. That would be four miles, maybe five. Not a bad ride on a horse. That was also further than any of the Fortier tenant farms. She knew those maps well now. "I was delivering some wool for my sister-in-law. There's a spinner down that way who likes our sheep above most others."

The name nagged at her for a moment, but Pullan was a common enough name in these parts - magical and non-magical - and Jim was exceedingly common, too. Probably he was a James formally, and that didn't help. He'd not gone to Schola. She'd have known him if he had, like she'd known every student since she was old enough to pay attention and remember. The last twelve years or so, she knew all of them reliably. She still knew the firsties, the ones she hadn't seen much at school, thanks to Mum and Dad and Leo's stories.

It meant she had to decide what to say now. "Ursula Fortier." Ursula was watching his face, and yes, he knew Uncle Garin's reputation. Not that it was particularly useful information, most people in Albion did, and the ones who lived within half a dozen miles even more so. He didn't give her much to work with, just a slight widening of his eyes. She let her mouth turn up in a smile. "Yes, those Fortiers. My Uncle Garin, specifically. Don't worry, he won't be appearing."

The way she put it got a smile in return from the man. "Kind of you to mention it." He took in a breath. "I'd heard you were living at Arundel now. The past year?"

"A year and a fortnight today," Ursula said cheerfully enough. "And he named me Heir, well, that'll be a year in forty days or so."

"A proper Biblical number," Jim replied, in a tone

that didn't tell her much at all. "And how are you liking Sussex, then?"

That was an interesting way to put the question. She posed one of her own, first. "You were fighting away the last few years?"

Jim startled, but then he nodded. "Left Snap in June of '42, enlisted. Went to America, after they let me out, with a mate and the girl he'd fallen for, a nurse. Been back a month or so." He was deliberately not precise, she thought.

"We've visited since I was little, but never for long at a time, a week, maybe. Uncle Garin doesn't do well with disruptions, and that goes about triple for small children." Also, Dad and Mum, both of them, had felt that it was best not to tempt fate when it came to anyone's temper. That had been true of Aunt Livia even more than Uncle Garin. They'd not stayed more than a day or two for key rites and gatherings until Ursula and Leo had understood how to behave when they were here. "But two years ago, we were here all summer, me and Mum and my brother Leo. Dad was on the Continent."

Jim let out a huff of breath. And oh, she'd confused him properly now. That was promising. She wanted to see what he did with it. "And you've been here for a year. Just spending time?"

"Oh, no." Ursula measured out her smile. She was enjoying herself, actually, seeing how the conversation played out, but she didn't want to overdo it. "I'm apprenticing in Incantation. My apprentice mistress is in Trellech, I'm there weekdays, supper twice a week, usually. Sometimes another evening or two if there's a lecture or something like."

"I suppose you get invited to all sorts of posh parties." Again, she couldn't read his tone at all. In some forms of this conversation, he might be jealous. In others, he might be dismissive, thinking it all foolish.

"These days, I'm as likely to be hosting them." She put her hand on her hip, making the pose a deliberate choice. She didn't choose the formal polite movements of her hands that women of her station — well, Uncle Garin's sort of station— did like breathing. "I do have plans. For the estate, for what I get up to, and I hope, what other people get up to."

"Plans." That was flat, not angry; she knew what angry sounded like. More than that, Dad and Mistress Renata had both trained her thoroughly in reading all the magical markers that went with anger, along with other emotions. Whatever he was feeling, he was both hiding it well, and it wasn't any of the emotions she'd have expected. "What about?"

Ursula cocked her head. "Well, for one thing, the new Agriculture Act, and what it means for our tenant farmers, and the leased farms, as well as the home farm. We're waiting to see what Albion's Ministry does with a parallel proposition focused on materia needs. Uncle Garin's got a particular interest in that, seeing as it's so tightly twined with his alchemy interests. He's been working on a series of potions, the most recent writeup in the Trellech Moon was last month, I can send along a copy if you like, to ease some of the damage from incendiary bombs. In aid of more complex research, of course. I've got my apprenticeship. And all those parties serve a purpose. It's so ever much easier to talk people into thinking you've had a good idea they should support if you've given them a pleasant time first."

She'd paced that just about right, because he was in fact grinning by the time she got to the last sentence, punctuated with a snort of a laugh. "Not just decorative, then." That seemed like praise. It was certainly moving in a promising direction. "I'd not mind a copy of the article, then. I've a journal, if you want to send it that way." He fumbled in his jacket and pulled out a battered bit of card with how to address him in the journal. It was uninformative, just a middle initial - C - to go with the names she knew.

"Journal." It suggested that his family had done reasonably well as farmers up to this point. The journals were less expensive than they'd been a decade or two, but they were not the sort of thing a family scrambling for every coin would buy, even for a son going off to war. "Your family land?"

"Aye. My da gave up farming in '44, one injury too many. It's my brother's now. I'm sorting what I do next." He didn't ask for a job or a character reference or anything like that. Some people would have. Estates had lots of work going, even in the changes with people returning from the fighting. Then he glanced at the sun. "I've a way to go, and I promised my brother I'd be home for the evening milking." That implied cows as well as sheep, plus whatever other things they grew.

Ursula noticed he was being careful not to give her more details than she actually needed, and that made her wonder if he'd done any sort of intelligence work in his war. Certainly, he'd picked up the precautionary tendencies.

Dad would approve, and Uncles Alexander, Claudio, and Orion. If she told any of them about this. If she told them about every conversation she had, they'd both fuss over some of the wrong bits and she'd never talk about anything else. "I'll copy it out and should have it this evening. I've got a clean copy put by." And Mum had absolutely drilled those charms into her. They'd been some of the first magic she'd learned. "Have a safe ride, then."

"Ah, Hare's a good sort." He patted the horse on his shoulder and then turned to mount. "Have a pleasant walk home, Miss Fortier." He swung up smoothly, settling into the saddle, touched his cap one more time, and then nudged the gelding into a walk across the bridge. Ursula looked after him for a moment, then shook her head and set off back home. She had an article to copy out and some research to prepare for. Some of what she wanted, she'd need to do in Trellech when she got a chance.

CHAPTER 6
THAT EVENING, AT THE PULLAN FARM

The long ride home gave Jim entirely too much time to think. Once he was home, however, there were chores to help with. The cows and the sheep and the pigs and the chickens didn't care that it was Sunday. They wanted their supper. Whatever else happened, Jim wanted to lend a hand and make it easier on his brother and the handful of farm workers he'd scraped together.

It wasn't until Alice had supper on the table that Paul turned up. Alice was in a somewhat better mood with Jim by then. He'd done her a favour, delivering the wool safely, and he'd got out from underfoot. Jim was thinking about how to do a bit more of that, maybe taking one or two of the kids with him for an afternoon. Fishing in the Arun, maybe, or walking the bounds of the fields and checking on the hedges and fences. There was a knock on the kitchen door, just as they were sitting down to eat.

"Paul!" Jim heard the comment before he turned round. "We didn't expect you."

"Don't worry about feeding me, ate on the way." He waved a hand. "Wanted a word with Jim, when there's a moment, but can I catch up with all of you? Bit of mint tea, I know you've plenty." He added, for Jim's benefit. "I helped dry a lot of it, last year."

Alice laughed at him and waved him into a chair tucked into the corner of the table. The meal itself was relaxed enough. Paul knew just how to tease Alice, how to make Luke smile, how to get the wary exhaustion to ebb for a little. And he was a grand one for teasing the children. He pulled a penny out from behind Tim's ear, made it disappear in front of Martha's eyes. Then he doubled it, handing one to each of them before producing another from behind his head to hand to David, the five-year-old. Agnes, as the baby, just watched and stared, but did not get any small objects of her own.

When the meal was over and Jim had washed up the dishes, Paul was talking with Luke. Jim came closer, not wanting to interrupt, before Paul patted Luke's shoulder. "We'll be a little. Enjoy the beer." He'd pulled a bottle out of somewhere, must have been his satchel, and there was one waiting for Alice. Then Paul gestured. "Outside? It's still nice out?"

"Sure." Jim followed him out, feeling a little like the tagalong younger brother. Paul went unerringly out toward the barn, past it, to where there was a bench by the horse pasture. Paul handed over a bottle of beer, then took half the bench, waiting until Jim did the same. There was a silence that grew until Jim sighed. "Why'd you come out? Just saw you yesterday. What've I done wrong?" Might as well get it over with.

"Gather you've not talked to our fellows much yet. When I was asking around in the journal last night." Paul kept his voice low.

"Nah. Haven't had much of a chance, have I? Luke's needed help. And I'm..." Jim shrugged. "We talked about that. Not sure how I fit right now."

Paul tilted his head. The thing about Paul was he was as perceptive as all get out. Luke was steady, Luke was an excellent farmer, but he wasn't perceptive like that. He was like a great draught horse with a plow, putting his weight into the work, but he did better with blinders to keep him focused. Paul watched more, saw more, and he acted on it.

It was, Jim thought, one reason that Paul was in the Society of the White Horse and Luke hadn't been invited. What that said about Jim, now, who'd also been invited, Jim did not know. Not now, especially. Paul was good at making the connections work, and Jim had never had that gift. Whatever skill he'd had at it had fallen away like a shed snakeskin in the war, and he'd come out with a different sort of scales or coat or whatever the metaphor was now.

"That's not all of it. What'd you do today, besides ride down to Greatham?" Alice had mentioned that. It wasn't Paul plucking it out of thin air this time.

"Met someone on the road. Actually. Let me go check something. Back in a minute." Jim got up without waiting for Paul's response, before he went back into the house, paused to take his boots off before he went upstairs, climbed to the attic, pulled his journal out from the shelf in the tiny little room, and brought it back down. He shoved his feet back in the boots on his way out, not bothering to lace them up.

Paul was staring off into the pasture when Jim came back. There was still plenty of light. The sun wouldn't set until twenty past ten, and it was only about eight now. Farmers got up early, which also made it suspicious Paul had come out here at night. Now, Paul twisted, looking at him.

"Why are you here?" Jim tried to keep it from being plaintive.

"People are a titch worried. Luke. Alice. Mistress Pipp. A dozen others. You've stuck to your own self since you got back. You weren't much in touch for a year, two years before that."

"Well, aye, nearly dying does that to a man," Jim said sharply, then he flinched. "Sorry. You don't deserve that." Then he added, more quietly. "And then I was working hard. The last month."

"But it's in you." Paul's voice was soft now. "There are thorns. No good wishing them away." Then he gestured, having made his point. "Why'd you want the journal?"

"I ran into someone on the road this afternoon." Jim took a breath. "Ursula Fortier. Tell me what you know about her, would you? And, I mean, the local bits."

"Huh." Paul took a long drink from his bottle, then tapped it. "The journal?"

"She said she'd copy something out for me." Jim flicked through the pages, toward the last one he'd used, about a third of the way through. It was true he didn't use it to write to too many people. He'd only got it his last year at Snap, so he could keep in touch with Luke and his parents and his family when he went to enlist.

He wrote to a handful of others and read the journal messages from the Society. A few others. There had been someone writing out of Trellech that shared the most important news. That had been a lifeline when he was fighting. Except that it had been the news that could be public, and Jim had known, by the time he needed it, just how much was being left out.

Now, he let his finger move over the pages. Yes, she'd written, and in a very workmanlike hand. Not fancy, like he'd expected, but readable. There were a couple of sentences of the context, the journal name, the date it had come out, the full title of the thing, which was half Latin. Jim couldn't decide what to make of the fact she'd glossed the title. The Latin bit was Prodesse quam videri. Did she think he had no Latin at all? Though admittedly, hers was probably much better, he only had enough for the relevant rituals.

He had to read the explanation twice to get it to make sense in his head. Ursula had written that the title was a reference to something her mother had written, some time ago. She added that it was Uncle Garin conceding a point in the sort of private way most people wouldn't notice. Why she was telling Jim that, Jim had no idea. He closed the journal, then looked at Paul. "Ursula."

"She kept her word. Wait, did she know who you were?"

"I gave her my name. Obviously." Jim tapped the cover of the journal. "Did she figure out we're both in the Society of the White Horse? I don't think so. I didn't give her a reason to. It wasn't the sort of thing I wanted to get into in the middle of the road by the Greatham bridge. Who knows who might have come along? And this message, there's no sign of that."

"And you're none too sure what you think of things yourself, are you?" Paul's comment was soft, but it cut. It was true, that was the problem. Jim didn't know how to talk to people who hadn't been in fighting, not anymore. Not about anything that mattered. If he tried and failed with the White Horse folk, it would break his heart. More than his heart was already broken. Not that he could say any of that, either. "How much did you see of her invitation? You were in training then, weren't you?"

"Jammed in with gods know how many others. I caught some of it, but not all the discussion. And I couldn't get away." He could have gone back and read it, but he hadn't, even when he'd had enough privacy when he was in America. It had seemed an unreachable world, then.

"Right. Some of this I knew at the time. Some of it I got from Master Isten and Mistress Farrar, who had most of her training. I caught up with Ivo Henry last winter. He's finishing at Schola next year. The only other in White Horse there right now." Paul shrugged. "We were hoping for two, but Master Isten offered to one of Ursula's brother's friends, and he turned it down, polite as anything."

Jim filed that away as not that relevant right now. "And Ursula?"

"Oh, there's a tale. Let's see, the summary in order." Paul's mouth twisted up. "You do like your tales in sequence. Everyone expected Dius Fidius would offer for her. It's that sort of family. Well, her father's side."

"Dad. She called him Dad." That was something that Jim had been chewing on all the way back. She'd been polite, but she'd referred to her Uncle fondly. In the same conversation, she'd called her parents Dad and Mum. Like Jim did, not whatever nonsense posh people said. Mater, Pater, Father, Mother.

"Anyway. We ignored all that, we always do, and we did our own divination and dreams and rites. You know how that goes." There was a whole system for it, to cover everyone of the right age. They did it in batches, names on little slips of paper, and then did more divinations on any of the names where something interesting came up. It took a week, usually, to work through them all. "And for Ursula Fortier, everything we got suggested something odd."

"What sort of odd?"

"Oh, Mistress Farrar got the story right and proper later. An invitation turns up on Ursula's bed, on her pillow. She was in Fox House, that wouldn't have been a bother for one of the fifth years, I gather. Next morning, she sends every single fifth year in Dius Fidius a note, politely declining. Never mind that she wasn't supposed to know who. Kicked over a right nest of hornets, from what Mistress Farrar said. Then we ran our divination again, and well. Five different people had dreams about it, besides the more deliberate efforts, and we invited her. Everything said we should offer to her, and be glad when she accepted, and so we did." Paul shrugged. "Don't know why, though."

"And you don't know her well yet."

"No. She wasn't able to get away much when she was in school, or even on hols. Her parents teach at Schola, both of them, and her father's the watchful sort. Warding and all that, he teaches it."

"And her mother?" Jim could look it up. That was the sort of thing that was published.

"Astronomy. She's head of their Horse House. If you're curious about her, ask Ivo. He ought to be at the Lammas rites. Ursula too, mind. She came last year, the first time. No one in our generation's sure what to do with her. Mostly she's quiet, listens and watches, she gets on well with the older folks. Does the dances well enough, the common ones. Some- times she goes out riding with Bess Nivens, up Trout- beck way in Cumbria. That's near some of her mother's family."

"And what's she doing to help the Society out?" That was the heart of it, really. Not that Jim had room to throw stones about it just yet.

"Hired on some people on recommendation. Got access to research a few times. Nothing big, but she's still learning some of the larger rites. Not the sort of thing they teach at Schola, some of the dances. She doesn't want to get it wrong, I'll give her that. She won't claim competence she doesn't have."

"So if she does claim it, she has it?" Jim asked thoughtfully. "She was—" He had to stop and think about it. "She was amiable on the road. Didn't tell me much I couldn't figure out if I dug for it, though. Who she was, the article." He tapped the journal cover again. "And she's Heir to her uncle, then? Not her brother?"

"She is. He named her last summer, um. Sometime between Lammas and equinox. No one's said much about why her and not her brother, but he's younger. She was pleased as punch about it, but not much detail. The older set are hoping it'll do some good. Especially things like the Agriculture Act, having someone who's got some leverage. Reach. Connections."

"Does she have any real sense of the land?" Jim expected not. He'd seen a little of that before. People who were all up in their heads, not with their hands in the dirt or a sheep's fleece or a cow's milk or whatever applied.

Paul shrugged. "Never had a chance to see her for certain. But she's taken it seriously enough, the parts I can see. You could write back to her, find out more. There's a bunch of us would be curious. She's been—you said amiable. Like that. Not standoffish, not nasty, but not inviting anyone closer. She and Bess and that lot talk, but it's all ordinary things. Clothing rations and what to do with them, and where they're riding that day. Nothing personal."

"Bess doesn't ask personal things because she doesn't want to be asked them," Jim pointed out. He'd walked out with Bess's sister at Snap for six months his last year. Until they'd both decided they didn't suit. And especially that Peg didn't want to be mourning him if he died in the war. Jim hadn't been able to argue with that.

"True enough." Paul shrugged. "There you are. If you see her again, I'm curious if she talks more to you. Or if you tell her. Before Lammas."

"Hah." Jim shrugged. "We'll see, I suppose. Not

that much chance we'll be on the same road at the same time again soon." Then he took a breath. "All right. Tell me a bit more about what other people have been up to, would you? Or what I should go read back on."

Paul didn't press him further, and they were out there for a good hour. None of it sparked a fire in Jim's heart for a line of work or even learning. But he felt a bit more settled at the end of the night, when Paul went off to ride home.

CHAPTER 7
JULY 10TH AT ARUNDEL

"You've been rather quiet this evening." Uncle Garin paused, having not only noticed but also decided it was worth a comment. Ursula had not actually been entirely quiet. She had been asking questions in the detailed discussion of three new journal articles and the pre-publication copy of an upcoming book. But she had to admit, she was not her most sparkling self this evening. Uncle Garin considered, his eyes narrowing slightly. "And you've been rather busy this week, yes?"

That was the thing about Uncle Garin. Even when she thought he was fully buried in his lab, he did notice things. He pulled them out of near enough thin air. Ursula knew at least some of how he was likely doing it. That was because she knew most of the tricks Mum and Dad used for a similar sort of omniscience as teachers.

She had been busy, though some of it was easier to explain than others. It was Thursday, her regular supper with Uncle Garin. It was the one time in the week when they both agreed to keep the time free. She'd insisted on it when she moved in, for half a dozen reasons.

It was interesting, fortunately. Besides learning about the estates, Uncle Garin's research was on the cutting edge of several parts of the field. His actual focus right now, a burning one that kept him working late most nights, had to do with cleansing radiation from the land. Along the way, he was also working on damage closer to home, addressing the way incendiary bombs and explosions had shattered so much of Britain and left shards of destruction through the land.

The suppers were work. Keeping up with advanced reading in a field that wasn't her own took her hours. On the other hand, the discussions were absolutely never boring. Between the alchemy that Uncle Garin was more comfortable talking about, she was learning a great deal about the estate and the family, in tiny pieces that she had to assemble afterwards like a jigsaw puzzle.

Sometimes, he'd stand up to fetch a book from near his desk, and she'd spot one more pattern in how he shelved things. Or he'd drop half a sentence of opinion into an otherwise entirely neutral evaluation. She had plenty of chances to notice how he spoke about other people, and which ones he liked more than he'd ever admit to. That was before how he talked about Mum and Dad, which were all sorts of informative and also not nearly enough yet. Ursula needed a lot more conversations to make sense of that.

"I have been busy." Ursula considered, setting

down her fork; she'd just finished a lovely poached peach. "I was out with Mistress Renata on Monday and Wednesday, of course."

"And you were back by half-seven both times," Uncle Garin replied. "I remind you, again, the warding is mine." He picked up his wineglass. "Speaking of, I am assuming you will be gone the evening of August first again?"

Ursula did not twitch. She had put hours and hours— weeks, in total— of work into not showing that kind of thing. But she came much closer than she wanted to. "Yes, Uncle." She didn't disclaim any of it, or protest that she wouldn't tell him where she was going, or any of it. It would give him entirely too much satisfaction, for one thing.

"I'm curious if you have the same depth of experience with our rites this year. I gather you were up most of the night." Uncle Garin shrugged minutely, setting it aside. "What else has occupied your time?"

Ursula considered her options here. "One small thing. I've been trying to place a name. And if you have a few minutes, I have something I'd like to ask you about." She'd been undecided about bringing it up, but if Uncle Garin were giving her an opening, she'd take it.

"The small thing first, yes. A name?"

"Jim Pullan. A few years older than I am, lives up beyond Pulborough. I ran into him on a ramble on Sunday. I've been trying to figure out if I know him."

"A steady farming family. They own their own land. Quietly prosperous, going back at least two generations. The father retired a few years ago, the oldest son has it now. He went to Snap, and both brothers, too. There's a sister in the middle, and I forget if she did as well." Honestly, that was more information than Ursula had expected, given it had nothing to do with their own tenant farmers or with alchemy. "Gerald Parker likes cross-breeding to both their sheep and their pigs." That explained at least some of why Uncle Garin knew it.

"And Jim's the younger brother." Ursula tried that out. If he were only a few years older than Ursula, it'd explain why he had enlisted in the army, rather than working on the farm. Farm work had been one of the reserved occupations, but only for those over twenty-five.

"Youngest, yes. Not sorts who make trouble. They keep to themselves, they tend their livestock and acres. Not the kind of family I'd invite for something here, of course."

Not that Uncle Garin did that terribly often in the first place, but no, such invitations when they came were for the closer connections. "If I ended up walking or riding up that way in future, is there anything you'd like me to pay attention to? When it comes to the land magic, of course. Beyond the hedges and the trees and whatever's in bloom if I do?"

"The bees, if you would. You've a good touch with them, and there are quite a few beekeepers up that way. Our hives are happy enough, but I wonder about establishing more, a little further out, if we could get a suitable queen." Uncle Garin turned his hand over. "If you've the time to talk to Bennett about it, you're welcome to take part of things over."

That, now, Ursula wanted very much. Mum

would be delighted, for one thing. Mum's family magics ran to apples and bees in particular, and Ursula had helped Mum with the Schola hives and orchards since she was tiny. "Oh, I'll absolutely make time for that. I can get free on Monday or Tuesday for a few hours. I'll check with her about a good time."

Eloise Bennett was in her sixties. She'd tended the hives at Arundel for decades, but she was getting a little slower on her feet. If they were to set up hives further out on the estate, asking her to take that on wasn't kind. Ursula, however, could do it handily. "I hadn't wanted to interfere." Also, it was the kind of step that Uncle Garin needed to offer her. It wasn't one she could ask for, in this intricate dance of demonstrating his trust in her and her suitability as Heir.

"You are delicate about that, yes. What was your other question?" As always, Uncle Garin's sharp shift in topic when he was done with the previous one jarred a little. Even though Ursula had been expecting it.

She gathered herself. "I had some questions about Grand-mère Laudine's journals. I've just got into reading them, the last week or so."

"You made it through Grand-mère Chrodechildis and her many notes, then?" Uncle Garin considered. "I looked through those. They cut off suddenly, of course. She had what they called an apoplexy, and she could not write after that. Or speak, though they worked out a system for her to share her wishes about food and what book to have read to her and all that."

"Did you see much of her, then?" It was odd to

think of Uncle Garin in this house as a child. Even though there was photographic evidence of it, for one thing.

"We lived at the Essex House before Father inherited. After, he lived here. Maman and Isembard lived at the Essex House, and I would go between them a bit more often. A day or two a week here, until I went to tutoring school, and then I spent most of the holidays here. Getting to know the land. Father was insistent on getting out on it every day, no matter how much rain or cold." Uncle Garin had not actually answered Ursula's question, and so Ursula waited.

Uncle Garin snorted. "Before her illness, before Father was Lord, we were here for family gatherings regularly. Two or three times a month, at least, sometimes much more. Supper, the weeks in between, usually on Wednesdays. So, yes, I saw a fair bit of her, but she was not a doting grandmother."

Ursula was fairly sure that no Fortier had ever actually been described as doting, not until Dad. But she certainly would not say that right now. "And Grand-mère Laudine?" She reflected again, as she said it, on the peculiar pattern of the family names. They meant that the women of the family were addressed in French, and the men were not, even though the descent from the Merovingians came through the paternal side.

"Maman." Uncle Garin closed his eyes for a moment, longer than she'd expected. Leo had made a suggestion a couple of weeks ago, right after he finished at Schola for the summer. He'd wondered if Ursula got as far with Uncle Garin as she did because she reminded Uncle Garin of his mother.

Ursula had asked Uncle Alexander about it a fortnight ago, when he'd taken her out for supper in Trellech. Well, supper and a dollop of useful gossip. He'd known Grand-mère Laudine and Grand-père Dagobert well, though they'd been a generation older. He'd snorted and said he'd had that thought earlier that spring. Particularly, he'd noted how much Ursula looked like Laudine in some ways.

Ursula had spent a lot of time looking at photographs since that conversation. They did look quite alike, about the face and cheekbones and eyes especially, once one adjusted for the fashions and the differences in the colours of their hair, and that Ursula was a good few inches taller and also more buxom. It was an odd way to think about the grandmother she'd never met, and who had been, by all accounts, nothing like Mum's mum. Now she waited for Uncle Garin to go on.

"Maman was exceedingly clever, but quiet about it. Her father was a master of talisman making. He didn't need to earn a living by it, of course, and he rarely made the pieces he designed. But she'd learned quite a lot of the art from him, without holding a formal mastery. You know enough of it, as a skill, that if I say it guided her well in layering what she was doing and anchoring it, you can follow?"

That description also gave Ursula something she would think about for some time. "And Grand-père was an alchemist." That was Uncle Garin's preference, and she wondered now how much of it had been his choice to start.

"Theoretical, mostly, by the time I was ten. He'd usually have someone working here, a journeyman who had use of the lab and the ordinary supplies in exchange for his assistance with testing what Father designed. They fit well together, magically. Both of them preferred to lay the groundwork slowly, over time. What are her journals like?"

"You've really never read them?" Grand-mère Laudine had died in 1911. Uncle Garin had been a grown man in his early thirties, but Dad had been only barely twenty-one. Surely Uncle Garin had been curious about what his mother had written.

"Father kept them in his rooms until he died. I didn't even know they existed when— when I might have put in the time. You've had a look now. They're not designed to be easy to read, not most of them."

"That was one of the curious things." There were some notes from before her grandfather had become Lord, after a series of deaths in the family in decidedly rapid succession. Four, in the course of seven months, in fact. "The early ones are brief, but easy enough to read. After she became Lady, not so much. I'm fairly sure they're encoded, but I haven't been able to figure out how."

"You see why I did not press the question." Uncle Garin was about to wave it away, but then paused and raised an eyebrow. "Go on?"

Ursula couldn't decide if she'd been insufficiently subtle or just the right amount of persistent. She wished she'd been able to see her expression in that moment, what he was reacting to, so she could dissect it with Mistress Renata properly tomorrow. "Would you mind if I took it to someone who could help with the decoding?"

"Who did you have in mind?" Uncle Garin didn't

say no right off. That was more promising than she'd feared.

"Aunt Cammie." Aunt Cammie had trained in cryptography with one of the best in the field. While it might well be a question for Major Lefton, it was much easier to ask Aunt Cammie as a favour. Even if calling her 'aunt' was a little oddly derived. She was the daughter by marriage of Uncle Ibis. She was most of a generation older than Ursula, and 'aunt' fit well enough. Uncle Garin didn't have remotely the same connection to her, though.

Now, he leaned back, tapping his forefingers together as he thought. He was giving it quite a lot of thought, and that was also interesting. She honestly had expected him to say no, and now she'd have to recalibrate half a dozen other matters under consideration. Finally, he nodded. "Select a few passages you do not think are particularly telling, if you would. Begin there. Report back to me about what you find, if you can work out substantive content." He lifted one hand. "And she may consult with Major Lefton, if she sees fit. I know your father considers them both entirely trustworthy."

"I appreciate that, Uncle Garin. I'm very curious now." And Ursula wasn't feigning this at all, but she was certainly saying it this way for a reason. "I'd like to get to know Grand-mère better, and this seems the only real way."

"True enough." Now Uncle Garin stood. "Shall we move to the sofa, and do you have another half hour for the alchemy? I'd like to talk out an idea at you, and see if I can solve one particular piece by explaining it."

That was also one of the things she did now. Ursula smiled, waiting for Uncle Garin to come around and pull her chair back as she stood. He tended to old-fashioned manners. She also set aside any plans of doing more of her own reading tonight. By the time they were done, she'd only be good for a mystery novel she'd already read twice, she was sure.

CHAPTER 8
JULY 12TH IN PULBOROUGH

On Saturday, Jim spent most of the afternoon out working on the hedges at the southern edge of their land. It was a slow process, but a steady one, going along both sides of the hedge and checking for breaches or breaks or damage. And also having an eye out for any worrying signs, blight or browning or land that wasn't draining properly, or was far too dry.

All looked well, actually. Better than he'd expected, in some ways. Once he'd got into the Society of the White Horse, he'd spent a lot of time thinking about the state of the land. Before the war, he'd had a feeling it was all right, but not what it could be. Now, there was a space there, something to grow into, despite the bombing. Despite how much woodland and meadow had been plowed up for food, which was solving an immediate problem— well, that would, probably— but created others, down the road.

He finished up with that around four and

decided he'd walk down to Pulborough for a drink. Luke had told him it was fine if he did; he had help with the cows tonight, and the sheep were being themselves. No particular worry. He had come down through the west side of the village, heading for the usual pub, the White Horse, ironically. It sat on a curve, where the road turned south toward Storrington.

As he came round the curve, he spotted a rider on horseback coming up from the south. At first, he couldn't make out who the rider was, though whoever it was seemed competent enough. The horse slowed to a walk, coming up into town, staying well to the side of the road. When they drew closer, Jim realised, too late to duck into the pub, that it was Ursula Fortier. He touched his cap as she drew up closer.

She had a good seat on a horse, solid enough. More to the point, she was gentle with the chestnut mare she was riding, bringing her to a tidy stop with no fuss. Then the woman nodded at him. "Mister Pullan." That was interesting. He'd have expected her not to be that cautious. She'd grown up entirely in the magical community, even more deeply in it than someone who grew up in Trellech.

Folks on Schola island lived and breathed magic, that was what all the gossip said. No one without magic even knew there was an island there. Trellech was in the middle of Wales, and while there were all sorts of illusions and warding to keep the non-magical out, it wasn't quite the same thing. That was more like Snap, a space of its own, but in a larger landscape.

Also, Jim had been to Trellech quite a few times, and never to Schola.

"Miss Fortier." He could match her anyway. "I didn't expect to see you this far north. A pleasant ride?"

She tilted her head for a second, and then dismounted, bringing her down to his level rather than talking down to him from the horse. It made him realise, he'd not really registered it last Sunday, that she was nearly his height. In a jacket, blouse, and breeches, with tall boots, she looked almost like a valkyrie out of legend, some sort of warrior, momentarily at rest.

She held the reins lightly with one hand, but he noticed, approvingly, that she didn't loop her arm through them. A moment later, she'd flipped both stirrups up to cross over the mare's withers, so they wouldn't bounce. Once she was facing him again, she smiled, and he didn't know what to do with the smile. "Yes, thank you. I didn't expect to see you, but our conversation last week made me a little curious about how things were up here."

There was something to the way she said it that made him think that was about the land magic and not just the land magic. He didn't know how to ask about that. He nodded once, trying not to be curt. "Something I could help with? I'm still catching up with people, but my brother and sister-in-law, a few family friends, they know most everyone in these parts."

"Actually, I might be looking for a queen in need of a hive. Uncle Garin and I are talking about expanding our beehives, further out than they are at the moment. I'm talking to our beekeeper on Tuesday, about what she thinks might work best."

"Do you know much about bees, then?" It wasn't the sort of thing he expected someone like her to know, and maybe a bit too much of that showed through. She was in the Society of the White Horse, she had to have some affinity for the land and all that lived and thrived on it.

"Oh, not as much as I'd like to." Her eyes lit up. "Mum's family has a lot of traditions about the bees. I've helped her out for years. Uncle Garin takes them seriously, the traditions, but he also doesn't suit up to go and do what's needed. I'm glad to."

It made Jim consider her a little differently. It was one thing to take the traditions seriously. He approved of that. But she also obviously enjoyed this one, looked forward to it, and he hadn't expected that. "I might know a couple of people. You'd not be looking for this year, though?"

She shook her head. "Not this late in the summer already. And longer, before we actually had hives ready to go. But I'd like to sort out where we'd want more, and get the hives made and placed. To be ready for whoever we're getting the queen from when they split their hive. Begin the working relationship. Though if there is a swarm or a reason to split, we could give that a try. We've plenty to keep them going overwinter." She tilted her head. "I suppose it depends a lot on the weather, too, if things settle a little."

"Miss Fortier..." Jim began, opening his mouth, before she spoke.

"Please, do call me Ursula. No need to be too

69

formal, not as country neighbours." Neighbours was stretching it, even by magical standards, there was a good five miles between them on the roads. Also, he wasn't at all sure he could call her by her first name.

Except, of course, that Lammas was coming up, and she'd certainly figure out they shared a society then, if she didn't before. Not that he could tell her now. He should have said in the journal, but that felt wrong, too. Now he coughed. "Ursula. Jim, then, if you like."

"Jim." She said it cheerfully, as if she were bestowing a charm blessing with it. She spoke deliberately. He'd started to notice that, even when she was saying quite ordinary things. "You were saying? Pardon for interrupting."

"I'd be glad to introduce you to a few people. Let me ask around, see who makes the most sense. Though I'm sure— it's Eloise Bennett you're meeting with? She'll know all the same people."

"Still. Sometimes a mention from someone else helps it along."

Jim had nothing useful to say to that. "So, you were out for a ride?"

"Mmm." Now she considered, taking her time in answering. There was a quick glance to see if there were others around, and there were a couple of people lingering outside the pub. She visibly decided not to chance it. "I'm still learning how things have been run on the estate. Also figuring out which things I want to change, and how much of an argument Uncle Garin will have with me about it. Seeing what's growing well around us is a help for some of that."

"And if that's different than you'd planned?" His

comment came out rougher than he'd meant. It wasn't that she was putting his back up, exactly, but she kept dancing near to doing the thing right, and then he couldn't tell how much she meant it. She said the right words, that was it. But he couldn't read how well the roots were anchored.

"Then I'd like to learn what's working. As much as I can. It's a little tricky. People don't expect me to take farming seriously." There she stood, decidedly posh, the breeches and jacket were good cloth, from before the clothes rationing. Before she was fully grown, actually, if he had to guess, which meant she'd got them from someone else.

Jim coughed. "Well. People make assumptions." It sounded entirely weak to him, and he looked away, down the road, to avoid looking at her.

"Maybe sometime you'd be willing to come down and consult a little? You know the land in these parts. Uncle Garin said your family's farm has done well, two generations back."

She'd asked about him, and Jim had no idea what to do with that. She'd asked her uncle, who was entirely terrifying, about him. Jim did not like being brought to Lord Fortier's attention, not one bit. Even if what he'd actually said, or at least what she quoted, was complimentary. But of course, he couldn't say that to her face.

There was an awkward quiet for a minute, until a door slammed well behind Jim, but not so far behind it didn't make him jump. He half-wheeled around, hearing the horse startle at the movement, before he got a grip on himself. It was a door. It wasn't anything worse. People slammed doors all the time. Now he'd made a fool of himself.

When he turned to her— running was tempting, but he didn't have anywhere to run to— she had taken a step or two back, giving him space. Her free hand was behind her back. Her face wasn't judging. Jim's reactions confused Luke. And Paul, though Paul didn't fuss about them as much, at least not yet. Frankly, Jim's reactions confused Jim himself, so he figured confusing other people was fair. But the woman in front of him wasn't confused. Not like them.

Jim forced himself to take a breath, and then another. He could hear his pulse pounding. It would take him a little while to settle. She didn't speak; she didn't try to insist everything was all right when it wasn't. She didn't say any of the stupid things. He'd heard plenty of that in America, people who'd never been near the midst of a war.

When he felt he could speak, Jim found himself asking, before he could think better of it, "Do you have family who fought?"

Her mouth twisted up on one side, the way he was beginning to think was a mix of amusement and complicated reality. "Depends what you mean by family and fought. But yes, enough that I know when fussing's not the thing."

She took a breath and let it out. "Dad, in the Great War. His best friend was killed. He was there. He still has bad days now and then. Uncle Alexander, he's actually my godfather. He was there too, but he doesn't let it show at all. Doesn't mean it isn't part of him. Uncle Orion, he was fighting in the Greek islands. More than that, I grew up with my parents teaching. I know a lot of people who fought, some of whom came back and some of whom didn't."

Jim hadn't thought about that bit of it. About much of what it must be like to grow up with teachers at Schola as parents. She'd know all the glory of the generation older than she was. More than that, depending on how many people kept in touch with her parents. It was like the farms in the neighbourhood, but magnified hundreds of times, in patterns he couldn't begin to make sense of, like a huge spiderweb sparkling with dew. Now he looked down.

"Oh." Then he let out a huff of breath. "Thank you, erm. Ursula. For, for..." He couldn't even finish the sentence. He didn't know what he was thanking her for. She'd been a decent person. That was all, and that was more than he'd expected, and he didn't know if he should thank her for it.

"One of Dad's first rules. Avoid making things worse. It's surprisingly useful in a lot of different settings." Then she tilted her head. "I think that man there might want your attention? And I ought to get back. Mum and Dad and Leo— that's my brother— are coming for supper. I should not smell like horse for that."

Jim felt that horsey outdoor air was a perfectly reasonable way to smell, but perhaps not for supper somewhere posh like Arundel. He made a tiny little bow. Then he turned, and yes, that was Mr Weeks, who might well have some work for Jim as they got a little further into harvest. He should have a word. He might get a beer out of it. That wouldn't hurt. So he waved to acknowledge it, before looking back at Ursula. "I'll write about some people to talk to about bees."

"Thank you." She turned around, pulling the stirrups back in place, and then mounting easily, without needing a mounting block or any help. Jim tried very hard not to think about the fluidity of that movement, or what it implied about the body under the jacket and breeches. Those were not things he should dare to consider.

He waited until she'd turned the mare around to head back south, and touched his cap once more. Then he went off to negotiate about the strength of his arms and the willingness of his back.

CHAPTER 9
JULY 16TH IN TRELLECH

"Come in, come in." Aunt Cammie opened the door, bouncing her daughter on her hip. "Let me take her back to Nanny, the office is that door on the right." Aunt Cammie looked entirely delighted with her world. Her hair was back, little tight curls escaping near her ears. She wore a daytime frock in a bright blue that looked stunning against brown skin, and a general joy at the day.

Kenna, the baby, also looked very happy, though she ducked her head, burying it in Aunt Cammie's shoulder as soon as she saw someone at the door. She was only eight months, and while Ursula didn't have vast experience of children that age, it was hard to explain things to them for a while yet. She was a paler brown, and she definitely had her father's hair and bright blue eyes.

Ursula immediately nodded and ducked into the room on the right through the open door. She had come for tea before going back to Mistress Renata's for supper. It'd give them an hour or two to talk.

She'd been to this house only a couple of times before. Aunt Cammie had a bit of family money from her father. When she and Duncan married last year, they'd bought this house; two floors, an attic for a nursery, and a bit of back garden. Nothing vast, but convenient for her work and for Portal Square.

Like everything Aunt Cammie touched, the office had a mix of chaos and absolute order. The desk nearest the door was tidy. That was Duncan's. But most of his work was away from home, running an aerodrome and teaching people to fly planes. Aunt Cammie's desk, in contrast, had five piles of paper, a typewriter, at least three notepads, and a roll of butcher paper tucked between the corner of the desk and the wall. There was a sofa and two easy chairs in the middle, in front of the fireplace. The chair nearest Aunt Cammie's desk had been pulled to one side, presumably to make more space on the floor.

A minute later, Aunt Cammie reappeared bearing a tea tray. "Start on the sofa, shall we? You look well. Is everything still good for you?"

"Yes, by and large. But I've found something, like I said, that's very much your sort of challenge. How are you? How's Duncan? Kenna is obviously adorable."

"Shy of strangers, but Mum assures me that's a common stage. She's likely to be a terror within a month or two. She's crawling and she's working on figuring out standing. We've already removed anything remotely dangerous to higher locations or other places. Mostly Giles and Kate's." That was part of why Cammie was here. The Leftons were just around the corner. Aunt Cammie had not only apprenticed with Major Lefton, but was back to collaborating with him regularly. "So, what have you found, then? Wait, let's back up. Do you know what you're asking me to do?"

"I do listen!" Not that Aunt Cammie talked about specifics, but she was a cryptographer, capable of decoding all sorts of things. During the war, she'd been running signals for a lot of it, both in the ATS and then in the magical community, though of course she didn't talk about any of the details at all, even where she'd been posted. "And the context matters, doesn't it?"

"You get the short lecture, then, for the moment. In any sort of personal encoding, there's always a trade-off between the ease of coding it and how likely someone is to crack it. Layered on top of that is someone's personal skills. It depends on how worried someone is about interception, or how portable it needs to be. A cypher can be worked with paper and the key. A code might need a referential book to make sense of it. Do you know which yours is?"

"A cypher would look like a jumble of letters, yes?" Ursula looked at Aunt Cammie, who nodded once. "Not that, then. It's in French, but the sentences mostly make sense? I mean, there are phrases, sometimes whole sections, where it doesn't, and I don't think that's a flaw in my French skills. It might be magical references I don't know. Grand-mère Laudine was trained as a talisman maker."

"No, you're fluent enough. I've tested you on that. But you're right, that's a form of magic that does like its metaphorical and oddly named references. Nearly as bad as alchemy." Aunt Cammie grinned toothily.

"Right. Tell me what you know about the source materials. Tell me again, I mean. I want to hear how you say it."

"It's my grandmother's journals, kept from when she married my grandfather, but they change rather suddenly after he became Lord. They've been kept up in a private library, just the Lord and the Heir have access. Even Dad doesn't now. The earlier ones, I brought a sample or two with me, are fairly ordinary. I can follow the French just fine, even when she's talking about a talisman or some ritual magic I'm not familiar with. Most of it's fairly ordinary, brief mentions of parties or events." Ursula glanced up. "What coding there is at this point, I think, is her griping about the family. My great-grandmother and great-uncle and so on. It'll be a sentence or two here or there, talking about the estate, but the references don't quite make sense if you look at the dates."

"Hah, you would think to check that. Well done. I'll look at the samples. It's handy to have a starting place. You said only samples, yes?"

"Uncle Garin agreed that if you want to bring it to Major Lefton, you could. But also that I need to choose samples I thought weren't too telling. That's the next part, I suppose."

"Oh, excellent. Giles needs a bit of a distraction, honestly." Aunt Cammie said it fondly. "He's lonely with Theo starting with the Guard. Kate gets to see him, on and off, but they're not allowed away from training for another six weeks yet." Ursula knew Artemis better of the two Lefton children, they'd been the same year at Schola, but Theo was a good sort. Both of them had gone straight for the Guard, like their mother.

Ursula had carefully avoided asking Mum and Dad if they had a hard time with her being away. She knew enough of the answer. Asking wouldn't help anything. And it was a necessary stage for all of them. She would not, however, have done well not seeing them for a couple of months all at once. Not without some compelling reason, like the war.

Aunt Cammie went on. "All right. I'm glad to make whatever oaths you like on the contents. I've got the usual set handy for you to look over. So is Giles, I checked." Her mouth curled up. "Alexander approves of them, if that saves steps."

"You know it does. But also Uncle Alexander taught me always to double check for myself." Aunt Cammie laughed and handed over a sheet of paper from the low table in front of them. Ursula read it carefully, then nodded, and Aunt Cammie made the oath promptly. That meant Ursula could go on with the rest of this. "Anyway. There was a whole string of deaths, all of them before Dad was actually born. After Grand-père became Lord, the journals change. They're a lot more coded. I could map some of it to events— Dad's birth, his naming, the seasonal rites, things I could confirm in other records."

"Are all the journals like that, or have you looked?"

"Honestly, Aunt Cammie. Like I'd shirk the prep." Ursula wasn't actually offended. She was teasing, but Aunt Cammie held her hands up in surrender. "They stay more or less the same, until she died - that was 1911. Dad had just turned twenty-one. But there's a stretch in..." Ursula paused to double check her notes. "1894. Summer solstice, 1894. Right after that, there's a long section, thirty-eight pages, that's even more densely coded. I couldn't make any sense out of it." Now Ursula took out her portfolio. "I brought you a couple of pages from the early journals as a sample. Here's five different examples from the ones after she became Lady, and a couple of sentences from the most complicated ones."

"May I ask what happened in 1894?" That was the key, of course.

"My great-grandmother died. I can do that maths easily. It suggests there was something she wasn't able or willing to write about until her mother-in-law had died. An oath, probably, but possibly also good sense. My great-grandmother had been ill for some time, an apoplexy, and not able to speak or write. That happened in early 1890, again, not long before Dad was born."

"The— you realise the dates are suggestive in several directions, yes?" Aunt Cammie leaned forward, sounding worried. "Are you sure you want me to look into this?"

Ursula cleared her throat. "Aunt Cammie, thank you for your concern, but honestly. Yes. I have thought about it. I want to know. Uncle Garin's given me permission, though I don't know if he expects me to have any success."

"And Isembard?" Aunt Cammie had relaxed minutely, but not enough for comfort.

"Dad isn't sure about it, but also— he only ever knew any of them, bar my grandparents, through other people's stories. It's personal for Uncle Garin.

He was nine or ten. Not old enough to know some things, but old enough to know something happened? Mum thinks I ought to look if I want to. The records are there. They were meant for someone to have access. That's her argument."

"It's a solid one." Aunt Cammie let out a puff of breath. "All right. I'll look. I'll braille your samples so Giles can have his own copy. What else can you tell me about Laudine, then? It might be a help with what she focused on for the code words. It's usually something someone knows well. Giles did one a while back— actually, you might know this one, that trip to Berlin in 1935. That was all art references, but nothing Geoffrey would have actually been interested in."

It did create an interesting puzzle. "Right. Well, I have a family tree and some notes. Grand-mère Laudine had a sister who ended up in Canada. There was some scandal in her husband's family. She was close to her parents. There are a lot of notes about them staying, both at Arundel and at the Essex house. That's where my grandparents lived before Grand-père inherited. It came down through her family. They were well off, but not landed families, had been for ages. Not a lot of cousins, either, though it's the Montagues, so there's a fair number of more extended lines around." Ursula kept track of that automatically, though the only Montague connections she talked with much were those she knew for other reasons, like overlapping in school.

"And what was her marriage like, do you know?"

"Dad always said rather distant. Uncle Garin basically never talks about their parents, not except occasionally pointing out a book or something. Once Grand-père inherited the title, he lived at Arundel, and she lived at the Essex house with Dad. They'd come for supper once a week, a little longer along the various rites. But Uncle Garin went to tutoring school only a year or two after, and he stayed at Arundel during hols. The Heir and all that. I do have a list of the titles from her part of the library. That was in the records. And there are a few people who knew her still around, but I'd have to see about introductions. We talked about it a little in the winter, but I didn't follow up."

"For that, you want to consult Lady Alysoun," Aunt Cammie said automatically, which was more or less what Ursula thought. "And she died in 1911? Was it a sudden illness? What are the last journals like?"

"It's a little hard to tell, the coding? But she writes up to almost the end, and the last one, I don't know. It felt like it stopped at a reasonable point? Like a book does, where the story and the characters go on, but that part of it is done? It's a little odd. I included that entry. Grand-père was ill for a while before he died in 1913. A year, maybe. Nothing the Healers could do anything about, I think. For her it was shorter, but maybe she knew it was coming? There are some references to regular Healer visits in the notes, but not about what. Or, now I think about it, who. It's just in the accounts. Once a month, maybe?"

"And you said the coding doesn't look very different across the decades. That's interesting, actually. Most people make changes." Aunt Cammie was increasingly distracted now, in a pleasant way. Then there was a sound from outside the office door and a brief rap on the door. "Yes, Nanny?"

The door opened, and an older woman ducked her head in. "Begging your pardon, but Kenna must be growing again. I'm sure she's hungry. I know you've a meeting, but..."

Aunt Cammie chuckled. "Oh, I think we're near enough done. Do you mind coming and sitting outside while I feed her, Ursula? We can chat a little more, but I think I have most of what I need to get started. If you want to leave your samples?"

Ursula shook her head, then stood, pulling out the portfolio and leaving it on the desk as Aunt Cammie reclaimed Kenna. That done, they headed down the hallway to the back garden. There were chairs out on the terrace, quite a pleasant spot and well shaded. Ursula said, "Have you been asked to demonstrate to me the joys of settling down with someone?"

"Oh, no. Now, there might be people who'd ask, or would if they thought of it. But none of your dearer folk would. They all have more sense. No plans in that direction, then?"

Ursula said, primly. "Oh, I have plans eventually. In due course." She did, too. She would have to sort out the question of marriage and children and a future generation in some form. None of her prospects on that front were at all promising, though. She'd honestly enjoyed the conversations, all two of them, with Jim more than the social rounds lately. They'd been a lot more honest, for one thing. For now, though, she could enjoy watching Aunt Cammie and her daughter. "But if you told me a bit about what it's like, this age, then it'd probably make Uncle Garin pleased that I'm not running away from the topic."

"Ah, well." Aunt Cammie grinned. "First off, you'd heard about my sister?"

"That Aunt Hypatia is expecting? Oh, yes. Mum told me last week. She said Aunt Hypatia said she could." Ursula leaned back. "I don't want to think about it for me yet. But I'm glad for them. How's she doing? I'll have to see about going out for a visit sometime again." Though she was booked through most of July at this rate, and into the second week of August.

That got Aunt Cammie into a companionable chat about how brilliant Kenna was. Also how she was sure to be climbing things as soon as she figured out how to resist gravity. How she was perhaps a little too ready with her current teeth, but that was Aunt Cammie's own choices coming back to haunt her. By the time Ursula left half an hour later to go back to Mistress Renata's for supper, she'd had an entirely pleasant interlude. It had actually helped to see someone being a good Mum without all sorts of complicated expectations.

CHAPTER 10
JULY 17TH AT THE PULLAN FARM

"Here." Luke slid a mug of bitter over. "Dad's." He pulled up the bench on the other side of the table. "Mind a word?"

Jim looked up, warily. He'd expected something like this. Alice and the littles were off for a visit to her parents for a day or two. He and Luke and Bill, the farmhand, had done all the evening chores. Bill was tucked up in his room over the barn. And here was Luke, being deliberate, like he was when he set out training a horse or whatever. Having it aimed at him did not make Jim feel any better.

Running from it wouldn't make anything better. "Sure."

"First." Luke looked at him, then down at his mug. "Look, this is bloody awkward."

"Alice?" Jim could at least ask the obvious question. "I know I'm getting on her nerves. Trying not to, but..." But it was one more person for the loo, one more grown man to feed, and someone who didn't know the rhythms of the family. "Don't blame her."

That came out sounding a bit more grudging than Jim had wanted to, but he couldn't do much about that now.

"Yeah." Luke let out a long breath. "Look. You need a place, you're handy with the work. We're not asking you to move on right now. But it'd be a help if you had a plan. If we helped you with a plan. She'll be a lot better when there's a date when you're not in the attic, just coming round for supper sometimes. Absence makes the heart fonder."

Jim snorted at that. Alice was a good woman, that was the thing, but she had the particular stubbornness of a farmwife. Jim might well marry someone like her some day in a future where he had steady work and had met anyone who might be interested in him. But Jim wasn't hers. Luke was. "Or at least, make me easier to deal with, because I'd go away again."

Luke grunted, agreeing enough without needing to speak against his wife. "So. Said I'd say it out to you, flat out, so we could sort the next things. Not all tonight. But some progress."

It made Jim pause, because he'd been thinking about that moment on the road where the door had slammed, and Ursula Fortier hadn't made it into his problem to deal with. That's the frame he'd finally put on it. It happened, he jumped, nothing bad came of it. She hadn't made it into her problem either. More like she'd refused to acknowledge it as a problem. Just a thing that happened. A fly biting, maybe. Not what you wanted in a day, but you kept going without it upending your plans.

The thing of it was, he needed a place, and being here maybe wasn't great for him. Being with Michael and their parents in Worthing would be worse, but being here wasn't great. He loved his brother. He loved getting to know his nieces and nephews better. Jim knew how to do the farm work, most of where everything was, how the land rose and fell. Here, he could do it without worrying he was doing something wrong for the farm. It wasn't enough. Or it wasn't the right thing enough, he wasn't sure. "I know it's hard to deal with me. And the noise gets me sometimes, the sudden ones."

"Ah." Luke looked away again, then took a long swallow of his beer. "Can't do much about that, not here."

Jim wished, for just a moment, that Luke had pretended they could. But Luke wasn't made for pretending. He knew that. Luke was solid, reliable, sturdy. He said the truth, without frills. Like their parents, actually, and Michael and Tess as well. It made Jim feel like a changeling child sometimes. There was a lot of good in that, and Jim knew it. But sometimes, just sometimes, he wanted the illusion of a different answer. Or someone who'd pretend with him that a different answer was even possible. "I know. 's not your fault." Then he took a breath. "I know what the obvious thing is, but I don't know how to make it happen."

"Which is?" Luke was going to make him spell it out, then. Which made sense, and Jim did his best to put his grumpiness aside. He'd gone and fought a war. He'd taken his time coming back. And if people here hadn't fought, they'd had bombs from the skies and endless threat of invasion, and that wasn't much good.

"Well, for one thing, I ought to apprentice." Jim swallowed. "But who to? No one near here's looking for one. Everyone's got enough of their people, or they're not going to take someone new on. I don't want—" His voice cut off. "I don't want to leave Sussex. Near enough to here to get back for an afternoon." Most of the portals near them were private or a good distance. Arundel was a reasonable walk, but he couldn't see himself asking Ursula Fortier for permission to use it. Or daring to use it even if she said it was all right.

"Good question." Luke chewed on it for a little. "We've the money for your apprenticeship. Dad put it aside, hasn't touched it, even when things got dicey for the brewing."

Jim hadn't known that, and he looked up, surprised. "Wouldn't have blamed anyone for it."

"You know how Dad is. Fair chance to each of us." And, well, if Jim had died, they'd have used it, and then he hadn't. Luke went on, his voice even. "So if you found someone, you could. What do you want to be doing?"

That was the thing. Jim wasn't sure he could find something that was enough what he wanted. "You got the farm here. And you're doing a fine job with it, you know that, yeah?" He looked up earnestly, because it mattered that Luke knew that, that he'd heard Jim say it.

"Aye." One of the better things about Luke was no false modesty. "Dad taught us well. And Snap."

"What I want is to run a place of my own. Not

right away. There are things I've never done myself, year in and year out. Helped with, sure, but that's different." Snap made sure each of them got experience at the parts they'd been learning. Luke was fine with the livestock, and he listened to advice, but he had an eye for a field that Jim couldn't match.

For his part, Jim was better with the livestock, and he thought he might be brilliant, eventually. Figuring out how to breed to type, for temperament, and how to train them to handling, those were all things he wanted more experience with, under someone else's eye. Dad had been good at them, but Jim had his own ideas he wanted to explore.

And he also wanted to think about a farm as a whole. What it'd be like to grow fodder, have vegetables, have livestock, have wool. It was tricky as all get out to do a bit of everything, but the land here, on the edge of the Weald, it could handle it, maybe. With the right staff and the right property and the right magic.

And anyway, he wouldn't be able to do that here, obviously. Luke nodded again. "Big Fred said you'd had a word with Lambert Knox. Anything come of that?"

"I was polite, like Mum would want. Dad too. He was a little curious about me. Nothing open right now." If Jim got a chance, it would be because someone else got sick or injured too badly to work, and he didn't wish that on anyone. Or that they expanded their farming a fair bit more, which didn't seem terribly likely. Ursula had talked about bees. That was different. Not that she'd have told him if they had plans that weren't public yet. "It's a well-run farm, though."

"Aye. I can have a word with Parker about it." Luke offered it carefully.

"He's not got space either. That's why Knox was willing to talk to me, partly. Knowing you and Dad, and what Parker thinks of our stock. But something like that would be grand. But there isn't, not here."

"Might have to give up on the here part?" Luke offered warily. "Or find some other line of work."

That was the problem, really. Jim didn't want to go away again. It might break him forever. He wasn't trained for other sorts of work, though if he could figure out what he wanted to do and get an apprenticeship in it, that might do. "What, though? Less and less call for a blacksmith or farrier. I want something that's on the land, not an office or a factory." A factory, likely also to destroy him. Being that cut off from the land, even before it got to the noise and the smell of metal. That probably ruled out black-smithing, too.

He couldn't talk about that fracturing of the land with Luke. He got all caught up in the feel and magic of it. That was a conversation for Paul. He couldn't talk about the rest of it with either of them, not without sounding like a coward.

"Well." Luke considered. "How about you make a point of going round the White Horse, at least once a week?" The pub named jarred again, but also it made sense. "Put out you're looking at your options, see if anything comes of it. I'll ask round. I did at the Midsummer Faire, but you're right, there's not much right now." He flipped his hand over. "The new Act might or might not help. Better prices for what we grow, at least."

"How tight are things?" Jim asked cautiously. He had the evidence of his own eyes, but he didn't have the last three or four years to measure it against, and the flooding had destroyed a lot.

"Tight, this year, though we're still making more than we've spent." Luke shrugged. "All our milk goes for rationing, done terrible things to the cheeses." Which ruled that out as an option for Jim, at least for a while. "Wool's still selling well enough, but you've done your shearing season."

"I have." And he'd do it again, almost certainly, but Jim didn't much fancy being out in the wet in lambing season. He'd had a lifetime of living out of a tent or whatever bit of cover he could get during the war, and also he wasn't sure his lungs would take that kind of abuse again. Then Jim cleared his throat. "There is one thing I hadn't mentioned?"

"Aye?" Luke looked up.

"Ursula Fortier. I've talked to her twice now. Met her on the road, both times." Jim met his brother's eyes, waiting.

"Paul said." Just the two words. Jim knew why Paul had mentioned it, and now that felt raw and edged, too. He took a breath, waiting to see what else Luke might say. "Gather she's taking an interest in the farming. Don't imagine she knows much to start."

"She was looking for people with a hive to split. More than one. She talked about it right enough, and Eloise Bennett's got the Arundel hives. She knows her bees."

"True." Luke considered. "Like to see her again?"

That put Jim on the spot, because yes, he would in a fortnight or so. "Maybe. But she doesn't owe me anything. And she's a Fortier. Who knows what she'd want in exchange?" Even as he said it, he knew there was something caught up in him about that, something that didn't make sense. "She was, she was..." No, there weren't words for that either.

"Haven't seen her around, not to talk to. The Faire, a bit. At a distance. She was keeping an eye out for her brother. That's a thing I liked." Luke glanced up at the end of it.

Jim ducked his chin, acknowledging that. "Like you do for me. Right. I don't know. It worth asking her if we do talk again?"

"What's she going to say? That she doesn't know anyone? No harm in that, right?" Luke pointed out, pragmatically. "And who knows what they're doing there? Not like Knox or Parker spill the estate secrets. She might put in a word for you with them, though, if there's hiring to be done."

Jim was quite sure, in that moment, he didn't want to owe her that kind of favour. It changed the feel of the ground under his feet. That was what it did, and he didn't like the idea at all. Even if, once she knew he was in the White Horse, she'd likely offer. It was what they were supposed to do for each other, along with all the rest of the rituals and traditions and understanding of the land. "If I get a chance."

He'd just have to see to it that the topic wouldn't come up.

Luke looked at him steadily, then shrugged. "I should get to bed. You too, yeah?"

"Let me finish my beer. I'll go up in a couple." Luke grunted once, patted Jim on the shoulder as he went by to rinse his mug, and then disappeared up to his and Alice's room. Jim took another few minutes, long enough to be sure Luke was done in the loo, and then went up to his attic room, closing the door behind him.

CHAPTER 11
JULY 25TH AT ARUNDEL

"Come up for a drink, would you? I'd like to talk through the evening." Uncle Garin took off his hat as they came into the entry. Ursula had been about to go up to her rooms and change into something more comfortable. Or a good less clothing overall. The outing had not been the most pleasant of weather. It had been thick fog with a hint of drizzle in Trellech. It was noticeably warmer back at Arundel, making her feel she was moving in her own personal steam cloud.

"May I go change first, Uncle? Quickly, of course." Ursula had a guess what he wanted to talk about. She would deal with it, but she would rather a moment to gather herself. Also, the sort of clothing required for making a proper turn at the Temple of Healing garden party was not the most comfortable to wear.

He waved a hand. "Be prompt, please. I'd like to get some work done tonight."

Ursula nodded and went promptly off to the stairs to her rooms, unpinning her own hat as she went. By the time she opened the warding on the door, she had the hat off, stepped out of the shoes, and had decided on which frock to change into. She stripped out of her clothes promptly, hanging them up to dry and be tended, and then shrugged on one of the dresses she'd brought with her when she'd moved, taken from Mum's closet.

She was going to have to argue with Uncle Garin and she needed the proper armour and weapons for it. This one was a deep green, with square folds that hung from the neck, framing her face and giving the whole a rather classical feel. Then she went to the jewellery box on her dressing table, pulling out the brooch Uncle Alexander had given her, which anchored a lot of her personal magical protections.

It was also, mind, gorgeous, a milky chalcedony talisman, meant to give her eloquence as well as protection. He'd given it to her when she began her apprenticeship. Then he'd sat down and explained the details of the work and a bit about who had made it. Slipping her feet into low shoes, she paused by the mirror to tidy her hair and refresh the cosmetic charms, and then went back across the house to knock on the door of his sitting room and office.

"Come." When she entered, Uncle Garin was standing in front of the unlit fireplace, a glass in his hand. He nodded at the glass of wine on the table. "We should discuss."

Ursula sat, crossing her ankles properly. The dress encouraged that sort of thing, which was a help, honestly. "Yes, Uncle?" She was going to make him work for it, not do it for him. He had been irritating enough about it all evening. She was not inclined to make this easier for him. Now, she picked up the glass, taking a small sip - she appreciated the Arundel cellars, of course. She wouldn't insult the wine. And she waited.

"You did not encourage any of the possible gentlemen who wanted your attention." The way he said it almost provoked her to laughter, he sounded like some villainous uncle out of a melodrama, with a plot to marry her off for his good. Oh, her being married and having future heirs was to the family's benefit, but not that way.

"No, Uncle Garin. I did not." Another night, she might have gone on, but no. Not tonight. Not if that was how he started.

"You know your duty." He turned now to face her, using his height and magic to create a bit of pressure. Only, well, Ursula had grown up with Dad right there. Dad had all the same height, a great deal more physical activity, and even more magic around on the average evening than Arundel had on offer. Not that Uncle Garin couldn't call more to his hand. She knew that. But she also knew he probably wouldn't. For one thing, he wouldn't want to risk damage to his own spaces. For another, well, she was reasonably protected against the minor slings and arrows of his magical temper.

"We've talked about this, Uncle Garin. You have agreed you will not press me on this point." She raised an eyebrow, the arch she'd practised in the mirror for hours, and then before Dad and Uncle Alexander for good measure. "Do I need to go through it?"

"Please." This was not a request, for all the word

suggested it. It was not quite an order, either, Uncle Garin knew better than to press that point.

"Xenophon Anders-Whyte would very much like my company, and I am not inclined to give it to him. Honestly, Uncle, hasn't Dad commented? He's well-bred, certainly, but he keeps trying to find the easy way to get things done. That sort can turn into a wastrel as quickly as a devoted husband."

Uncle Garin barely moved, but there was a slight nod at that. Right, Uncle Garin would not defend Anders-Whyte. Ursula still held a particular matter against him, on behalf of her brother. Not that she'd bring that up. It wouldn't help Uncle Garin's temper at all. She went on. "And Samuel Baddock-Martin's a nice sort, but he's the eldest son. His brother's far too young for me, especially if you want a marriage in the next three years. Besides, I know you're dubious about him." Samuel was Heir to his mother, and besides, she'd heard last week that he had another romance in mind. But he was easy to tick off the list.

"Bertie Winslow?" Uncle Garin offered it cautiously. He was the younger son of the current Lord who held South Hampshire. That demesne ran along the border.

"All about automobiles, aeroplanes, and films. That's all fine, but I'm not entirely sure I want to live with it day in and day out. I'm quite sure he'd find life here tedious. Not inclined to farming or the land," Ursula said promptly. "Also, I'm sure someone finds him attractive, but I certainly don't." He had the sort of brittle brashness that would be a lot more under-standable if he'd actually served in combat somewhere.

"Being attracted is not, shall we say, actually a requirement." Now her uncle's voice had gone soft, almost dangerously so. Ursula bit her lip, holding still in caution. "Helios Thanet seemed pleased to see you, and you to see him."

"I enjoy conversations with Helios. But he's Heir in his own right. I can't imagine him giving it up." He'd been engaged before the war. Ursula was enough younger that she hadn't heard details at the time, but had pieced together some of it since. The whole thing had made her think better of him, but it had been a complete mess. His fiancée had been the sort that thought appeasement was a fine idea and that the Nazis were delightful. Helios had broken things off as soon as that became obvious. She'd disappeared into Germany, and Ursula wasn't sure what had happened to her since. It had left Helios in a slightly odd position, though, and still unmarried. Now, Ursula shrugged and went on. "Besides, his parents don't think Mum's breeding is good enough." Which was entirely ridiculous, but some people insisted on being like that.

"You can't just dismiss every eligible man so abruptly." Uncle Garin stood, and here was the temper. The roiling wave of his magic hit her own protections first, then the sound. "You promised me you would duly consider marrying, promptly enough to ensure the continuation of the line."

The thing of it was, he was being an utter hypocrite. He and Aunt Livia had never had children. Dad had told her, before she moved here, that there had been three losses, early in her pregnancies, before they stopped trying. Ursula could never throw that in Uncle Garin's face, not if she ever wanted to talk to him again. And she did, because whatever else was true, she loved her uncle. Even more, she respected all the sacrifices he'd made— and the ones he'd been made into— by and for the family. She would do the same if it was actually necessary. She just didn't think it was, and she was certainly not going to go to an extremity that her uncle had never managed himself.

Now, he'd worked himself up well and proper. He began by listing all the families who might have been matches, if only looking purely at charts and trees and annotations in the Gold Book mattered. "The Farrells are an impeccable line, and their estates are doing well."

"And I do not want any of them as in-laws. You don't either. You were complaining about them just last week." That came out a touch too curt. She'd have to refine that. Ursula took a deep breath. She'd have plenty to discuss and dissect with Mistress Renata tomorrow. Uncle Garin ran on through another half-dozen names, his voice getting deeper and louder with each set, laying out their particular benefits like a man eager to make a deal. It did not suit him at all.

Ursula waited for a pause in the declamation. "Shall I go, Uncle? There's not much of a conversation here."

"Stay." That was a flat order. Ursula looked at him, steadily, considered his current state, and then set down her wineglass. Slowly and deliberately, she picked up the book on the side table next to it and flipped it open. It was, thankfully, at least in English and not in Latin. Reading Latin while Uncle Garin shouted was not at all her idea of a pleasant evening. It was not a topic she'd expected, something about the traditional planting customs and traditions of the county, but that was all to the good at the moment.

He did not quite yell, but his voice filled the room, echoing back at her. Every so often, a sentence had an interrogative lift and a pause. Then she'd make some brief and suitable comment about why she'd considered that man and decided against him. Parents, quite often. Debts, in three cases. Gossip about the sort of habits she didn't want to share a house with, even one as large as Arundel. Someone she was certain would never remotely be faithful. He also couldn't be trusted to be sensible about his health, or hers, in the process. The first part of that wasn't to her taste, but might be managed, but she refused to deal with the second.

She listened, of course, because above everything else she was waiting for when he began to calm down. Twice, she'd had to pull her magics in around her more firmly, as he raged and fumed. Eventually, he began to run out of even vaguely plausible names, ending with "Tiberius Warren?"

"No, Uncle Garin. A bit young for me, and he deserves a chance to figure out what he wants in life." Then she brought her chin up and waited.

"Is that all you are going to say tonight? Thank you, but no?" Uncle Garin took a breath, picked up the glass he'd set down somewhere in the process, and took a long sip from it.

"I made my position on this topic plain when I moved in. You agreed." Ursula knew she had to hold her ground here, or the next argument like this would be far worse. "I am giving due thought to it, and to each and every implication of a match." Even if that meant discarding everyone who seemed plausible.

Any given choice not only had consequences for half her other plans, but she also just plain wasn't very taken with any of the obvious candidates. Oh, Helios and Edmund and a number of others were a good time at a party, for a dance or intelligent conversation. But that wasn't the same as a marriage.

There was a long silence, then the clink of the glass being set down on wood. "We are not going to get further on this tonight."

"Nor any time soon, Uncle. Let's not do it again. Surely we have better ways to spend our time." She tapped the book in her hand. "This, for example. Were you reading this for the bees? The bit about how the lore here says hives must be paid for in gold."

"That is how we've always done it. A trifle tricky, these days, we have to get the gold made up suitably." Uncle Garin took a breath. "We keep the customs."

"Of course, Uncle. That's something I appreciate, always." They went back and forth like that for a few minutes until she was sure he was no longer so tangled in the argument.

"Lammas." Now Uncle Garin looked up. "Be ready to begin at half-nine, please. I've made arrangements for the gathering, same as last year. You are welcome to discuss with Mrs Borrowsmith. It's a bother that we can't be generous with the food, but she has come up with some ideas. There are berries in stasis."

Ursula certainly hoped so. She'd helped pick rather a lot of them, baskets full from the bushes on the estate. They'd make do with a token amount of bread, and whatever else they could put together. The point of the rites was to help there be more food in the coming year, at least. When they'd finished those details, Uncle Garin cleared his throat. "Have you made any progress on reading Maman's journals?"

"A little. Aunt Cammie sent along a number of suggestions of ways to approach it, and some of them help. Others, not as much as I was hoping. It's hard to tell who she's talking about in a lot of passages. We think she's using, oh, a dozen references for the same person or situation." And Ursula hadn't even tried to tackle the most complicated and dense section yet.

"Ah." Uncle Garin cleared his throat. "I'm sure you have things to prepare for tomorrow?"

"Yes, Uncle Garin." It was a dismissal, but at least he was no longer upset. She offered him a kiss on the cheek, she was tall enough she didn't have to strain for that too much. Then he walked her toward the door, bringing the glasses with him to leave for one of the staff to clear and wash. "Good night, I hope you sleep well."

Once his door closed behind her, she made her way steadily back to her own rooms. It wasn't until she was inside that she closed the door and let out a long sigh. She'd had other plans for the evening. But now she needed at least a thorough wash and some sort of novel that had no hint of romance in it whatsoever until she could sleep.

CHAPTER 12

AUGUST 1ST AT A FARM NEAR WALLINGFORD

"Pullan! Jim Pullan, let me have a proper good look at you." Jim had been doing a good job of keeping his back to one of the barn's walls. But he'd turned round for a moment to pass a bench over to Matt. He didn't drop the bench, and he counted that as a victory. Then, a moment later, his mind caught up with him, and he had to smile.

"Mistress Pipp!" Jim took several steps over and then braced himself. She'd been one of his favourite teachers at Snap, even before he'd joined the White Horse and discovered she was a particularly notable member. She was shorter than he'd remembered, more grey in her hair for certain, but she still nearly threw him off balance in an enthusiastic hug.

Then she stepped back to have a good look at him. "There you are, then." She patted his shoulder, the way she did to size up a horse or a cow, and there was something soothing about that, actually. She treated them proper well. "It's good to see you back."

Her voice got softer. "Last of the ones likely to come home."

He'd not known that, actually. Paul had been careful not to mention it, Jim thought, because that was a comment full of dark drops into grief Jim couldn't count. Here and now, he ducked his chin. "I know I've barely written, Mistress Pipp."

"Barely written." She tsked, but agreeably. "And you're a grown man now. You can be calling me Milly." She added, a second later. "Formally it's Milia, but there you are. Some parents have odd ideas about names. At least it's not Pomona. Pomona Pipp would be silly, even if they didn't plan on me marrying a man named Pipp."

"And how is Master Pipp?" Jim could tell a cue. "And your children?" Her children were all grown up. They'd been both enough older and in sufficiently agricultural fields that they'd all been dealing with Land Girls and rationing and finding enough staff, but not going off to fight.

"All well and safe, thanks be. I'll be telling Alfred you asked after him." That had visibly pleased her, and Jim was glad he hadn't completely mangled the social chat. "Now, let's see, there's so much to catch you up on. Can you spare Jim for a few minutes, Matt?" She called it out over his shoulder, and Jim heard Matt's agreeable reply. Milly took his hand and steered him outside, where there'd be a bit more quiet.

The site of the White Horse gatherings, the big ones, like this, varied each time. Today, the instructions had been to go to the Wallingford portal. Then he'd been told to walk west to the far edge of the cemetery, north along the road, and look for a barn. He didn't know whose it was. They were close enough to a couple of villages he was sure it must be someone in the White Horse proper, not a loan. Jim had felt the keep-away when he got close, but he also thought he could feel the damage to the land here.

Standing here, now, he could see the destruction of the flooding. It must have taken out all the fields around here, plus likely whatever was stored in the barn. Mistress Pipp— Milly— saw him figure it out, and she nodded. "It was bad here. While a flood can be good for the land, this wasn't so much."

"Or for the year's growth." Jim rummaged in his head, trying to figure out what to say next. "That's why we're here, then?"

"Mmhmm. Spread the magic along the Thames. There's a few from Many Are The Waters lending a hand with that, up and down river from us. They're easy enough to coordinate with, thankfully."

That made Jim's chin jerk up. "You're senior, Mistress?" He'd somehow missed that news, going back through the journal and the conversation amongst those of the White Horse.

"One of them." Now her eyes were gleaming. "See, if you'd come and had tea, we could have had this conversation with more comfortable chairs and no demands on our time."

"I've had work to be doing." Jim looked away. There was something too determined in her expression to be comfortable for him right now. "So I suppose you're one of the people Paul's been talking to."

"He's been worried about you. I have been too.

Here, tell me what you get from the ground, what you think it needs right now. Magic and not, both."

Jim had known this sort of on-the-spot exam was coming. Doing it here meant there were many people around, but it also meant this couldn't drag out. He'd mess up, he knew that. He wasn't what he ought to be. "May I have a minute?"

Milly nodded once, and more usefully she took a step or two back, giving him space. Jim took a deep breath, then another, doing his best to get a feel for the land. Then he gave up, and squatted down to touch it, fingers pressing into the ground. It was soft enough, even up here by the barn where it'd not have been ploughed. Closing his eyes, he gave himself over to listening to the magic, to touching it. He'd done best with touch all along. Sometimes also sounds, but there was far too much chatter in the background for that to work here.

He gave it a good minute or two before standing up. "I'm sorry. Not much. I know about the flood, everything's all jumbled. I don't know what the land's good for right now. It mostly wants to be left alone, I think. The slow road to recovery, not being poked at and prodded and muddled more."

"That's a good starting place." Milly tilted her head. "And it's not like it used to be for you."

Jim couldn't look at her, but he shook his head slightly. Then, a little braver if he didn't have to say it directly to her face, with her looking at him. "I don't see how it could be."

There was a silence, but Jim didn't think it was a pity sort of silence. It was something different from that. It was like the land under his feet, or he was.

Prodding wasn't helpful. Milly realised that, maybe. After a good minute, she said, "My Alfred fought in the last war. Might do you both a bit of good to talk about coming back. When you're ready. Even if that's not for a little while."

Jim took a deep breath again and let it out. "Not yet, ma'am. But thank you for the offer. Knowing someone might, that's a thing."

What he said, or maybe how he said it, provoked her into a snort of amusement. "Aye, well, you both sound the same about it. That's a start." Then she gestured with the hand well away from him. "What would make the evening best for you?"

It was his turn to snort. "I'm not sure, honest." Now Jim looked out across the fields toward the river, not that he could see that far in the bits of fog and mist coming up. He considered his options, but she'd been his teacher, she'd been an excellent teacher, and she'd asked. That was three good reasons to actually say the next bit. "I don't know what I'm good for anymore. Not work, not magic, not anything else. And being here, that might be a help with some of that, or it might make it worse."

"But you're here anyway." There was a note in her voice now, something interested and curious. "Well. We'll be doing the dancing out here, that side. Best to do it on the earth proper. Food inside, like you were setting up, and benches and all. You can take a step away when you need to. Watch." Then she clucked her tongue. "You've always had an eye for what needs tending. It's hard to get a good look at yourself, but let yourself look at everyone tonight, see what needs a little help. There are worse places to start."

"And will there be people looking at me like that?" Jim asked, still not turning toward her.

"Oh, sweet goodness, there already are. But we don't have all the answers. I'm thinking on it. You know Paul has been. Others too. If we think of a thing might be a help, we'll tell you. I can promise that."

Jim wanted something far more solid and certain, but he would not get it. That much was obvious. "Perhaps a dance, later?"

Milly laughed. "I'd love that. There you go. Sounds like Matt needs a hand again."

When Jim made it back inside, they were at the stage of setting up tables. Food would be in short supply, but having some mattered. Matt was busy getting a couple of casks of beer into place. That was more to drink than Jim had expected, the way people went on about it. He came over to help take one in hand, and once they got them settled, considered the labels. One was from his dad's brewery, several others from good Sussex brewers. "Might not have a lot to eat, but we can drink our grain?" He offered it cautiously to Matt.

Matt shrugged. "Someone was generous with the coin. The brewers can use it." Though of course, a lot of the current barrels would have been made last year sometime, before the flooding. But the brewers would have a lean year this year. Dad had been worrying over it.

Then he looked around. "Isaac's got some bread, and someone managed the charms to filter the flour better, so it's not all stodgy. Think that's most of it. How've you been, then?"

"Settling back in. Getting used to the rain." Jim gestured broadly. "You?"

"Well enough. Looking at settling down, maybe. You remember Ellie Webb?" She'd been the year between them at Snap. Jim remembered her as quiet, but always pleasant, steady.

"Congrats." Jim made it brief. "Wish you very happy, then."

It made Matt smile, anyway. "Could use a bit of that, couldn't we all? I've got a place working for the Kitterings, up in Oxfordshire. You should come have a look if you get a chance. They've a portal. It's easy enough on that end."

"Not so much from mine. But yeah, I'd like to. Maybe after we've got all the harvest in, when there's a bit more time?" It would mean he might figure out how to make small talk again properly before he had to do it with strangers.

"You've got some work, then? That's good." It was pleasant enough, but Matt didn't press for details, and Jim certainly didn't want to get into them. He had picked up days here or there. Whatever tedious work needed an extra set of hands. But nothing steady, nothing that'd let him put down roots anywhere. Certainly nothing that was keeping him out of Luke and Alice's attic for more than a day or two at a time.

For the moment, he shrugged. "Still looking for the right place long-term, if you hear of anything. I'd rather Sussex, but I'd not mind hearing about anywhere."

"Right." Then Matt looked back past Jim's shoulder. "Ah. More folks got here. You want to go check on the dance space, make sure there're benches there? If I see Paul, I'll tell him you're out there."

Jim glanced at where he was looking. There, at the other end of the barn, was Ursula Fortier. She hadn't seen him yet, and whatever conversation might happen about that, he'd prefer it was somewhere with fewer people over his shoulder. It was the third time he'd seen her, and each time he'd been startled by how well she looked. Tonight, she was wearing a green frock, something older. Her hair was braided in a coil around the crown of her head, like a queen or a farmwife in charge of her space.

Only then, he realised something. She was scared. Jim couldn't have explained why he was sure, but he was. Maybe it was having seen enough men about to go into battle, knowing what it felt like in his own body. He didn't think it showed to the others, who kept chattering. No one was greeting her, at least not immediately, though she'd made eye contact with a couple.

Jim wasn't sure what to do with that, either. He retreated out the barn door nearest him. He could go stand in the dancing circle and figure out what else it needed for comfort and the proper charms.

CHAPTER 13
THAT EVENING

The thing about this was that Ursula should not feel so alone. At the same time, her plans allowed for the fact that she expected it to take a decade for the Society of the White Horse to have any idea what to do with her.

Four years ago— four years and three months ago — she'd gone through the initiation on her own with a handful of adults. There had been six people crammed into the front room of Master Isten's cottage before they'd set off for the orchards at the far end of the island. The weather had been unsettled, threats of storms, though the downpour had held off until they were on the way back. She'd slunk into Schola's encompassing walls, getting in just before curfew.

If she'd gone through with Dius Fidius, it would have been a celebration of dozens of people she knew, including Dad and Uncles Garin, Alexander, and Claudio. There would have been the best food they could lay hands on, even given rationing, and plenty of wine and other drink. There'd have been fancy robes, a beautifully decorated house, all the comforts that magic and money could provide.

But she'd known that wasn't for her. Dad and Uncle Alexander and Uncle Claudio certainly did a fair bit in keeping with the focus of Dius Fidius. They all had an expansive generosity with their skills and resources for the larger community. Uncle Garin did, too, though it was less obvious with him. He'd spent his entire adult life, nearly, in service of the Council. Now, it was hours and days trying to come up with alchemical solutions to the horrors of modern warfare.

But the rest of them? Certainly the people near her age saw the glory and not so much the service. Or they thought that doing good was about the show of it. A fête that raised money decorously for some noble cause that could have used something else more.

Ursula wanted to get her hands dirty. Quite literally. Her initiation into the White Horse hadn't been fancy. It hadn't had plenty of people. But she'd done it because she was driven to it. She kept turning toward it, the way she knew how to follow the Wain to Polaris and north. Ursula couldn't explain it, but no one had ever asked her to.

Even when she'd told Mum and Dad last month, as part of talking to Leo about his own choices when it came to secret societies, they'd not prodded at her about why. They'd let her share what she chose. Mum and Dad just wanted to know she was happy.

She was. Only, she was also lonely. She'd be lonely for a while yet, almost certainly. If her plans went more quickly than she had any right to expect, five years. More likely ten, maybe fifteen. It would be longer if she slipped up, and they thought she had the wrong intentions, hurtful, manipulative ones. It rather depended on whether she could do anything that was visibly helpful, beyond paying for the beer and offering jobs when there were jobs to offer. Which there weren't right now, so that wasn't much help.

It was easier with the older generation, the people around Mum and Dad's age. They didn't consider her a threat, maybe. Mistress Farrar and Master Isten had made it clear to her that the younger generation had argued about her invitation. But most of them had been terribly busy with fighting or tending the land. The elders of the society were better able to take a long view and, as Mistress Farrar had said, keep their focus on what the divination had told them. That Ursula could bring something new and needed.

If she could only figure out what that was. She kept having a feeling about it, one like in her initiation, of the earth beneath her feet telling her things. But it was bees, buzzing. She knew it meant things, but she had no idea what. Maybe there'd be something in the dance this year that would make more sense than last year. It kept rolling off her fingers, making her want to grab desperately for something she couldn't see, only to fail to catch it before it shattered on the ground.

Now, she took a breath, and began to move through the gathering, nodding to several people. She hovered at the edge of half a dozen conversations, never quite part of them, though she greeted people and made a comment or two here or there. Ursula was letting herself be seen, demonstrating that she wouldn't try to take over what wasn't hers to touch.

Maybe half an hour after she'd arrived, she'd got as far as the middle of the barn when the music struck up in earnest. Roger Hemming had been angling over toward her, and now he caught her eye. "May I have the first dance?" He was in his late forties. Roger had been more at ease with her because he knew her Uncle Seth, who'd made his clever prosthetic wooden hand.

Ursula snorted. "It's a circle dance, yes? As is tradition?" Given something to work with, it was easier to keep going. "But of course, I'd love to lead off with you. How have you been? And how's Judy? The rest of the family?" His wife was not a member of the society, but as she took his arm, Roger chatted amiably about his children and their families.

As they made their way outside, he tilted his head. "It's been a year for you. Does it feel different yet?"

"Yes and no." It was the true answer and also a quick one. It was taking her a minute to get used to the charmlights in lanterns hung from poles. They moved in the breeze or when people brushed too near them, shifting the light. It was hard to see anyone's face. Before she could say anything more, the music struck up, and she was flung into the necessary steps.

It took ferocious concentration for the first three dances, then something in her shifted. Like Dad got when duelling, from all he'd said, knowing where feet and hands ought to go without having to think about it. By the sixth, she was in the swing of it, trusting that her feet would twist through the patterns. The seventh dance, the last in the first set, was begun with a partner, then the partners changed, repeat by repeat.

On the seventh time through, the change of part-ners brought her face to face with Jim Pullan. He was not shocked to see her, but she was sure she was letting it show. The music gave them no time or breath for conversation. She had to focus on picking up and dropping hands as they wove through the other dancers, split, and came back together again. By the time they were done, she could feel her hair coming down in wisps from the crown braid around her head. The back of her frock was damp with sweat.

They ended face to face again, and Jim bowed as she curtsied, remembering at the last moment to make it the right sort for a country dance, not for the Council rites. She stared at him, not certain what to say, as the others around them moved away, laughing and chattering.

"Here, have a seat, here. Do you drink beer?"

Ursula nodded weakly, and he steered her to a bale of straw at the far edge of the dancing circle. The musicians had left their instruments on the other side, out of the way, and the sky was too cloudy for the stars to be enough comfort. She was sure Jim would disappear into the knot of happy people. She was startled when he came back much faster than she'd thought possible, with two sturdy mugs of beer. He handed one to her, then lifted his before offering a wary, "To necessary conversations?"

Something about how he said it made her laugh, despite herself. "To necessary conversations." She took a long drink from it, then waited. What he said next would be telling, but she didn't know what to expect.

"I couldn't figure out the right way to tell you. Not on the road. Not in the journal." Then Jim's chin jerked back toward the rest of the crowd. "How do you feel about that, then?"

Ursula shrugged. She wasn't inclined to drag her feelings about that, uncomfortable and jagged as they were, out in front of him. Instead, she answered the question he hadn't asked. "The people here have no reason to trust me, to, to..." Words failed her for a moment. That was a sign the evening was still spinning out of control. "To expect I won't mess things up. For them, for the land. I knew coming in it'd take time."

"You've been coming for a year. I asked. And out riding with Bess, and some of them all." Jim turned away, toward the barn, then looked back at her. "How much time?"

"Years, I figure." There was no reason not to be honest. She'd weighed that out already. If she told him and he spread it around, well, it was the truth. If he didn't tell anyone, that was interestingly informative. If he asked her about it, that was a different sort of information.

Now he took a step back, and she was startled to realise he was angry. He hadn't been. The first time they'd met, she'd been sure of it. She was more sure that he was now, because this looked and felt different. There was a coiled tension here. It was so much

CELIA LAKE

like Uncle Alexander or Uncle Orion that it made Ursula want to cry with a twisted sort of relief at knowing where she was. Most of all, she was confused. It made her scramble up, wanting to put space between him and where she was sitting. She absolutely wanted to be on her feet for this, able to move.

Jim backed off almost immediately, putting his hands up, one of them still holding the wooden mug. "You expected that?" His voice had an edge to it still, but something contained and walled off, not threatening her.

"No one here has reason to trust me. Not properly. Well, most people don't." Ursula took a breath, then another. She called on all the tricks Mum and Dad had taught her for weaving through a complicated conversation. Ursula wanted desperately to know who he was angry at and why, and she absolutely couldn't figure out how to ask. She needed to change the subject, she knew that. "You've been a member since your time at Snap? You'd have come in knowing other people, then."

It did not help as much as she'd hoped, but he nodded, lowering one hand and taking a good long sip from his beer. "Not my brother, but one of my brother's best friends. Some people my own year, the ones around it." His chin jerked. "Bess. Some of the others."

Ursula wondered what would be different if he introduced her to them, if she had someone her own age to vouch for her. That she was tidy and didn't go mucking around with other people's magic without permission or understanding. Not that he had a lot of

118

evidence of that yet. It wasn't as if they'd had more than two conversations.

That was the rub, here. If she'd gone into Dius Fidius, it would have been like it was at the Council Keep. She'd be a known quantity, more or less. People would know what she was expected to do, and that she had been trained to do it. Here, no one knew, not enough. "And it's your first ritual back?"

He nodded once, and she'd hit some sore spot, she could see him react to it. But again, she couldn't figure out what or how to avoid doing that in the future. "I've changed, being away. More than some people did." Jim lifted the mug and gestured with it, a little hitch of it. "Will you dance with me again when they pick up? The partner dances?"

No one else was likely to ask her, for one thing. She'd sat most of them out last year, but she knew them. The next set was a series of patterns, but keeping the same partner throughout. Also, dancing would mean she wouldn't need to figure out safer conversational topics. Ursula nodded once. "If you wish. I believe I know the steps."

Jim's eyes went wider for a moment, but then he just nodded, encouraging her to finish her beer and taking the mugs back. He returned to her side just as the musicians started forming up again. When he held out his hand, she put hers into it, to find his grip was strong and steady.

CHAPTER 14
THE NEXT MORNING NOT LONG
AFTER DAWN

"Blessed Lammas." Jim waited by the portal until the magic had flared and dissipated. It was right around dawn, perhaps twenty minutes past. Ursula had stayed that long, but she'd said she had obligations later that morning and she had to wash up first.

She hadn't said what, but Jim knew Arundel had some sort of Lammas rite as a demesne. He did not know what it involved, but she'd want to change, yes. The dress had flattered her, and her hair up like that had too.

But those weren't the sort of things posh people wore when they were doing posh things. Different shoes, for one, and her hair done differently, and probably sparkling jewels. Though when he'd seen her so far, she'd been dressed sensibly for what she'd been doing. Maybe that was a different sort of sense for a different sort of task. He'd be thinking about that for a good bit.

First, though, he'd be thinking about the dark

hours of the night. The partnered dances had gone smoothly. Either she was an incredibly quick study, or she'd put a great deal of time in. With someone else, because that was the thing about a partner dance, you had to track where the other person was. With her, everything had been smooth. They'd flowed. The land had liked it. Jim had liked it.

None of the dances the White Horse used were unique to them. They used the same country dance moves as a number of others, the sort widely done at the Midsummer Faire or whatever other gatherings came up. Maybe out at Schola, too, though the idea of rows of people swirling in country dances in the academic robe they wore made him snort.

Jim hadn't wanted to crowd her. In the breaks between the dancing, and then the hours of quiet, before dawn, he hadn't wanted to hang on her elbow. She'd talked with perhaps a dozen people, no one their own age except for Bess. That had seemed pleasant, but was fairly quick, more like checking in about something later. No one their age had made her particularly welcome, or invited her into a conversation, or gone out of their way to notice what she was up to.

And that made Jim angry. He could feel it boiling up again, walking back to the barn. He'd been warned that coming back from war could make a man angry about odd things. But this was an entirely reasonable and justified anger. They were a society, sworn to the same goals. They'd made the same oaths, and it was supposed to make them brothers and sisters in the work. Now he couldn't understand why she had just accepted it.

Which meant that when someone jogged his elbow, Jim almost snarled at whoever it was, before he got himself under better control. It was Paul, who immediately stepped back, as if he'd seen something he didn't like much. "Hey."

Jim did not know what to say to that. Paul had to know what the score was. He'd talked with Jim about some of it, but he apparently hadn't done anything to make it better. Jim had been watching her near all night, even before the dancing. "What?" He could hear the irritation in his voice, and he took a breath, before repeating it more moderately. "What? Something the matter?"

"Tell me why you're angry?" Paul took half a step back, then added. "You walked her back?"

"The portal." She'd made a point of showing him the settings for Arundel and telling him he could come through there if he wanted. It was miles closer than the one just outside Horsham. Jim had been warned not to try the one outside Petworth, it hadn't been stable since 1942.

Horsham was a good ten-mile walk. He'd done it last night, well hitched a ride for more than half of it. Not that he felt he could trust the invitation to use the Arundel one. Not sensibly. But the Arundel estate, that was four miles back home. Or home for now. It was an easy walk, roads he knew well.

He'd probably give into the temptation, at least if he got away early enough that he was unlikely to run into whoever was arriving at Arundel for the day. Now he waited to see what Paul did.

"And why are you angry?" The thing about Paul was that he had a way of putting distance between himself and what was going on. It was protective, Jim knew that. Given Paul's Dad, and his Mum, for that matter, he'd learned how to let things flow around him. Things were better now, they had been for a while, but what a body learned early stuck.

Jim took a breath. "Why isn't she made welcome? She's one of us."

"She's not." Then Paul inhaled, Jim heard it, and said, carefully. "You disagree."

"Of course I disagree. Come on, Paul. You've had enough of the same lessons about introducing a new horse or sheep or chicken to a herd or flock. You've done it more than enough. Every last one of you, within a decade of your age, is treating her like she can't be trusted. Certainly can't be included. Of course I'm angry. How in all the bloody muck of the world did you let it get this bad here? All of you."

Jim turned away, feeling his heart pounding, because he knew now he wasn't fit for being around other people. Yesterday evening, he'd have said decent people, but that might or might not be true. Paul didn't reach out, didn't try to say anything. Jim took a couple of steps back toward the door, intending to go back to the Wallingford portal, and to Horsham, and a long walk home. By the time he got back, he'd be too exhausted to do much to annoy Alice and Luke.

There were steps behind him, but he was past the door, maybe three or five feet, when he heard Milly's voice. "Can I have a word then, Jim?"

Probably no one else could have got him to stop. Jim closed his eyes, hovering there without moving a muscle, before he turned slowly around. There was

Milly, Mistress Pipp. Paul was on one side, and a couple of others of the men between their ages. Next to Milly was Roger Hemming, who Jim didn't know well. He did crafting, not farming. And Bess Nivens, next to him, and two women round her age.

Jim let out a huff of breath, not moving beyond the twitch of his shoulders. "I'm not fit for company, don't you think?"

"And that's when you need some. Bess, can you sort out another round of beer? There's still some. Jim, will you come and sit down, so we can talk? Ten minutes. If that's not working, we'll wish you well and see you on your way for now."

The thing of it was, he'd sworn oaths, the same ones they had, and those oaths had commitments to sorting a thing out. Making an honest attempt, anyway. He could feel the power of the magic coiling around him for just an instant as a reminder, then he nodded once and took step after slow step back inside. Milly made her way to one of the smaller and rickety tables with benches on each side. She sat facing Jim, Roger sliding in to a seat next to her. Paul stood just behind, but Bess was brave enough to sit on the same side as Jim.

To his surprise, it wasn't Milly who spoke. Roger cleared his throat. "We couldn't help overhearing some of that. And you're right. The problem is, we don't know what to do about it."

"Treat her like any other member? Get someone to introduce her round, properly? Talk to her about—about all of it? I suppose someone did some of that. She knows the dances."

"She's a quick study, actually." Milly folded her

hands on the table. "Gwen Farrar taught her most of it. Henry Isten's known her since she was tiny. But last August was her first time at one of our larger rites. And it's..." She shrugged. "It's no excuse, but we've all got our own things keeping us busy. Stretched to the limit. Especially this spring."

"And still, none of you could take twenty minutes tonight?" Jim said. "Pardon, sir." He nodded to Roger. "You did, I'm thinking?"

"Oh, I did." Roger said. "But I have a bit of an advantage. I know her uncle. Not the Fortier one, one of the Wain ones. Up near where Bess lives, Trout-beck way."

Jim nodded once, chewing that over. "And what did that change for you, then?"

Roger chuckled warmly. "Ah, you're a quick study too, aren't you?" He spread his hands out, and Jim saw one of them was wood. "Seth made this for me. Doesn't do all a flesh and blood hand does, but it's handy as anything, pun intended, for holding something steady while I work. I don't need to worry so much about the awl going astray." That was right, he did leatherwork, some harness fitting, other work like that. He uncurled the fingers, then brought them back to a loose fist. "And Seth, now, he's so proud of his children and his nieces and his nephews. I heard a bit about her before we looked at an invitation. And more since."

"I asked her to go out riding, after last year. When, yeah, she was all on her own. She'd talked down her uncle, the Fortier one, this time, to let her come without pushing to find out where. No one knew what to make of that. Matt made a fuss about it until Roger called him on it." Bess lifted a finger. "And we've gone riding every month or so. But not the last couple. I've had to be at home. Grandmum's needed someone with her all the time. You're right, that's not much, over a year."

It saved Jim from saying it, at least. Now he looked at a spot on the table. "It's not right. Either she's one of us or she's not. She's made the oaths, so she is. She needs to be." As he said the last sentence, he felt something stronger than he'd expected. It wasn't just personal, whatever this was. It was something larger than him or Ursula, or anyone at the table.

Jim felt someone shift, not physically, but magically, and then he heard Paul's voice. "You feel that, then? I do too. Now you've, um. Called me on it." It helped to hear Paul admit that, but then Paul went on. "We owe her better. We owe a bunch of people better. There's something..." He let out a breath. "Can't get a grip on it."

Milly nodded. "Will you try what you can to name it, Paul?" He nodded once, without specifying what. There was a fair chance it'd mean Paul sleeping out on the ground on some hilltop with lore behind it. But it wasn't as if Sussex was lacking in options for that. "And you, Jim. We've no right to ask you to take more on right now."

"I made oaths too." Jim looked up to meet her eyes. "What do you want to ask?"

"How did it feel, dancing with Ursula tonight? You too, Roger."

Jim had to think about the right words for it. "Good. Better than good. I enjoyed it for one. I wasn't

—" He stopped because the next bit was true, and it was admitting a vulnerability he wanted to bury deep. "I felt like she was watching my back. The way my friends did— back." Back during the war, back on the continent, back when not doing that ended in death. "I felt like I could trust her to know what she was doing. She was doing the magic of it right, too. The flow. I didn't expect that."

A lot of people went through the motions, and that wasn't wrong, it wasn't bad. Just making the right motions stirred the magic up, and people with more sensitivity and skill could guide it. Ursula had been doing it all for herself, near as naturally as breathing, as far as he'd been able to tell.

Roger snorted. "Well. There are some things they teach at Schola might be a help to us. I asked Seth about it last month. I was curious. He went there himself, besides his sister teaching. No, she's got some sense for it. And for the land. Though that's maybe less formed."

Jim wasn't so sure that was the case, but he also didn't have evidence to argue with. "So you want me to— go talk to her more?"

"If you would. About whatever seems right to you. The Society, lore, Sussex. Whatever makes sense."

"Bees," Jim said, amiably. "She was looking for bees."

"I'll ask around." Paul said, immediately. "More, anyway. Luke already mentioned." He added that to Jim.

"And you write and let me know how things are getting on. Maybe we can sort out something smaller, better for getting to know her and her to get to know us, for Harvest Home, somewhere?" It was a more flexible sort of gathering. There'd be dozens around Albion. "A plan to be getting on with."

"Yes'm." The honorific came out automatically, and now Milly reached across to pat his hand.

"Right. We should all do our bit tidying up, I think, and get on home. You let me know when you want to come visit, Jim. It'd do you good to have a chat, my Alfred and you both."

"Yes'm." Jim knew when he was outmanoeuvred. But then he could stand up and put himself to work and do something he was competent at for a bit.

CHAPTER 15
AUGUST 2ND AT ARUNDEL

Ursula woke slowly, curled up on her side in the same position she'd fallen asleep in. The incense in the tent was much lighter now. Time had obviously passed. She didn't open her eyes yet, holding the memories of the vivid dream she'd had in her memory. Before she could move, there was a voice near her head. "Notebook and pencil." Then they were pressed into her hands.

"Thank you, Uncle Alexander." Before she did anything else, she wrote out what she remembered, quick strokes of the pencil forming both words and sketches. There had been bees, metal ones, dozens of them. The pile was mostly copper or bronze, but as she'd watched, others dropped down one by one. Gold, gold, silver, gold, silver. Then, when she thought they'd stopped, gold and silver that fell beside each other, a distance from the others. There was one underneath them that kept catching at her attention, a different sheen, but she never got a good look at it. There was a rumbling, like a thunderstorm, and flashes of lightning.

She took a breath and brought her mind back to the rest of it. The best description she had, and the word she wrote down, was wistful. Like she was reaching out for something that was needed, but she didn't know the shape of it. Not yet, anyway. There was a shadowy figure in the distance, out of reach, too far to see clearly. Closer in, she had got flickers of places around the estate and the various properties owned by the family.

Some of those she knew, some of them she didn't. That involved more sketches, descriptions, anything she could think of that would hold the space in her mind long enough to recognise it again. What she did know was that the points would help make a net. Something that would hold and support other magic, necessary magic. She didn't know what that magic was or how to do it, but she could get a sense of the container, at least.

She kept coming back to a particular feeling. It was like when she'd taken Jim Pullan's hand for the dancing, last night. A root that went deep and strong, steady in a way she didn't always feel about Arundel. Arundel was ancient, but it was also battered, with places that were weaker than they ought to be. She wanted to sit with that feeling for a long time, and now was not the moment for it. Instead, she went back to sketching, capturing all the fleeting glimpses before they faded.

It took her a while. Long enough that when she looked up again, Uncle Alexander was perched on a stool. There was a cup of tea steaming gently on the small table next to him. Ursula pushed herself upright, automatically folding up the light wool blanket that had been over her feet as she looked around. "Dad and Uncle Garin and Leo?"

"All finished much before you did. As did I. Everyone's chatting outside. I let them know you'd be a few more minutes. Take your time, there's no rush." Ursula considered him, wondering why he was the one in here, and Dad wasn't. She hadn't expected Uncle Garin to be the one doing the tending here, of course, but Uncle Alexander was unexpected.

"Are you all right, Uncle Alexander?" This was the first time he'd joined them inside the tent. The Fortier Lammas rites had a number of other traditional pieces. When she emerged, there'd be bread made from wheat grown on the demesne estate, honey from the hives, butter from the dairy. She and Uncle Garin had already walked the bounds in token, just one field. But they'd been working their way around the entire outer border, piece by piece, all last week and they'd finish it this week. There'd been the libation, of course.

And then there was the core of today's rituals. That went back to the Merovingians, where the Fortiers traced their magical lineage, and a series of visionary dreams. Each Lammas key members of the family had a divinatory nap. Cots were brought out, a pavilion, alchemically tuned incense to encourage the right sort of state. Uncle Garin made that himself, of course, adjusting an ancient family recipe depending on who would be there. Last year had been Ursula's first time, along with just Uncle Garin and Dad.

This year, she'd asked whether Leo and Uncle Alexander could join. If they wanted. Uncle Garin had considered it; he'd taken a fortnight to do so, and talked to both Dad and Mum about it. Possibly also Uncle Alexander. And then he'd agreed. Now, Ursula wasn't sure if it had been a good idea. On the other hand, Uncle Alexander could have said no.

Now he turned his hand palm up, palm down. "You know what day it is. I dreamed of Perry, among other people. It was a good dream. I am glad I had it. But it aches, waking."

"Oh." Ursula reached out to touch his hand. "Oh." It was the anniversary of Uncle Perry's death, Dad had been feeling it hard too. Uncle Perry was the uncle she'd never met, died a decade before she was born, on Lammas in 1917. He and Dad had been best friends all through school, inseparable, and, as Dad said, making each other better. Dad and Uncle Perry and Uncle Alexander and two others had been fighting, doing the kind of fighting Dad didn't talk about, during the Great War. Dad still thought it was chance he was alive and Uncle Perry wasn't. Then she cleared her throat. "Should I apologise for asking you to join us?"

"No, no." Uncle Alexander's voice was both very gentle and so solid it was ageless and potent, all at once. He went on, not calling attention to that. "I'm glad I did. I'm still thinking about some of what I saw, but that's fine. I'll be at Ytene tonight. You needn't worry I'll be lonely." The trick of being here was that he couldn't be at Ytene for the Carillons' rites. But Ytene's Lammas rites were less involved, on the whole.

"Come for supper, sometime? I'll sort it out with Uncle Garin. After this week, obviously." She was spending a day or two with Aunt Hypatia and Uncle Orion while her apprentice mistress was on holiday. It was a chance to see a little more of how Fairlight worked as a demesne estate. Also, Ursula wanted to pick Aunt Hypatia's brain about half a dozen bits of magical theory they never ordinarily got time for. Besides, she loved watching the two of them, and the expression Uncle Orion got on his face. It was the way Dad looked at Mum, as if he were amazed she was right there, loving him back just as hard.

The thing she hadn't been able to explain to Uncle Garin was that whoever she married, she wanted to look at them like that. Have them look at her that way. Both. Because Mum and Aunt Hypatia did it too.

Which brought her back to that slightly wistful and undefined feeling. Reaching for the teacup, she took a breath. "How's Dad? And Leo? And Uncle Garin?"

Uncle Alexander chuckled. "Leo's bursting with questions about it, and Garin was talking through some of it with him when I came back in. Your father is talking to your mother and the uncles on her side. Garin seemed in quite a good mood, actually. Though it's always a trick to tell with him. Anything you want to talk out now?"

Ursula shook her head. "It's the sort of thing I want to think through. Ask Dad, maybe, later. And of course, I'll tell Uncle Garin, too."

"There we are, then." He hesitated, and Ursula could hear the weight of the pause better, thanks to her ongoing apprenticeship. "I'm glad you asked if I would." Then he coughed and added. "Why did you? You never said."

"It's your own fault you've been a model for not answering questions my whole life and then some, Uncle Alexander." Ursula pointed out. But then she softened, because he had his reasons for that, and those weren't her reasons. "You lived here, growing up. And you're my godfather. That's a familial relationship of a particular kind. You never had been part of this bit of the rites, before?"

He shook his head, just the once. "Laudine and Dagobert considered it, I suspect. But it would have made a statement that had consequences, with whoever was here as a guest. It's certainly not something I'd ask for. But you're right. I was born here, in the gatehouse. We lived here all the time until I was nine or so and Ummi got the townhouse in Trellech. I've many happy memories to go with the ones that were less so." The gatehouse had been empty ever since, not that Ursula was going to ask about that right now. They sat in silence as Ursula finished her tea, and then Uncle Alexander offered his arm, all elegant formality.

Once she came out, she was thrust into a conversation about bees, but living ones this time. Mum had been talking to her mum and Eloise and Aunt Dilly, all of whom had thoughts about bees, and where best to consider new hives. The question was how widely to spread them, and also which places they could do particular wonders.

Fortunately, everyone seemed to be roughly on the same page about the way to go about it. Mum

and Grandmum planned to come down in a fortnight and go look at sites, as well as maybe seeing
about swarms. Bringing them to and through a
portal from Cumbria would be a trick, but it was
possible, and Grandmum knew all the bee gossip
from near her. It was from Grandmum that Mum
and Ursula got their love of beekeeping and the
magic that went with it. Ursula liked having that
connection coming from both sides, making the land
more whole and healthy.

The rest of the afternoon went on smoothly
enough. Ursula had read enough of the journals to
know that sometimes things went wrong or at least
oddly. Those were the sort of omens people stared at
for months afterward to try to interpret. There was
none of that today. Everyone agreed the land needed
support and help and tending. The war had done so
much damage, along with turning over fields to agriculture that weren't used to it. But that was different
than some great problem no one had noticed.

By the time most people had left, going back to
their own homes and rations for supper, it was just
Uncle Garin, Mum, Dad, and Leo. Uncle Garin agreed
to talk out the dreams tomorrow after breakfast and
went off to his lab. Mum and Dad and Leo came up to
Ursula's sitting room for a simple supper and more
conversation. Once they'd mostly finished eating,
Dad leaned back, putting his feet up on one of the
stools. "How does it feel to have been here a full
year's cycle, then?"

"Good, Dad. Still really good." She nudged Leo's
foot with one of her toes, to get a little more room on
the smaller sofa for both of them. Leo had gained

another inch again, she was sure of it. "And Leo, glad you joined us. It wasn't too much?"

Leo shook his head. "It was, um. Distant? Sort of like stars, I felt like I had enough time to figure out what I was seeing?" He glanced at Mum, who grinned back at him. She had said, so many times, that one thing she liked about stars is that they were a long way away and she generally had time to figure out what she thought about what they were doing. "Thanks. For asking me." He flushed a little, more shy than Ursula had expected.

"Hey, maybe you'll have a piece of what's going on that I don't. Or that Uncle Garin doesn't. Besides, it felt silly last year, to set up the pavilion and all for just three people."

Mum chuckled. "See, there's the practicality I like to see. Though you could fit another half-dozen cots in there without trying. I'm glad you invited more people down."

"It used to be one of the showy feasts of the year," Dad said slowly. "Even when I was little. May Day was showing off art and style, and also a particular sort of romantic battle, done in poetry. Solstice was the Council rites, of course. Lammas was a chance to show off the largesse of the estate, which works better with a crowd. Making people stand around waiting for you, which is one of those shows of power that's not as subtle as people think it is."

"Sorry, Mum, for making you wait," Ursula said. Though Mum had been waiting for Dad to dream ever since they got married. That wasn't Ursula's fault.

"That, love, is why I'm glad Mum and Dad came

down. I loved talking more to Eloise and the bees. Really, we ought to figure out a proper tour of the orchards here. Maybe not the same day, though."

"I'll sort out a map for you and send you a copy. Some spots we're thinking of for bees overlap with the orchards. Some don't, but that's bees for you."

Mum snorted. "Quite. Can you get free for a day sometime for the mead? We have enough honey we can, even with what we're keeping for the school's use." That was a family tradition, and there were various incentives to encourage honey right now, given the sugar rationing. That was the kind of tradition Ursula particularly loved, something made with care and attention, to nourish a new marriage and sweeten it. It reminded her, though, of something she'd meant to ask Dad.

"Week after next, maybe? Send me a couple of days and times and I'll see when I can get free?" She was going to be terribly busy, actually, between the visit, keeping up on reading for her apprenticeship, being out on the land, and whatever else happened. Something would, she was sure. She could feel it sort of itching at her, the potential. "Dad? Can I ask you a question? About your parents."

"Oh?" Dad pushed himself a little more upright. "Have you got further in Maman's notes?"

"A bit. Aunt Cammie gave me some ideas, but then we got to where I need to stare at it some more." Ursula paused. "There's that long bit I told you about, after great-grandmother died."

"I was four then." Dad rubbed his nose, slowly. "I barely remember it, mostly everything draped in black."

"Something changed, but I've no idea what." Ursula didn't even know what she was asking for here.

"What does Garin say?" Dad asked, quite reasonably.

"I asked. He was just back from Schola, after his first year." Ursula thought about what Uncle Garin had and hadn't said. "From what I got out of him, he was, um. Dutiful's the right word. But she'd been more ill that spring, and of course, she couldn't say anything back. Just peer at him."

"The person who might know more is Alexander." Dad said. "Give him a week or two, though, would you? Today was—" Dad stopped. "He wouldn't let anyone see him hurting, for so long. Even when..."

Before Dad had to go on, Mum said, softly. "Even when you were hurting for the same reason. Now he will let people see and help. That's much better than the alternative. I'm glad he's off with Geoffrey and Lizzie and Edmund and Merry and Ros tonight. Not alone with it." Mum considered, "Have you ever seen the gatehouse, Ursula?"

She shook her head. "Should I ask to? Ask him?"

"It seems a shame to have it empty for so long. Your rooms here are lovely, but maybe that would do well for a larger workroom or consulting space, if you wanted to do that. A separate entry, distinct from the house, all that. Might just shake something loose for him, to show you."

Dad snorted, amused. "I remember when the idea of setting up our rooms at Schola overwhelmed you.

Now you're having architectural ideas of your very own."

"I have spent time chatting with one of the best architectural magic specialists of our age, you." Mum said, teasing back. "I'm still not—" She stopped. "I'm not easy with it, exactly. But it's Ursula doing it now. And Garin, who is no longer so inclined to roar or snipe at me." And there was no Aunt Livia, who would have been difficult. All of them could fill that in without Mum saying it. "I don't know. Go have a look sometime."

"I'll ask Uncle Garin about it." Then she nudged Leo's foot. "All right, you. Tell me what you've been up to. Besides reading. How was your trip to London in more detail?"

CHAPTER 16
AUGUST 10TH NEAR ARUNDEL

Jim was not at all sure what he'd got himself into. He had heard nothing from Ursula Fortier for nearly a week. Then on Wednesday, she'd written to ask if he could meet up with her to talk further. By the time she'd written, he'd already found himself work through Saturday, so he'd offered Sunday. Then he'd asked where.

It was a tricky question. He had no desire to go anywhere near the Arundel demesne estate. It wasn't exactly about trust, though that was part of it. Getting too near it had made him feel odd for years, well before he'd gone to fight. He didn't want to test that now.

At the same time, they couldn't go into a pub together. There wasn't a magical one this side of Crawley. He certainly couldn't invite her to come up to the farm. There'd be a dozen people sticking their noses in. No matter that only seven lived there, besides Jim. So instead, he'd posed the question, asking for somewhere quiet, maybe with a roof.

She hadn't replied for hours, then she'd written back with a suggestion of a shepherd's hut, near enough to the Arun he could come down along the river. She'd added "Tenant farm, no sheep there this year." Which, he supposed, gave her a reasonable right to make use of the hut. Jim couldn't decide what to make of the fact she'd picked somewhere near enough halfway between them, not that she knew exactly where he lived. Probably. Now he was starting to wonder. She certainly had people she could ask, since she not only had his full name but the White Horse connection.

When he turned up early, she was already waiting. This time, there was no horse, and she was in a calf-length green split skirt, rather like the Guard's uniform, with calf-high brown boots and a cream blouse. A straw hat was firmly on her head, with green ribbon holding it in place under a braid down her back. It suited her unreasonably well. He felt shy of his clean but patched hard-wearing trousers and scuffed boots and the shirtsleeves rolled up to his elbows.

"Afternoon. I've a flask of black currant squash, if you like?" Jim wondered what she was like, being hospitable with posh people. He nodded, cautiously, and she handed a flask over, another in the basket beside her. "I hope this wasn't too out of the way for you."

Jim shook his head, feeling like he was already well behind in this conversation, but he certainly would not point that out to her. "A pleasant walk today, though with any luck the rain holds off until evening. I hope you've been well?"

"Very busy, but quite well. I spent a couple of days with Aunt Hypatia and Uncle Orion. That was grand. And I've been thinking about the Lammas rites rather a lot. I'm glad you were willing to talk more. I've a few questions for you." Jim stiffened, and suddenly her voice changed. "Pardon. I'm being fearfully rude. May I start again?"

Cautiously, Jim nodded once, as much because he wondered what on earth she meant.

"Good afternoon. I'm Ursula Fortier, and I've been thinking a great deal about the land, both the bits of it I have some say in, and all the bits they touch. Now that I know you share some of the same particular interests, I'm hoping you'd be willing to help me with some of what I'm trying to figure out. Also, you went to Snap. Which I want to ask you a lot about, actually."

On the one hand, that was rather a tidy summary, assuming that was actually what she wanted to say. On the other hand, he had absolutely no idea where to start with it. "Why are you asking me, then?"

Ursula considered, then pulled one of the crates outside the hut over, leaving Jim to take the steps if he wanted. He did, which put his head just about level with hers. "You asked me to dance." That was also true, and it was also no help at all. He already knew that part. Not that he could put into words all of why he'd done that.

"You're a fine dancer, those dances." Jim ducked his head at the end, not sure how she'd take it.

"You're better." The thing of it was, he kept looking for something in her tone that was condescending, posh. Something that was her assuming she was better at whatever it was they were talking about because of her birth or her going to Schola or who knows what else. He'd certainly met enough of that type. But she kept not doing it, and he kept looking for the trap. "It's the flow of them that matters, doesn't it? And there are ways people enhance that, but I don't know those yet. Not enough to do them reliably, and I won't do it badly."

Jim let out a little sigh, despite himself. "Tell me what you know about the land, then. Start somewhere." Maybe, just maybe, he could figure out what to say next, given that.

She folded her hands in her lap, the way he assumed ladies did at fancy teas or whatever they did. But when she spoke, it was clear, thoughtful, and correct. "What I know is that I do not know enough. I do not have the language to describe what I do know. I can touch the ground, especially on the demesne lands, and know that what we have isn't good enough. It's the strain of having been pushed beyond a sensible limit already, and with more effort needed. I have glimpses of what might help— more beehives, for example. But I don't know which choices are, what's the word, looking at longevity, rather than the next season or two. Uncle Garin had some thoughts about fertilisers, alchemical ones, but I think that might be too much. It would work for a year or three, but then it would deplete the ground."

"Like what?" The question came out of him, even though he wasn't sure he could follow the answer.

Immediately a tangle of Latin names followed, but before he had to admit he wasn't following that, not that way, she stopped. "Uncle Jehan's not actually sure it would work properly, for one thing, not that it's an easy conversation to have with Uncle Garin. I can send it along in the journal, and the common names, and the research and all that. Not that I don't think there are specific spots it might help? But there are other spots, and they sort of suck magic into them, oddly. I was asking Uncle Orion about it a few days ago, and he's got spots like that, too. He's in northern East Sussex. Though we think a lot fewer or more shallow, or whatever the right word is. Then I asked Uncle Alexander what he knew, and Uncle Seth and Uncle Golshan. Because Cumbria's different again, isn't it, and they got less of the Blitz."

The rush of names, at least these weren't Latin, mostly, made him blink. "That seems a lot of uncles?" It was the first thing out of his mouth.

She laughed, and he liked her laugh. He liked her laugh too much, maybe. There was something completely honest about it. It had a chime like some of the lore about bells lost to the coast or some deep pond, ringing despite everything. "Also a lot of aunts." She said it like it was a shared joke, not a correction or her knowing more than he did, even if, obviously, in this case, she did.

Ursula ticked off on her fingers. "Most of them I'm not blood related to. Uncle Garin, who I live with now, on Dad's side. Mum's the middle of seven, three brothers, three sisters, all of them married with children. Uncle Seth is Mum's favourite brother, and Uncle Golshan lives with him and Aunt Dilly. They're the ones I talk to most. Uncle Alexander's my godfather. But there are also family friends, and I call most all of the other teachers at Schola aunt or uncle.

Growing up there, I mean, they were right there. I had supper with them most nights. Usually other meals, too."

It made a certain sort of sense, if one were going to call many people aunt and uncle. After a moment, she added. "Uncle Orion is, um. On the one hand, he was one of Dad's particular students. Aunt Hypatia was an aunt to me before she married him. Her older brother teaches at Schola."

Something nagged at Jim about Orion, but it was a common enough name, and certainly plenty of them must live in other parts of Sussex. "Right." It came out weakly. "I have— I mean, there are lots of people who take an interest. But my parents moved to Worthing with my middle brother. I'm living with my older brother and his wife and their kids."

"So you get to be uncle!" Ursula seemed honestly delighted by that. "Leo, my brother, is younger. So I have to make do with cousins, and I don't get to see them nearly enough. Though it must have been hard, coming back, when they hadn't seen you for an age."

Jim swallowed hard, remembering what that had been like. He hadn't expected anyone to rush to hug him, though Luke and Alice had been welcoming enough. But the little ones had hung back, hiding behind Alice's skirts, for a good couple of days. "It took a little. I thought it was something I did wrong."

"Not that I'm an expert here, but I gather that's pretty normal. Especially very young kids. Mum said it's how they're not really as connected to linear time as adults have to be, and so the gaps get to be odd shapes in their heads? But Mum says things like that about time." She shrugged, as if that were an ordinary sort of conversation to have. "Anyway. I know that the land needs help. I do not want to give the wrong help. You are in the Society of the White Horse. You went to Snap. Also, you live nearby. Three excellent reasons to ask you. You know more than I do, and I would like to learn, please."

This time, he flinched. He couldn't help it. Everything she wanted was everything he doubted about himself. Now he looked down at the ground between them, focusing on that rather than on the tips of her boots or anything higher. There was a silence then. She didn't rush in to fill it. When it stretched on and on, she cleared her throat quietly before asking, "Why did you get angry last week?"

Jim flinched again, but she'd said it gently. That was the thing. He knew what terror felt like, down to his bones. He knew what it was like to be certain someone was watching him, who'd make him dead if they could. Jim knew the betrayal of his own body, when even breathing was something he was failing at. This was something different. If she could feel through things with the same touch when it came to the land, he wasn't sure he had anything to teach her.

Without looking up, he managed to fumble for words. "You're one of us. Our sister. You made the oaths, you went through the rites, you've learned enough to get started. I got angry because you should have had a welcome, long since. And they hadn't." He swallowed hard, something bitter in his mouth, and then fumbled for the flask for a bit of the black currant squash. "I got angry at them, too, once I walked back from the portal."

It took him a minute to look up. She was sitting

there, her head tilted, obviously thinking. "Well. That just makes it obvious you're the one I should talk to." She almost went on to say something else, but then she stopped. "Look, part of why I wanted to talk to you was, do you know anything about the Arundel Lammas rites?"

Jim shook his head. "Not the sort of thing I'd be invited to."

At least then he could sit and listen while she explained. The thing of it was, it was all dressed up fancy. A pavilion and special cots, the kind of thing you needed to have space to store between times. But the basic idea of it wasn't so different from some of what Jim did, some of what Paul did. What the Society of the White Horse did, at least half of them, regularly enough. Laying out on the land, giving yourself to dream or silence, to listen to the land. The way she talked about it, she took it seriously, the right kind of serious, and so did Lord Fortier. Jim hadn't expected that.

When she talked about what she'd seen and felt, she talked most about specific spots. About wanting to identify them. She had brought the notes she'd made. He recognised a couple of spots, from the curve of the hill and the older trees, but he didn't know all of them. "Can you tell me how to get to them? Or take me round to them, sometime?"

"I've work." He wasn't sure if he was asking her to pay for his time, or whether he didn't want that between them. The White Horse folks were practical. Sometimes coin was a sensible trade for time, but he didn't know how she saw that.

"And I've got my apprenticeship. And things with

Uncle Garin. Perhaps another Sunday? Whatever would do for you and be fair?" She leaned forward. "We could go by horseback, if that helped. I don't know what makes things easier for you, or more possible, but I'm open to discuss."

He was not sure that seeing more of her in breeches would actually help him concentrate on any other topic, but he certainly wasn't going to say that. It wasn't as if her conversation were less prone to making him feel tongue-tied and like he was thirteen or fourteen again. The age he'd been when he had just noticed girls were interesting for being girls, and not for all the other reasons he might want to talk to someone. He nodded. "Another Sunday, sure. We can sort that out in the journals."

"Good. Then can we talk through, I don't know." She tapped the notebook. "This bit? What I should pay attention to when I go there?" That, at least, got him onto something that felt like more solid footing. Jim could talk about how to spot a healthy hedgerow or field much more comfortably once he got started. She listened, making brief notes and asking him questions, until the light changed enough that he coughed. "I need to get home. Sheep and cows and all."

"Of course." Then Ursula smiled at him, focusing directly on him in a way she hadn't done. It was like getting the full sun on his face, after a cloudy day, and he blinked twice. "Thank you. For sharing what you know and for asking me to dance." Before he could say much of anything back, she stood up. "I'll write." Then she was immediately off, down the path away from him, as if she didn't want to linger.

He watched her go, the sway of the skirts and the way she walked quickly over the path, even the bits of roots and stones in the way. She knew where her feet were, and he'd be thinking about that metaphor for ages now.

CHAPTER 17

AUGUST 12TH AT ALEXANDER'S
TOWNHOME, TRELLECH

"If you want to borrow that, you may." Ursula looked over her shoulder at Uncle Alexander. She'd thought he'd been entirely focused on the other set of bookshelves. Then she glanced down at the book in her hands.

"How full of nonsense do you think it actually is?" The title in question had to do with theories about folklore and the land magic, but the chapter headings had been a tad dubious. For one thing, they were the long Victorian headings that went on for a paragraph, scattered with commas and entirely unnecessary capitals.

"Geoffrey thinks there's some meat there. In those words, actually, which I'm fairly sure applies to at least some of the commentary. Take that as you will." Uncle Alexander pulled a volume off the shelf he'd been looking at, a much more slender one. "And you want this as well. Though I take no blame for the headache it will give you."

Ursula turned to face him, setting the book in her

hand on the side table carefully. "What sort of headache, please, so I may properly arrange my diary to accommodate?"

"In every life, and every apprenticeship, there must be at least a few books that have you waking up at three in the morning cursing. Tell me if I'm wrong once you've read it properly." Uncle Alexander was chuckling, though, which meant that at least the loss of sleep would be rewarded by an excellent conversation or three after. "Not one I recommended to your father, for the record."

That was also exceedingly interesting information. Then Ursula tilted her head. "Has Mum read it?"

Uncle Alexander started laughing properly then, the kind that was contagious and had them both out of breath in moments. When he got a grip on his laughter, Uncle Alexander nodded. "Tell her I gave it to you, and that I promise not to talk to you about it until she can be there. It has to do with the implications of cyclical magic, though admittedly in one of the more abstruse forms. Ummi considered it formative."

"Thank you, Uncle Alexander. Such a lovely present for both of us!" Ursula said it chirpily on purpose, the bright tone of an ingénue complimenting a vase of flowers or some such thing. It was, in fact, one of her exercises of the week, to get used to saying things in ways she never would normally. Stretching her range, Mistress Renata had said.

She'd warned Uncle Alexander when she got to the townhouse, of course, that she might practice as the opportunity arose. Now, he waved her toward her usual chair, setting the second book on top of the first and moving to pour cups of peppermint tea. Ursula settled down. Once she was sitting, she tilted her head. "You've not talked much about your own apprenticeship."

"No, and there are reasons for that." Uncle Alexander held up a finger. "You know the custom for these chats. Your side first." One joy of being out of Schola, Ursula had found, was that Uncle Alexander had arranged for her to come to tea on a regular basis, just the two of them. They scheduled it fortnightly and missed perhaps one in three.

She did know the custom. Ursula got to browse in the library, then she talked about what was currently occupying her mind. Then, and only then, Uncle Alexander would consider answering a question or two. That was because he was her godfather, and she got particular privileges not available to most people.

It meant Ursula had to figure out how to put what she was thinking, and what she had been thinking about since yesterday. That hadn't been a waking at three in the morning. It was more like she'd gone to sleep thinking about it and woken up a paragraph or two later in the analysis. It would have been nice if her sleeping mind had made a tad more progress, honestly. "I'm still thinking about the Lammas rites, and the dreaming, and what it means."

"And you said, last you wrote, you were hoping to talk to someone about it. Not Garin, I assume, or you'd have said it differently."

The annoying thing about conversations with Uncle Alexander was that he'd notice things about that. Ursula was fairly sure he couldn't help it. If he didn't spot the framing, she'd worry he was dead or replaced by a doppelgänger. At least she'd given thought to how to talk about Jim. "Someone local. He went to Snap a few years ahead of me."

"In combat, or was he farming?" Uncle Alexander asked it without any particular inflection.

"Fighting." She thought about saying more, but she didn't actually know details. "Just came back. His family has a farm north of Pulborough." She was deliberately using the phrasing he'd used, though by now she knew just where it was.

"And why were you talking to him in particular?" Uncle Alexander turned that focused stare on her. Ursula had a certain amount of resistance to the implications of that stare compared to most people. That was not nearly as much help as it ought to be.

"Because he knows the local area, because he went to Snap and knows a lot of things I don't know. I gather he's very good with sheep, as well as keeping an ear out for people with beehives they'd like to split." She had asked around, of course, for all sorts of reasons. Mostly— she'd admit this to herself and not to anyone else except maybe Mum or Aunt Dilly— because she was trying to make sense of him. More information from different angles wouldn't hurt.

The thing of it was that she'd enjoyed talking to him. She'd looked forward to yesterday's conversation once they'd scheduled it. Talking with Jim was like Mum with a new piece of light in the sky she was trying to get to make sense. "He knows things I don't. I want to learn them." She wanted to talk to him more, and that meant finding more good reasons to. Not that she didn't have a good start at a list that would keep them chatting for a while.

Uncle Alexander tilted his head, weighing that. It had a density to it, like all the images of the heart and the feather on Maat's scales that Ursula knew from some of his mother's books. "And how are you beginning the learning?"

"I asked him about some spots I saw in the vision at Lammas. He knew a few of them, I had the sketches with me. He might know some others. Then we talked about, I don't know how to talk about it properly yet. The patterns of it." She gestured at the books waiting for her. "If the book you're lending me is about that, your foreknowledge is doing well."

"So why are you asking me about this, then? The land is not usually our topic of choice." He leaned back a bit in his chair.

"Come off it, Uncle Alexander. The land is very much your business, just not the same way it is for Uncle Garin." Ursula wriggled her fingers. "I am not limited to a single point of perspective. I am applying as many as I can find." Then she coughed. "Though."

"Is this your question for the day?" His voice was amused, and Ursula was sorry she'd have to at least dent his mood. But this was Uncle Alexander, and he had a lifetime of moving from challenge to difficult to complication. And in this case, she really did want to know.

"You know I've been reading Grand-mère Laudine's journals. I'd like to put them in better context, if I can. Information, not the more personal parts, at least today."

Now Uncle Alexander shifted, focusing on her. "Information." Then he nodded once. "Go ahead."

"I haven't made sense of everything yet. Certainly

not the more complicated part. But it's clear there was something messy and complicated, and it hurt the land." She hesitated "It hurt Uncle Garin, too. Not directly, I think? Not Dad so much."

"No. Isembard didn't— he was born after most of it. I don't know all the details, mind you, I was away. It was all arranged before Phillip died." Ursula listened closely to him, the way he was picking absolutely neutral words. True ones, but neutral. "But you're likely right about Garin. He was old enough to be aware of changes, some of them sweeping. No one's ever said Garin's not observant. But he wasn't old enough he'd be told what was going on." Uncle Alexander considered. "To be fair, there was a fair bit Dagobert and Laudine couldn't talk about. You have worked out what it means that there's that long stretch of more complex writing, after Chrodechildis died?"

That was not a difficult maths problem, not remotely. "That there was some oath that ended at her death. But even then, Grand-mère Laudine couldn't write about it directly. Hence the code. And that only two people could access the room it was in."

"And Dagobert knew. Whatever is in there, Garin has some right to know. Whether he wants to, that's a question all my magics can't answer." Uncle Alexander shook his head. "I can give you a timeline, if you like, of what I know about. Apprenticeships and betrothals and deaths and such. Though you could work out most of it from the accounts."

"I'd like to check what I worked out against your dates, please." It would be foolish not to. She did think she had most of it. The account books were a lot easier to work though. Both betrothals and funerals made a mark on the accounts. Then she took a breath. "Am I doing the wrong thing, looking into it?"

Uncle Alexander went still again. "It's old wounds, long scarred over. Hidden, buried, and for some good cause, even if I don't know all of why or what happened. But you're doing it for a reason."

"I keep thinking it has to do with the land. With things I can't get a grip on, for the land. I don't think that's a failing in me. I think that I'm missing, I don't know. A source of light to measure everything else with. That's the wrong metaphor." Ursula grimaced.

"Then trust that." Uncle Alexander leaned forward. "If I can give you any gift, learning to trust that sense of your own magic is the one I'd choose." Then, without her needing to ask, he said, "By the time I finished Schola, I'd completed two apprentice-ships to Ummi's standards. In Ritual and in Naming. I picked up a fair bit of Materia work in my travels. When I came home, I apprenticed. Do I need to name her?"

That was a particular thing. Uncle Alexander had never said Magistra Renthorn's name, not in all the time Ursula had been around him. She knew it because she'd looked up the announcement when he'd come through his Council challenge, and that had named her. Uncle Alexander hadn't written it, though, and she'd still been alive then. "No, Uncle Alexander. She was excessively rigid, I gathered. From what I could find."

It made him chuckle, though the sort of laugh

that had uncomfortable echoes. "That's all truth. She made me go back to the beginning. I had to do every exercise perfectly, in structured progression, and give her all the expected answers. She had— she had no care for me. We shared no meals, we talked about no books other than my direct assignments. She offered nothing of herself beyond her contracted time and the least amount of space and attention she could get away with. It was a political decision. The Fortiers had arranged it, and it did open doors for me. Laudine and Dagobert made it clear that if I couldn't abide dealing with her, they'd help make other arrangements. But I could not be seen to fail."

That phrase, those barren eight words, said a great deal about how Uncle Alexander had come into adulthood. "I'm sorry." It wasn't hers to apologise for, but then Ursula figured out how to ask what she actually wanted to know. "Does it bother you to see other people having a better experience?"

"Gods, no. Garin was the hardest, I think. The first, of course. But Dagobert was also an alchemist. He could find someone who was a good fit. Isembard struggled a little more, I think, but they respected each other. Teaching Perry was an utter delight." Uncle Alexander glanced away. "Being for him what I'd not had, not after Ummi died."

"And Edmund?" Uncle Alexander had taken Edmund on formally as his own apprentice, the first he'd had since Uncle Perry.

"Just so." Now he spoke more gently. "I know some Incantation work, but not nearly enough to teach you all you want to know, the way you want to use it. And honestly, in your case, I think you need to learn from another woman. There are subtleties of dress and manner that are beyond me. But I will offer you what I can."

It made her smile, because she could not imagine the detailed analysis that Mistress Renata did, of all those things and more, coming from Uncle Alexander. "It is why I enjoy our teas together." Because Ursula loved this particular kind of closeness, a time set aside for learning and talking and growing. A season for it, in her life and her week, to keep up with the earlier agricultural focus.

"Good. And looking at Merry and Leo and Ros in due course, I hope I can help find you all mentors who delight in teaching you, as the individuals you are. If I do it with a bit of spite driving me, to do the opposite of what she did, well. I hope I might be pardoned."

"I think you've earned every bit of spite about it." Ursula said, loyally. "It's making the teaching better, the way Mum and Dad do."

"Thesan has been a model in this, as in a number of other things." Then Uncle Alexander pushed upright. "Come on, if you're working on Laudine's journals, let's take a little circuit around the streets and you can practice your French with me." That was him changing the subject. On the other hand, he was offering, so he'd be bringing some of the relevant vocabulary to the surface. It was a particular kind of closeness and care. She would wrap herself up in that as well as the books and the tea and the occasional answers to questions asked.

CHAPTER 18
AUGUST 14TH AT PAUL'S FARM

"You can stay the night, if you don't mind the spare room." Paul nudged Jim's foot with his own boot. Jim had flopped down on his back on the straw in the hayloft. They'd spent the day moving hay bales around for long-term storage. Then they'd done a circuit of the woodland to the north with an eye to coppicing later in the year. It had been years, apparently, 1940 or '41, depending on which bit of wood. It'd produce some nice long poles and staves, both for crafting use and for shoring up some of the fencing. Plenty of extra fuel for the fireplaces, too.

Jim nodded, his eyes half-closed. "Emma doesn't mind?"

"Nah. She'd like to see you a bit more. We've enough to feed you. Mum said to tell you."

"I've got the ration book on me." Jim had kept forgetting it. It hadn't been too much of a bother in America. By the time he made it there, sugar was the only thing rationed. In Albion, it seemed near every food was, except vegetables and fish. It wasn't as if he could afford a meal out the way some people apparently did.

He wondered, suddenly, what sort of things Ursula ate. They had a home farm, obviously, which meant the estate was likely kept up well in eggs and such. Obviously there was honey to make up for the sugar. If not as much honey as she was hoping for next year. "Thanks."

"I'll go tell her. Back in a couple."

Jim nodded, and let his eyes close all the way, just drifting. It had been good to give Luke and Alice a break, and to get a bit of quiet on his own. Paul didn't talk much when he was working, just what was needed for the task at hand. He and Emma and their daughter, just five, had a smaller cottage. Paul's father and mother and two widowed sisters had the main house, and the whole family usually ate together. It'd be pleasant to talk to all of them, someone different. Though Jim was also glad he had half an hour before he had to move again. Most of him ached.

He might in fact have dozed until Paul came back, startling awake with too-rapid alertness when he heard Paul's feet on the ladder. His heart was still racing when he pushed up on one elbow. "Em's making up the spare bed, and Hazel's helping. Or making it take three times as long, but she's looking forward to you telling a bedtime story, if you don't mind."

Jim shook his head. "I've been practising a bit more." He tried to will his heart to slow down, not that it worked. It never did. While he wanted to stay, to feel his way toward some sense of normalcy, it wasn't like that would make for an easy evening, either. He kept having to work at it, in a way he'd never expected.

Or maybe he had, and that was why he'd fled to America's southwest for so long before coming home. Nothing here worked quite like he expected, and he was more and more sure he was the one who'd changed in unfathomable ways. He took a breath, trying not to be obvious, while Paul sat down, one leg sticking out, leaning back on his other hand.

Paul was quiet for a long time. Longer than was comfortable, certainly. Then, softly, he said, "You were— what were you, when I came up?"

"Dozing. And then startled." Jim couldn't lie to Paul. He didn't much want to talk about it, but Paul had some right to know. If he didn't talk about it to Paul, he'd never talk about it to anyone. He couldn't imagine having this conversation with Luke, too much separated them. Certainly not Alice. Not his parents, who'd worry over things they couldn't possibly change. He took a breath. "You don't want to know."

"Probably not." Paul's voice was a whisper now. "Is now a good time? We've an hour to supper."

The phrasing made Jim snort. "Not really a good time for any of it." Then he took a breath. "What was it like here?"

"You were— you've never said where you were. Just that you were here until just after the Normandy landings?" Paul's voice turned up, making it a question.

"In training, yeah. Can't tell you where. But the

first part, right when I got in, we got the Blitz, the bombs they'd drop on the way out of London or away from whatever other obvious target. And—" Jim swallowed. "They'd had huge losses at Dunkirk. Whole bunch of us got assigned, then training. Lots of training. Living sort of rough. Tents and all, with buildings, the officers up at some local estate. Up in Scotland, for a bunch of the training. East Anglia for a bit." He could say that much, anyway. It wasn't giving any specifics.

And that had been land. He'd found some of it soothing. But some of it wasn't like any land he understood, in ways he'd failed to find words for. Or to do much with. The land— rock— up there had tolerated him, and the coast had felt actively uncertain. He didn't really know what to do with an ocean, other than give it a wide berth. People joked, not really joking, about the dangers of going down by the greenwood or the river or whatever, but an ocean? He didn't go near. East Anglia had been better, that was at least land more than sea.

"And the fighting?" Paul's voice was tentative now.

"Tell me what it was like here first. Would you?" Jim wasn't entirely sure why he needed that. Well, partly to figure out how to calibrate.

"A lot of hard work. Worse, bringing on people who don't know farming. Some of them are fine, we had a couple of Land Girls picked up fast enough. But some of them kept doing bloody foolish things. Not just leaving gates open, that's bad enough, but not realising what could get them hurt or dead. Or animals."

"And the animals were shaken up by the bombs and the changes and all that."

"Aye." Paul sighed. "If you make me come up with words about it, and it's fair you're asking, so I'm trying, it wasn't steady. We couldn't use the customs to pull us forward, like a good rope. We couldn't lean into what was coming, the next harvest or the next planting or what have you, because what we could do changed over and over again. We aren't as reliant on petrol here, but we never knew if we'd have enough to get food to market. Or what we'd get paid for, what we could sell. Or if we'd lose a cow or sheep or chicken to some injury or panic. Got woken up, middle of the night, not just for an air raid, but for all of that."

Jim grunted softly. He'd had all of that— well, not the cows or sheep— and a tent. He did not miss the tent one bit, nor having his tent mates so close at hand. "We had schedules. Routines. Expectations. Most of that was all right, when we were training." He waved a hand. "Too many people too close. Too many people with nerves. Or doing things to keep their nerves to a dull roar. Drinking and smoking whenever we could get it."

"You too?" Paul's question was soft, but pointed.

"Sometimes." Jim's shoulder twitched. "Gave up the smoking when I got sick, mostly. You've seen me drinking."

There was a long pause. "I've seen you when I'm around. Doesn't mean you're not drinking more when I'm not."

The thing of it was, Paul was right to be worried. Jim tried to figure out how to put it. "Don't drink much. Don't have the money for it, for one thing. Or can get it easy enough. Puts a damper on the thing when what you can get besides beer is a long, long walk." Paul snorted at that, but Jim made himself go on. "But there were nights, in America, mostly, when it was the only thing knocked me out long enough to get some sleep. Everything ached, otherwise."

"Your body or the rest of you?"

"Body. Lungs. My heart, but not the physical one." Jim stared up at the timbers of the barn's roof. "I couldn't have come home right after. Not if you'd given me all the gold and gems and treasure in one of the banks. It'd have killed me to come back."

"But you did. Eventually." Paul was being unyielding here.

"Also couldn't not." Jim had to take a deep breath after that, and that pushed him into coughing. He turned away from Paul, to his side, to get everything back under control, then pushed himself to sit up, facing his friend again. "And now I don't know how to be here."

Paul started pulling a few bits of straw out to twist them against each other. "You talked to Alfred yet?"

"Yesterday, a bit. We're planning on more." Jim had found that soothing. Milly had been right they'd had more in common. "Having someone who was— he was in the trenches. I think that was mostly worse."

"You'd not have liked being pinned down in one place, no," Paul said. And Paul was right.

Jim looked past him. "We went in ten days behind the first of the invasion. It was a lot of fighting. Never knowing where anything safe was, or rather knowing because nothing was. It took us weeks, and hacking across hedges and deep old growth. Every time we had to do it I hated it." Jim understood a hedge, and those had been old bushes, well-tended until the war had descended on them. They'd been dense and thick, and they'd had to come down enough to make sure the enemy wasn't hiding behind them. They had been stuck for nearly a month near Rauray.

"What was it like, being around so many people without magic?" Paul sounded cautious. Both of them knew plenty of people who weren't, most of the farms near them, for one thing. Or all the people they traded with, or bred pigs or sheep or cattle with.

Jim shrugged. "It was hard to have people so close. Not to be able to write in the journal, people would have seen. And my magic..." He looked away again, down at the straw under him this time. "It ached a lot. Like something was swollen that I couldn't ease, sometimes. Or like a drought, other times, when everything hardened and dried up."

"An imbalance of the humours." Paul said it lightly enough, because Snap mocked that sort of theory. Nevermind that they were all perfectly well aware that a balance of water and earth and sunlight and air was needed for growing things.

"Yeah." Jim sighed. "I had to, I had to make walls between things. Other people and me. But not too many, because I— they kept me alive." And he hadn't known everyone in the brigade well, not most of them. Not when he hadn't been able to talk about a good two-thirds of his life at home. But they'd

165

depended on each other. Jim's breath hitched. "I saw too many die. Alfred and I talked about that part."

He hadn't, much. Not with anyone but Mark, who'd been there. They'd only managed to do that sitting out watching a glorious red and gold sunset in mountains unlike anything Jim had ever known, all desert and sandy-coloured rock. It had felt alien and different enough that it wasn't like he was the same person or remotely near the same place. Here and now, he couldn't do that.

"Did it break your land sense?" Paul hesitated after he said that much. "Like the Great War?"

Jim shrugged. "I don't know. I'm not the same man who went into the Army. But I don't rightly know what did which piece. Or who I am now." Quietly, he added. "I've killed men. I know that for a fact. It's the sort of thing that ought to change me, isn't it?"

Paul had no answer for that. Jim didn't know what he felt, having said it. Having made it clear that he had. Before either of them had to figure out what to say next, there was a call from downstairs, Emma's voice. "Come down, would you? Food's coming out on the table. You want to wash up."

CHAPTER 19
AUGUST 16TH AT VERITAS IN KENT

Ursula thought the garden party was going well, really. The Edgartons had taken to hosting something seasonally. Or rather, and more specifically, Gabe and Rathna had taken to hosting something distinct from what his parents hosted. Now there were twenty or thirty people gathered on the lawn with drinks and seasonal fruit, enjoying a pleasant afternoon.

Leo and his friends were off nearer the house, chatting and laughing. Mum and Dad were talking to several of the Penelopes, along with Uncle Alexander. Lord and Lady Carillon were talking to Lord Richard and the Leftons. It was the sort of conversation that left little space for anyone to join them, but made it clear they enjoyed the company. Edmund and Anthony had found a bit of lawn to themselves, catching up along with both Theo and Artemis Lefton.

The invitation list was an interesting split, actually. It was one that made Ursula reflect on the question of names. Over the winter, Uncle Garin had proposed a conversation of several of the current Lords and their Heirs. It had been nine of them in the end.

Lord Richard and Gabe had hosted Uncle Garin and Ursula, along with Lord Carillon and Edmund and Uncle Orion and his brother Achilles. Plus Uncle Alexander, who had definitely wanted to be a fly on the wall for the conversation. It had been productive, far more than Ursula had expected, and it had also been a gesture in a direction of more connection, rather than less. At that gathering, Gabe had made it clear she should use his first name. She was an adult. His wife had followed promptly after, the next time Ursula had visited.

Figuring out what to call everyone else was a bit more of a trick. The Penelopes went by last name, in general. That was easy enough. Ursula had talked enough to Mason and Witt and Doyle among the others that it was easy. But what to call Gabe's colleagues on the Council was a unique problem. For one thing, Uncle Garin might well have keeled over if he thought she was being disrespectful. Not all the Council came, but a fair number of them, and a few who'd retired in the last couple of years. Uncle Garin, for example, as well as Theo Carrington.

Over near the pond, she could see Cyrus Smythe-Clive, who'd retired as head of the Council last year. His daughter Gemma, who was the same age as Dad, roughly, was laughing at something he'd said. Then she explained it to Mabyn Teague, with whom she shared a passion for Materia as a field and a certain interest in Alchemy. The energy of the conversation was drawing Uncle Garin closer, which was all to the good. It was important for him to get out and see people and talk to them about what he was up to. Here, at least, everyone understood him well enough to keep to the less tender topics.

Silvia Warren was nowhere to be seen, but that was to be expected. Ursula was fairly sure the Edgartons had invited her, though. Magistra Warren was still frustrated beyond measure that her son, Uncle Claudio, had changed directions in his career. He'd recently finished up an apprenticeship as a Penelope under Gabe himself. That wasn't the only reason she was frustrated, mind, but it was why she wasn't at the party.

Uncle Claudio and Uncle Orion were off chatting with a few other people, and Uncle Orion's arm was firmly around Aunt Hypatia's waist. Ursula had been delighted to see Aunt Hypatia, who'd apparently declared this the one portal trip she was taking this week, given her pregnancy.

Aunt Cammie had checked in earlier about how the decoding was getting on. Ursula had made a bit more progress since she'd talked to Uncle Alexander, but she was still daunted by the long passage that likely held at least some of the information she was searching for. She was contemplating that, when Lady Alysoun made her way across the lawn, gesturing at chairs set off to the side made of comfortable wickerwork. "Come keep me company?" She had her cane with her, but she was walking a bit more slowly and uncertainly than usual.

"Of course, Lady Alysoun." With Gabe's parents, she absolutely preferred to give them the title. They were the same generation as Uncle Alexander, a generation older than Mum and Dad. Lord Richard and Lady Alysoun both had that sense of formality and an older era about them. Today she was wearing a lovely dress, pre-war, in twilight blue. Her silver hair was pulled up in a bun with soft waves.

Ursula had shaped no small part of her own presentation on how Lady Alysoun managed things. Not the specific details, of course. Ursula was taller and broader-shouldered. The same styles didn't work, never mind their ages. But she absolutely wanted to have the same comfortable confidence that she was suited for the setting, adding to it in some indefinable way. "May I fetch you another drink?"

"Oh, that would be very kind. Another of the punch, please." Ursula went and traded her own empty glass for two fresh ones, coming back to sit in the chair. Lady Alysoun leaned forward. "Garin seems to be keeping an eye on how long you talk to eligible young men. Is that a bother?"

"Mum reminds him at intervals what he agreed to when I moved in. Besides, there are a limited number of suitable men here, given everything."

"Given that Edmund is his father's Heir. Anthony will be Gabe's, though we hope still many years from now." Lady Alysoun's gaze went directly to her own husband, the current Lord. Ursula murmured her agreement to that. "Orion is happily married. Claudio would be— well." Uncle Claudio was working his way toward an actual divorce. That was public knowledge now and not just in his closer social circles.

"Uncle Claudio is entirely my uncle, and no." Ursula nodded. "And while I'm glad to see Tiberius is here, no to him as well. Uncle Claudio's clear what Mum and Dad would say if he even suggested it. We talked about that this spring, actually, when he was asking for some advice."

"He mentioned you'd been helpful in suggesting some joint projects. You've a good eye for it. Neither Gabe nor I wanted to be too heavy-handed about a suggestion. Or rather, Gabe has said he's been pushing Claudio hard about other things. That was not one that was his to chase."

The conversation about Tiberius had gone better with Ursula, who knew him as a fellow student in Fox House, as well as through his father. It was good to see them now. Tiberius had been brought into that knot of conversation now, with people laughing.

Lady Alysoun glanced around the lawn. She made it look casual, but Ursula wasn't fooled. She was keeping track of everything. Ursula considered who else was nearby— no one within fifteen feet. Then she cleared her throat. "Actually, Lady Alysoun, I had a question about something you might help with. Aunt Cammie suggested it."

"I am sure she has her reasons." Lady Alysoun chuckled at that. Aunt Cammie made friends like breathing. There was something about her that brought people closer. "Do, please, tell me, if you'd like? Or we can find a more private time if you'd rather."

Looking around the lawn, Ursula felt the examples here might actually be helpful. "I have been looking at some family records. My grandmother

Laudine's journals. They're both in French and in code, and Aunt Cammie— and Giles— had helped me sort out some of it. It's not a cypher, it's proper words, just she's obviously using a number of phrases and sentences to mean other things."

"I know that sort of thing, yes. We've used it a few times. Giles is quite clever at designing them. I'm not surprised he and Cammie are as much help deciphering them. Have you found anything interesting?"

"Yes and no? A fair bit of what I've made sense of is Grand-mère Laudine complaining about her mother-in-law. But there are other parts that seem to be about more sensitive topics. I'm wondering if talking to someone who was aware of what was going on, or at least knew more of the people, might help."

"Oh, that's an excellent question, isn't it? Let me think about that for a moment." Lady Alysoun's fingers moved slightly in her lap, counting out something with tiny brushes of thumb against each finger in turn as a personal abacus. "You're talking about before the deaths in 1889 and 1890."

"Yes, please." Ursula gestured. "Though I'm curious about my great-grandfather, too. But his records are in a straightforward sort of French, and they give me a better sense of him as a person."

"Right. Hmm. Richard was in his last year at Schola when everything happened. He was at the Council rites, though, through that period. Alexander was a year older, but I'm sure you've already asked him?"

"Asked, and— each time I ask, he gives me a little more information. But it's clear it's a difficult topic for him. We have so many other things to talk about." Ursula leaned forward. "Though if you suggested I press a little more, I'd consider it."

Lady Alysoun glanced over toward where Uncle Alexander was. "Mmm. You might try other sources for a bit. You should talk to Cyrus, though. For one thing, his Challenge was that year. Theo Carrington was in the same Challenge, though his successful one was some years later. The Fortiers wouldn't have had either family as allies— the Smythe-Clives were a step down, and the Carringtons a touch new."

"By which my ancestors meant rising in power since the Pact, rather than the Conquest. Or before the Conquest, there's rather a lot of people going on about Merovingian traditions." Ursula considered. "I could translate out some of the funny parts if it would amuse?"

"Oh, it would, if you have a chance. A fine repayment for this puzzle." Lady Alysoun tapped her fingers on her wrist, considering. "You might ask Geoffrey if his parents had records. They'd have been of the right age and status to have had some interactions with the Fortiers. House parties, maybe, that might give you ideas of other names. I'm sure he and Lizzie could turn up that sort of thing fairly quickly."

Ursula snorted. "By which mean you're certain she's got them all catalogued properly in an index?" Lord and Lady Carillon were known, at least among their closer circles, for the attention to detail they brought to everything they touched. Ursula certainly had stories from Edmund, who took after his parents that way as well.

"A well-indexed library is a joy and a gift every

time it's used. I commend it to you now." Lady Alysoun turned her palm up.

"I have already taken that well in hand. Well, except for the coded journals that resist telling me anything useful," Ursula said. "I'll certainly speak to Magister Smythe-Clive then, if you don't think I'd be imposing."

"Gods, no," Lady Alysoun said. "He'd like a project, Gabe's sure of that. He's been doing a lot with Mabyn, organising the Council library better, but there's only so much of that one can do in a day. He'd know the Council from that era, as people, and whether they have family who might be willing to talk. A delicate question, in this case."

Ursula took a breath. "What was their reputation, then, please? I have some sense of it, but it's all— it's all public things, outside the family papers."

"Honestly, you can see a fair bit of it in how people treat Garin. Well, everyone other than you and your parents and brother, honestly. As if there's something a little frightening lurking in the background. Not a temper out of control, exactly, but a rage that could be brought awake in an instant and funnelled into a goal."

"And Great-Aunt Bradamante's line?" She'd died in 1895, at only fifty-five, but her children had children about the same age as Dad. The Fortiers saw them once a year, on Boxing Day, in an awkward, uncomfortable tradition that could not be broken. Always hosted at Arundel, never anywhere else. As long as Ursula had been going to it, it had been two hours of tea, small cakes very much in the French style, and extremely limited conversation.

"Slightly less terrifying, but they've held themselves apart. They've had as much focus on France and Canada as Albion, that's part of it." Lady Alysoun pursed her lips, considering that. "It's interesting, actually. They're competent in their respective fields, but none of them draw attention. It is rather telling."

"Not like Dad and Uncle Garin," Ursula said, bemused. Because while Dad used that deliberately, being charming and approachable to get done what he wanted, he definitely was visible, he always had been. "Not the same way, but both of them draw the eye."

"And yet, also, the sort of family who built out plans over a decade or three, depending on their goals." Lady Alysoun focused on Ursula. "That part, I believe, you share."

Ursula blushed, but she did not demur. "I won't argue with it, no. Mum and Dad do long-term plans too, though. Remaking Schola the way they have, I've heard a lot of the stories there." Then she considered. "Uncle Garin doesn't understand that it's why I won't rush into a betrothal. Anyone I might pick affects at least three of my long-term goals. Unless and until I can see a way around that, I won't risk them."

Lady Alysoun raised an eyebrow, tilting her head slightly. "That's not the way I've done things, but of course, it was a different time when I married in. Gabe now, I suspect Gabe would agree with you, with that 'how else would you do it' expression of his. Any of your plans you're willing to share at the moment?"

"Let's see, you've already heard about our trading visits to the demesne estates. That's been very helpful. I know Mum mentioned we're talking about more beehives. I wonder about our orchards, though, and there's a stretch of the fields nearer the river that's been tending to flood, even before this past spring. All marshy land, and I'm wondering what we could plant that might do better at draining the water back to the river. And then there's the sheep."

Talking about the sheep made her think of Jim again. Suddenly. "But there's also something I came across in the notes, about some of the warding on the estate, the boundaries. I talked it through with Dad and Uncle Garin, of course, but we're wondering what other approaches might be less bothered by changes nearby."

"Ah, now that's a question I think Richard would be interested in. Likely also Gabe." She lifted her hand, made a quick gesture with her fingers, not quite crooking them, and her husband and son both immediately detached themselves from the conversations they'd been in. The details quickly got far enough above Ursula's head that she went and rounded up Dad and Uncle Orion, with Uncle Claudio and Uncle Alexander trailing along amiably.

CHAPTER 20
AUGUST 17TH IN THE SUSSEX COUNTRYSIDE

"There's all sorts of lore about the knucker holes." Jim had goals for this conversation, and he wasn't sure how to get from the stated reason to all the other ones. He'd come down to Worthing on Friday afternoon to spend a day or two with Mum and Dad and Michael.

Then he'd found himself with an afternoon at loose ends. Mum and Dad had ended up with plans, and he'd not wanted to tread on Alice's afternoon by getting home too early on the Sunday. On the spur of the moment, he'd written to Ivo Henry last night. Jim had wondered if the young man might want a ramble to look at some spots with a particularly large amount of folklore.

He wanted to get to know Ivo a bit better. For one thing, he worried that if Ursula had found little welcome, Ivo might have found even less. For another, there were things he maybe wanted to know about Schola, and he wasn't sure about asking Ursula herself. Or at least not yet.

But when he'd met the train from Brighton, it had been near as hard as going over the Channel had been. It was silly; he knew that. This was a conversation, nothing more. Mum had sent along a bit of a snack, including some apples. If Ivo wanted, he could head home at any time.

Ivo turned out to be more self-possessed than Jim remembered being at that age. Though to be fair, in 1941, he'd shot up in height and was all elbows and clumsiness. He'd been looking at leaving school and enlisting, and he'd felt tumbled around by that.

Now there was a world where Ivo could choose what he did with his time. They'd spent the first part of the walk chatting about who Ivo had talked to, and how he'd been spending his summer. That involved a grandmother in Brighton who'd needed some help around the house. Ivo had been polite. He'd asked what Jim had been doing. The fact Jim didn't like admitting he didn't have plans wasn't Ivo's fault.

It had just made it time to mention their goal, the knucker hole. "I was reading about them last year. One of my classes. Dragons, right?" Ivo said.

"Aye. Though no one's entirely sure what the dragons looked like," Jim said. "What did you learn about them in school?" It seemed a reasonable way into it.

Ivo glanced over at him. "How much do you know about Schola, sir?" Being called sir made Jim blink. He supposed it was plausible enough. He was, what, six years older, give or take, with a war between them.

"No need for that, right? I'm not going to tell people you were rude unless you actually are. Doesn't seem that likely from what I've heard." Jim waved it off, and Ivo grinned suddenly.

"Schola?" The young man persisted.

"I've been talking a little with Ursula Fortier," Jim admitted. "Not about Schola, much."

"Ah." Ivo walked along a bit; they were up into the country roads, maybe half a mile from the knucker pond now. Jim was keeping an eye out on the hedges, because he couldn't get those comments Paul had been making out of his head. They were well out of his usual rambling range, about five miles south of Arundel, a good ten from the family farm. After they'd walked along for a minute or two, Ivo said, "The thing is, I'm not sure what you're looking for. You went to Snap." It wasn't a question.

"I did. Going away to school, that's like you and Schola. And also not at all like. I gather from Master Isten that there's not so much staying up for the lambing or the calving or all that."

It made Ivo snort. "Not so much, no. Though we've all been helping with the chores— finding eggs, feeding, that sort of thing. Some of them complain something awful. Not me, though, I like it. It's real. In a way a lot of the classes aren't always." Before Jim could ask about that, Ivo went on. "There's more focus on book learning, I guess. Not that it's wrong, not that we don't have to do things with it. But we start with the books first, the head, and then move to the heart. Mostly."

"Mostly?" Jim asked. "Do you like it there?"

It made Ivo snort. "My grandmum has a whole speech about how this stage of life, it isn't for liking or not liking. It's for learning so I can figure out what

I'm doing. They're all very proud of me. The Schola connections matter. And I love the land and the lore." He gestured at the ground they were walking on. "But, beg pardon, I don't want to be a farmer."

"Not everyone's meant to be," Jim said, quietly. "What do you want to do?"

"Materia or Flora, probably. Things that are grown, but for magical use, figuring out how to tend them. I've talked with Ursula a bit about that, though she's going in a different direction." Ivo glanced over. "There are people at Schola who are posh, all the way through, won't talk to anyone who doesn't meet their social standards. She's not like that."

"Well, she talks to me, so I suppose that makes some sort of sense." It sat uncomfortably on Jim's shoulders, mind, and he wasn't sure what to do about that.

"She's been right nice to me. Even if she terrifies a lot of people my year or so."

"Terrifies?" Jim considered. He could see a number of ways Ursula Fortier could be imposing, but he wasn't sure which applied here.

Ivo nodded. "You know her parents are both professors there, right?"

"We've not talked much about that, but yes. She's got a brother. Still in school?" Jim glanced over, then focused on the road. This conversation was easier without managing his face so attentively.

"Leo," Ivo said, amiably. "Two years behind me. They both grew up there. I've heard Leo going on about the land, there, the island? The way the White Horse goes on about other land. Also maybe like a demesne land? I'm not sure about that. It's not the sort of thing I could ask about." He shrugged. "Anyway. Professor Wain, that's Ursula's mum, is head of Horse House. That's the House I'm in. Ursula was in Fox. Half of them are still sure she's going to call them to task for something when she turns up. She was a prefect, and everyone swore she had eyes in the back of her head."

"Did she want everyone to behave all the time, then? I knew people like that at Snap, all about doing the thing right. Safety matters, aye? But sometimes people take it too far." Jim offered it a little cautiously, because that sort of rigidity didn't seem to match what he'd seen of Ursula.

"Ursula comes out to tea once a month or so, with her parents and her brother. She doesn't stick around for supper, usually, but she talks to Professor Knox, he's head of Fox House. And the other professors. They like seeing her, she enjoys seeing them? She'd check in with me last year, too. Make sure things were all right. Sometimes I'd give her bits of gossip." Ivo walked along, kicking a stone or two out of the road to the verge. "Not the sort of prissy eyes in the back of her head. But she'd not let someone bullying sit, or someone being nasty. Or any of the things that can get you hurt, and there's a lot of those at Schola."

"Huh." Jim was caught again about what it might be like growing up in a school. And with the sort of chaos that he thought most schools must have, when the teachers weren't actually looking. "Have you had problems with the people being mean?"

"Oh, no. Not so much. But she made a point of checking with me about it." Ivo shrugged. "And she's talked about the White Horse things a few times.

Some of the lore and the dancing rites? More last year, once she'd been able to do them properly. She's got a whole bit about how they're like some of the Council rites and the dances they do, and how they're different? I don't follow most of it, though."

By this point, they were coming up toward the church, and Jim gestured them down the church lane, toward the ponds. "So, tell me what you know about the Knucker Ponds. Then I'll tell you what I know."

"They're deep, they're clear, they're supposed to have dragons in them. One of my teachers—Professor Leonard— said the name goes back to the Anglo-Saxon. Nicor, I think it is? And there's lots of lore about how the dragons get killed, some of it more recent than you'd think? But we don't have any near where I live, not proper."

"I suggested this one because the hero's named Jim," Jim said, amused. "Actually, two different heroes named Jim. One version of the story, there's a knucker. It keeps coming up out of the water and eating livestock, or maybe some of the people nearby. That's no good, so they needed someone to kill it."

"Before the Pact?" Ivo asked, after a moment.

"Aye. There are some versions of it say it's before the Conquest, even, but that's never made as much sense. Not as many people living round here yet then, as I understand it. Now, one version of the tale has a wandering knight doing the deed, and he's buried in the churchyard with a great stone slab over him. Or there's the version I like more, with Jim."

"It's a good name," Ivo offered after a moment. "What does Jim do?"

"So, in that version, he's a farmer's boy. Some say

Jim Pulk, some say Jim Puttock, maybe from Wick or Lyminster or even Arundel town. Now that Jim, he's clever. He makes up a pie with poison berries in it. The dragon sticks its head out of the pond, wondering what's up, and Jim gets him to eat the pie. When the poison's had a chance, he kills the dragon, cuts the head off, and takes it off to the pub."

"Does he have a good life?" That was the crux of it, actually.

"Depends on the story. In some, he gets some of the poison in him, or maybe the dragon's blood kills him. But in the version I like better, he has a happy life. Though that doesn't explain the gravestone, does it?" Now they'd come up to the hole, which had clear crystal water, but deep enough the bottom couldn't be seen. "There's a tale that Jim lowered something on the ropes of six church bells tied together and didn't find the bottom."

"Do you know the charms about sorting out good water?" Jim asked after a moment. They worked through a dozen of those. Ivo knew several, but it was a good exercise, and they were handy things to know. That done, they made a circuit of the pond, then came back through the courtyard. They'd been talking a bit about yarrow and some of the lore. Before he thought better of it, Jim circled through to one of the newer graves— a death in the war, a young man— and cut off a stalk, gone to seed.

Ivo tilted his head. "One of the old charms?"

Jim startled, then turned over his shoulder. "Maybe. I don't know." He didn't say, though he suspected Ivo knew, that putting a stalk of yarrow under your pillow was a love charm, to call up a dream of who one was meant to be with. He didn't really believe it, and besides, whatever sorts of dreams he had, they never had people he knew in them. And yet, he had no idea where he should aim his life. Maybe a dream would tell him. If he didn't like that answer, maybe he could run as hard as he could the other way.

Jim offered to walk Ivo back to the train, but the younger man shrugged. "No reason to make you go out of your way, or, what, wait for the train to Pulborough? It's Sunday, after all."

It was. Jim left him where the road turned north, setting off to walk through Arundel town, then further north to Pulborough. It'd take a fair bit, but he'd have time to think as he walked. Talking with Ivo hadn't answered the fundamental questions of his life, but talking through some of it had been a help. He could feel wheels spinning, deep in the back of his head, about what might make sense next. If only he could both put words to it and find someone to hire him for whatever was relevant. That was the trick.

By the time he got back to the farm, everyone else had eaten, and he had a bit of the vegetable pie for his supper. When he went to bed, he pulled the yarrow out of his bag, his handkerchief keeping the seeds from going everywhere. He put it under his pillow, not expecting much. When he woke in the morning, what he had dreamt of wasn't a person. It was a room he didn't know, in a building with a view he'd never seen. Sussex, he was fairly sure, this bit of Sussex, but there was a lot of land to go around.

CHAPTER 21
AUGUST 24TH IN RURAL SUSSEX

"Afternoon!" Ursula waved cheerfully as she came up the hill. She was glad to have arrived. The satchel on her back was getting a tad heavy. Jim was waiting on the crown of the hill, the same horse he'd ridden before tied up to the fence post. She'd walked, taking the train bridge over the river at Amberley, and that was not suitable for a horse.

"G'day." Jim touched his cap, waiting until she got closer. "Nice day for it?"

"Lovely day." Ursula felt she was coming across a bit much like a schoolgirl in one of those stories. But it was lovely, in the low seventies, with blue skies. It was a day that was created for being out on the land. "I'm glad you were willing to meet me." She'd realised, at about four in the morning on Tuesday, that he must not have a lot of free time, not if he was doing farm work.

"It's my day off, so long as I'm back for the evening chores. Not until seven." Jim shrugged. "And

I'd— it's not bad for me to be away from Luke's for a bit. Out of the house."

It wasn't Ursula's place to ask. They didn't have that kind of whatever, surely. But now she was curious. "You don't have someone else you'd rather spend time with? A friend." She almost stopped there, then some impulse led her on. And she did actually want to know. "A sweetheart?"

He was about to answer the first, when the second question brought him up short. "No. Ma'am. Who'd be interested?" The ma'am was, she thought, an instinctive term of trained submission. She'd been talking about that sort of thing with Mistress Renata that week.

"None of that." Ursula put some effort into getting the tone right, tricky to do in three words. She wasn't sure she'd managed it, either. "We're friends, aren't we? I hope." Then she sailed on, because she wanted to know the answer to the next question too. "Might I ask why you're willing? I'd hate to guess wrong."

Jim looked at her, obviously baffled. But it was the sort of baffled that meant he replied, that was fine. "I'm curious about you, it turns out. I know I've no right."

"None of that either." This time, she let herself be a bit sharper. "We're both of the White Horse. You've been kind and helpful, and as I've said, you know all sorts of things I don't." Then it hit her, and she closed her eyes, shaken off balance in a way she hadn't expected.

Before she could open her eyes again, there was a hand under her elbow, steadying her. It was a good thing too. Her heel had gone down in a little bump of the land, and she'd almost toppled. Dad would not approve of that. "You all right?"

Ursula nodded promptly. Dad had drilled into her that she oughtn't worry people out of season. Also, all her uncles had reinforced that one. Except maybe Uncle Garin, who did not so much acknowledge other people's emotions. She focused on him as she opened her eyes, and now she had to figure out how to say what had hit her, and she wasn't remotely ready. "You're not seeing anyone. Walking out with anyone. May I say something, touching on the personal?"

Jim kept hold of her elbow for a moment, then released it, his hand dropping to his side as he took a half-step back, warily. "I don't see how I can stop you?"

Ursula took a breath. She hadn't been able to practise this, though even if she had, she wouldn't have planned for this shape of the conversation. She'd have to just be kind and blunt and hope it worked well enough. "The thing is, I've been looking forward to seeing you." She sucked in a breath, and then added, as clearly enunciated as she could manage. "Interested."

Now he took two more steps back. He looked at her as if she'd transformed utterly into some creature he didn't know, and that certainly shouldn't be wandering around the Sussex countryside. A great boar or a wolf or a bear, some animal that hadn't lived free on the land in centuries and centuries. A dragon, maybe. That was why they'd started on this hill. It had had a dragon once, so the lore said. "I must be misunderstanding."

All of his movements were guarded now, as if he'd plummeted back into the midst of a combat he was utterly ill-prepared for. Ursula said, softly, "I'm interested. In you, in specific, in friendship and whatever else we might decide we like. Shall we sit down and talk about it?" At least if they were sitting, she wouldn't have to worry about either set of knees giving out. "I've a blanket."

Jim gave a little sigh, and she took that as sufficient permission. There was a nice bit of grass, near enough the top of the hill that wasn't too sloped. She took the thin wool blanket out of her satchel, spreading it out. Next she weighted down the bottom centre with the bag, the far side with her own self, and left the other half for him. A moment later, he joined her, though he left as much space between them as the blanket allowed.

Once he was settled, Jim spoke again, but looking off down the hill toward Bignor. "We come from different worlds. You can't imagine we could— we could find a place where anything would let us—" His voice trailed off. "Anything, anyone. Your uncle. Your parents. I'm a vole on the ground, you're a bird. The earth and the air don't mix."

It was, of course, a reasonable concern. And it was quite a well-put argument, if one were only considering the question as a rhetorical exercise. "I am not saying we run off and get married today. Goodness, no. Besides, Mum would be horrified. She hasn't put up mead for me yet. And I'd never hear the end of it from Grandmum. Let's not do that."

The oddness of the comment— and the fact she'd used the horatory subjunctive in a way Uncle Alexander would entirely approve of— wasn't what Jim was expecting. The idea that this was something the two of them were doing together, whatever it was they decided on, that mattered. He inhaled more deeply. That was excellent.

Ursula went on, keeping her voice steady. "What I'm saying is that I've been looking forward to seeing you. And I'd love to make plans to do more of that. Figure out how we go on from there, when that makes sense."

"But, there's no point, you can't possibly. They wouldn't let you." Now he was stammering, but Ursula noticed, had already noticed, that he wasn't arguing about not wanting to. There, that would give them a way forward.

"Do you want to spend more time with me?" It was blunt, but she wanted to hear what he said to it.

Jim held still for a good long moment, then he nodded once before he spoke, his voice soft and rumbling. "Wanting is not the problem, sweet." The endearment surprised both of them, though she thought it surprised him more. His hand came up to cover his mouth, and she counted it as a point very much in her favour.

"I like hearing that." Ursula let her voice soften and deepen, finding an unexpected use for some of the training she hadn't expected to need for ages yet. "Very much, actually." She gave it a moment to sink in. "We don't have to do anything about it now. Not more than we'd already arranged, meeting up to explore the land. But may I make some plans in that direction?"

Jim put his hand down again, behind him, leaning on it, as if leaning on his hands meant he knew where they were. "What would you do if I said no? Would you stop making plans?"

"Well, I'd focus on convincing you in ways you agreed to listen to. And I'd keep the other plans for later." Ursula would tell him the truth. That was the only way to go on. She hoped, very much, that not too far in the future, she'd be able to tell her parents about this. She wanted them to approve of how she'd done things.

Ursula wanted to be sure she'd done everything in kindness and hope. And yes, a fair bit of growing interest about a number of ways she and Jim might get on. Though she was trying not to think too much about some of that right now, it was becoming distracting. He was strong and broad-shouldered. He moved like he knew what he was doing. And he'd been great fun to dance with. For a start.

Jim hesitated, then he said, "You must have other things you need to do. Besides coax me round."

"Well, yes. Though, to be fair, they're in fairly good order at the moment. Mostly." Ursula considered whether to bring the next point up now or wait, but she could feel it lurking. "Uncle Garin is rather insistent about me marrying sooner than later. Dad — and Mum, but Dad counts more here— have both made it clear I know my obligations and I'll sort it out in my own time. But what you need to know is that none of the people Uncle Garin's thinking of appeal to me. Not remotely."

"You must have— you're gorgeous." He lifted the hand nearer to her, gesturing. "I've been thinking that— um. Trying not to think it, actually. Since we met when you were out riding. You must have men dancing attendance on you. Fancy parties, houses, horses, automobiles, I don't know what else. Gems." Jim gestured at her, though he was stammering a little by the end.

Ursula began smiling at that, at the thought he'd noticed then. When he fell silent, she cleared her throat. "At some point, I'm glad to give the potted discourse on what those things do and don't signify, and when I might actually care about them. But in terms of someone courting? I don't need any of them. What I want is someone who pays attention to me. Not the show of me. And someone who cares about the land. I know some people who do, the way I do— they're not in the White Horse, but they do. But they've got other bits of land to tend." She hesitated, then added, "Other Heirs. But the posh set that Uncle Garin thinks I ought to consider? Not what I find attractive."

"And I am?" Jim blinked at her now.

"Mmm. I know I enjoy dancing with you. We've done that. You lead well. You certainly didn't step on my feet. I felt like I knew where I was with you, that we were dancing together, not just in the same place. And you're handsome. Strong. I know you work hard. I know you think about what you're doing and why you're doing it that way."

Just as she finished speaking, she felt his fingers touch her hand, where it was leaning on the blanket. His hand covered hers, and she could feel the strength there, both of his arm and his magic. It reminded her of something else to say. "Mmm, yes. And I like how your magic feels. Like a purring cat. Warm and rumbly and like sunlight."

Jim's fingers twitched, but he left them there. Then he moved a little closer. There was a good silence before he said, "I'd like to know more about what you're up to, then. So I can understand what that means for— for whatever we're doing."

"That's entirely fair. You tell me next, all right?" Ursula considered. "There's my apprenticeship, of course. A whole set of things dealing with the estate, from the bees to the implications of the Agriculture Act. Whether we can turn over more land for Materia and Flora use, as well as food. Ducking Uncle Garin trying to matchmake— and all right, maybe being a little difficult to a couple of those. I hold grudges on behalf of my little brother, with good reason." She glanced over at him at that, because it was in fact a thing an otherwise reasonable person might have concerns about.

"Why do you hold the grudge? And your brother's how much younger?"

"Leo's a third year starting next week. He's in the Dwellers, if that gives you a sense of his personality." As a society devoted to charging at social issues that needed improvement, the Dwellers in the Forge were less secret than some. Ursula had his permission to share it, though not about his friends. "He wants everyone to share in what's good. And— mmm. The grudge is about people who bullied his friends or who put pressure on Leo to do things they wanted him to do. We're not having any of that."

"As a younger brother, I think I'm obliged to approve." Jim swallowed. "Mostly, I'm trying to figure myself out right now. I'm living with Luke, that's my oldest brother, and Alice, and their children. And they can use a hand. But come winter, it's going to be tight quarters. Alice is already grumpy about me being about." Before Ursula could say anything, he added quickly. "I want to be useful. No grace and favour."

"I wasn't going to." Ursula said it immediately. "It wouldn't suit. You're like Mum is. Need to be doing something that matters, the way you define it. Dad learned it. Mum's always been like that, I think. Even though her worthwhile is stars, and not everyone agrees how important they are."

"They teach at Schola, both of them," Jim offered it hesitantly. "I was talking to Ivo a little last week."

"Oh, I can give you all sorts of stories. They're about to be tremendously busy, all the new firsties arrive on Wednesday. But if I start with those, we'll be here for days. How about we look at the view from the hill? I'm wondering if that's one of the glimpses I got in the dreams at Lammas. Then you wanted to go down toward Coates, didn't you?"

Jim nodded. "That's not too far for you, coming back?"

"Oh, no. I can cross the bridge at Greatham. A hearty walk, but that's fine." There, it would give them something to talk about, without getting too far into more personal topics too fast. She wanted to talk about Mum and Dad and Leo, but it was also a little tender. Ursula didn't know enough about Jim's home life or his parents. She just knew people had all sorts of different families, and some of them were much easier to talk about than others.

CHAPTER 22

AUGUST 28TH AT PETWORTH HOUSE, SUSSEX

"Well, now, does that give you a place to be starting? I'd be glad to talk about grafts in the spring, assuming we come through the winter well enough. Especially for local." Mr Streeter looked out toward the orchards where they'd just been walking.

Jim let out a slight sigh of relief. Paul, who'd come along for good reason, had somehow got an introduction. Even more implausibly, Mr Streeter had been willing to spend an hour with the two of them, showing them around the Petworth House orchards.

On the one hand, it shouldn't entirely be a surprise. Mr Streeter was famous in horticultural circles. He'd been on the radio for more than a decade now, sharing gardening knowledge in an enthusiastic rolling Sussex voice unlike the posh accents more normal with the BBC.

Jim had fond memories of sitting around the kitchen table, when the farm was Mum and Dad's, listening to it. And it had been solid gardening advice. He suggested nothing he hadn't tried, and he put things kindly. That was far too rare in the world. Mr Streeter had come into his own during the war, guiding people in the Dig for Victory campaign, as the phrase went.

And he'd been willing enough to give a little more of his time, generously, when he'd heard Jim was a veteran, trying to sort out what he was doing next. Jim knew what a gift that was. He wished the man had magic, so they could talk about that, but even without it, the hour had sped by.

"It does, sir. Thank you." Jim put all the warmth into it he could. "I know someone a little further south, toward Amberley, who's looking to add to their orchards. I thought I'd see what the options might be."

"Ah, well. On the banks of the Arun, or further in?" Mr Streeter considered. "I'm sorry I can't be sharing any of the fruit just yet. Ours come to harvest in October. Perhaps you might bring him out then, and we can talk about the grafting."

Jim swallowed. "Her, actually." He tried not to draw attention to it. "She's living with her uncle. He's said she can make a go of trying it." Then he added, since the information was relevant, "Two different orchards, one near the Arun, the other maybe a mile away. I've not seen them yet myself, though she gave me a detailed description."

"Huh." Mr Streeter said, considering. "Thought I knew most of the orchards near here."

"Her uncle keeps to himself." That was actually true, though Jim hoped that phrasing never got back to Lord Fortier. Paul, beside him, was twitching every so often, though mostly just his hand shoved into his pocket. "They've got a bit of land, but it's walled, most of it." Or at least warded and protected by illusions and who knew what else.

"Well." Mr Streeter looked him up and down. "A woman you're interested in? Apples have their lore, don't they?"

Put like that, Jim would not lie, even though he hadn't figured out how to talk to Paul about this yet. Any of it. Or the implications. Now he nodded once. "We're getting to know each other, but she's said she likes my company. And I'd like..." Jim gestured at the apples. "I'd like to do something to help her. And show I've got my own, my own..." Skills wasn't quite the right word.

"Ah, there's that." Mr Streeter nodded. "I don't know of anyone hiring, not long-term, not right now, but you give me your address, and I'll let you know if I hear of anything. You ask the proper sort of questions. Now, what you and the lass ought to do is go up to Jessamine Cottage in Pulborough. The tree there, they've just had the apple entered at the National Fruit Trials, it's been called Keed's Cottage, properly. It's just coming ripe, and it's a fine sweet apple. Rich. Pale yellow, the skin is, and flushed orange and streaked red. That's an ancient tree, now."

"Thank you, sir," Jim said it enthusiastically.

"And, mmm. If you end up Horsham way, I could see about an introduction, there's several good varieties near there. Crawley's too far, maybe, but you'd already know about Joseph Cheal and Sons and their apples."

"I do, sir. Though I'll be honest, I prefer the Petworth apples rather more. That Non Pareil, for example. I know people don't always consider it the best eating apple, but it's one I missed particularly."

"Ah, now." That comment had a softness to it. "You come back in October, then, and we'll have a talk about grafting. The trees here are getting on. Best to spread it a little, perhaps." Before he could say anything else, one of the other gardeners was waving, and he turned. "I'd best be getting back to it. You write and let me know where a word might be a help, would you? A pleasure to meet you both."

They shook hands all round, and Paul and Jim set off back onto the road for the walk back home. Paul waited until they were well down the road, no one near them, before he said, "Apples, is it, as a gift?"

Jim turned, stopping on the verge. "Don't tease." In a better world, one that had been kinder for years, he thought his voice wouldn't sound plaintive, pushed to the last thread holding everything together. Paul heard it. Jim could see his eyes widen.

He started with the apples. He could talk about the apples. "The thing about apples, you know this, is that you have to graft them. There's a magic in the grafting, even if you don't use magic to steady it. Taking something, bringing it somewhere new, and setting it to flourish. And then there's the varieties of apples, the ways we can use them. Eat it fresh, cook or bake it, make cider. Many are the apples." Jim spread his hands.

Paul nodded. "And there are the magical applications. How the varieties can be spread, which ones last, all that. But also how they can anchor specific things, better than many a crop. That variety. Set your apple, tend it, and there's a patience to it, too. A slow change, not a fast one."

"Yeah." Jim lifted his hat, ran his hand through his hair, and put it back. "The magic of it. And she's reaching for that sort of thing. In a variety of ways." He couldn't quite put it into words, not that bluntly, but he was thinking about the variety of things Ursula apparently wanted. "We talked on Sunday. She made it plain she'd been looking forward to seeing me. Not, um. Not just as someone in the White Horse who had an ear for her."

"Huh." Paul rocked back on his heels. "You know you're going to get hurt. She can't— whatever— anything serious with you."

Jim thought, immediately, of how she'd talked about the men who'd been paying court to her, not that she'd quite put it that way. "She's been clear with me about what she doesn't want." He shrugged. "It's tender. Will be. But she likes talking to me. I like talking to her. She's got a sense for the land, though not as good a one as she wants. And not as good a one as we all ought to want her to have. So. Apples. Bees. Whatever other horticulture or livestock I might know something about or find someone to talk to or, well, whatever."

Paul let out a sigh. "White Horse doesn't get tangled up with the Council and the demesne estates."

"We haven't in a while," Jim said. "I asked Milly and Alfred about it a bit. We used to, more. Because how else is the land supposed to work best?" He let out a huff of breath. "Ursula and I met up because there's a thing in the Arundel Lammas rites, and she's trying to figure it out."

"That's not the sort of thing it's safe to talk about." Paul lifted a hand.

"Safe?" Jim could feel frustration boiling up in him. "I've not been safe for years. You weren't either, though that was bombs from the air, not guns booming left and right and front and back. Or—" He twisted his fingers, gesturing at his chest, his own body barely managing to breathe. "Don't think I'll ever have safe again. Might as well do something useful with it."

Paul stepped back another step, looking Jim up and down. "If her uncle finds out, there'll be— it'll come down on you."

"Not like he can get me fired, now, can he? Or tossed out of the house. We're not tenant farmers. And besides, the new laws." Jim shrugged. "All right, I admit, there's a risk if I get a job somewhere, but..." He shrugged. "That's not now." And Jim had got, over the past five years, extremely good at staying in the now.

"Give me a min." Paul moved to the edge of the verge as well. They could hear a truck rattling down. It rolled past, not stopping to offer a lift. When the dust had begun to settle a bit, Paul cleared his throat. "Will you tell me? Strikes me as the sort of thing you shouldn't be shouldering alone. And I can't deny you're right about the land needing every bit of help we can give."

Jim let out a long breath. "Right. So, some of their rites aren't that odd. Walking the bounds— a field all the way round, a bit of beer on the ground, same sorts of things we all do."

"Right," Paul agreed. "But there's more? Fancy ritual?"

Jim snorted. "We didn't talk much about that, though I'm clear she knows a lot more about that sort of thing than I do. No, this is old. Her people, her dad's side, they go back to kings, well before the Conquest. With all sorts of legends about dreams telling them things in symbols. Also bees, but there was a whole thing about bees we didn't actually get into. We got off on other topics. Apples. Her mum's side. They care about apples and bees."

"I can't actually argue with someone caring about apples and bees," Paul said. "Gran would rise from her grave and haunt me, for one." He nodded. "And their rites?"

"There's a part where they all go into a big fancy tent. A pavilion, I guess, like you hear about in tales about knights and all. There are cots, and there's some incense to help with dreaming. And they see what the dreams say."

"That's a bit more like what we do than I'd have thought," Paul said.

Jim couldn't help chuckling. "That's what I said when she told me the first time." He nodded. "She had a lot of specific places. Landscapes, where you could see how the buildings and the hills and the river and the fields lay. She made sketches of most of them, enough to have an idea if she saw them again. That's why we met up, Sunday, to look at a couple. She's sure of two spots, and had an idea about a third. So far."

"So, not just the dreaming, but having some sense of what to do about it. Not just for show or the public fuss, posh people." Paul was poking at that more, and would be for a while, Jim thought.

"Yeah. And it's not just her. From what she said, Lord Fortier took it proper serious, too. And her father, and her brother, and her uncle. One of her other uncles, not blood related." That was still confusing to Jim, though Ursula had referenced half a dozen of them on Sunday, casually and fondly in conversation as they came up. Then he took a breath and went on. "The week before, I put a bit of yarrow under my pillow."

Paul knew what that meant, as well as Jim did. "Did you now. And did you dream?"

"Not of a person? A view, like Ursula had, but mine was a building, an old one, with stone walls and a window. But I've never seen it before. I was standing in the window, looking out at the world outside. It was green, and it ..." He hadn't actually consciously realised this part, not until he had to put it into words. "It felt good to be there. Even though it was like nowhere I've ever been. Big and ancient and solid, like a yew or an oak, it'd see centuries through. And I could feel the magic of it, in the ground and the stone, and it felt good."

"What sort of good?" Paul would press, and Jim had known he would.

"Ursula said dancing with me, our rites, my magic felt like a purring cat. Maybe the kindest thing anyone's said. It felt like that. Not like it was all mine, though, but it had that rumble and soft to it." Jim swallowed. "I don't know how to get there, but that's a place I'd like to be, if I can just figure out how."

"Huh." Paul hesitated, then he patted Jim on the shoulder. "All right. Let's sort out finding more people to talk to about apples. And whatever other work seems to be a good idea." Then he said, carefully, "Would you be willing to work through some notes on the White Horse, when we've done more with other parts of the land magic? Look at the records, sort out when we stopped and why?"

"Why me?" Jim asked.

"You've got the time and the interest. And it sounds like Ursula Fortier's willing enough to explain things to you, the parts that aren't what we do. Enough to be getting on with."

Jim couldn't argue with that. "Glad to give it a try."

"I'll see about if we can get you paid for it, too. At least a bit. Give you a bit of coin for your pocket." That, of course, would make it a good bit easier on Jim, though he'd have to figure out how to explain it to Luke and Alice. That too was a problem for tomorrow or the next day.

"Ta. Shall we get back?" Jim barely waited for Paul's nod, before they set back off on the road. By mutual agreement, they turned the conversation back to what they'd seen at Petworth. Both of them wondered what the estate must have been like in its full glory, thirty-five gardeners to the six they had now. And far more of it given over to flowers and decorative plants.

CHAPTER 23
AUGUST 31ST ON A HILL IN SUSSEX

"Are you sure this is all right? There are said to be pharisees here." It took Ursula just a moment to make sense of Jim's penultimate word, the local term for fairies.

"The Fatae? Oh, yes. I checked." When she'd moved to Arundel last summer, she'd made a point of asking Uncle Alexander and Uncle Orion about which spots she should be cautious about. She'd asked Uncle Alexander because he knew. He had maps he pulled out with no need to rummage for them at all. She'd done it while Uncle Orion was there, because watching Uncle Alexander be informative to multiple people at the same time was always good fun and also useful knowledge.

Jim had met her an hour ago on the Pulborough Road as it went through Southam, partly so they could look at an apple variety together. He'd left his horse at The Crown in Cootham, just east of the orchard, before they'd begun walking toward Harrow Hill, a bit to the southeast.

He'd made no direct comment about the distance, some ten miles each way for him, but the way he'd looked at her when she'd turned up was reassuring. Jim had been visibly delighted, if also perhaps a tad startled. She had worn nothing unusual, a green and gold skirt Grandmum had made for Mum years ago, and a blouse and sturdy shoes. She'd been thinking about seeing him again, and she'd been delighted her memory had matched up to the reality. He was in shirt sleeves and trousers, a hat on his head, but he'd looked like he belonged to the land.

Starting with an apple orchard had given the two of them a chance to practise talking to people together. That had been easy enough. The woman who had shown them the orchard knew Jim's parents. Ursula got the sense that was true of quite a lot of people, certainly anyone with family in the area for a generation or five back.

Jim had introduced her as a friend who'd moved to the area to live with her uncle, 'up at the manor house, just west'. Ursula had wondered if the circumlocution of names was a matter of dodging questions about the magical community or local nerves about Uncle Garin in specific. But then they'd got caught up in other topics, as they walked down to Harrow Hill, and she had set the question aside for later.

There were apples to talk about, for one thing. This particular one had been an interesting addition to her list of local varieties. The Golden Pippin was quite venerable, first identified in 1629, and with an intensity to the taste that Ursula looked forward to understanding better when they ripened in October. And Cootham was quite close enough for her to walk down there whenever convenient, only a mile and a half from the eastern edge of the estate. She was sure that now she'd been introduced, she'd find it a tad easier to talk to people in the nearest villages.

They'd walked along, hand in hand once they'd cut across the right of way on the fields, and that was also entirely distracting. It was a thing people did with sweethearts. She knew that. She'd seen more than enough of that kind of touch, from Mum and Dad, from Aunt Dilly and Uncle Seth and Uncle Golshan. Never mind a number of others. But it was the first time Ursula had had it for her very self, with someone she was interested in that way. It was an entirely different set of stars to steer by.

But now, of course, they were at the foot of Harrow Hill, and there was the question of the Fatae. Jim was waiting for her to go on, apparently, and she shifted to look at him. "Are you worried?"

"I. Yes?" His voice turned upwards uneasily. "Though it's not any of the traditional dates when it's good to be cautious."

"There is a Fatae portal near here, but the surface is just fine. Going down into the mines, that would take an offering or two and best not without permission. But I am also not dressed for Iron Age mines. And neither are you, actually." Ursula had been well trained in the potential dangers of caves, mines, and other underground surfaces, even before worrying about being rude to the Fatae.

Something in how she put that made Jim smile, maybe despite himself. "All right. So why did you want to come here?"

"First, it's a reasonable convenient distance to see you, but also remote enough that we're less likely to run into someone who knows either of us. Second, part of my continuing tour of the remaining sites. I want a look from the top of the hill when we get up there." She had a thought that maybe it was a spot she'd seen in the Lammas dream.

"And? That's only two. I've not known you long, sweet, but I know you've got more than two of whatever it is you're counting." Jim said it with a straight face before bursting into a broad grin.

He was absolutely right, though, and that made Ursula bounce slightly on her toes with an utterly childish delight. She wanted to say more, she certainly had more on the list. But what came out of her mouth was, "Three. Will you kiss me? May I kiss you?"

It was terribly forward. But before she could step back, he moved his other hand, just to her upper back, tugging her a little closer, before his hand was touching her cheek. "Here. Like this."

Kissing was absurdly different from what she'd expected. He was right there, so close, and she could feel not only his mouth but his magic, curling up around her like a glowing, bubbling mist. She opened her mouth to it, just slightly, to feel his tongue trace her lips, then press gently inside, all while he was guiding the angle of her head. They were near enough the same height, making something in the kiss feel equal and evenly yoked.

When he pulled back, he was breathing a little hard, but watching her so intently that she felt tender. His hand shifted to her shoulder, resting there lightly, as if he'd disappear if she so much as hinted it was unwanted. Ursula gathered her words as best she could, fumbling. "Again, please?"

The second time was less entirely new. His hand came down between her shoulders, then at her waist, pulling her a bit more into his embrace. The kissing was easier. Now she had more of an idea what to do. They kept at it, with little pauses for breath and changing the angle a hair, until he let out a sigh of pleasure and drew back.

"More later." Jim's fingers brushed her cheek. "Have you done that before, with anyone?" Then he went still. "Is it? May I ask that?"

"You may ask me anything you like. If I can't tell you, I'll say so. Or if I don't want to." Ursula swallowed. "No. Nothing like that."

"I'd have thought you'd have boys trailing you round," Jim said, leaving his hand on her waist. She liked it there, very much, a comforting solidity that was making it obvious why Mum and Dad did the same thing so often.

"No one I liked well enough to encourage. And Dad was something of a, mmm. Visible presence. You needn't worry about that, though. He's made it clear I have my head in deciding who I like and choose, and he'll not loom at them. More to the point, Mum's promised to make sure he doesn't do so accidentally. Also, they're at Schola and especially busy this week and next."

Jim snorted at that. "All right. I allow as how the remote location was an excellent idea. What was your other reason? Reasons. There's probably more than three."

Ursula laughed, feeling free to show her delight. Jim wouldn't use it against her, as some people might. "Four, there's the feel of your magic, and I want to try something. Five, it's a beautiful day, and why not enjoy the countryside?" She waited just a beat, then she added. "And six, I was rather curious about the lore here, but I promise I checked. Nothing I intend to try will be a problem."

"All right, all right." Jim lifted his free hand. "Shall we walk up to the top, then?" She nodded; most of the land around them had been turned over to agriculture, and Ursula had an idea about magic cascading down. Jim took her hand, and they went up between two rows of trees that were absolutely deliberate. Ursula made a slight bow, but that was because she had manners suitable to the setting. Once they were up at the top, after a fair bit of a climb, it was near enough flat.

"What do you have in mind, then?" Jim sounded nervous, but he also wasn't suggesting she not do whatever was worrying him. He more than deserved an explanation.

"I want to sing." He blinked at her, as if he'd heard something more like 'I'd like to teach a pig to fly'. She repeated. "I'm apprenticing in Incantation. I want to sing and see what it does."

"A particular song?" Jim frowned. "I know most of the traditional songs. And the ones the White Horse uses. But nothing I'd sing somewhere like here. It might do something. Wake something up."

"Do you trust me?" Ursula was watching him

closely now. There was a terrible silence, when he was entirely still. Then, deliberately, making it visible, he nodded.

Without saying anything else, she planted her feet properly, feeling the strength of her stance down through her heels. Her feet were angled just right to create openness and flexibility. Then Ursula took a breath and sang. She'd decided on this song because of Jim, because he was a farmer, and sometimes a ploughboy, along with his other skills. "Come all you jolly ploughboys, come listen to my lays. And join with me in chorus, I'll sing the ploughboy's praise." He knew the song, of course he did. His hand lifted, dropped, and she kept singing.

She was not the most skilled singer, the kind who made their living on the stage or entirely with their art. But she was more than simply competent. She'd worked with Aunt Tabitha from the time she was ten, when she'd first suspected she might want to go into Incantation in particular. And the song sat well in her voice, neither too high nor too low, with a delightful ornamentation she could lean into, both triplets and little burrs of trills.

By the time she'd finished the first verse, she could feel the magic steadying, beginning to spread out like a carpet, changing everything it touched, just slightly. The idea she'd talked out with Mistress Renata was having it roll downhill from the top. Ursula thought of it like a glaze on a cake might flow to lie gently on the land around the hill and all it touched. As she began the third verse, she could feel Jim's magic begin to join with hers. She didn't dare look at him and lose her place, but she reached for his hand and squeezed it.

On the fifth verse, as the song moved into the celebratory delight in hard work done well and rewarded properly, he sang. He had a glorious baritone. She'd discovered that at Lammas. When it was just the two of them, though, his voice gave hers a foundation, letting her better soar. He wasn't singing the melody, either. He had a counterpoint that made the whole thing better and better. It certainly made their magic near enough glow and burble, the way a cheerful, healthy river did. Ursula could near enough see the cascade of it.

By the time they started the sixth and final verse, his hand was on her back again, the two of them singing like there was nothing else in the world. It was making shapes, like a magnificent castle or cathedral. If she'd done this at Schola, the magic would have come out in learning and conversation. Here, it was coming out in the earthy pleasures. It was all about good food eaten in better company, or a mug of black tea on a brisk day.

When Jim came to the end of the final verse, he fell silent. Ursula let the last note ring for just a second, before she shifted into one of the ritual chants Uncle Alexander had taught her. It was one all about offering to share, being generous and open-hearted. She had no idea where he'd learned it. When she let the last note of that fade, she found herself with tears running down her face.

Jim hadn't moved his hand. Now he moved to stand closer, a little behind her, to support her. She leaned her head back on his shoulder, just feeling and listening to the world around them. There were the ordinary sounds of birds and the rustling of the late summer grass and grain. But they'd done good. She knew that, as surely as she knew her name.

"Thank you." Ursula breathed it. "For trusting me."

"Ah." The sound was breathy, tickling a bit, right next to her ear. "I'll do that with you any day you like, and twice on Sundays."

The way he put it made her laugh, turning to peer over her shoulder at him.

"How did you know that'd do that?" Jim said after he'd just stared at her— and let her stare at him— for a dozen heartbeats.

"Incantation is the song of the world, by some ways of thinking. Sometimes the song needs another voice or two to lend a hand." She let out a long huff of a breath. "Though that's work. Effort. Joy. But also." She gestured with one hand. "That."

"And now you're tired, and you don't know what to do next, and your heart's still beating too fast." Jim nuzzled at her ear for a moment, before shifting to move. "How about we go back down and find somewhere to sit?"

It was an excellent idea, and Ursula let him lead her off. They found a patch of flat ground where they could look at the hill. It looked unchanged, but Ursula could feel that the land was happier. Easier. It wasn't a big flashy magic. But it was a little more light, earth that could soften rather than flood, a bit of a boost to the harvest still to come in. It wasn't until they'd gone through a bottle of black currant squash and half a sandwich each that she remembered her earlier question.

"Before, talking to Mrs Parker in the orchard. You mentioned the manor to the west. Is that because of the magic, or because no one talks about Uncle Garin?"

Jim snorted. "Both. Arundel's got magic on it, you know that, to keep people away. A vague sense of a large manor, walls and fences and such around, and big dogs to chase people away. No one dares go scrumping there for apples, or poaching. They haven't for centuries."

"There are, in fact, no actual dogs," Ursula said. "Though the warding's solid. Dad keeps it up now, and he talked me through all of it. And some of the illusion work, though that's not as good as it was, apparently."

"And you like living there? All alone with your uncle?" Jim was asking. He sounded more nervous, but the fact he was asking was excellent.

"Not entirely alone," Ursula said. "We still have staff. Not many these days. A cook, a housekeeper, a couple of people to keep the place up, cleaning and the garden. And people working the farms, of course, many more there, now." She shrugged. "And being with Uncle Garin doesn't bother me. Far from it."

"Your uncle is— he's supposed to be terrifying." Jim hesitated. "Is that all right to say?"

"If that's what you feel, then yes," Ursula said immediately. "Best to talk about it." She then considered the next thing she wanted to say. "He's less terrifying than he was, in general. Oh, he's touchy if he's interrupted. So I don't. We write in the journals about ordinary things. We have supper together every Thursday, and sometimes other days. Just don't go near his wing without an invitation."

"I was not anticipating an invitation to Arundel this century, actually. He— he doesn't scare you?" Jim said the first one with a fair bit of humour, before the worrying came back.

"Ah. No, don't worry. I have ways to manage Uncle Garin. Being his niece, being Mum's daughter even more than Dad's. And the fact that I'm his best choice for Heir. He generally remembers it." Ursula considered, then added. "And to be honest, he's— he needs someone around who wants him happy. Plus, he's doing incredibly important research."

"Research?" Jim hesitated. "What sort?"

"He might not always have had the most, mmm, sensitive relationship with the land and the land magic? He did his duty, but by ritual, rather than by feel? But he's got better the last few years. But no, the atomic bombs, they - they infuriated him? The implications of them. Since we got the news, he's been working on ways to help the land recover, even a bit, the places touched by it. And on other things, like the damage the incendiary bombs did here. He'll work far into the night, go to sleep, wake up, and do even more the next day. Someone," she added, "needs to make sure he eats and sees sunlight outside sometimes. And he'll listen to me about that well enough." Mostly. Usually after a fair bit of grumbling, but that was Uncle Garin being consistently himself.

Jim let out a soft sigh. "That's not the man people tell stories about." He sounded plaintive. "But all right. If you say so." Then he cleared his throat.

"Could you be telling me a bit of how you were doing what you did? Is it something we could teach more people?"

That got them into a delightful discussion, circling back every third or fourth sentence to some bit of the underlying theory or the variations people had tried. The topic kept them busy until they got back to Cootham and she had to turn for home on her own.

CHAPTER 24

SEPTEMBER 2ND ON A ROAD NEAR GREATHAM

Two days later, Jim was entirely caught up again in the work of the day. He'd gone home on Sunday bursting with wanting to talk about his afternoon. But Luke and Alice wouldn't have done more than give the barest shred of time to the magic of it. And talking about Ursula as someone he had kissed, that was far too tender and complicated. Instead, he'd come home, done his share of the evening chores, and gone to lie on his bed in the attic and stare at the ceiling.

He'd hoped to have time to talk with Paul. But there'd been no rain for the better part of a week. There was no more in the immediate future, so Jim had been needed to do some watering through their vegetables. Then he'd had to make sure there was plenty handy for the livestock, and keep checking. That morning, Luke had sent him off down to Slindon, to the estate there, to deliver a horse. He made good time, at least, getting down there not long after noon.

It had taken him a good half hour to find the right person to take the gelding. He'd had to circle the estate twice in the process. Much of the nearby land had been turned to farming, of course, like every flat enough field or meadow or bit of woodland had been. What Jim hadn't expected were the signs of the war in other ways. There was what looked all the world like an airfield. But Jim thought it might have been a dummy one, like those he'd seen and heard of a few other places. Marks on the ground suggested tents had been there long enough to kill the grass. Seeing those, remembering living out of them for months at a time, in the run up to the Normandy landings, was worse.

He'd got through the necessary transactions, finally, but no one was going back up toward Pulborough. Jim set off on the eleven miles home. He was dusty and tired enough already he didn't bother to stop at the pub in Slindon. He was all over dust by the time he got to Bury, and he wanted to press on for home. At least there he could wash up, and take some cleaning charms to his clothes, and stop feeling grit in places that shouldn't have it.

Jim was somewhere between Coldwaltham and Pulborough when he heard horses coming up ahead. The dust and the angle of the light made it hard to see him, but he heard two, and moved to the side of the road, rubbing at his face with a handkerchief that came away muddy with sweat and dust. He could see better, though, and the horses resolved into two people riding side by side. He recognised Ursula first, riding the same chestnut mare she'd ridden before.

Beside her, though, that was her uncle. Jim had

seen enough pictures here and there in the papers. He was riding a blood bay hunter, no white on him, a good hand and a half taller than Ursula's mare. It put Lord Fortier's head a good bit above hers. Both of them were turned out formally, jackets and breeches and tall black leather boots.

Jim was utterly unprepared for meeting Ursula, and especially not with Lord Fortier looming right there. But he couldn't be rude, he wouldn't be, so he tugged on his cap, and offered. "Good day." Not using Lord Fortier's title was complicated, but the title would show something, since the Fortiers didn't hold a title in non-magical Britain anymore, and it was a main road. And it saved him trying to figure out how to address Ursula. He ought to be formal, and he couldn't bring himself to.

"Jim!" She sounded delighted, pulling up her mare to a square halt. "Uncle Garin, just a moment, do you mind?"

Lord Fortier brought his own mount to a halt a step later. He was an excellent rider, Jim thought. The sort of rider who made unflustered steady commands. The horse obeyed immediately, but without a sign of fear. Ursula's mare stomped once, and he was caught about how the two were obviously from distinct lines of breeding. The mare was shorter and stockier, definitely with one of the native ponies in her bloodline. Lord Fortier's gelding was of far more rarified breeding, likely a race horse and a warmblood. The evaluation didn't take him more than a second or two. Then Ursula was speaking again.

"Uncle Garin, this is Jim Pullan. Jim, my Uncle

Garin, Lord Fortier." She spoke quietly enough, and he supposed she had more than enough magic to tell if people were too nearby. "What brings you down this way?"

"Lord Fortier." Jim nodded, then risked the name. "Ursula. I was taking a horse down to the Slindon Estate for my brother." He saw, as soon as he said her name, that he'd done something wrong. It wasn't anything Lord Fortier said, it wasn't even anything obvious in his body. The horse beneath him didn't move or twitch an ear. But Jim had overstepped.

"And now you have to walk all the way back? Bad luck." Ursula, on the other hand, sounded comfortable. Not visibly fond, and of course, he didn't expect that. He assumed she hadn't run home to tell her uncle all about her first kiss, and this was scarcely the time to bring it up.

"Beg pardon about the dust. It's worse on the road itself. It wasn't near so bad when I was riding. And yes, on the walk, but I'll be home in an hour." Jim could at least reply and be civil. And while eleven miles was a fair bit, it was certainly a lot easier than anything he'd done in France or as they marched and fought their way towards Germany. No one was shooting at him, and he didn't have to carry all his gear on his back.

"How do you know my niece, then?" Lord Fortier's voice was quiet, but it made Jim shiver with it. Some people had that kind of weight to everything they said. It made sense that Lord Fortier was one of them, but it certainly didn't make it easy to deal with.

"Uncle Garin..." Ursula cleared her throat.

"It's a simple question, Ursula. Mister Pullan?"

And that was pointed as well, making it clear Jim hadn't completed a proper apprenticeship. Jim couldn't think how to answer it for a moment. Ursula was between him and her Uncle. She could scarcely gesture much. She did mouth something, one word he couldn't make out, then tapped her left wrist with her fingers, halfway up the forearm. That gave him the hint.

"We know some people in common, Lord Fortier, including someone who knows Master Wain's carving work. Master Henning, he's a leatherworker, highly respected for his harness work. He has a hand Master Wain carved out of wood, with clever charms on it."

"Ah." Lord Fortier nodded once, but Jim could not for the life of him read anything in that usefully. "Ursula?"

"Uncle Seth knows a lot of people. Almost as many as Uncle Golshan." Her voice had a definite note of amusement, as if there was some joke there that Jim wasn't getting. She wasn't doing it to make Jim feel left out, though. He was fairly sure she was teasing her uncle. It made her a very brave woman. She went on, apparently blithely, "Jim came back from the war earlier this summer. Just in time for the shearing, wasn't it?"

"A few weeks before, yes." Jim bobbed his head and avoided names.

"And Jim's been very helpful with some of what I've been learning about bees and apples. He, and his family, know a lot of the other farmers in the area. Always useful, don't you think? Lambert recommended learning more about their livestock, you remember."

"Other than that? Or delivering a horse? What are you doing with yourself?" Lord Fortier just moved a couple of fingers, gesturing down the road.

"Currently, sir, staying with my brother and sister-in-law and their children. Luke took over our father's farm while I was in the Army. I'm looking for an apprenticeship, but they're scarce right now, the way the farming's changed."

"Indeed." Lord Fortier was fond of a single word answer, and they gave almost nothing away. "Your family aren't tenant farmers, are you?" It was nominally a question, but Jim was certain he knew exactly how things were.

"No, sir. We've owned our land proper since my great-grandfather. But my brother has a knack for the fields, and I'd prefer the livestock. Harder to find a place there. I went into the Army straight from Snap, and my teachers are keeping an ear out. There have been a few places open elsewhere, but I'd rather stay in West Sussex. The rest of my family's in Worthing now. And I've friends nearby." Now he was babbling, he could feel it. That was going to get him into trouble.

Lord Fortier nodded once, abruptly. "We should get home, Ursula. You had plans for the evening."

Ursula did not sigh, and she did not grumble. Jim thought that showed a great deal of self-control, honestly, though also a skill she obviously needed several times a day. However, she nodded. "As you say, Uncle. Jim, I'll write about the next round of apples, shall I?"

CELIA LAKE

He certainly couldn't say no, and he wasn't about to. He nodded once. "When convenient, of course." Then he touched his cap again. "Good day."

"Take care, Jim." Ursula's voice was a little more insistent. Lord Fortier just nodded once and then his horse moved smoothly off. Ursula joined him, half a head behind, twisting in the saddle to look at Jim before her uncle asked her something and she had to focus on her reply. Jim watched them both disappear down the road, entirely unsure how badly he'd done there. Some amount of it, he was certain. Perhaps Ursula would tell him more.

An hour and a half later, he was back in the cottage, and at least the hot water was plentiful. When he finally came downstairs, all the dust scrubbed off, he found Luke at the kitchen table. "Can you do the pigs and the evening milking?"

"Sure." Jim would rather not, it had been a very long day already, but that wasn't the fault of the pigs or the cows. "Something the matter?"

"Worried about the fields. More. Still." Luke shook his head. "There's a touch of might be blight in the north field."

"What?" Jim slid onto the bench. "Gods. I hope not. Did someone let some barberry get established then?" It wasn't a sure thing, but Snap's professors had argued for the connection for some time, even though no one quite knew why it was a problem. It was a horrible sort of explanation, like explaining the birds and bees to children. Barberry and wheat liked each other very much, but weren't any good for each other.

Luke wriggled his hand. "Dunno. How are you with the charms to spot it these days?"

"Good enough," Jim said. The way he'd sung with Ursula, that might be a help too. "I'll write to a couple of people, check on the best ones right now, if you like?"

"Please. And first thing tomorrow, soon as the chores are done, let's go have a thorough look. We might need to look at harvesting this week, tend to it, before we get the winter wheat crop in."

Jim grunted. "Yeah. Makes sense. I'll be ready, first thing." He stood again. "Oh, right." He passed over the note from Slindon, confirming that the horse had been delivered in good shape, and that the last of the payment would be transferred.

Luke nodded, and then sat there, chin in his hands, staring at the mug in front of him. Jim patted his shoulder awkwardly as he went by and went out to get set up for the feeding and milking.

CHAPTER 25
THAT AFTERNOON AT ARUNDEL

"That boy was entirely too familiar with you. You are not to see him again." Ursula stood where Uncle Garin had indicated, and she refused to give into the temptation of an immediate reply. They had ridden home mostly in silence, but when they'd dismounted, Uncle Garin had told her to wash up, change, and come to his rooms.

It did not suggest anything she wanted, but of course she hadn't argued with him then. She was saving her arguments for now, when she might have more specific information. She'd dressed for it, too, in a dress that had been Mum's and that was fitted to make her look like a polished mature woman. Her hair had been dried with a charm and tucked up into a chignon, to encourage the overall effect. Ursula had chosen her Schola pendant as her only visible jewellery, along with the ring that tied into her personal protection charms.

Most of Fox House favoured amethyst for their

stone. Uncle Garin certainly had, and Dad, though Uncle Alexander's was a purple garnet. Ursula's held a purple star sapphire. She'd picked it originally for the unusual form and the beauty of it. But in the years since, she'd come to see it as a reminder of aligning herself in the proper direction, using it as a compass for her heart and her mind. And the blue-purple of it made her think of hydrangeas and the bright warmth and joy of the summer.

Now she took another breath. She had to make it clear that Uncle Garin had crossed a line. The question was how. She did not want to give him even a hint that she might be agreeing. At the same time, she would not, could not, put Jim at risk by telling the entire truth. Uncle Garin was absolutely not fit for that.

She wished she had put on the brooch Uncle Alexander had given her. It had even more protection and warding charms imbued into it, a proper talismanic piece. It was a simple thing, of white and gold made into a flower. But the magic it held was far more complex, much beyond anything Ursula could do on her own. Because, as Uncle Alexander had said, when he'd given it to her on her eighteenth birthday, if she needed what it did, she'd need that help badly and comprehensively.

"Uncle Garin, why do you say that?" When in doubt, borrow Uncle Alexander's habit of answering a question with a question.

It was absolutely not the response Uncle Garin had expected. And decidedly not one he approved of. He took two steps forward, fast, the way he might in a duel. Ursula stood her ground like Dad had taught her.

The thing with Uncle Garin, Mum had said, when they'd been discussing Ursula moving in, was that he had strong opinions. Some of them, but not all of them, were right. And many of the wrong ones, he was coming from something sensible. Uncle Garin worried about the line of the family. He'd gnawed at the attenuation for decades. He wasn't wrong to do so.

But if she let him have so much as a quarter inch now, the rest of her life here would be that much more difficult, magnified over the years. It was why she'd been so specific in the agreements they'd made when she moved in. It was definitely why Uncle Alexander and several other people had gone over them a dozen times to catch every possible loophole.

Fortunately, Uncle Garin remembered himself in time, stopping a good six feet from her. Ursula had called up her own personal protections, tapping the ring that helped with her thumb, hidden behind her fingers and the fold of her skirt.

"He was too familiar. He has no right to be so. A boy who went to Snap, of all things." Uncle Garin near hissed the name.

"We need all the ways to help the land we can get," Ursula countered, keeping her voice as steady as she could. Though there was a quaver there, because in the middle of the sentence, she couldn't help thinking of some of the sites of the bombing she'd seen. Or the flooding that spring, and the devastation after. She hadn't been allowed to go help magically. To be fair, that's not where her skills lay. But she'd ladled out soup and helped people in the shelters where she could.

"How much time have you spent with him? I dislike it." Uncle Garin turned away, stalking over to his desk. He'd changed as well, the sleeveless ritual robe over his suit now flowing out behind him.

"We said, when I moved in, that I will spend time with whomever I wish. You agreed to that." Now she pressed, quoting from part of the agreements. "Ursula may come and go freely, keeping company in all forms with whom she chooses." There were clauses about not interfering with the needs of the estate, but those had spelled out her obligations, rather than limiting who she talked to. At the time, Uncle Alexander had been thinking of the non-magical as much as anyone else, or people she might meet in London. Visits to the theatre and various performances were a common part of Incantation training.

"I expected it would not be a problem. Now, it is." He turned again, bringing a piece of paper. "How much time, Ursula?"

"Shan't." Folding her arms would have been too obvious and too childish. Neither of those were acceptable. Then she considered her options. "It is not the world you grew up in, Uncle Garin. We've had two wars. Albion and Britain are scarred by the one that just ended. The land is cracking apart, and the land magic even more so. It's not just here, and you know that too."

Uncle Garin grunted, but at least that was a different response than she'd been getting. She did not dare suggest they sit down. She needed to be able to move at speed. Ursula didn't want to suggest he have a drink. There was a small but real chance she didn't want him to have anything in his hand he might throw before he thought better of it. He hadn't done that in a terribly long time, Dad said. But once someone had done a thing once, it was easier to do it again.

"Please. Tell me why you're upset about who I talk to?" There, that was the way Mum would go at it, a bit sideways but focused on the actual problem, not all the shrouding storm and fuss.

"You insist on defying good sense." He turned away for a moment, before turning back, now leaning slightly on the back of one armchair. That was also promising. It suggested he was settling down a little. "You show no interest in any of the eligible men. And then you are friendly— he called you by your first name— with a farmer."

"Farmers are also people. Worthwhile people. Don't be a snob, Uncle Garin. It doesn't suit you." Now she pressed a little. Because whether or not it suited, it was the way he'd lived his whole life. He flinched, almost imperceptibly, but that was a sign he was at least listening. The question was where to go from here.

"Why do you care?" There was a fresh note to his voice now. She rarely heard Uncle Garin speak with anything less than certainty. Both Mum and Dad had told her he'd been bending a little more over the last few years. But Ursula knew that was far more often with her parents. She didn't have enough direct observation to entirely trust her judgement of him in this sort of mood. No matter, she'd have to make do with what she had to work with.

"Jim is a person. Our mutual friends are people. A wide range of skills, good for rebuilding what needs it, and taking care of their people and the land. With any luck, getting things so we can stop rationing most of our food." That was hard to argue with. Everyone was long since exhausted with it by now. "And we've talked about the people you think eligible." Ursula tilted her head. "Do you want me to talk about that more directly, then?"

His hand came up, twisting, and then he moved to sit in the chair. "We might as well."

Ursula took her time moving to sit. She kept to the nearer side of the sofa, closest to the door, just in case. Not that she wanted to turn her back to him, not yet. Ursula loved her uncle, but she sensibly did not entirely trust him when he was in this sort of mood.

It made her consider, yet again, what Uncle Garin and Aunt Livia had been like while she was alive. Her death had changed a great deal for him, but Mum had thought that, along with whatever else, he'd honed himself on the arguments with her.

There had been, for all their marriage, at least one a week, sometimes with other people around. They'd use their words. There would be sparks of magic flying, and no one with any sense wanted to be too near when that happened. Now, she thought Uncle Garin kept reaching for that fight. Ursula could not be the one to give it to him. It would destroy all her carefully laid groundwork, possibly forever.

"We talked this out a month ago. No new suitable

young man, or even a slightly older one, has appeared, sprung from the land like Athena from the head of Zeus. You know the lists in the Gold Book as well as I do. And, you agreed, it needs someone who will marry in. Not Heir in his own right." Ursula folded her hands in her lap, her fingers now covering her ring.

"You made your arguments. That does not, however, solve the need for you to marry." He mirrored her, his hands folded, feet tucked under the chair, rather than out, the way Dad preferred to sit.

"And the Heirs of the Great Families, or their brothers, are not actually the only option. There are plenty of well-born young men I have not yet actually met." She considered for a second before taking a risk. "Jim— and Uncle Seth's friend— know a different set of people. I have considered all the ones you considered more likely. And for various reasons, they do not suit."

Uncle Garin opened his mouth, closed it with a snap. Then, his voice in the sort of perfect neutrality that made Ursula certain it was covering a dozen other emotions, he said, "In my day, our elders decided for us."

Ah. At least he'd said that much, rather than ignoring that lurking dragon in the corner. "I had the gift of growing up with Mum and Dad. I know you must have given so much to do what was needed, what your parents felt must be done. I wish you'd had the things Dad got to have." Which started with a great deal more honest affection, and very few arguments indeed. Her parents were not perfect. But they were, as Mum had put it last year, mutually well suited to working out problems before they became unmanageable.

Uncle Garin said nothing to that, which suggested she'd balanced it right. Then he stood, moving to the drinks cabinet and pouring himself a brandy before returning to his seat. He didn't offer her one, but she wouldn't have taken it. She still needed all her wits and some extra. "Livia was considered to be a suitable match." Someone else might have given a platitude, that they'd done their best, or they'd gone forward together. Uncle Garin was at least not a hypocrite, because when he went on, he said simply, "We tried to do our duty. I feel the weight of the estate. I have since I was young."

That was Ursula's cue. She stood, crossing to bend and kiss his cheek. "I want Arundel, and all the land around us, to flourish. I promise you that. Not just this year, not just in a decade, but for centuries to come. But that means choosing wisely, now, not quickly. Finding someone who has as much love of the land as I do. This land, in specific."

She would not get a better closing line, not if she tried for hours. "I'll see you for supper on Thursday, Uncle Garin."

He didn't stop her, and she walked out with her back straight. Ursula made her way back to her rooms, stopping only to seal the warding as she came through the door. Then she flung herself on the bed, face down. She was utterly exhausted, drained in a way she hated.

Most of all, she desperately wanted to talk to Mum and Dad. But if she went out there, for one thing, it was already getting on for supper. Second, and more important, it was the second day of classes at Schola, and both Mum and Dad had obligations this evening. Worse, Ursula knew Mum wasn't entirely sure how things were going to go with the second years tonight.

She wanted to write, and she really shouldn't do even that. Not over something that would keep for a few days. She could go out for tea on Thursday if she still needed to talk. The other part was that Ursula knew this was something that, fundamentally, she had to figure out herself. Mum and Dad and Uncle Alexander and all could give advice. But they all had their own relationships with Uncle Garin, and those were like briars and tangles.

It had not gone as badly tonight as it could have. She'd have to take that victory for what it was and hold fast for whatever the next argument was. She was sure there'd be one.

CHAPTER 26

SEPTEMBER 3RD IN THE PULLAN ORCHARD

Jim was waiting, more than a little uncertainly, up by the orchard. It was just coming up for seven, misty and surprisingly cool. He felt it was good he'd grabbed his cloak from his room on the way out. It meant he could bury his hands in the wool of it. It wasn't sensible to be out here waiting, and yet, he was going to stay until he was sure Ursula wouldn't be coming.

He'd woken in the middle of the night out of something that wasn't really a bad dream, but certainly wasn't a comfortable one. He'd lain in bed staring at the ceiling for a good ten minutes before thinking to check the journal and see if there was any news. Before he'd even glanced at the page for the White Horse, or the news, he'd realised there was a note from Ursula.

She hadn't explained what had happened, not on paper, but it was fairly obvious she'd been in a state. Her handwriting had gone jagged, rather than the smooth, readable hand she'd used everywhere else.

And there was also something in which words she was using. He'd offered, before thinking through the practicalities, to meet her first thing in the morning. Then he'd had to write back five minutes later, to see if she could come up close to the farm.

He'd gone short on sleep, but that was fine. Jim had got up at five, seen to the livestock, done the milking. Then he'd set off a mile north, to the edge of the orchard, leaving a note saying he'd meet Luke at eight to look at the grain. He'd picked the orchard because it was well away from the cottage. It had a bench, and there weren't likely to be people coming by unless they got particularly unlucky. As it turned out, there was a fair bit of mist, which would also hide them from anyone too far away.

Jim had checked the journal twice now, and he was trying to be patient before checking again. He wasn't used to carrying the thing around, though it was, in fact, quite handy. The second time, Ursula had said she was about to mount up, and that had been right at six. She'd given the time. She wouldn't be writing while she was riding. That was ridiculous, and there wasn't much he could do to help her from here. He kept doing the maths in his head. A good horse, six miles, having to jog around where the roads were, probably just about an hour.

Before he could talk himself into checking again, he heard hoofbeats. Then they slowed, coming up to the entrance to the orchard. He called out, hoping her mare wouldn't startle. "Here. Let me get the gate."

The mare was well-trained, more than he'd expected. When Jim opened the gate, he found Ursula already dismounted, tucking the stirrups up and pulling the reins over the mare's head. She looked at him, then suddenly looked incredibly relieved. Jim wasn't at all sure what to do with that expression before he coughed and pulled the gate. "Here. I don't suppose you've a halter?"

"I do." Ursula's voice caught for a second, then she said, "I have checklists for this sort of thing. In my head, at least. Though I admit, I didn't expect to apply this one quite this way."

Jim had even less idea what to do with that, other than lend a hand Ursula got a halter and lead from a saddlebag and got them on the mare. Ursula did all of it deftly, after pulling her hands out from leather gloves. It wasn't until she had the mare tied up to the fence and the two of them had retreated to the bench that Jim figured out where to begin. "Are you all right?" Of course, then he muffed it, because the next thing was "I don't have terribly long, I need to help Luke, I told him I'd be back around eight."

"That gives us an hour. I've got to get back, Mistress Renata's expecting me at half-nine. That's barely enough time to change and get through the portal." Ursula took in a long breath, then let it out before she twisted to better look at him. "I had an argument with Uncle Garin last night. When we got home. He tried to forbid me from seeing you."

Jim listened, then the last part hit him, and he was standing before he realised it. "I shouldn't, you shouldn't—" It was an entirely instinctive reaction, before he got a grip on himself and swallowed. "I can't have him angry at me."

Ursula had tilted her head, observing like a crow or raven might. Then she said, softly, "I'll understand if you can't take the risk of it." Each word was carefully enunciated, spaced out, like blows of a hammer on an anvil. By the last one, something in the world was fit to shatter.

"I, wait, no." Jim tried to get a grip on his emotions and his words, and he felt he was failing at both. He stood there for a second, all his muscles quivering like he wanted to run as fast as he could away from an ambush. This wasn't an ambush. She'd given him more than enough warning of the scope, even though she hadn't given details. It wasn't as if Jim didn't know what Lord Fortier probably thought of people like him. Hearing it was true shouldn't be this much of a shock.

He made himself take a breath, then another one. On the third one, he realised Ursula was matching him, breath for breath, and that her hands were trembling just slightly. And they must be cold, she had her riding jacket on, but nothing over it, no cloak or cape or heavier coat. It was well under fifty yet this morning. Jim took a step forward again. Then he folded himself onto the bench, pulling the cloak free as he sat, so he could offer some of it to her, draping across her knees. He kept his hands to himself, but she looked down, and he had to figure out how to ask something. "What would help?"

There was a catch in her voice now, not the steady competent words he'd expected from her. "Not to be alone with it."

Before Jim could think of anything else, his hands were moving to cup hers, under the folds of the cloak, just holding on. "All right. Let's talk about it. He forbade you from seeing me. Here you are."

"He tried to forbid me. That's the key part. He's not allowed to, for one thing. And for another, it's bad for him to get away with things like that. Third, it's even worse for both of us if he does, so no. Shan't. Which is not what I said last night, exactly, but not that far from it."

"You've lost me, sweet." Jim said it softly. "Can you explain it differently? He's allowed to do near anything he likes, isn't he? Lord, and he was on the Council, and I don't know what else."

It drew a snort from Ursula, though she kept a tight hold of his hands. That was fine. He enjoyed having her holding on, rather a lot. Being that connected to him. "When I moved in, we set out agreements. He needs me, he desperately needs someone to be Heir. I want to be. I want to figure out how to make things better for the land, for the land magic." She looked up and met his eyes. "Which is not all of why I'm in the White Horse, but it certainly seems relevant, doesn't it?"

Jim didn't have an answer for that one, partly because, so far as he knew, no one had ever quite done that. Not in at least half a century. "And your father?" Jim frowned. "Are there other people?"

"Most of Dad and Uncle Garin's family died before Dad was born. All in a row, the sort of thing that makes you sure there's some reason even if it's not obvious. There are some distant cousins we see once a year, or if something overlaps, but they don't actually talk to us? They really don't know what to do with Mum. Dad was Uncle Garin's Heir from 1913, when their father died." Jim could do those maths, at least. That was well before Ursula had been born.

"But he— he wore himself to bits taking care of Schola. Dad loves Schola. Leo does too. The way I love Arundel, or at least the way I'll love Arundel when I've had a bit more time. There are fast loves and slower loves, and I'm greedy enough to want both. There's only so much even I can learn in a year."

There was a great deal there that Jim was trying to get his head around, but he had to agree with the general theory of some things taking more time. He sat there, blinking at her, before she went on. "Here's a thing. I know I love you. I knew as soon as we sang together up on the hill. I don't necessarily know all the ways I love you yet, or what that means for both of us. I know it has to be complicated for you. And I'm not—" She made a gesture at her figure and her height. "I'm a valkyrie, near enough, and that's not to everyone's taste."

The last bit, at least, he had an answer for. "Oh, trust me, your figure is absolutely not a problem for me. Especially when you're in breeches. I, erm. Realised that the first time I saw you riding?"

"Did you really?" Ursula favoured him with a glowing smile, as if he'd said the thing just right. He hadn't thought he'd manage that. "Anyway. I'm not expecting either of us to know what we want to be to each other. Though I do like that you got up early, or at least made time for me, when I know you've other things to do. And you were there, in the night, when I wrote."

"Not fast enough, though." Jim shook his head. Then he tried again. "Don't you have other people, friends?"

"Yes? And no. It's the first week of classes. Mum

and Dad are rushed off their feet. Aunt Dilly's been bouncing back and forth between Linden and Lars—those are the two cousins I'm closest to, Mum's side. They both have small babies."

"So, never enough sleep for anyone," Jim said. "I've an idea of that, even if my nieces and nephews are older now. And other people?"

"Have their own lives. Or..." She shifted a little, and Jim offered her his shoulder to lean on, which meant he could pull the cloak around her from the back. It made it far more snug and warm, and he did not object one bit to her nestled up close to him. "Telling them would have consequences." She let out a huff of breath. "The thing is, if I married any of the people Uncle Garin thinks I ought to, hmm. How to put this?" Her hand twitched. "It's a whole cascade of choices, and I don't like where they lead. I don't like how they'd limit me. People would see me as taking sides in an entire line of arguments and disagreements."

"And you want to be free to manoeuvre," Jim said promptly. "But how, where do I fit into that?"

"First, I like doing magic with you. Or rather, based on a small sample size, I would like very much to explore a great deal more in a variety of settings and situations. It might take decades, though."

"Well. Decades." Jim didn't want to tease her, but he was, actually, now he was over the initial shock, enjoying the teasing a great deal. "I suppose I might make room in my packed social life for that." He was rewarded by her head properly on his shoulder, putting weight on it now, after an initial tentative test. "And your agreements?"

"I know I need to marry someone who's willing to marry into the land. And have children, ideally, because honestly, I'd rather spare Leo the trouble of worrying about it. You're the first person I've looked at I've actually wanted. And I've been thinking about different people, in an academic sense, for years."

"You barely know me," Jim pointed out. But then, he realised it was a lie, or at least a partial one. "I mean."

"I know we share the same oaths to the White Horse. I know I like talking to you, I knew that from the first time. I wanted more of it. Also, I continue to want more, and I will want even more in the future, if you're willing. All the verb tenses of wanting. Then we danced, and I knew more about you. Now we've sung. Your magic and mine, they do well together. I'm not saying we should run off and get married right now. But I'm wanting to figure things out with you. And I haven't with anyone else."

"Huh." She was exceedingly fervent about it, a determination showing through more and more as she got through that. "And the others you considered? The sorts your Uncle approves of?"

"The ones I like enough are Heirs in their own right. That won't work. Or I like them, but they have horrific relatives, and thank you, no," Ursula said. "Then there's a whole set I dislike and do not wish to spend more time with than is necessary for my various plots and goals." She contemplated. "The ones in the first category, they'd be fine with the White Horse part, I suspect. So long as I told them sensibly. But the others? Probably not."

That comment about the White Horse made Jim

think of several things, but he started with the most immediate question in his mind. "Does your family know?" Before she answered, he added, "Mine doesn't. Not about the White Horse. They didn't ask Luke. I always wondered if he felt hurt. But Paul was his friend, first, at school."

"I told Mum and Dad and Leo over the summer. Because Leo's in the Dwellers. Uncle Garin would throw eight kinds of fit, instead of the usual three or four, so no. Not unless it actually serves a purpose. He hasn't earned it."

"And you think you can make him hold to agreements?" It was, on the face of it, absurd. Ursula was, as far as Jim could tell, exceptionally well-educated and competent for twenty. Or not yet twenty, he'd looked it up. Her birthday was in November. But Lord Fortier had been Lord for decades and on the Council for longer than that. He terrified basically everyone who had ever talked about him in Jim's presence. Or at least intimidated them.

"Oh, yes. In this case." Ursula pulled back enough to peer at him. "Explaining why I'm sure would take more time than we've got this morning. A couple of hours and a family tree and a timeline and half a dozen charms Mum mostly uses to explain orbits and planets. I promise I will, though."

Jim saw the sense in that, at least. She was so earnest about it; he was fairly sure she wasn't trying to duck the question. "All right. Is he going to be angry at me? Or my family? What do I need to know about that?"

Ursula considered that, giving it weight. "He's generally not spiteful. Not like that. I might ask Mum and Dad about it, not, um. I want to tell them about you, and I want to wait a little. Does that make any sense at all?"

"If we tell people, whatever we're telling them," Jim agreed. "They'll have opinions. I like figuring ourselves out without everyone sharing their thoughts for a bit. Might talk to Paul about it, but not anyone else yet."

"Fair," Ursula said. "Anyway, I can talk about Uncle Garin being difficult without that. I'll let you know? We have a tradition of family tea on Thursdays. I wasn't planning on going this week. I usually go once a month now? Getting out to Schola's something of a trek, the portal's a mile or so from the school itself. But maybe I will. And on Thursday nights, I have supper with Uncle Garin. Mostly we talk alchemy." She sounded less certain about that.

"All right. That's enough of a plan to be going on with. We can write in the journals. And if there's— if you ever need to be somewhere else, you come to the cottage. Whatever time it is. I'll make it right with Luke and Alice."

She kissed his cheek once. "Thank you." Then she moved, angling for his lips. That was a far, far better way to spend the time they had left in the morning. By the time they both had to get on with their day, he'd had a good twenty minutes of her in his lap, his arms and cloak around her. They'd spent the time nuzzling and kissing and not saying much else of consequence.

CHAPTER 27
OCTOBER 4TH AT SCHOLA

"Mum?" Ursula knocked on the door frame of the office. Mum took her time looking up, but Ursula knew Mum was expecting her. For one thing, Ursula had arranged it by journal yesterday. For another, Mum knew everyone who made it past the fifth floor, and especially her own children. Then Mum was smiling warmly. "Is this the sort of chat you want to have up here or downstairs? Your dad's got a duelling student until five, and Leo's hoping you can stay long enough he can have a word with you."

"Uncle Garin cancelled supper, that's part of what I want to talk to you about," Ursula said, because she was frustrated by that. "And of course. We need to find another day for tea, don't we? Or some option." Leo had Materia class until supper on Thursdays this year. It meant the usual family tea time wouldn't do, or at least not if she wanted to see her brother, which she did. Then she contemplated.

"More privacy, please, but can you let me know when Dad's on his way up?"

Mum nodded, and set about tidying up her desk. It was in a good state, but of course, they were only a few days into term. Only one of the chart scrolls was threatening to topple off the desk onto the floor. Mum scooped it up, rolling it up and tucking it into a cubby to her left. She picked up two books and then waved a hand. "Downstairs, shall we?"

Five minutes later, Ursula was curled up on the sofa, a bottle of cider in her hands rather than a mug of tisane. Which suggested Mum knew enough about the complexities of the conversation to start with. Ursula, for her part, had given a fair bit of thought to what to say and where to start. "We probably want to talk about this when Dad's here." This was the delicate part, oddly. "But Uncle Garin tried to forbid me to talk to someone."

"And then he cancelled on you tonight. I assume he's sulking." The way Mum said it was so matter of fact. "What did you say, then?"

"That we'd agreed he wasn't to do that. He doesn't even have good reason, other than snobbishness," Ursula said.

"For Garin, that is, oh, not the top tier of reasons. But certainly a common enough one." Mum had held up under quite a lot of that, especially when she and Dad were first seeing each other. "May I ask who, or would you rather not talk about it?"

"One of the White Horse people. Well, one in specific, I'm sure Uncle Garin would object about the others if he knew about them. Most of them." Ursula wiggled her fingers. "Lives north of Pulborough, back a couple of months. He was in France and Germany after the Normandy landings. Not in the first wave of it."

There was a pause, during which Ursula watched her mother attentively for any signs Mum had guessed Ursula's actual feelings. Mum gave her no hint, worse luck. Instead, she said, "Snap, or apprentice?"

"Snap. Enlisted as soon as he left school, so he's now trying to figure out the apprenticing. I've asked Uncle Seth and Uncle Golshan, but he wants to stay in Sussex." Ursula found this part a little easier to talk about.

"And they've not the same range of connections down there." Mum clucked her tongue twice. "I gather it's hard going. The agriculture's been so unsettled, people aren't taking on new apprentices as freely. We were talking about it when we were aligning the astronomy exams last week." Astronomy was one of the few topics taught at all five schools. One of the exams was standard across all five, about how to use the stars for navigation and the other key calculations that kept people alive. She opened her mouth, then shook her head. "What do you want to do about Garin?"

"I don't want you or Dad to talk to him. Not yet, anyway. It— it makes all the gravity wrong." She fell back on Mum's astronomy metaphors, and it got a smile. "But I needed you to know, and I wanted..." Ursula let out a puff of breath. "I wanted to come see you. Well, for other reasons too, but I don't know what Dad's going to think about them."

"All right, so the question is, do you want to wait

on it until he's here and talk about it once, or repeat yourself?"

Put that way, it wasn't much of a choice. Ursula snorted. "I'll wait. He'll be what, twenty or thirty minutes?" Mum nodded, and they settled into amiable conversation about what Ursula had been learning. And on Mum's side, she got the chaos of the beginning of the year, and the other usual conversation that Ursula honestly missed.

She loved Uncle Garin, even if she didn't like him much right at the moment, but conversations with him were a constant challenge. She had to be on the top of her game. Talking with Mum and Dad was easy. It flowed. Like it did when she talked with Jim, and she tucked that away for later thought, well away from Mum's observation.

Twenty-five minutes later, they both heard the steps outside, the soft chime, and then Dad was sweeping in, kissing Mum's forehead and then Ursula's. "Let me clean up, five minutes. Shall I put the kettle on?" He did, and when he came back out, he collapsed onto the sofa next to Mum, peering at Ursula. She knew perfectly well Mum and Dad hadn't actually had a chance to share any information directly, and yet he began with, "Not just Garin on your mind, then?"

"How do you do that?" Ursula shook her head. "Not just Uncle Garin, no. Um. I'm into some tricky bits with the journals. The sort of thing where it's about time I talked to you."

Dad immediately sat up straighter, leaning forward with his elbows on his knees. "All right." The way he switched focus was fascinating, in one way, and she knew he was doing some of it deliberately. He'd been the one to teach her the things to pay attention to there. Mostly.

Ursula rummaged inside her head for what she'd sorted out about how to say this on the way here. "The other part of it is that Uncle Garin tried to be difficult on Tuesday, and Mum said he's sulking. I was cranky, and so I took the day off with Mistress Renata today, and I spent time in the library with the journals instead. I'm working on that bit where they get difficult. It's slow going, but I've got about five pages. Enough that I think I see more of how she's talking around things."

"A big enough sample, as Cammie says." Dad agreed. Then he swallowed. "What does she say?"

"It's clear, almost immediately, that there were oaths that dissipated when Great-grand-mère Chrodechildis died. Grand-mère Laudine doesn't say so, not straight out, in the parts I've got translated, but it's like a dam breaking."

Dad nodded once. "You thought that must be it, I know." He waved a hand. "If it makes you feel better to just use their names, go ahead. I won't be offended. And Garin's not here to be snippy about it."

It would cut down on the number of words required. And maybe give Ursula a little more emotional distance, which would be handy about now. "Are you sure you want me to talk about it, Dad?"

"I'd rather you talk about it with me than deal with it all yourself." Dad leaned forward to take

Ursula's hand. "You've an excellent head on your shoulders, but you don't need to take it all on. Honestly, I ought to have looked long since. What did you find?"

"She talks about, um. First, she talks about there being something wrong with Childeric." Childeric had died in his Council challenge. Everyone had expected him to come out shining, the golden pinnacle of his generation. "She hasn't got up to the challenge itself yet. She's sort of laying things out."

"Ah." Mum and Dad glanced at each other. "We know a little about that. Not the sort of thing we'd talk about while you were a student. It's complicated. We don't know all of it, either. We were working at it from the other direction, his records here."

Ursula blinked. She knew, of course, that teachers could see those. But she also knew that they were kept strictly private. There was no need to have someone's school choices chasing them down as an adult. Mum pointed out that while some things stayed steady in a person, they weren't always the expected threads when they left school. It wasn't fair to make someone carry around who they were at fifteen or eighteen in their forties or fifties. Or even, to be fair, twenties.

"Oh?" When in doubt, follow Uncle Alexander's habit and make an interrogatory noise. Not that it'd fool Mum and Dad, but they'd take it as she meant it.

Mum took over explaining. "Back in 1925, we discovered that there was a piece of magical teaching that was in play for a few years. A new teacher with no idea of how students actually work, exciting new untested theories. Beginning in 1881." Ursula did the math quickly in her head. Childeric would have been a fourth year.

Mum went on with the explanation. "In 1884, Andrew Fowler came on, teaching both Martial and Protective magics." It had been during the various wars of the Empire, many and awful, and Ursula supposed they might need three professors between the two fields. "He spotted that a number of students weren't, well, the language we use in reports home is 'living up to their potential'. But in this case, it wasn't because they weren't paying attention in class, it was something about their magic. Subtle, mostly."

Dad cut in, "Not only subtle, but varied. Fowler brought it to the other staff, and by the end of that year, they'd cut all of that out of the classwork." He added after a moment. "If you want to read it—please don't try any of it, even if you think it's safe—it's Algernon Morris-White's *An Exhaustive Discourse on the Proper Education of Young Minds and Magic*."

"A title of its era," Ursula said, wrinkling her nose. "And of course I won't try it, Dad. What happened?"

"No one talked about it. Of course the Great Families wouldn't. Admit that something had gone terribly wrong? And Schola didn't talk much about it. There are notes in the files. They advised particular parents to have a Healer go over things thoroughly, they suggested remedial exercises. They were particularly cautious with the next years, all of them. Best we can tell, about one in seven had ongoing effects from it. Helena was a student at the time, so these are people she knew as classmates. Some people got ill more often or stayed unwell. Some, their magic just wasn't what it should have been, based on the initial exams."

"Only the exams were different then, too." Easier to manipulate. That was something Ursula knew about them.

Dad's mouth twisted. "Exactly. Plenty of ways to cover for it. And some people, it didn't seem to bother them much. They had good lives, marriages, children whose magic doesn't seem to have been affected. But Childeric?" He spread his hands. "Which brings us to us figuring some of this out."

"When I came across the commentary in 1925, we knew the method was badly designed. And plagiarised. With exceedingly poor citations. But a few years ago..." Mum shrugged. "It was a bad few months. '43. We all— the staff— we needed something to distract us. We started looking at, I don't know. The deaths out of season. Because we'd had so many others."

Ursula hesitated for a second. "I'm sorry, Mum. Dad." She'd had some idea of that, but they'd protected her from a lot of it. She'd heard the names, read out in the Great Hall, the moments of silence. And she'd known a lot of them, far more than her fellow students. She knew every single one weighed on both Mum and Dad, but it wasn't something she could usually ask about. Now she swallowed. "Will you, not tonight, maybe tell me a bit more about some of them?"

Mum nodded once. "Come out on Remembrance Sunday, all right? We'll tell you a bit more. Leo too, if he likes." Ursula nodded. She knew both of them also did more private things on the eleventh, but they had that right. Mum went on. "Anyway. Still not the sort of thing we want to talk about among too many people; a loss of confidence in the school would be a problem. And we were certain, by the time we were done talking through all the individuals, that that kind of problem couldn't repeat. There are too many independent checks and balances now. But what we don't know is what the Fortiers thought about any of it. No one would talk about it."

"Why won't people? It would have been easier to fix." Ursula grimaced. "I know the answer. Power, fear, strategy. The usual answers." Dad patted her knee once, in mute agreement. She sighed, considering whether to go on with what else she'd begun to see in the notes.

Mum caught that, of course she did. "Can we help you work it out? Or is there information we might have come across that would help? I don't know if you want to see our notes from that yet, if it'd bias your decoding or help."

"I don't know either, honestly, Mum," Ursula said. "There is a comment in there. There are some phrases I'm not entirely sure of yet. Laudine says clearly that Childeric needed to make a good marriage to a woman with strong magic. Thessaly Lytton-Powell. Strong magic on both sides, families known for it."

"She was a gifted duellist. Magically, not just the learned forms. It was visible in her, I gather." Dad said that evenly. "I looked up her records here when we were looking at Childeric. She was enough younger she wasn't affected by the whole problem, too. The same year as Cyrus, if you'd not put that together."

"Huh." Ursula would, she thought, need to go through and map out the people who were prominent now from around those years, and see what it said. There, she'd absolutely ask Mum for the notes, because she was sure Mum and Dad had already made those lists. "Do you know, were there other people who might have been considered?"

Dad's eyes widened. "I'm not sure. We weren't going at it from that angle. The family would have evaluated her thoroughly, though, in a dozen ways. Conversations with the professors here. Some of that's in the file, their own evaluations. A check with the Healers before the betrothal. I'm sure of that."

Mum said, amiably, "Garin made some noises about those traditions at your father, who was having none of it. Worked out well enough for us."

Ursula snorted at that. She knew perfectly well that both she and Leo put in a lot of hard work in their studies. But they both had solidly been near the top of their respective years. She didn't see that changing for Leo. "But it meant they were looking for something to balance Childeric." She frowned. "Now I want to look at the next generation of the people who were affected. If it carried down to their children."

"That, my love, is a massive research project." Mum considered. "Give me a week or two. I can get the lists for you. It's all in the Gold Book, the people you're thinking of, but I'll pull the class rankings for you." Those were in fact available in the library, just

Mum would have an easier time putting the list in order than Ursula would.

"Thanks. I think..." Ursula had to think about the maths. People in that sort of family often waited until after apprenticeship to marry, certainly to have children. That meant it'd be people maybe five years older than Dad down to about Mum's age that would be particularly of interest. "All people you know, right?"

Mum's mouth twitched. "Nothing wrong with your maths, no. And I will add some private comments if I think of anything relevant. I might ask Lizzie, too. She may have more. Is that enough for you to take back to your notes and look at with a fresh eye?"

"She keeps talking around the essential problem, but yes, I think that helps."

Dad cleared his throat. "One other thing. I've told Garin this, actually, though not until recently. A year and a half ago, it came up." Now he was looking at the wall above Ursula's head. "Childeric had two problems, besides whatever it was with his magic. First, he had a nasty streak. The sort of thing that ought to have him sent down or his magic bound for a good stretch. At the time, no one pressed the point."

Ursula had grown up knowing the internal politics of Schola as much as she knew its staircases and rooms. "Master Norton and Headmaster Osborne." Both of whom had been long gone by the time she'd been old enough to notice anything. But she could see the reactions to how they'd been in Uncle Jehan and Aunt Helena and Mum and Dad and so many others here.

"Exactly. He was a golden child, he was permitted liberties others weren't. Then he didn't have a good sense of his own skills, because he'd been allowed to slide so often. It doesn't do favours."

Mum pursed her lips, then said, "Isembard, love. How much of that did you know, or guess at, when you were dealing with Orion early on? Also Claudio?"

Dad blinked at her. "I guess. Ursula," He focused on her. "The thing you want to look for, in Laudine's comments, would be something about that. How he didn't care who he hurt, to get what he wanted. That he thought he should have all the good things for the asking. And yes, love." That was back to Mum. "I was worried about it with Orion. You were too, I remember that."

Ursula thought about what Uncle Orion would have been like at that age, uncertain and unsteady, and what it must have taken to teach him something different. Now, she just said, softly, "I'll look, Dad. Laudine must have seen a lot more, I'm almost sure of it."

"Let me know when you want to talk about more of it. Now, why's Garin upset?" Dad leaned back again, and Ursula explained, letting the more historical topic drop. Once Ursula laid it out, he shook his head. "Honestly, Garin would probably be better off if he knew more people from Snap. I know Alexander and Gabe think the Council would be vastly better off with more folks from Snap and Forvie. By which they mean any." There had been a couple of challengers from both in the past few years, but none successful yet. That devolved into a general conversation about various gossips, until it was time to go down for supper.

After supper, Leo dragged Ursula off to one of the workrooms, partly to get her to help with something, and partly so he could talk to her about half a dozen things, all tumbling over each other. She spent half of the time leaning on the table, watching Leo gesturing as he did his best to explain a ritual theory he'd been working out and glad he was so happy.

CHAPTER 28
SEPTEMBER 7TH IN ONE OF THE PULLAN BARNS

"Paul has an excellent rant about that. In about three different versions, depending on how much time you have." Jim was not, at the moment, looking at Ursula. They were up in the loft of one of the further storage barns, well away from the house. Ursula's mare was tied up comfortably downstairs. It was drizzling out, which made outside less than desirable. Ursula had insisted she didn't mind the surroundings. It was at least nice clean hay and straw here, waiting to be moved elsewhere on the farm.

Currently, she was using his shoulder for a pillow, the two of them stretched out together. He hadn't quite dared to be more direct about the cuddling, but he liked this, rather a lot. The two of them, quiet, somewhere they wouldn't be interrupted.

"I'm thinking," Ursula said, "I should talk to Paul about it sometime, if there's a chance."

Jim snorted. "You have every right to ask to talk to him. White Horse to White Horse. He's got a journal. Tell him I told you about his rants. Not that he's not right."

"Oh, I agree. Just, I bet we could get something actually moving if we went at it from more than one direction. Let me lay this out, make sure I got all the pieces. We have the land magic that the demesne estates anchor. Which I know a fair bit about now, though there's more to learn."

"That's one part, yes. And honestly, we don't know a lot about that, other than the things everyone knows. Though Paul found what you told me about Lammas really interesting, how it overlaps what White Horse does."

"Yes, but that's a Fortier thing, not a general demesne estate thing. Though I'm fairly sure I could get a comparative list out of…" She counted up on her fingers. "Veritas, Fairlight, Ytene, for certain, for this. Baddock Hall, almost certainly. Maybe the Thanets if Lord Richard can catch Lord Thanet in a good mood, Helios wouldn't without his father's permission. Half a dozen others, maybe."

Jim was struck again with the sense of being plunged into a deep cold pool, shocking to the system but somehow also glorious. Possibly also dangerous. He closed his eyes, focusing on the weight of her against his shoulder. "Just like that?"

"Yes, and no? The first three, we've already agreed to share some of that kind of thing, if there's need. The others, there'd be a bit more trading. But I can think of reasons people would listen. Me, in my own right, even, not because of Uncle Garin."

"Did you see him since you wrote yesterday?" Ursula had, Jim had to admit, learned good habits

CELIA LAKE

about sharing information somewhere along the line. Just about the point he started wondering about something, he was likely to get a note in the journal at least touching on whatever it was.

"Still in the lab. That's fine. He likes the lab, he's doing terribly useful things, even though he's frustrated with his actual goal still. I had a note from him this morning when I said I'd be out most of the afternoon, telling me to let him know if I'd be back late. By which I suspect he wants to lurk and talk to me, but he is entirely competent at lurking while reading a book. So I'd like to be home before supper, at seven or so. You need your own supper, so I don't want to keep you."

Jim wished he could invite her home. But for one, he wasn't at all ready to deal with Luke and Alice's opinions. For two, he wasn't sure Ursula was up for dealing with the little ones. And anyway, the ration books made having someone over for a meal far trickier than it used to be. Especially on short notice. Now he just nodded. "That's one part. That implies more."

"You and your attention to my counting." Ursula said it fondly, turning her head. A moment later, he felt a kiss on his cheek before she settled down again. He very much wanted to let his hand shift to cup her hip and tug her a little closer, and that would not do any good for the conversation. Which, in fact, he also wanted to have.

"Second, we have the general tending of the land, agriculture and sensible people who went to Snap and so on. Third, we have people aware that the land magic could use some help, the Council and

258

various other specialists." Then she went suddenly silent, the sort of consuming silence that rather worried Jim, even while he was absolutely unsure what to do about it. It was a sniper's sort of silence, or the quiet before a shot rang out. That was the problem with it. He could feel his heart beginning to beat faster.

She must have felt something, because she spoke a bit faster than maybe she'd meant to. "Jim, can I ask you a question I'm fairly sure you haven't considered? Just talking about it right now. I won't do anything about it unless you and Paul are both willing."

Jim sucked in a breath, then said, "Let me look at you, then, while we talk?" As much as he enjoyed lying there, side by side, he needed to see her face for this. He was sure of it. He needed as much information as he could get. She pushed back a little, turned on her side, propping herself up on her elbow, and he did the same on his left, leaving his right hand free. Once they'd both moved, Jim took a slower breath, then nodded. "All right. What's the question?"

Precisely, carefully, spacing the words, she said, "Would Paul consider making a challenge for the Council next month? On the fourteenth, the new moon."

"You. Wait. What?" Jim heard himself get higher pitched, more scattered, just in three words. "You can't be serious. They wouldn't let him in. Um. Wherever it is. The Council Keep."

"Will you trust me that if Paul's willing, that part can be sorted?" Ursula seemed entirely sincere. Not, Jim thought, that he'd be able to tell reliably if she were wanting to keep something from him. She would, he suspected, be an excellent card player, if she could convince people to let her play.

He closed his eyes, trying to figure out what to say. "Why? And why Paul?" Jim couldn't ask why not him. For one thing, Jim had absolutely no idea what was involved, but he was sure he didn't want to. "And don't people prepare for that sort of thing for months? Fancy clothing and potions and charms and — we've nothing like that."

"Oh, those are excellent questions. May I kiss you, first?"

"That's unfair." It was, but on the other hand, kissing her made sense, and this conversation didn't. Before he finished saying anything, Jim scooted closer to her, letting his right arm come down around her waist again, tilting his head to kiss her. He took his time, just enjoying that.

That was the thing. He was fairly sure he was going to say yes to whatever she proposed here, and she wasn't even trying to talk him round yet. She had a reason, and she valued her oaths. Everything else would fall into place.

When she finally pulled back, she nudged his shoulder with her free fingers. "Better?"

"Kissing you reliably improves things." Jim let out a sigh. "All right. Answer my questions, please?" He rearranged, so she could curl up against him. This time she stayed on her side, so his arm went under her head and down her back. Hers went across his stomach. The whole thing was a fair bit more intimate, even if both of them still had all their clothes firmly on and in place.

"Why the Council? Magistra Mabyn Teague— her

son is Lord Teague, in Devon— retired last year. No one succeeded at the Challenge, and they've been desperately wanting to find a different range of people. I know that for a fact. Mum said something on Thursday that made me think of it just now, so I know it's still a thing."

"They don't let the likes of us turn up at Council challenges. You know that. You must know that." Jim felt it was both true and a very weak argument.

Her fingers ran along his jawbone, as if exploring. "Will you trust me if I say I know the right people to ask? If they also think it's a good idea, they can make it happen."

Jim sighed. "I trust you. I just don't know how to persuade Paul to trust you."

"Oh, I'll make oath on it, if it helps. Let me tell you the other two things first." Ursula offered it so simply. If someone had asked Jim, he'd have been weighing whether it was an insult. She just assumed that it might help. "Second, why Paul? I read three of the Sussex papers regularly, plus the Trellech Moon, and I've been paying attention to all the White Horse people I knew about since I started. Notes and all that."

Jim was suddenly unsure what sort of things might be meant by notes, but if she were getting it from the papers, at least it was all public. "More about the notes, sometime?" he asked. "But why Paul?"

"Paul knows an awful lot of people. Not just magical, and I'm sure that matters a lot more than people have been thinking. He's got good relationships with farmers for miles in every direction. He's a decade older than you, he's established. But if he is successful— yes, that's about seven layers of 'if' there. Let's work with the idea for a minute." Jim chuckled at that and let Ursula roll on without interruption. "If he's successful, his father's got the farm well in hand. They're not dependent on Paul to keep it going, not like some. And it'll be October. There's all winter to sort out how to go forward. The trick's probably more about easy access to a portal. Plenty of people on the Council do other work, so long as they can get free when needed. He's what, six miles to Arundel?"

"About that, depends on how he cuts across country. You can't imagine your Uncle would..." Jim then stopped. "If you can solve the rest of it and talk Paul into the idea, I'm just going to assume for now you can figure out the portal."

Ursula laughed, sounding delighted. "I have some ideas, yes. Right. Third question and the fourth you didn't ask, too. Third, on preparation, I think it depends on the person. The people I'd want to talk about it can advise. And almost certainly help. If there are things it would be good to have on hand. A lot, though, gets puffed up and exaggerated. It's a serious thing, a thing that changes gravity. That can mean dangerous, but it doesn't actually have to."

"You make the idea sound so reasonable," Jim said, quietly. "But Paul's good at serious. I'll give you that."

"And fourth, why not you? That being what you're not asking, don't think I didn't notice. For one thing, I can tell you can't even get your head around the idea. But beyond that, you've only been home a season. That's not really enough time to get yourself steady. Right now, for next month? Paul's in a better place to try and see how it goes. Steady. If he succeeds, he's got the connections and leverage to do something powerful with it. If he doesn't succeed, maybe he'll learn something that will help. If we were Mum and Dad, I'd ask for a bet about it, on him learning something useful. They like bets she's likely going to win."

"What happens when she does?" Jim let his hand shift a little, because the way she talked about that, the comfortable glow of mutual enjoyment, made him want her closer.

"Some sort of forfeit, usually. Dad enjoys losing to her. They're usually fun. They only tell me about half of them, though, which means the other half are things in the bedroom or something like." All right, Jim also liked, rather a lot, that Ursula took that tone about that sort of thing. It suggested that when— if, but probably when, given the two of them— they got to that point, they could enjoy themselves in several dimensions.

Now he nuzzled at her hair. "All right. I'll talk to Paul. You talk to whoever you need to talk to." Then he cleared his throat. "And now, maybe, I—" His voice caught.

"Something entirely about the two of us, not the rest of the world?" Ursula shifted a little in his arms. "Your hand's kept twitching a little, wanting a bit more touch."

It drew a groan out of him before he could stop himself. "How do you fit so much being persuasive and glorious inside you?" Jim inhaled, exhaled, and then pushed himself to ask. "I'd like to touch you more. Kissing as well. See what you think about that. Not the most comfortable place to spread out, even with the blanket, but it's private enough."

"Mmmm." Ursula shifted in a stretch that was entirely unselfconscious. "I like that very much. Where did you have in mind?" She was like a cat, contented, sure that the results would suit, and if not, she'd be clear.

"Oh. Your hip." He let his hand move, twisting a little as she gave him more space, daring to let his hand move there once she nodded. Jim rearranged himself, his body just far enough away not to distract too much with his own reactions. He could feel the thicker fabric of the breeches against his hand, and of course they didn't hide any of her curves at all.

"I like that. And?" Her own hand mirrored him well enough.

"Your back?" That earned him another nod. He followed the touch with a kiss, letting his hand wander against her back, petting slowly, feeling the curve of muscle and bone. Then he let his fingers drift, following the line of her bra, exploring cautiously. She arched against him, and he groaned into the kiss again. When she pulled back again, giving them a chance to catch their breaths, he got out, much more quietly. "Your breast?"

Her agreement was more gasp than sound, but it was definitely enthusiastic. Jim hesitated for a second, then rearranged so he could move both hands a little more comfortably. Watching her intently now, he let his hand move to cup her breast. He held there for a second, enjoying the tender intimacy of it, beginning to get a sense of the feel of her. Ursula's chin went up a little, exposing more of the skin at her neck, and that made it easier for him to fumble with a button or two. Then he was nuzzling at her neck, down to her collarbone, feeling her arch into his touch, both of them throwing themselves into the sensations.

Jim didn't want to take it too much further, for all sorts of reasons. She had to get back. He had to get to supper. And she was wearing riding breeches, which gave him a lot to look at, but complicated touching skin. Before too long, he got a grip on his desires, enough for the moment to kiss her cheek. "We both have places to be, even if I wish we didn't."

Ursula had ended up on her back, blinking up at him, with a languid smile that promised even more plans. "Anticipation. It's an excellent word." She then let her eyes closed. "Mmm. Promise me something?"

"Yes?" It was half a question, but really, they both knew he'd be meaning that as agreement.

"If you think of me, in private, later, I'll think of you?" Ursula demonstrated what she was implying with an evocative shift of her hips. Even if it was mostly to get ready to stand.

"That's not just thinking. Minx." Jim kissed her nose. "Yes. I like you telling me I might." Then he pushed himself upright, glad his layers more or less hid just how urgent some of that thinking might get. A moment later, he offered a hand up. "I'll walk you back to the road. How's that?" He could cut back across the fields easily from there.

"Grand." It took her a moment to straighten out her clothes once she was standing and tidy her hair.

Then she let him escort her down out of the loft, re-bridling her mare and walking hand in hand with him until they were at the road. She swung up smoothly into the saddle after one more quick kiss, and he stood there, watching her ride away, until she disappeared into the mist.

CHAPTER 29
SEPTEMBER 10TH AT YTENE IN THE
NEW FOREST

"Edmund will be sorry he missed you. He's in London for the week, working on a couple of projects." Lady Carillon sat down next to her husband. Now she'd made certain Ursula had something to drink. "You'd mentioned you were hoping for our eye on something?"

Both of them wore comfortable country clothes, nothing remotely fancy, but they looked as if every detail of the space and setting had been tailored to their preferences. It had, of course, from the books on the shelves to the shades of green, brown, and cream of the room and their clothing. The New Forest, going into autumn, with a few hints of the changing leaves outside. They were echoed in the choices of vases and decorative art put out for the season.

Ursula had several goals tonight, though that was one of them. It had taken some careful timing, because another of her goals involved being here when Uncle Alexander arrived after the usual Wednesday Council meeting. Timing that was three kinds of tricky, at least. But she'd asked Uncle Orion about the agenda, and asked Gabe how long he thought a piece or two of it would run. Hopefully, the two of them wouldn't put it together in Uncle Alexander's hearing until at least tomorrow.

Now, she was in the Carillon's library at Ytene, after a pleasant look at the current mares and foals out in the paddocks. Her own mare had come from these stables, as had Leo's. Besides, watching the foals was always a delight. Matters with Lord and Lady Carillon were trickier, however. Mum and Dad considered them good friends. Uncle Alexander spent about half his week here, when there wasn't a crisis.

Ursula enjoyed time with all three of the Carillon children, though she was closest to Edmund in both age and interests. But there was always a slight sense of distance with their parents. Witness, for example, the fact they were Lord and Lady Carillon to her, where the Edgartons, nearly a generation older, were Lord Richard and Lady Alysoun. No matter, she was here for multiple reasons. She would see it through.

Ursula took a breath, gathering herself. "I'm working on a project, and I've come to a point where it needs an outside perspective. And I can't ask Dad or Uncle Alexander. They're too tightly tangled with it." There was a moment before she admitted. "Particularly, I'm worried it might be a problem for Uncle Alexander."

"Ah." Lord Carillon leaned forward, one hand on his wife's knee. "Begin with a summary, then, please."

Ursula laid it out as neatly as she could. She pulled out her notebook with a sketch of what she'd figured out so far. She began with how she'd consulted with Aunt Cammie and Giles about the coding, how she was working through the most challenging parts, and, of course, the timeframe. "I have looked at Laudine's notes, from 1889 and 1890, and Chrodechildis's, but they're not very helpful. There are names there I haven't been able to track down, for one thing. Maylis's records mention that a Thessaly Lytton-Powell was engaged to Childeric. But the last thing I could find by that name is a brief marriage notice; it doesn't list her husband. There's no update in the Gold Book, no further details."

Something in that surprised Lord Carillon. "People do not, as a rule, just disappear like that." He tapped his fingers on the arm of the chair. "It was the sort of announcement that suggested a scandal of some kind?"

"I think so. Not having made a wide study of the type in the period, it's a little hard to tell. I copied it out, though." Lady Carillon stood, and Ursula handed over the notebook with that in it, opened to the right page.

Lady Carillon clucked at it several times, handed it to her husband, and then brought it back. "Also not my usual period, but you're right. That suggests a scandal."

"Alexander was away then." Lord Carillon said it quietly, but deliberately loud enough that Ursula was intended to hear it. "Otherwise, I'd consider Naming magic to be involved."

Ursula nodded. "His mother had died six months before, and his brother about a year before." She spread out her free hand. "And even if I sorted that out, I'm not sure it matters for the part that Laudine is talking about when she's writing in 1894."

"I knew neither of them, not more than by sight. I was twenty-eight when Lord Dagobert Fortier died, and his wife died two years before that. And he was in poor health by that point, easily winded. A different generation, and I'd been doing a fair bit of travel." Lord Carillon spoke carefully, as if working through a series of memories.

"He'd been in poor health for a long time," Ursula said. "Though more quietly, I think, for most of it. There are notes about them going to lectures in Trel-lech, though most of their social entertaining was on a smaller scale. Not unlike you do here."

It made Lady Carillon snort. "All right, let's talk through it, then." The next forty-five minutes were filled up with the two of them applying their quite substantial analytical skills to the larger shape of the problem. Watching them do that, together, was decidedly educational, in a way Ursula had never quite seen before.

She'd heard about Lady Carillon's skills, of course, Mum had been clear about them. But hearing the two of them together was like listening to Mum and Dad, or Uncle Orion and Aunt Hypatia. Each sentence built smoothly on something the other had said.

It made her more certain of what she wanted with Jim. She could feel their chance at that, almost within her grasp. She couldn't put words to it, not the sort of words that would persuade Uncle Garin, but that was a problem for slightly later. Now, she was put through her paces, having to thumb through to check dates and details, confirm details of the estate, all sorts of things she hadn't necessarily considered together yet.

Right around nine, there was a chime from one of the journals. Lady Carillon's, to be precise. She lifted a finger, elegantly, then opened it, and glanced at it. "Alexander should be back in about twenty minutes, give or take a conversation." Before Ursula could do anything, those blue-green eyes were fixed on Ursula. "I am assuming you'd still like to be chatting when he appears?"

With most other people, Ursula would have bluffed about this. And she'd probably have succeeded with most of them. Here, she took a breath. "Yes, Lady Carillon. If that's not a bother."

The laugh startled her. Lady Carillon began, a comfortable burble of amusement, joined by her husband's lower voice almost immediately. Then, without hesitation, Lady Carillon said, "Ursula, dear, I think at the point you invite yourself to our library for an evening, partly to ambush Alexander, you might as well call us by our first names." She didn't, so far as Ursula could see, consult her husband.

But he immediately echoed it. "Geoffrey and Lizzie, if you please. It will startle Edmund, but that's no matter. Now, what did you want to speak to Alexander about?"

That involved an entirely different approach. "I have a potential candidate to be considered for the open Council seat, but it will take some persuading in several directions."

Watching them, she saw the surprise in both sets of eyes. Then Geoffrey gestured. "In that case, I particularly appreciate your care with Alexander's comfort, in the earlier conversation. Shall we continue with that until he comes home?" He then picked up smoothly, with a query about the specialities of the various members of the family, who they'd apprenticed with, and that particular network of connections.

Just about twenty minutes later, there was a voice in the hallway, then the library door opened. "Geoffrey, Lizzie, I didn't expect." Then the most minute of pauses, followed by, "Ursula, good evening."

Ursula looked up at her godfather and smiled, her best calm and controlled expression. "Lizzie and Geoffrey have been extremely helpful with one of my current projects, but I was hoping for a word with you about another of them?"

Uncle Alexander's eyebrows went up further, expressively, then he glanced at Geoffrey and Lizzie on the sofa. She stood, promptly, moving to pour a glass of brandy for Uncle Alexander. Uncle Alexander folded himself onto the sofa, in the spot she'd just left, and leaned forward. "Out with it, please? Thank you, Lizzie, of course." Lizzie put the glass in his hand, then took the other remaining easy chair, a few feet to one side of Ursula's.

"Uncle Alexander, I was wondering if you— and perhaps Uncle Orion and Gabe— might have a conversation with a potential Challenger for the open Council seat." Ursula kept her voice even, but she was entirely uncertain which direction he would go from here.

"Name, age, background?" That, at least, did not assume male or female, and Ursula appreciated that.

"Master Paul Wicken, top marks at Snap, left school in 1932, apprenticed and has been helping his father with the farming ever since. He's got an excellent reputation in the local area. Their farm's about six miles from Arundel as the crow flies. Well established, wife and a daughter." She didn't share that he was in the Society of the White Horse. She didn't have his permission for that. Ursula suspected all three of the other people in the room might spot a certain gap.

"And how do you know him and why do you think he's a candidate of interest? There's barely a month left." Uncle Alexander leaned back now, which was probably a good sign, and he took a sip from his glass with a sigh of relief.

"We've friends in common." She hesitated for a moment, then added, "Uncle Garin threw a fit about one of them, a man named Jim, last week. He's talking to me again, but he disappeared into his lab from Tuesday to Monday morning, to help you calibrate. Though he has said I should plan on supper with him tomorrow."

Uncle Alexander snorted at that. "I appreciate your precision with the most relevant measurements, yes. All right. Does this man know you're proposing the idea?"

"In truth, not quite yet. Tomorrow, most likely. Jim's expecting to have a word. I know they're both planning to be in Trellech next Wednesday and into Thursday. They're staying overnight at one of the inns. For those discussions about the applications of the Agriculture Act, and which crops might get particular consideration." Ursula's chin came up. "If you wanted, I thought you might manage to get Uncle Orion and Gabe to join you in a conversation. Save time all round?"

The first response was a massive snort, followed by a rolling laughter, that went on and on. It lasted until Ursula was three parts relieved and one part worried that Uncle Alexander had finally lost all grip on himself. Geoffrey leaned over and patted Uncle Alexander's hand. "Do remember to breathe, dear chap." That did not help the laughter one bit. Now there were tears streaming down Uncle Alexander's face. Finally, though, he managed to stop laughing.

"Ursula, remind me to tell your father that he is to blame for having brilliant children who are sometimes a trial to their elders."

"Surely Mum too?" Ursula said cheerfully.

"I prefer not to trouble your mother with such comments," Uncle Alexander said. "Though in this case, it has a certain amount of her touch in the observation. Do they know you're proposing this?"

"That I've been talking more with Jim and Paul and a few others, yes. That I had this particular idea, no. I had it on Sunday, and it's not the sort of thing I wanted to talk about by journal." Then she folded her hands again, properly. "Will you please consider it?"

"Not with the eyes, imp, and that tone of voice." Her godfather waved a hand. "Geoffrey, Lizzie, what do you think of the idea?"

"I think you've been complaining about a lack of sensible candidates from Snap for years. The man sounds steady." Geoffrey said. "Have you been on his farm, then?" That was directed at Ursula.

"No, but I've got a sense from some conversations

about how he goes about his magic. I gather he did well at Snap. His father's farm is doing solidly well, allowing for the year's weather. And it's not his alone, so they could spare him for Council work, I think, with a little planning. There's no portal nearer than Arundel, though." That was the last detail Ursula needed to mention, she thought.

"Which means Garin has to at least not be that kind of difficult about it. We can probably work round to that. Lizzie?" She'd been quiet, and Uncle Alexander, of course, had noticed.

"What sort of magical work have you done with them? Both Paul and your friend Jim?" Like with Mum last week, Ursula could not for the life of her tell if Lizzie had accurately figured out the difference between the two of them. She wouldn't lie. This was too important.

"I've done more with Jim, applying some of the Incantation techniques I've been learning, in song, to bless the land. Up on Harrow Hill, Uncle Alexander, that's why I was asking about locations." He waved a hand, and Ursula went on. "A bit early to be sure of results. I plan to go back in a fortnight and see what's different. But I've done some of the country dances for blessing with both of them. Paul's got a nice feel to his magic, measured. Unforced, spacing things out." She might not have danced with him directly at Lammas. That had all been Jim. But she'd certainly got a good sense of him there.

"That, for our sins, is something we could use," Uncle Alexander said. "Seeing as how I do not run to moderation except as an occasional surprise, and Orion and Gabe certainly don't either."

275

Geoffrey was the one to chuckle this time, but then he nodded. "I think that's all that's needed for the discussion for the moment?" They kept fairly early hours at Ytene most of the time, and it was getting late.

"Thank you, that's all I had. If you have other questions, journal or send a note round? If you'd rather not alert Uncle Garin, I check my box at the Fox's Den most days."

"That will do. And Ursula?" She stood, carefully smoothing out her skirts, before going over to Uncle Alexander when he crooked his finger. "It is an excellent idea, assuming the man himself is willing and as you say in other respects. Certainly worth discussing. Let me know what he says, and if we can arrange a teatime conversation next Wednesday. And yes, you may come. It is, after all, your plot."

She laughed and bent to kiss his cheek. "Thank you, Uncle Alexander. For taking me seriously. And thank you, Geoffrey and Lizzie, for both the time and your ideas. Those are a great help."

No one lingered over the goodbyes, but Lizzie walked her out to the portal, asking one or two questions about Ursula's plans for the autumn and winter social seasons. Ursula was certain they'd be up some time longer discussing her and her plots, but she'd expected that. It was entirely polite to make sure they had time to do so without too much awkwardness.

CHAPTER 30
SEPTEMBER 11TH AT PAUL'S FARM

"You can't be serious." Paul had been lying on his back on the blanket. Jim had come out to help in the orchard— and for this conversation. They'd had their lunch. It was the best time to bring up the impossible topic. The sky was blue. They had another fifteen minutes before needing to get back to work, and most importantly, they were alone right now. "You can't."

"Swear. On the Silence, on my magic, on the White Horse." Jim watched his friend carefully now.

"She can't mean it. She's not even twenty. How can she suggest something like that?" Paul spluttered, a little more, then picked up his flask of tea and had a long drink from it. "You... you mean it?"

"I think you should consider it. And talk to people about it." Jim turned his palms out. "Ursula knows people to talk to. They're glad to talk to you on Wednesday. We'll be in Trellech anyway, after the meetings. Ursula said she'd take us out for supper, after, somewhere quiet." Jim was, honestly, not entirely sure what he felt about that, he ought to be taking her out. But for one, she definitely had more in the way of ready money than he did. And for two, she actually knew places to go in Trellech and he certainly didn't. "If you decide you don't want to after that, everyone will let it drop."

"Including Ursula?" Paul sighed, closing his eyes but settling down on the blanket again.

"She'd stop fussing at you. Whether she'd stop looking for someone else from Snap and the White Horse, well, I won't take bets on that. She's got plots in every direction I can see and about eight others I didn't know existed." The thing was, Jim was beginning to get used to that idea. That Ursula was a woman who thought expansively, but also with a deep practicality. It was certainly anything but boring.

"Why are you making her arguments, then? And what's her actual goal here? I mean, what's the plot?" Paul hadn't moved. He appeared to be talking as much to the apple trees as to Jim.

"For one thing, I'm here. And we both thought, she talked it through with me, that you might take the question better coming from me."

"If by better you mean I now think you're both batty," Paul said. "You can't think this will work."

This was the crux of it. Ursula had talked through all the variations with him. Now he had to see if he could do the same with Paul. "Here's the thing. I think it's a good thing, probably, even if it doesn't work all the way."

"Probably." Paul snorted. "People die in challenges."

"They haven't for a good while. Ursula double checked. The last actual death was her cousin, Childeric." Jim concentrated. "Her grandfather's older brother's elder son. He died in 1889."

"Not at all reassuring, Jim." Paul grunted. "How'd he die? Why'd he die? How can I avoid doing that?"

"It's all unusually obscure? Ursula's working on figuring out some notes that might help. But she promises the people to talk to on Wednesday can talk about it sensibly. What the risks are, the range of them." Jim tried to put that as simply as he could. But now he could feel his own ability to judge risk tangled up. Most people survived Council challenges. They might not succeed, but they generally came out in one piece. Compared to fighting across Normandy, it struck him as actually remarkably sensible odds for a few hours effort.

It didn't sneak past Paul, though. That was the thing about Paul being observant. And, to be fair, having known Jim pretty well before the war. "Tell me?" Paul's voice was softer now.

"All right." Jim let himself fall back onto the blanket, so both of them were staring up at the boughs full of apples, not needing to look at each other. "I've done a lot of dangerous things the past few years. This one— it's serious, it matters. It's complicated, it's ancient magic. But I don't know that it's any more dangerous than some of the White Horse rites. No one's shooting a gun at you, there are no bombs exploding around you. If you go in, polite and respectful, understanding why you're there, I don't know what the range of risks is."

"You think people go in there all rude?" Paul grimaced. "Really?"

"I wouldn't put it past some. Some people, bravado pushes them into things that make no sense. And for a long time, the Council challenges have been especially like that. Ursula was telling me it's not that long ago that they started trying hard to get anyone who'd gone somewhere other than Schola."

"And now, do you know? I haven't really kept track." Paul's voice was at least quieter now, more thoughtful.

"Ursula double checked, last night. One from Dunwich, one from Alethorpe. Um. Magistra Maisie Wallace. She was at Dunwich, she challenged in 1941. Magister Warren Michaelton was at Alethorpe, he challenged in 1943. She said they were hoping for Betony Harris in '45."

"Ten years older than me. She got appendicitis, I remember that. I didn't know she'd been hoping to Challenge. I could write to her, maybe. After I talk to them."

That 'after' was gloriously telling, and Jim was pleased with it. "You could. And Ursula said the people we're talking to, if you're willing, want to hear you out, and they can give advice."

"And who are they?" Paul glanced over, then snorted. "She didn't tell you, did she?"

"She did not. I suspect at least one of them's someone she calls Uncle, but she has an awful lot of people she calls uncle. Also aunt. Most of whom she's not actually related to."

"Well, only the one uncle on her dad's side. So

long as it's not him. Though I suppose he'd have opinions."

"Possibly, um. Maybe probably? Not the helpful ones." Jim interlaced his fingers and put them under his head. "I asked her about it this morning, in the journal, what he'd think. She hadn't answered yet, last time I looked."

"Have a look now?" Paul suggested. "All right. So uncles on the other side, the one Bess knows more about. They seem a lot more reasonable. Not farmers, but they come from people who were. And sensible trades, mostly. Woodworking and things. But what'd they know about Council things?"

Jim pushed himself upright, reaching to rummage in his satchel. He'd brought it, partly because Ursula might write, and partly because he'd be bringing some apples back home. He pulled out his somewhat battered journal, flipping through it, then set it on his knee. "She said she's not talking to Lord Fortier about it yet. She expects he'll throw a fit. Her words, not mine."

"Makes him sound like a toddler. Glad Hazel's grown out of that stage, honest. Mostly." Paul sounded terribly fond, though, which was as it ought to be. "Anything else?"

"If you're willing, three people to talk to, at four next Wednesday. She says it's a townhome in Trellech, private, but not that far off one of the main streets. She can meet us and show us." And stick around to translate, Jim rather hoped.

Paul let out another sigh. "I'm going to have to talk it through with Emma. Doing anything about it. Does she have to turn up for this, for one thing? I mean, I don't even know what's involved. Not like a White Horse gathering."

"More wine than beer, I bet," Jim said. "And what do we know about wine and that, eh?" He then added, "Ursula wrote about that too. She's being informative about lots of it, just not who we're meeting with. That you can invite whoever you like. Most people invite their immediate family or mentors. Apprentice master or mistress, close friends, things like that. And she says if you wanted her there, she'd be glad to be. She's just never been at an actual Challenge before. The last one she might have, she was in school for it, and getting away was a problem. But her parents were."

"Huh." Paul nodded. "Expect I might like some company. And Emma definitely would, if she's willing to go. You too." Then he sighed. "I'm talking myself into it, aren't I?"

"I wasn't going to say anything. Might have talked you out of it." Jim leaned over to put the journal back. "I'm glad you're willing to listen."

"It's what you said earlier," Paul said. When Jim had first laid out the idea, before Paul had spluttered. "About how the land needs the help. And needs people who understand farming, working the earth, getting it under our nails. I mean, I can't argue with that. How many people on the Council, year after year, and none of them farmers?"

"Some of the Lords of the land. But that's not the same thing at all. Even if Ursula thinks there could be more cross-pollination there, too."

"Does she want to challenge for the Council sometime?" Paul asked it, looking away, as if he suddenly wasn't sure he wanted to know the answer to that question.

"I have no bloody idea." Jim let out a breath. "I mean. She's got at least a dozen plots I know about. Plenty I don't. Or plenty of plots that aren't, um. Active, yet? I'm pretty sure she rotates some of them, like fields."

The phrasing made Paul chuckle. That was something. "Ask her sometime. Not because of me. Or, I mean, yes, because that made me wonder. But it's not, um. Her answer's not going to change mine."

"When I get a chance. We don't exactly have a lot of time together. Sunday, for a bit, if it's not pouring with rain." Jim shrugged. "It is what it is."

"You're really gone on her, aren't you?" Paul was speaking carefully now. "Too far?"

"Too far to turn back. I know it's impossible. Or I keep thinking it is. She keeps thinking it isn't. And maybe she's terribly naïve, or— I don't know. But when she says she wants more of it, I just want to do my best to live up to that. It's not just the..." His fingers twitched. "We haven't even done that much beyond kissing. I mean, no privacy, not enough."

"And we're sharing a room, Wednesday. I don't really want to go wandering the Trellech streets for hours, to give you space." Paul sounded apologetic, though. "Must be hard, snatching time. Em was at least just a mile or two. And we had plenty of space. Shepherd's hut, for one."

Jim shrugged one shoulder. "Wouldn't ask you to. It's going to be busy days, and she's got to get back after supper, anyway." He had, in fact, sort of wondered about it in her direction. Writing last night, she'd let down his hopes lightly. Her parents didn't have space in Trellech. Apparently borrowing someone else's would mean telling them enough of why. And Lord Fortier would notice if she were out too late. All excellent reasons that did nothing to ease either of their desire for more time. Because she'd been blunt about that, in the paragraphs that followed, about some of the things she was looking forward to when they had the chance. "She's got some ideas, just not the sort that are fast to figure out."

"Odd world, when she can sort a conversation about a Council challenge on a few days' notice, and not a private room. Sort of feel sorry for her, actually. Can't be kind, being seen, observed like that, all the time."

"It'd help if we had a portal closer, or if Arundel were, um. Not so closely observable. That's not an easy fix." Jim shrugged one more time. "All right. Can I write her back that you're willing, sort out the details? She said whatever we're wearing for the meetings is fine. Clean, tidy, no one expects anything fancy. The right proper tie for the season or whatever nonsense that is."

"Good. Don't have one, don't want it." Paul pushed himself up. "Let me stretch out, and we'll get back to the apples. Will and Bert should be back along in a few." They were from the next farm over, lending a hand.

CHAPTER 31
SEPTEMBER 14TH IN A SUSSEX FIELD

J im cut through the last of the woods, to come
out in a field, blinking. There was a fair bit of
mist, but up ahead he could see something
brighter. Light, out of windows, and that was
confusing as anything. But Ursula had given him
clear directions, and those included walking up the
hill.

Once he got within fifteen feet, the shape got
clearer: a shepherd's hut, door and a few steps on one
end, a window facing out down the slope of the field,
tucked back against the treeline. The glow was light
from the window. Ursula must have been looking
out, because she was on the steps a moment later.

"Come in. It's not much, but it's clean?"

Jim came up the steps, and then immediately
took off his shoes, which was not a thing he'd ever
felt inclined to in a shepherd's hut. It wasn't large at
all, a bed across the far end, though broader than the
narrow cot bench some huts had. There was a slender
table under the window with a single chair with a

pot-bellied stove halfway along the other wall. The near wall had a cabinet with a teakettle and pot and a couple of mugs. And a metal water jug and basin, but of course no running water. None of it was fancy, but the whole place smelled clean, polished with something that involved beeswax and herbs, and there were linens on the bed, clean and white.

"What is this?" Jim glanced around again.

"We own the land, but they've been keeping the sheep down closer to Fittleworth the last year or two. No one's been using the hut much— what was the name? Harry Whitsun?"

"Had to give up the sheep two years ago. He's got a bad leg." Jim said it automatically. He'd picked that up. "And this is— it's safe for us?"

"Warded, when we're not here. There's an outhouse, tucked in the trees, about twenty feet that way, with the bog. No running water, but we can use the pump at the farm at the bottom of the hill, or just get water from the Rother. There's a jug or two there." Ursula pointed.

"You did all this?" Jim was still struck by it, the number of things she'd been thinking of. "One of your plots?"

"Well. I wanted somewhere we could be private, a bit more comfy than on a hay bale. And it's not too far for either of us?" It was, in fact, about as much in the middle as was probably feasible, though Jim certainly didn't know all the bits of land that the Fortiers owned.

"Five miles. No, that's as good as we were going to get, wasn't it? Not too far for you, to be gone when your uncle might notice?"

"Not all the time. But on a Sunday, probably. When you can get free for a couple of hours. It wants curtains still. I need to look for some old fabric in the attics."

Jim took a step forward, then hugged her hard. He'd been trying to figure out something like this, a place that they could rely on. They were halfway through September. The mist and rain and drizzle were likely to get more so. He hadn't fancied any of the options, and he certainly didn't have space to have her over, even if he'd talked to Luke and Alice about it.

Part of him felt like he'd failed, not providing. On the other hand, his head was most clear on the idea that he could never provide for Ursula better than she was already provided for, not when it came to money or things. Instead, he just buried his face against her neck, holding on, before he got out a "Thank you."

She pulled back just enough to peer at him. "Come sit? Let's talk." She closed the door, and within a minute, they were both sitting on the same bed, surprisingly comfortable, thigh and hip against each other. He poked at the mattress cautiously. Ursula snorted and added. "Wool, cleaned and repacked, and about six charms. Aunt Dilly was very informative about the process."

"I, um. I didn't know you knew how to do things like this?" Jim coughed. "Is there anything I can do?"

"Paint the shutters, if you like, sometime. Or the rest of it, again. I whitewashed, but I only managed one coat, and it could really use more. And I don't know about getting a rag rug or something up here. Too big for me to get up by myself. Maybe some more hooks for hanging things. Do you know a blacksmith that does them?"

That at least gave him something to aim for. Now he looked around. He realised that most of the items except the stove, which would have been here, were small enough to bring up in two, maybe three trips. Especially if she'd brought the wool for the mattress loose and packed it here. "I'm feeling like I'm not doing my share. Here. With us. Whatever we're doing." It came out of him awkwardly, in a burst, and then he looked down at his hands.

"Is that going to be a problem?" Ursula asked, without weight on any of it, making it impossible for him to figure out what she felt about it. But then her hand covered his, before her fingers laced through, and she squeezed once. He was still looking at his hands. He couldn't look up at her, but now it was their hands, and that was in fact different.

"I feel like I ought to be doing more. Providing. Making things happen. But I'm so pleased you figured this out, because I couldn't have. I don't know where it leaves me."

"Ah." That was still very neutral. Then she spoke again. "All the expectations, are they gnawing at you? What walking out with someone ought to look like? I'm sorry I can't give you the ordinary sort of thing, the way most people do it. I'm never going to be able to. Family, and how I was brought up, and what I'm doing with my life."

"And a lot of money," Jim said, still not looking up. "More money and space and land and everything than I can get my head round."

Ursula was quiet for a long moment, but she

squeezed his hand, so he thought maybe she was thinking. She wasn't pulling away. She certainly wasn't obviously upset at him. Finally, softly, there were just a few words. "Would it help to meet my family? Mum and Dad and Leo, I mean, first. Not all the aunts and uncles, though probably a couple in passing, if we go out to Schola."

Jim let out a huff of breath, and then he sat with what he was feeling for a good minute. He squeezed her hand back, hoping she'd understand, and got the brush of her thumb with no words, so probably that was working both ways. "I don't know, honestly. Do you want to? What'd they think of me? Um. What would meeting them mean?"

"It's term time, and it's really hard for both of them to get away. They come out for supper with Uncle Garin, and with me, now, once a month. Usually I go out there once a month, but we're still figuring out timing. Leo's got class until supper, the day we've been doing it, and then I have supper with Uncle Garin on Thursdays."

Her voice caught. "I'm rattling on. That doesn't help. We could go there, especially if you're willing to come to the Arundel portal. On the other end, it's about a mile walk from Schola village to the keep, and then the family rooms are on the fourth floor. It's Mum's birthday on Friday, so I bet Dad's doing something nice for her then, or maybe Saturday. Usually they go down to one of the pubs in the village on a Saturday and do their marking. That's how they started, and Mum says why mess with a wonderful tradition?"

"What does nice look like, then? For them? For you?"

"Supper out, somewhere. Mum likes cooking when she can, but of course the ration cards go to the school. Mum and Dad eat most of their meals down in the Great Hall. Leo, obviously, too. Before the war, Mum would bake biscuits for family tea, things like that. " Ursula let out a breath, then said, "Would you hold me? That's a thing I love you doing."

It was a thing Jim felt he could do, so he extracted his hand from hers, slipping his arm around her back. She immediately leaned into him a bit, comfortably. "Mum feels odd when Dad gets her fancy things. He has a few times. Her engagement ring, he worked with a good friend of hers about an amazing new telescope about ten years ago. Books, specific books. But mostly it makes her feel odd, so he doesn't. He has a lot of money. And I do, though sort of sideways."

Ursula hesitated, and Jim shifted to hold her a bit more. "What does that mean, sideways?"

"An allowance I can't really get my head around, right now, still, as the Heir." She didn't put a number on it, but Jim couldn't have got his head around that any better. "But I didn't grow up with lots of fancy things. Knowing the family had estates, and big houses, and all that, yes. But we live in rooms that are about the same size as Uncle Seth and Aunt Dilly and Uncle Golshan's cottage, just laid out differently. I have nice party frocks, because I have to go to fancy parties sometimes, but you've seen what I usually wear."

"Which is about six steps nicer than what I wear,

but I see your point. Practical, sturdy." Jim had noticed that, then he added. "And it looks gorgeous on you. Not hand-me-down."

Something in that made her laugh. "Actually, about half of what you've seen is. Mum just knows a great dressmaker, and she's done the alterations. Makes a lot of difference. And Mum's blonde, but Aunt Dilly isn't, and I have things from both their closets." Ursula turned her head to nuzzle at his jaw for a moment. "The one I was wearing at Lammas, for example."

"Couldn't stop watching you," Jim agreed, his voice less creaky now. "For other reasons, too, but the dress made it easy to keep looking. And you, in the dress."

"There." Ursula sounded pleased. "What will Mum and Dad think of you? I can't say for sure. But I can say that if I tell them I am bringing someone I want them to meet, that sort of someone, they'll pay a lot of attention. And ask questions, and want to get to know you. They're good at listening and learning. Teachers, right? And Mum has already promised, before there was you to be specific about, that Dad knows he might want to get overprotective. She gets to remind him if he looks like that."

"Bet your Dad can be proper terrifying if he feels the need to be." That was the thing. Her parents sounded ordinary enough for teachers, which wasn't a thing he knew a lot of people who did. Though talking more with Milly and Alfred had been helping, getting to know them as people, not his teachers. Maybe that was good practice. "And they know about you being in White Horse?"

"This summer, yeah. After Leo told about being in the Dwellers. I hadn't told them, but it didn't feel fair to tell him and not them. I do, I love them. Not fashionable, sometimes, but I do. They mess up here or there, or they're busy when I want to talk to them, and they're always worrying about lots of people besides me and Leo. But they're good parents, and they're good people, and being upset because they care about a lot of people seems pretty selfish."

Jim snorted. "And you do not seem to run to selfish, no. Generous. Did you get that from them?"

There was a pause, again, then he felt her nod, her cheek rubbing against his shoulder. "I like to think. Thinking about not just right now, but ten years or twenty years, and what makes things better. I think teaching makes that easier, sometimes? You're doing it in one place, one way? And what I want to do is more scattered than that." Then she took a breath. "Does that help?"

"A bit more. All right. If we go see them, when. And what do I wear, and what do I need to know, and all that?" Jim took a breath.

"We could go on Thursday, after your other meetings? Leaving Trellech around half-three would be great. I could meet you? Mum and Dad are free from four. We could catch Leo for a few minutes before he goes into supper. I'd have to be back for supper with Uncle Garin by seven. So you'd be dressed to be in Trellech. We don't need to bring anything. Mum will have cider. And apples, this time of year."

Jim nodded. "All right. If you think this is when you want to do it."

Ursula's answer was to twist, touch his cheek,

and then rearrange herself to kiss him. The kiss was, in fact, exceedingly persuasive, and it didn't take long before they were rearranging themselves to take advantage of the width and length of the bed. This was, in fact, a great deal more enjoyable as a place to explore than a hayloft.

CHAPTER 32
SEPTEMBER 17TH IN TRELLECH

"Last chance." Ursula came to a stop by the door to Uncle Alexander's townhome, the bright blue standing out against the brick and stone of the street's houses. It was only a few blocks from the inn they were staying at, and not on the main streets at all. That was good for Ursula's nerves, at least. She wasn't in the mood for dealing with gossip about who she'd been with. Not yet. Both Paul and Jim had cleaned up nicely— Jim especially, she thought. They were neatly dressed and not too exhausted from the day's meetings.

Paul shook his head. "I'll talk, at least."

"Excellent." Ursula beamed at him, then turned to touch the bell pull. Uncle Orion opened the door a bare second later. He must have been lurking there, waiting.

"Uncle Orion!" Ursula waved a hand and turned to gesture for Jim and Paul to go in before her. "Do come in, please. Introductions inside." Uncle Orion raised an eyebrow as she passed him, directing them into the library on the left.

Coming in, she was struck by how they must look. Uncle Orion in his late thirties now, five years older than Paul, give or take, and fifteen older than Jim. But despite being dressed for a peacetime afternoon tea, he still moved like there was a war on. Dad had commented on it over the summer. The way he kept an eye out, and how he balanced on his feet. It showed how he thought.

Gabe was leaning against one side of the fireplace—unlit, of course, given the weather. He was in his later forties now, old enough for gravitas and not too far out of the same generation. He was wearing country tweeds, not the usual working uniform of the Penelopes, looking deceptively at ease. Uncle Alexander was posed against one of the bookshelves. As always, Ursula admired the gorgeous and well-kept black ebony, with the jewel tone leather bindings made to suit. Now it made a particular picture. He had one of the faience blue over robes on, which only highlighted the silver in his hair and beard when set against the black of the suit under it.

There were six chairs waiting, two of them pulled in from the dining room across the hall. Uncle Alexander nodded at her, taking in Jim and Paul. "You are both welcome to my home and to my library at the heart of it. Ursula has vouched for both of you and we," He nodded at Uncle Orion and Gabe, "are very interested in this conversation and where it might lead. We wish you no harm. If there is anything we might do to ease a concern, please let us know."

If Jim and Paul had been Schola men, especially of Fox House, that would have sent up all sorts of alarms in their heads. They weren't, though. It meant that Paul cleared his throat. "Sir." He didn't turn to look at her, which was rather nicely done, actually. "Ursula did not actually explain who you were."

"Ursula may do the introductions, then," Uncle Alexander said, but she could tell he was laughing. Or would have been, if they weren't in exactly this situation.

"Paul, Jim. I am pleased to introduce you to my godfather and uncle by mutual choice, Magister Alexander Landry. This is Penelope Gabriel Edgarton, Heir to his father and the demesne of Veritas. And this is Lord Orion Sisley, also an uncle by choice, one of Dad's favourite students, and Lord of Fairlight and its demesne. All three are members of the Council; Uncle Alexander is the longest-serving, now."

She was watching to see when Jim and Paul realised what she'd done. It didn't take long, Uncle Alexander's name did most of it. Then Gabe and Uncle Orion's summaries did the rest. Jim turned to her, blinking, but he didn't actually say anything to her before turning back. Paul gathered himself a little faster, making a slight bow. "Sirs."

That meant Ursula could go on. "May I introduce you to Master Paul Wickens, a farmer of Sussex, and to Jim Pullan, the same. At the moment." She had explained to Jim and Paul that she intended to keep the White Horse out of it unless it became directly relevant. First, that was more fun for her, to keep her uncles guessing. And second, it gave them all a bit more space for elbows, if needed later.

"Sit, sit. Ursula, you know where the tea cart is, if you'd offer it round? Mint tisane and some biscuits to go with it." Uncle Alexander waved a hand.

Paul was braver than Ursula had feared. He sat, waiting just long enough for the three older men to take their own seats, leaving one for Ursula. Gabe crossed one ankle over the other knee, cane tucked at his side. Uncle Orion leaned back, letting his legs stretch out, though he'd kept his gloves on as she'd expected. Uncle Alexander was angled forward, watching Jim and Paul intently.

She, for her part, was watching just as closely when Paul spoke. It would be telling how this would go, in how Paul began. "Sirs, may I ask why you three in particular?" There was the slightest hesitation, a horse gathering itself before a great leap. "Ursula has been persuasive about the power of my making an attempt at a Challenge. What say you? And what advice would you give?"

Uncle Alexander's smile turned glorious. There were not many times she'd had the chance to see him like that, as if someone had just released him on a hunt that he'd been yearning for. One he'd wanted for years, she suspected. When he spoke, his voice was made of gentleness, the way he got when he was teaching Leo. It was the voice he used when laying out the spread of the cosmos and the dance of the most potent magics piece by piece. Ursula made quick work of pouring out cups of tea and adding a biscuit to each saucer, distributing them in order of seniority before retreating to her own chair.

"The three of us because we are inclined, for excellent reason, not just fondness, to take Ursula's suggestions seriously. She ambushed me with the idea last week, for the record." Paul did not know what to make of that. His face was terribly easy to read. Uncle Alexander went on comfortably. "Gabe and Orion have their own comments, but all three of us have been hoping for a challenger from Snap. And, for reasons of our own, we think that this moment, this seat, might be a particularly relevant time."

Gabe spoke up at that. "In brief, and Ursula does not, I think, know more than the broadest outline of this, we have a theory about the nature of the Council seats. Developed with Orion's best friend, Claudio, two years ago. We are still gathering more substantive data, but we believe that there are a range of people who might flourish in a seat, but that each seat has, mmm. Tendencies."

"And Mabyn Teague, whose seat this was, resigned last year. She's well, but she'd served a long time, and may she have a joyful retirement," Uncle Alexander said. "She is primarily a Flora specialist."

Uncle Orion nodded. "When no one succeeded at the Challenge for her seat last autumn, everyone agreed to take a while and see if we could have a different range of candidates. But with the war, with other challenges in people's lives, it's been hard to find people we thought might suit."

"Farmers having had a rough few years of it," Paul said, no hint of deference in his voice. Ursula was delighted at that, that he wasn't showing any signs of being intimidated or cowed. Not that her uncles and Gabe were trying to be difficult. Actually, they were all deliberately framing themselves as ordinary folks with thoughts. As much as they could, which in Uncle Alexander's case was a trick and a half, but one he was used to. "Will they even let me Challenge?"

"Last year also brought us a change in the head of the Council. Cyrus Smythe-Clive retired. May he also have a long and joyful retirement," Uncle Alexander said. "He's a good friend, so is Mabyn. Our new head is, well. Gabe. Your turn."

Gabe snorted, leaning one elbow on the arm of the chair. "Our new Head, you've seen the news, is Silvia Warren. Widow of Hesperidon Warren, who was our Head for nearly thirty-six years before Cyrus. Silvia is still figuring out how to be Head in her way, not in his." Jim and Paul didn't have context for this, and Ursula only had some. "She's learning. She won't like you Challenging, but she can't forbid you. The only way to do that is for no one to tell you when and where to turn up. Where is obvious, I hope, Dinas Emrys. Accessible by portal from the location of your choice. Ursula knows the settings, for one. And we'll tell you all the rest of it, ourselves. She can't stop us."

"But the question, if you're willing, is more about which of us you would prefer to have proposing you as a candidate, sponsoring you, all that. There's a bit of show about it, on the day." Uncle Orion was speaking plainly, and Ursula thought that was reassuring Paul in particular. Jim, mind, had said nothing, but she hadn't entirely expected him to. "As for preparation, that's a good question. The experience is unique for everyone. We don't talk about all of it, even now. It used to be not at all, but Alexander and Gabe set a new fashion there, a few years before my own Challenge."

It made Uncle Alexander snort with amusement, and Gabe grinned, adding in the pause, "Silvia is still terribly annoyed at me for that. But she might grant now that it was in fact good and necessary."

Orion went on, "She's none too fond of me, either, but we do well enough working together, even if I never expected to say that. Claudio, her son, he and I've been friends since we were at Schola, had each other's backs all the ways that matter and then some more." That, Ursula thought, might be compelling to Jim and Paul. That there was space for that. Ursula wasn't entirely clear on all the ways Jim saw Paul, or vice versa. But she'd been able to tell that they trusted each other. And that trust had more to it than just being in the White Horse and near each other suggested.

Paul hesitated. "I'm no fighter, sir. Or duellist. And I'm thinking all three of you are." Something in that made Jim's chin come up. He blinked at Paul, before Paul gestured at Jim. "Jim said something, when we were talking about it. I want to be brave, but I'm not tested like that."

"No," Gabe said, softly. "You were helping keep us all fed. That matters a great deal, too."

"Alexander fought in the Great War. We all three did our various parts in this one. But I'm the one who fought, artillery and guns." Uncle Orion didn't hesitate, he just set to work pulling the glove off his left hand. "One of the things where I hold a grudge with Silvia— and she knows it, I've said it to her face often enough now— is this."

He turned his hand over, showing the scars where his pinkie and ring finger had been, and how he was missing half of his middle finger. "She had it stuck in her head that anyone visibly imperfect shouldn't be on the Council. Couldn't be. Gabe sponsored me, despite that, and pointed out that the land— the Lady, as we think of her— would choose. Worked out well for me. I wasn't sure about doing it, going in. But I did, because if Gabe and Claudio were right, it needed doing. I needed to try, you understand? Not necessarily succeed."

Paul grunted, an uncontrolled sound, then he reached almost blindly for his tea, sipping it. Uncle Alexander considered, then nodded at Gabe. "If you'd grab the cider?" Gabe disappeared off to the hall and across to the dining room.

By the time he came back with three bottles to fill glasses on the sideboard, Paul had recovered most of his composure. "You do understand, sir."

"I do." Uncle Orion was utterly in earnest. "I've done a lot of things in my days, so far. Some of them, I'm quite good at. But I always felt like there was something I was missing. Now, well. I'll be busy at that for decades to come. I can't promise you this is that for you. But I think you trying is an excellent idea. You'll learn more. We will too. And if you come out successful? I'll be glad to have you as a colleague."

Paul went quiet— a little pale, now, as if he'd crossed some great barrier he hadn't expected to, and come out on the other side. He nodded once, and then Gabe offered him the cider. "From up near Ursula's mother's home. I'd offer you Sussex-made, but Alexander doesn't yet keep it in stock."

"Beer." Paul said, after a moment. "Beer's fine too. Jim's dad's a brewer now."

"Glad to get some in for future conversations," Uncle Alexander said. "So, now, we ought to talk about the practicalities." That conversation wandered a fair bit for nearly an hour. It was much more of a back and forth, with Uncle Alexander laying out the formalities of each step; he'd seen dozens of challenges by now. Gabe chimed in with more about the different people involved. All three of them agreed that what mattered in the preparation was Paul being himself. Bring apples, bring the fruits of his fields, but he didn't need fancy clothing or potions or tools.

Once that had been going for a bit, Jim finally asked a couple of questions about how what the Council did affected the land, and the other way around. Somewhat to Ursula's surprise, it had been Uncle Orion who'd answered that one, talking about the cycles and the seasons, having a feel for it. Then, there was the next question Jim had. "What will Lord Fortier think of it? We're—"

"You're right there." Uncle Orion snorted. "He cares a great deal about the land, as well. Don't forget that, no matter how terrifying he looks. That's a thing he and I have in common. Now, Lady Fortier, Ursula's Aunt Livia…"

"She was unafraid to sacrifice herself. That's how she died, getting magical items out of Paris in June 1940." Gabe picked that up smoothly. "I have what was her seat, and trust me, I've given a lot of thought to that particular question. I didn't like her as a person. She was nasty about my wife, both in public and in private, and I hold a grudge. But I respect how she died, and I respect what she died doing, and it turns out that matters to me too. None of us are saints, whatever language you use for that. Gods know I annoy people all the time. Silvia, mostly, but these two as well, and plenty of others. We're all human, but hopefully we'll all buck up and work on the goals we share. That's been going well enough."

In another twenty minutes, a soft alarm went off from Uncle Alexander's desk. "The three of us have a meeting. Regular Council meeting, Wednesday nights. Shall we put in a formal request for you, after?"

Paul sucked in a breath, then he nodded. "I talked it over with my wife and parents already. What do I need to do?" There was a form, a bit of teasing about who would sponsor, and Uncle Alexander eventually took it on, with a comment about how it was Ursula's doing.

And then, somehow, they were all out on the walkway, watching the three Council Members walk up toward Portal Square, all at a good clip. Neither Jim nor Paul moved, just starting.

"DId that just happen?" Jim's voice came out with a squeak at the end. "It's real?" Then he turned to Ursula, and said, "They just—"

She let out a slow breath. "They took me seriously. All three of them." Intellectually, she'd trusted they would, but the emotion was an entirely different thing, it turned out. "And you were wonderful, Paul. The questions you were asking, right off, that got Uncle Alexander on your side immediately."

Paul glanced back at her. "If you say so. I feel like

I've leapt off the cliff and won't land until October fourteenth. I hope."

"Well. As Uncle Alexander said, no thinking on an empty stomach. I've got a private room at a restaurant Gabe's sister and her husband like. He doesn't care for crowds and noise, and the food's grand. This way, it's this side of the big squares." She did not look to take Jim's arm, again, she couldn't, in public, and risk someone seeing. But they trailed after her, beginning to talk a bit more normally.

Food, decent beer, and some quiet helped get them both more comfortable again, to the point that the last half of the supper was an energetic debate about the pros and cons of various points under discussion with the Agriculture Act. It also gave Ursula several things to take back to Uncle Garin for further investigation. When they left, Jim hesitated, and then kissed her cheek once. "See you tomorrow?"

That, mind, was a whole distinct thing. She'd arranged for him to come out to Schola, to meet Mum and Dad. She'd been feeling more and more uncertain about not about keeping things from them. And Paul challenging gave a bit of an excuse. Tomorrow, Jim would be near a portal at the end of the day, in time to make it to tea. Ursula would have to head home for dinner with Uncle Garin, but Jim could reasonably walk from Arundel. It was ragged as a plan, but it would do.

CHAPTER 33
SEPTEMBER 18TH AT SCHOLA

"Come on. We're exactly at the right time." Jim felt Ursula tug on his hand. He'd stalled, looking up at Schola. Snap was a farm with a wide range of low buildings. Schola was an actual castle, actively in use, bustling with magic. At the moment, there weren't many actual people visible, but he could feel them. Just the way he'd felt the thousands of people in Trellech before they'd come through the portal.

"Um. Yes?" Jim managed a reply, but he was still craning his neck.

"Over on the left, that's the salle, but it's the Martial class in there right now, not Dad. This way, we're going up the stairs. They have a lift now or do you mind four flights? I should have asked."

Climbing that many flights of stairs regularly might have something to do with how shapely Ursula's legs were, now she mentioned it. That was definitely not the sort of thought he ought to have in his head bare minutes before meeting her parents. Jim shook his head. "Stairs are fine." Then Ursula was leading him inside a massive hall, with stairs leading up from both sides. There were not, at least, many students in the halls, barely any. "Class in session?"

"Mmhmm. Which means no students to dodge, and also fewer of my professorial aunts and uncles to be introduced to right away. Here we go." They reached the third floor, when it got much quieter, then up to the fourth. This was part of the tower, because there were windows now. Ursula halted in the open space in front of a wall with a door set in the centre. "Ready? Need to catch your breath?"

Jim nodded, just once, and Ursula just waited, without fussing at him, for a good minute or two. It gave Jim a chance to look around; this was a neutral space, a few pieces of art on the walls, but nothing at all personal. Finally, he said, "Ready as I'm getting."

"Here we go." She opened the door in the wall, revealing a long hallway with a window at one end. There was a door to the right and one to the left, with others further down. Ursula knocked once, sharply, on the door, then put her hand on the warding panel to the right of the door, resting her palm there for a count of three. Jim could feel something shift, though he'd never have been able to describe what.

The door opened, and there was someone right behind it, beaming. Ursula's mother looked very like her, except for the hair. Her mum was a bit shorter, blonde, wearing a dress in deep blue that was similar to Ursula's in cut and design. "Ursula, there you are. To the minute. Come in, and introduce us, please."

Ursula glanced at him, then tugged him in. The room inside was the absolute opposite of where they'd just been. Everywhere he looked, there was something with colour or shape, but it wasn't cluttered or busy. It was like Mum and Dad's cottage, down in Worthing. Down to the basket with mending in it, tucked away under one of the side tables. The colours were comfortable, more greens and golds and warm-coloured wood than the posh purples he'd expected.

There was a sitting area right by the door. It was big enough for six, maybe eight people comfortably, a table and chairs beyond that, and desks and books. There were a lot more photos of people, some of whom must be family, and some who must have been former students or something of the kind. And, standing, but waiting by one chair, was a tall man, with dark hair speckled with some silver. He was definitely where Ursula got her height.

"Mum, Dad, this is Jim Pullan. Jim, my mother, Professor Thesan Wain, professionally, and Fortier socially. My dad, Professor Isembard Fortier." Ursula indicated them appropriately, even though Jim knew they all knew each other's names.

"Ma'am." Jim immediately made a little uncertain bow towards Ursula's mum, then offered his hand when she extended hers, shaking it. Then he turned and took a few steps to offer his hand to her dad. "Sir." The handshake he got back was firm, measured, and came with a nod of the older man's head.

"There's no need to be formal if you'd rather not. Please call us whatever you're comfortable with. But we understand Ursula is currently being a whirlwind and you're probably not sure what to do about that.

The guest loo is the first actual door on the left. The curtains are the kitchen. Ursula thought you'd like the cider, and we've apples, and I scrounged a little flour for biscuits earlier this afternoon. Have a seat." Ursula's mum waved a hand.

Ursula, thankfully, sat first, patting the bit of sofa next to her, and Jim sat, before saying, cautiously, "If it's not a bother, ma'am. And I'm getting used to the way Ursula does things."

"Oh!" Ursula said, cheerfully. "Happy birthday a day in advance, Mum, and I have something for you. Dad can give it to you tomorrow." She rummaged in her satchel, pulling out something tidily wrapped in brown paper, and handing it over to her dad, who tucked it away on a shelf beside him. He had said nothing yet, and that was worrying Jim.

Before Jim had to figure out anything else to say, her mum came back. She had a tray with bottles of cider, sliced apples, and biscuits that definitely had something in the way of spices in them. When Professor Wain sat down, next to her husband, she patted him on the thigh. "For our part, the state of the whirlwind is that Ursula wrote on Sunday asking if she could bring you out. She gave us your name and a few sentences of your background, and not much else. You might have noticed she does that. I don't know if it's a help that she does it to us as well."

"It, um. Seems fair, ma'am?" Jim offered. "Consistent, anyway." That got him a warm smile. He was sure it was approving. He then went on, after Ursula slipped her hand into his, pointedly. "Ursula's keeping me on my toes. She has from the first time we met."

"You're recently come back from the war, then?" Ursula's dad's voice wasn't sharp, and that was curious.

"Sir, yes. I had pneumonia near the tail end, and a mate, a good friend, met a nurse in hospital, from America. I went back with them to see him married, and to see if it helped me recover. But then I couldn't bear to be away from Albion too much longer. My brother has our family farm, north of Pulborough. There's not really space for me, but we've friends near there. I'm figuring out the next thing. An apprenticeship, if I can, with an eye to managing a farm of my own, long-term."

"And Garin's met you once, I gather, and disapproved. Garin disapproves of almost everything, as I'm sure Ursula has mentioned. If she hasn't, we need to have a chat about the difference between relevant privacy and necessary groundwork. Again." It had the sound of him teasing Ursula, and when Jim turned to glance at her, she was grinning right back. Then there was a snort from her dad, who went on. "We were not expecting her to bring someone home with long-term intentions with so little warning, shall we say? And I suppose I ought to ask you many prying questions. Promise me you won't do anything too hasty like getting married? I will never hear the end of it from Thesan's mum if she can't put mead up for the wedding properly. Again."

"Again, sir? You married quickly?" Jim could at least follow that, though he was glancing from one to the other to figure out if he'd overstepped.

"We'd been planning, oh, a year's engagement. I'd fallen for Thesan, good and hard, but we'd been friends for a year already by then. And I knew marrying me was a big change from what she'd expected."

"To be fair, I wasn't expecting to marry at all. Astronomy is not entirely congenial with taking care of small children in most circumstances, and teaching and astronomy certainly isn't," Ursula's mum said. "My family has a tradition of putting up mead for weddings and all the other times we might need a bit of the blessing of it during the year. All the occasions happy and sad. Two bottles, at least, one for the wedding day and one for the ten-year anniversary or first child or some such. Only some-one..." She glanced at her husband. "Came to me that summer and wondered if he could hurry things up a lot. He proposed at the end of the summer, and we got married in December. And had Ursula two years later, almost."

Which tidily answered if they'd married because the contraception charm had failed or some such. That was an entire other conversation he really needed to have with Ursula soon, the way she liked to spring things on people. Jim, in specific, though apparently not just Jim.

"I gather there'd be a certain amount of fuss expected, before a wedding, sir. I can't deny that I'd like to be worthy of marrying Ursula, and I'm doing my best to make that solid." Jim hesitated, then swallowed. "Even if I'm not at all sure why she decided on me."

It got him an elbow in his side. "Mum and Dad do know where we danced the first time. I liked you before that. I was a great deal more interested in a longer-term partnership as soon as we'd danced." There was something so insistent in her voice that it brought Jim's chin up, before he heard Ursula's mum chuckling.

"Ah, now, that's a grand tradition in the family. Isembard looks like that. I sometimes catch him at it. Orion, too, with his wife, and that's something I wasn't ever sure I'd see. I know I do it too, the 'how on earth did I get this lucky and surely I'm going to spoil it in a minute' look. Isembard hasn't yet."

"I got a great deal of excellent advice on marriage from Thesan's mum and dad." Ursula's dad put that in quietly. "As you might have guessed, what I got from my parents wasn't as much help as I'd needed."

"Sir," Jim said, then he let out a breath. "My mum and dad don't know yet, though now I've met you, I suppose I ought to tell them a bit more. And my brother and his wife. My best friend knows."

"Ursula has, in fact, told us about Paul and the cat among the pigeons she arranged yesterday," Thesan's dad said. "Alexander trained me, if you didn't know that. I had a lot of the training of Orion. And Gabe— well, Gabe has many skills, but mostly they're not my fault, except for a couple of the duelling approaches."

"While we're on family, though, Dad?" Ursula offered. "Can I ask about something? And then maybe we can swap over to school stories. Jim and I keep getting distracted about other topics. I haven't really explained all of what you do?"

"Yes? You said you were having supper with Garin tonight, as usual, right? Leo's hoping to snag you right at six when we go down." Ursula's dad switched modes, comfortably enough, and it was interesting watching him do that, and see where Ursula must have learned some of it from. He'd gone from watchful at the beginning to relaxed, and now to something more focused.

"I was working through Grand-mère Laudine's journals, the later bits, the last few years, while I'm stuck on a bit in the tricky part." Ursula said, though now she made a point of settling her hand on Jim's leg. It let him have time to drink some of the excellent cider and have a delightfully crumbly biscuit. Jim's mum would approve. Maybe even be slightly envious and want the recipe. "Were you talking with her a lot about the warding at Arundel when you were apprenticing?"

Thesan's dad tilted his head, rubbing his nose with two fingers. "I was. It was, for one thing, it was a safe enough topic to talk to them about." He glanced over at Jim. "My parents were, by the time I can remember, anyway, fairly distant. I lived with Maman at the Essex House, and Garin lived with Father at Arundel. And of course, he was here at Schola by the time I can remember much, or apprenticing himself, and then on the Council. A lot of the warding magic rewards working through it, piece by piece. I wasn't permitted access to the private library, of course. But Father would bring some things out for me to look at. He let me go along with the specialist they had in to do it. And Alexander, of course. Why do you ask in specific?"

"There are a number of references. I think it's all the second and third year of your apprenticeship. Right, right before she died? She's reflecting on what I think must have been Uncle Alexander's mother, and how she'd been tending to the warding. I hadn't realised she'd done so much of it."

"Ah." Thesan's dad considered. "You'd want to look in the journals in 1870, then, when she arrived. I know there were formal agreements there, and those copies should be part of Grand-père's records. I'm sure they'd both have signed them. Possibly Philip as well, but he was young enough I'm not sure." He added directly to Jim, "Old enough to make the Pact, but legally, not quite an adult. He was not yet thirteen, I know that much." His wife nudged his hand with a bottle of the cider. He took a drink and went on, "They had been worried about the warding for a long time, at that point. Is there anything about that in the journals?"

"A lot of worries about keeping the family safe," Ursula said. "The sort of safe that— I'm sort of glad they died before the Great War. I don't think they'd have handled you going to fight well, Dad." Jim twitched at that, for just an instant. Then he caught Ursula's dad doing almost exactly the same thing.

"Ah, well. That's true enough." Then he shook his head. "That is a not a topic for a first meeting. Though Jim, I assume Ursula has explained what her Uncle Golshan does."

"Haven't managed to introduce them yet, but yes, of course, Dad," Ursula said, sounding mock-offended. Jim had appreciated that explanation, of that set of uncles having an eye on what veterans needed, far beyond what the Ministry or the British government thought was sufficient.

"He was a great help to me, well after. And still is. And Seth. Anyway, I understand the part about getting your feet under you taking some time. I gather you're avoiding all the things I did that were horrible ideas, so I shan't throw stones from a glass house." That suggested topics Jim ought to ask Ursula about cautiously in private some other time. "As you say, Ursula, stories about the school. You first, love."

Ursula's mum picked up with explaining what she did— teaching, but also being one of the Heads of House, and what that meant here. She was comfortable explaining it, in a way that made Jim wonder how many times she'd done that explanation. Once she got through the first bit, she added, "Astronomy's one of the only classes taught more or less the same way at all the Five Schools. At least for the first couple of years. I do a good bit more talking with people about teaching than most of us."

From there, it wandered into tales about students settling in and the various things people got up to in class. Then there was a rather wide-ranging discussion of which students they expected to be more in need of attention this year. It wasn't anything terribly private or personal, it was all about public things like extra courses or performances. They kept up talking until there was a rap on the door, and before anyone could answer, someone bursting in. "You're still here!"

Ursula laughed. "Jim. That'd be Leo, who has better manners, we swear. Leo, this is Jim. You got out of class early?"

"We did. And hello, Jim, I'm Leo, and I have questions for you. Ursula said you might talk to me about them, about some of your wassailing rituals, and how they're different from ours?"

Jim glanced around to see that the adults were all looking quite interested. "Sure. Though that's a longer topic than we've got time for now. Ursula's got to get back."

"You'll just have to visit again? Sometime I can spend more time." Leo seemed very much in earnest, and at least not upset by Jim's presence.

At that point, Ursula's mum stood up. "How about I walk you down to the portal? Leo, you need to eat. You wanted to go to the lecture. And Isembard, it's your night." He stood, snorting.

Twenty minutes later, they were down by the portal again. They'd made their farewells properly on the ground floor, with Ursula waving at several dozen people heading into the main keep for supper. Just before Ursula went through the portal, her mum put a hand on Jim's arm and said, "Let me have a word, Ursula, before I send him through?"

Ursula did not complain at all, and that was fascinating. She just nodded, kissed her mum on the cheek, and disappeared through the portal. Professor Wain cleared her throat, leaving her hand where it was. "Isembard was right. We didn't expect her to find someone as quickly as she did. But you've made an excellent showing. We look forward to getting to know you better. Most of all, we trust Ursula knows what she wants. Not that we haven't arranged some suitable precautions around people who'd only be interested in her money or status."

"It'd be a great deal easier without them, honestly, ma'am. I'd have a much better idea where I was and what I was standing on," Jim said with utter honesty.

"That, love, is how I felt about Isembard. So I've some experience making it work out, and the places it felt overwhelming. As long as you treat our daughter well, we wish you the best. I make no promises about whether Leo will want to talk your ear off next time, though. Tell us if you mind."

"I liked what I saw of him, ma'am, and I'd like to get to know him better. Being a younger brother, I've an idea what that feels like, someone wanting to bring a wife in." That was revealing, but, well, it had been the undercurrent all along. That Ursula was serious about him, even if they weren't going to be official about that until it made more sense. Certainly, Jim was terribly serious about her, or he'd have fled from yesterday's meeting and today's as fast as he could.

"That's a fine place to start. Now we've met you, do feel free to write in the journal. Leo doesn't have one yet, but if you want to write to him, we can set you up with a copy that can. Mostly, he doesn't have a journal so Garin can't write to him in the middle of the night and make him deal with whatever it is before he's properly awake. As to Garin..." Ursula's mum considered. "He's going to be difficult, but I believe Ursula's got ideas about that, and also we'll help. It is not at all good for Garin to cling to certain assumptions."

"Ma'am." This was not a conversation he wanted to have while Ursula was waiting at Arundel. "I shouldn't keep her."

"No. We hope we get to see you again sooner than

later. Have a good evening!" That last was cheerful, and she stepped back, waiting until Jim walked through the portal. He didn't dare kiss Ursula on the other side, in case her uncle was somehow watching. But he reassured her he was fine and that he'd see her Sunday. Then he set back off for the walk home. At least Paul had taken his suitcase home for him. He didn't have to carry it all the way back.

CHAPTER 34
LATER THAT EVENING AT ARUNDEL

"Come." It was difficult to tell Uncle Garin's mood through a door, especially one of the heavy oak doors common to this house. It meant Ursula was not sure about his state from just the one word. She'd knocked precisely at seven after washing up and pinning her hair back in place.

At the last moment, she'd added Uncle Alexander's pin, trusting to the intuition that suggested it as a good idea. She had her satchel, just in case Uncle Garin wanted to talk about a couple of the alchemical papers he'd mentioned this week. She opened the door to find the table set as usual.

Uncle Garin was still down at his desk at the far end of the room. As she closed the door behind her, he stood and walked down to join her. Now she was certain he was upset about something. If someone— Dad— had made her spell it out, she'd have talked about the length of his stride, and the way his arms weren't moving freely. There was something clipped and too tight. Mostly, she just knew. "Good evening." The question, now, was whether she acknowledged his mood or asked the reason for it.

"Please, have a seat." She lowered the satchel to tuck it under the table, permitting him to push the chair in for her as she sat down and smoothed out her skirt. Uncle Garin preferred the formalities, and she had better things to do than waste her time arguing with him about it. He moved around to set out the dishes, his hands moving a bit more briskly than usual, for a simple meal. Chicken, vegetables, a mustard and wine sauce, all of those were usual for this time of year.

The first part of the meal went smoothly enough, at least for anyone who wasn't entirely aware of the undercurrents. Ursula was. Uncle Garin was. They were both pretending everything was ordinary. Finally, when she'd finished her chicken, she set her fork down. "May I ask what is bothering you, Uncle Garin?"

His chin came up sharply, as if he wanted to tell her to be quiet. Ursula, for her part, began gathering her own protective charms, just on principle. There was something hovering in his expression, far more electrical than usual, and that suggested caution was a good friend for the moment.

What Ursula could not tell was the source of the worry. She didn't think he'd have found out about Jim yet. For one thing, her parents— and Leo— had been entirely clear that the timing of that conversation was Ursula's to decide. It was possible he'd heard about Paul and the challenge. It might be something else, entirely unrelated, because Uncle Garin certainly had fierce opinions about dozens of things that were not Ursula's immediate concerns. Instead, his jaw twitched once. "I had some unpleasant news. About the upcoming Council challenge for Mabyn's seat."

"Oh?" At least that let her classify which matter he was concerned about. Maybe she would start labelling them that way in her head, the way scholars referred to groups of legends. There was the Matter of Britain, the Matter of France, the Matter of Rome, the Matter of Albion, the Matter of Dinas Emrys.

"Some nothing, went to Snap, thinks he can challenge for Mabyn's seat. Thinks he has a right to. Silvia was telling me about it today. I had to see about the quality of supplies. I ran into her at Gordon and Harris." That was Uncle Garin's preferred alchemical supplies shop in Trellech. It was an excellent thing Ursula hadn't run into him. "Upstart."

There were two ways this could go, rhetorically speaking. Well, there were more than that, with a dozen fancy names, but it came down to two. She could challenge him or she could let him complain, inaccurately and awfully. Put that way, there really was only one choice. "I thought that the goal these days was to have a wider range of challengers, surely? Especially when the last challenge was unsuccessful for whatever reason."

His fork clattered on the plate. "You don't understand. How dare you sit there and presume? I should — you—" There was a moment, like the quiet before a crash of thunder. Then he was standing, his hands grabbing at the tablecloth, before all the china went flying. She heard at least one plate crack and the delicate shattering of one of the wine glasses. Ursula pushed backwards, away from the table, barely managing to kick her satchel toward the door. All her personal protections and wards had sprung up, both the ones she had trained, and the ones Uncle Alexander had given her.

Ursula found herself standing about five feet from the door, close enough she could fling herself at it and possibly get through it before too much else happened. But it also pinned her in place, while he had the entire rest of the room to use. Worse, this was fundamentally his castle. Certainly these rooms were his personal fortress, every single magic in them, all of the floors, tuned to his preference over decades. She couldn't fight that. She could barely anticipate what it meant. Even Dad didn't know all of it, not for certain.

Her breath was coming fast now, the little jerky breaths that meant she needed to fix that, or her body would panic more than was sensible. Ursula forced herself to take a deeper breath, keeping her hands out, palms down. Not a sign of surrender, and it certainly wouldn't fool Uncle Garin, who knew perfectly well she could do a number of things, magical and otherwise, without moving her hands.

For the moment, he didn't move either. He was glaring at her, his feet in a proper duelling stance. All his magic was flaring out around him, into the visible range, as shadowy shapes of twisting, poisonous vines with a crackle of something else behind them. Lightning.

She'd heard about Uncle Garin's temper from Dad and from Uncle Alexander. The fights he'd had with Aunt Livia had been epic and whispered about for weeks or months after. But Ursula had never before seen him in full rage. "Get out." His voice was fierce now, but she knew if she left now, it would be forever, and she wouldn't have that. None of them could afford that.

If she let him win this fight, it would warp and twist and poison every single other conversation they had, until one of them was dead. She refused. "No."

"Go." This time it was rougher, louder, with all the weight of his own magic behind it. She almost ran, wanting to bolt for the portal and Schola and somewhere safe.

Instead, she ground her heel into the floor behind her, hearing a crunch of some glass. "No." She repeated it again.

"You don't understand. Everything I worked for. Everything Livia wanted. Everything that was supposed to be.... Some peasant, barely enough magic to make the Pact, wants to come in and challenge."

That, at least, gave her a hook to hang a comment on, and she would. "You're making assumptions, Uncle." Ursula fought to keep her voice as smooth and even as she could, and she knew it wavered twice that he'd catch. And possibly once that he might just miss.

"You can't know." Then, all of a sudden, something in her brought him up short. "You know who

I'm talking about." Uncle Garin took a step or two back, leaving a good ten feet between them now, almost the width of the room.

"I do." Then, she added, "Uncle Alexander's met him. Liked him." She wouldn't bring Uncle Orion into this. He didn't need the difficulty.

Uncle Garin stared at her, his eyes bulging a little. "You can't mean you have an opinion about this." Now he sounded incredulous, as if Ursula were a toddler, with a current favourite colour that would change in three days. Ursula had never been that sort of child, and she was certainly not that sort of adult.

Then it came to her. It was one of those absurd whirlwind sparks of inspiration. "Paul Wicken is my society's pick for the Challenge." Nine words. Nine was an excellent number.

It hit Uncle Garin much like a bomb might have, a shuddering that was physical and metaphysical at once. He took another half step back, and another, until his back was up against the wall. Ursula took the chance to strengthen her stance and to risk bending just enough, never taking her eyes off her uncle, to grab her satchel and swing it over her shoulder.

"Which society?"

Not that she'd tell him, not in this mood. "Come on, Uncle Garin. That's not how things are done. You can't argue for tradition on one hand and demand a new era the next breath." It was provoking him, and that was certainly dangerous, but it was what she had to work with. "Paul has strong magic, excellent connections."

"I should disown you." That, now, at least meant

he was working down to less deadly options. Also entirely weak arguments.

It let Ursula shift her body from a protective stance to an easier one, the way she'd tease with a friend, or at least someone friendly. Helios Thanet, for example, not quite an ally but certainly sometimes aligned. "You know better, Uncle Garin. Besides, you threatened Dad with the same thing." Her uncle gaped for a moment. Surely he must have realised Dad would have told her. "And it's even worse now. You are not going to disown me. It's me, or it's maybe one of Great-Aunt Bradamante's line. You can't stand to be in the same room with any of them for more than two hours a year. You care about your land duty, you understand it. You won't disown me over it, in a fit of spite. You have no choices, here. Me, or nothing. And you love the land too much for it to be nothing."

He let her get all of it out before he started spluttering. "Your father."

"Dad told me you tried to forbid him from marrying Mum. He pointed out it was Mum or no one. If you wanted the line to continue, Mum was your choice. You backed down. He certainly told me that part. Dad puts every tool in my hand he can give me. He always has."

There was a silence, one that dragged on and on. It was quiet enough she could hear the soft ticking of the clock over the fireplace. Ursula began counting, and she got to seventy-seven before she spoke again. Uncle Garin obviously wasn't going to. "There are two things you should know."

He didn't reply, but he also didn't try to stop

her. Ursula drew on all the magic she'd ever been taught, and on the connection she'd been nurturing to this land, the land that she had sworn to tend. She could feel the quiet strength of it beginning to bubble up through the stone of the manor, a resting green and brown behind her eyelids. "First, you know that there was something desperately wrong when you were young. You lash out, because you know things were almost far, far worse. I don't know all the details, I'm still working on Grand-mère Laudine's journals. But I know this. Others in the family were working on forbidden magic. The kind of thing that's locked away forever after, because it will taint and poison everything else around it. I am almost certain that whatever happened hurt Grand-père. And you knew some of it."

The expression on his face told her enough. She couldn't make sense of all of it. He had far too many decades of protecting himself and keeping anything he felt from showing. But she could see there was something there, for just an instant.

She pressed what advantage she had, doing her best to keep her voice steady. "They were going around every rule you've set up for how you live your life. Worse, they were doing it to be selfish. You are better than that, Uncle Garin. I know you care. About the land, about the Council, about all the people you've shared that with." Even Aunt Livia, not that she'd mention that name right now. "I know you want to mend the land, from all the damage from the war, and that is so wonderful. But the land needs every help it can get. Maybe Paul can do something you don't know, that you've never learned, that you're not shaped to do."

Uncle Garin inhaled sharply, but he didn't yell or shout. Instead, slowly, he took a step or two, before moving to sink down into the chair he'd pushed aside what seemed like hours ago.

If she got this right, maybe a lot of things would change for the best. She had to try. Ursula took a breath, ignoring the way her own heart was pounding. "You made your own Challenge, Uncle Garin. Twice. You know that if Paul isn't the right person, it will be obvious. To him, to everyone else. But if he's what the Land needs, what the Council needs, and he doesn't try? We all lose. We can't afford to. Another year of flooding, and we won't recover. Or maybe there's disease, or drought, or who knows what else."

He just stared at her, like she'd taken on some stature out of legend. He wasn't moving, his fingers weren't even twitching.

"I am going out. Out of the house. Don't try to follow me. You'll regret it if you do. If you actually get worried, you know Mum and Dad can trace me fast. But you'll have to explain why." And oh, they wouldn't like that one bit.

With that, she took several steps backwards, trusting entirely to her memory of the room. She opened the door, etching the scene into her memory. The table was crooked, nearly up against the near wall, two plates and a wine glass shattered, the remaining food and wine gone everywhere. And then, remote and distant, there was Uncle Garin, like some faded and ancient statue, the world unlike anything he'd known.

Ursula slipped out of the door. As fast as she could, she made for the door out, pulling every charm Dad had ever taught her for privacy and secrecy in her wake. She paused only to grab her cloak on the way by, shrugging it on over her shoulders as she near-ran.

CHAPTER 35
LATER THAT EVENING IN SUSSEX

Ursula hesitated as she came to the portal, just outside the edge of the demesne estate proper. She had choices. Her parents would welcome her. They'd be confused and probably worried, but they always would give her space. She could go to the Essex House, which would confuse the staff, but where she wouldn't otherwise be bothered.

Honestly, if she turned up at Fairlight or Veritas or Ytene, anyone there would sort out a guest room, for that matter. And while Uncle Claudio might, at Auctoritas, she definitely didn't want to run into his mother. Besides, she had no idea if Uncle Claudio was at home this evening.

She did not want to do any of those things. Everyone at any of those places— bar Silvia Warren — would want her to be somewhere comfortable and safe for the evening. But she'd have to explain. And above all, Ursula did not want to explain herself. Not just yet.

That left three options. She could get a room at the Fox's Den, in Trellech. Her house club had uses, and she kept a suitcase with a spare set of clothing in storage. But the chances she'd run into someone who would gossip were entirely too high. She could get a room at one of Trellech's inns, but she didn't have a spare set of clothes with her. Or she could go to the shepherd's hut, see if Jim had got all the way home yet, and spend the night there.

Right. That was a decision. Glancing over her shoulder one more time— there was no sign of anything changing in the manor— she set off up the road. There was just enough traffic, and it was still close enough to the new moon, that she didn't find anywhere to stop and write a note until she was in the hut itself. After she'd checked her shoes for slivers of glass, they didn't need that on the floor here.

Ursula did not want to worry him unduly, but she would vastly prefer Jim's company right now, even if she couldn't manage to explain what had happened. Finally, after staring at the page, she managed something brief enough. "Had an argument with Uncle Garin. I'm fine, but spending the night in the hut. If you're free, I could use the company. If not, write and let me know you made it home safe?"

Ursula had taken out her book and managed to not read the same three pages four times before there was a reply. He was briefer, but absolutely reassuring. All he wrote was "On my way, under an hour."

That at least gave her something to work with. He must have been up near Pulborough or a bit further already. He'd made good time. But that gave her a chance to take a jug down to the river and get some water, and then to put some on to boil for tea. By the time Jim actually knocked, she'd had a mug, and more in the pot, keeping warm. There was a knock. She knew it was Jim, not just because of the warding, but because of the feel of his magic through the door. It had an edge, but it was absolutely him, a fuzzy steady warmth.

"Jim?" Even though she knew it was him, it was good to check.

"May I come in?" Ursula nodded, forgetting he couldn't see that— she was off balance still, she could feel it— before calling out "Please." As soon as the door opened, she let herself exhale fully. She wasn't on her own, and that turned out to matter far more than she'd calculated so far. He took a step toward her, then hesitated. "Might want to take off your shoes and check near mine? There might still be glass shards. There's tea in the pot. Well, mint." Mint was what she'd had in her bag.

Jim hesitated, then bent to take his shoes off, closing the hut's door behind him. He poured a mug of tea for himself before crossing the few feet to the bed. Ursula pushed herself to sit, legs tucked to one side, giving him plenty of room. Then he was right there, next to her, putting the mug down on the table against the window before his other arm went around her. "What happened? Why are you here?"

"Uncle Garin was—" Then she stopped, because there were so many things she wanted to say, and they weren't actually fair to put out into the world. Once she said them, Jim would remember them, and it would shape how he saw Uncle Garin. And even though she was still furious, that wouldn't do, not for now and certainly not for the future. "Uncle Garin is full of assumptions. I pointed that out and we argued. He needs time to figure out where he's wrong."

Jim listened, tugging her a little more against him. "So you're here, and not— could you have gone elsewhere?"

"I could. I didn't want to. There are plenty of people who'd have given me space. Mum and Dad. Just."

"Just, you wanted to sort it out yourself. Needed to?" Now there was a question there, and this wasn't just about her, was it? That was fascinating, if perhaps also more information than she was quite ready to deal with at the moment.

"You too? You feel like that?" Ursula swallowed. "I'm glad you came." That part was tremendously simple. "You don't mind?"

"Not at all." Jim's hand slipped down to cup her hip, the way he handled a horse or an apple or probably a sheep. Steady and comfortable, confident in what he was doing, and she leaned into that. "More time with you? And we barely had a chance to talk about any of the last two days. I was thinking we'd have to wait for Sunday at the earliest. Or the journals, but it's not at all the same."

"Do you need to be there in the morning?" Ursula asked.

"Nah. I wrote to Luke. And we're getting into the quieter season. He can manage the feeding and milking." Jim took a breath. "Your mum, earlier, she said it wasn't good for Lord Fortier to cling to assumptions. Same ones? Different ones?"

"Different ones. About Paul, about how he wasn't fit to challenge. I, I think I handled it right? But I don't know." Ursula sighed, and she felt all the strength go out of her.

Jim immediately patted her hip. "Look, let's both get comfortable and talk. And, and." He glanced down. "I don't want to ask you for something you don't want."

Ursula considered, then said, "I think a bit of physical company might be very welcome in a few minutes. Certainly delightfully distracting. That's an excellent idea." She wriggled away from him enough to strip off the cardigan, her socks, and then after a moment's hesitation, everything except her slip and panties. It was the least clothing she'd worn around him ever, but she wanted Uncle Alexander's pin somewhere safe, and the blankets she'd brought for the bed should be plenty warm. A minute or two later, he joined her, having stripped down to his undershirt but leaving his trousers on. Once they were properly under the covers, she snuggled in close to him, and his arm went around her, and she could just breathe in something comfortable.

"Your mum and dad love you a lot. I'd— I'd like you to meet mine. And Luke and Alice. If we're like that about each other." There was a hint of a question behind it. "Your mum implied we were."

Ursula snorted. "Wouldn't have brought you to meet them if I wasn't like that about you. I don't need — I don't need to rush the formal. There are reasons to take a bit of time. After the Challenge, certainly, time for you to meet people and get used to some of what it looks like in my bit of the world. But I'd like to meet your family. If you think they'd like to meet me."

"Like's not quite the word, sweet. You'll confuse them a fair bit. But that's all right. No one's going to, um, argue with you?" Jim said. "They're worried about me, mind."

Before Ursula could say anything back to that, she heard the chime of her journal and sighed. "I— can you hand me that from the table?" She'd left it out, because there might have been a message from Jim, or someone else. "It's Uncle Alexander."

Jim pushed up on an elbow and obliged, not trying to read over her shoulder. She considered the message, rereading it several times while she decided what to do about it. "At Arundel, at Garin's request. Are you all right? You needn't tell me where you are, but if there is relevant information, I would appreciate it. A."

Then, she read it out loud, glancing up to see Jim's expression. "To translate, he's with Uncle Garin - I wonder how that happened - and he's somewhat at a loss. It's certainly not the sort of thing I can explain well in the journal, and I'm not going back there tonight."

"No?" Jim hesitated. "I'd walk you back."

"No." Ursula said, firmly. "Uncle Garin needs time to be more sensible. And now that we're here, and we've space and time, I do not want to give that up. Uncle Garin's entirely a grown man. He can cope with whatever he's feeling for a night." Her voice softened a little. "Though I feel better that Uncle Alexander's there."

"If you're sure." It was a statement. That was one

of the things she loved about Jim. One of an increasing number. He checked with her, but he didn't question her decisions. That was far too rare. She'd learned that years ago.

"Am." Ursula said. "Let me write back, though, moment." She considered what to say. Then she pulled out the pen in the edge of the cover, and wrote back in her tidiest handwriting, reading it out as she wrote each phrase. "I am fine, thank you. I expect to be occupied the rest of the evening. If you'd like to talk in the morning, I'll check for a message when I wake up. Mistress Renata isn't expecting me." As soon as she put the pen down, she added to Jim, "She isn't, but I expect I'll want to talk to Uncle Alexander tomorrow. And then Uncle Garin. I need to think about how to do that best." She handed the journal back to Jim. "Come back here and curl up? Please?"

He snorted softly at that last. "You don't need to ask twice. Are you sure you don't need anything else? To think out your uncles?"

"That's for tomorrow." Ursula said that part firmly. "Tonight is for other things. Like what we're doing next. One of the things on my list is finding you somewhere that suits you, longer-term. Either near Arundel or near a portal, ideally, because I certainly do not want to give up seeing you regularly and closely." Ursula wriggled to demonstrate her point, and felt Jim react to that, a twitch of his hips. "Mmmm." That gave her ideas, actually.

"You're considering some new plan, aren't you? I am getting to know that sound." Jim did not sound upset, more amused. But it was the sort of thing she had to check about. Now he'd brought it up.

"I'm going to keep doing that. Do you mind?" Ursula let her hand settle on his chest, mostly to see what that did to his reactions. She felt his breath catch, and let her hand drift lower.

"How far are you intending to go with that then, tonight?" His voice had a little edge to it, not unhappy, but wanting to know the lay of the land.

"We've more privacy than we've had yet. And I was doing research on charms for this kind of thing. There's more than one I'd like to try out. I find I want to, mmm, how to put this, stomp a few more of Uncle Garin's assumptions into dust."

Jim made an awkward sound in his chest. "Are you propositioning me, then? Are you— this isn't, you haven't before. You should be somewhere far nicer. It might not, you might want a bath or something after, I don't know."

He was stammering now, and that was both adorable and not getting Ursula what she increasingly wanted. "Are you saying no?" Then she shifted, to peer at him, her hand coming up to touch his cheek. "Brand new plan, just hatched in the last few moments. I would, in fact, very much like to explore all the things we can do in this bed. Here. On a bit of the Fortier lands. It's not the demesne estate proper, but that's honestly all to the good right now. And I can tell you want, too."

"I want so much with you." It came out as a groan, before he could stop himself, his hips moving again against the air. This, now, this was entirely unfair, but she moved her hand again, down his body, until she could cup him, feel exactly how much he wanted, watching his face for the reaction. He closed his eyes, screwing them shut, making the most fascinating sound deep in his chest. She left her hand where it was, not moving, to see what he'd do.

Slowly, carefully, he got one eye open, then the other, then he sighed. "It may not be good for you. First times aren't always."

"Don't care. Fairly sure I'll like it. I do know charms. I've done a lot of reading about it. Now I want to actually understand. With you. Only with you. And there really is a charm I found in some of the White Horse records, for blessings and, I don't know. Channelling the love of the land." Ursula tilted her head. "Please?"

It was the 'please' that undid him. A moment later, she was being pushed onto her back and he was stretching out against her. One of his hands was fumbling to undo his trousers and get them off his body, then all over her upper body. He was cupping a breast, touching and stroking down the curve to her hip, beginning to shift and arrange her, all while he was kissing her, urgently.

It was like getting flung into the air, the way Aunt Cammie's Duncan described flying an aeroplane, an absolute glory of everything moving at once. It was far too much for her to pay attention to all the different threads. Despite all the delight of it, and all their mutual eagerness, it took a bit for them to get to anything they hadn't done before. Eventually, though, he was nudging at her to pull down her panties, then to help her strip off the slip. His own pants were next. Finally they were entirely naked, skin against skin, hot and damp and entirely new.

"More?" Jim lifted on his elbow. "Tell me you're certain."

"More." Ursula put all the weight into it she could, all the ways she wanted this, and it was bubbling up in her heart and her body. And while she didn't forget, she wasn't made to forget, how it fit into all her other plans, this wasn't about any of those plots at all. This was about the two of them, and all that meant. Before she could dwell on that, though, his mouth was back against hers. His tongue pressing into her. A moment later, his fingers were slipping deliberately between her legs and then one inside.

He pulled back, just for a moment, to murmur in her ear, "Getting you ready for me. I, oh, this is..." He dissolved into incoherence, nuzzling at her neck and ear before going back to kissing. Kissing, apparently, did not confuse him. Having something solid and warm inside her, though, that was something she'd explored a little on her own. But her own fingers couldn't get nearly the same angles, and also it was Jim. She didn't know what he'd be doing, how he'd be touching, and that was a whole new landscape to begin to learn.

Finally, he pulled back to look at her, bracing now on both hands, as he looked down. Jim was breathing a little shallowly, flushed, and she could feel the heat of him against her lower body, the hardness of his cock. "Tell me you want this."

"Oh, far more than I've words for." Ursula tried, though, because she wanted to find some, and because she could tell he wanted to hear it. A clever well-trained tongue had to have uses here, too, didn't it? "I want to feel you inside me. I want to be that close to you, know exactly where you are. You make me feel wonderful, rooted, solid, all the song of the land and the greening of the world, and the flourishing. Blessing."

Jim grunted, as if that hit him in places he had no armour against. Then he nodded, just once. "I'll take this gently." She felt him notch against her, then push in, the stretch far bigger than fingers. It was an utterly novel sensation. It took her more than a breath or two to figure out even what she was feeling. Then she got her eyes open again, to find him watching her as if he wanted to swallow her. His hips rocked, just a little out and deeper in, and she whimpered in pleasure. "More. Slow to start? More."

"More." That brought an arch of his hips— Ursula was now certain that horseback riding, competent riding— had to have some benefits here. He filled her and pulled back, keeping the rhythm steady until she was rocking with him. None of this was simple. Of course it wasn't. The best things had layers. She'd heard stories about young men taking a disappointingly short time with sex; people did giggle about it, even if that wasn't fair. Jim, though, seemed to be pacing himself.

They'd settled into exploring more, this touch or that. Then whether her legs made the angle feel that much better. He nuzzled at her breast again, along the top of it. "Do you want to try the charm?"

"Oh. Oh yes." The incantation wasn't complicated, a blessing in the ancient Anglo-Saxon, a fragment passed down through centuries and faded manuscripts. It had caught her memory, and she began saying it, more than chanting it, barely pitched. Jim shuddered as she began, and then he picked it up, repeating it with her. They arched against each other for three repetitions, four. He reached between them, doing his best to stroke her and to bring her to a climax, as if he couldn't hold back longer.

That wasn't quite enough, somehow, until he pushed into her hard, grinding until she felt as if there was nothing else in the world but him wanting her. His mouth came down against the edge of her neck, sucking, and that pushed her over into a series of shudders. It was entirely like what she'd done to herself, what seemed like decades ago, and utterly different. This time there was his body to clench around, his shoulders and strength and warmth to cling to. His full attention was on her, and that was glory. As soon as she'd begun to quiet, he was picking up speed, a last few urgent thrusts that left her gasping, and then he spilled inside her. That was a feeling she wanted more of, those instants of something made only of potential.

He came to rest above her, propped on his elbow, before tugging her so they could both rest on their sides, with him still more or less inside her.

CHAPTER 36
A SHEPHERD'S HUT

J im lay there, gathering his breath and his wits, unable to let Ursula go. He wanted to stay like this forever, even if that wasn't remotely practical. His heart was still rushing, a rhythm like the best of the White Horse dances, where the magic carried the music and the music wove charms. It was not at all what he'd expected from this evening. He wouldn't have dared wish for any of it. Been brave enough to.

And yet, here was Ursula, nestled against him, entirely trusting and relaxed. Here he was, wanting to do that again, in any form he could imagine and any she could. Likely, she'd have a whole range of ideas he hadn't considered yet, given the way she was about every other part of her life. A man could get used to that, he thought.

Slowly, not wanting to startle her, he nuzzled at her shoulder again. He might have left a mark, but he supposed that could be managed. Jim would be shocked if she didn't know a dozen charms for bruises. He knew a few. He let his hand shift slowly. "Ursula." Then more hesitantly. "Love?"

"Mmmm." That got him a sound like a purr, a muzzy contented noise. "Again, when we can?"

That, now, made him chuckle enough he slipped out of her with some regret. "Again. Might take me a bit."

"We've a lot of forever to work with." Hearing her put it like that should have felt binding or restrictive, and it didn't. It felt like they were walking down a road near here. Hedges on both sides, gates or places a road split off. But they were going forward together, sharing what they saw and heard and knew.

Jim sucked in a breath, then he made himself nod and say it out loud. "I like that idea. How do you feel, then?"

"Splendid." Ursula's voice turned a little more thoughtful. "The sort that would like further experimental data to work with. But I'm like that."

"You are." He moved now to kiss her nose. "I have learned that you are full of plots, and full of observations, and full of a desire to learn more. I'm glad this was, that this was like you'd wanted. And the charm...."

"A lot more of the charm? In a variety of locations?" Ursula said hopefully.

"I would prefer not to scandalise people I know, please. Or people you know." He added the last one hurriedly, because honestly, that changed the field a great deal. It made her laugh, so that was all right. "But yes. It was—" Jim hesitated. "Sharing the White Horse with you, knowing that's at our heart. Matters, more than a little."

"Me too." Her voice went very soft. "I'm not - this isn't - too much for you?"

"It's a lot," Jim admitted. "You have so much you want to do, and you're, you're from a world that I don't understand. And." He kissed her nose again. "You don't necessarily explain yourself. But I trust there's a reason for that."

"I'll do my best. But you can also ask. Neither you nor Paul asked who I was introducing you to. You should know Uncle Alexander's a horrible influence when it comes to not answering questions." Ursula was watching him closely now.

"No. We didn't. And we could have. What would you have said, anyway?"

"Depends how you asked." There, that was Ursula relaxed again, trusting, and sure that he trusted her. He'd go a long way to hear that. "If you'd asked, though, that it was people on the Council, inclined to take me seriously."

"Alexander Landry's your godfather." Jim tried it out, feeling for the relationships. "And Lord Orion Sisley is..."

"One of Dad's favourite students, one of his first, too. His father was on the Council. Uncle Claudio's his best friend. I grew up with both of them coming to visit, when they needed space from their families. And Gabe is— he's curious about a lot. It turns out he and Uncle Alexander and Uncle Orion have similar approaches about what they want. Uncle Alexander's been on the Council for ages, since 1897. Uncle Orion's one of the newest. He challenged for Uncle Garin's seat when Uncle Garin retired right after the war. Gabe in 1940. For the seat that was Aunt Livia's. Uncle Garin's wife."

"I will never get over you calling them all aunt and uncle. I'll make it be fine in public, just." Then Jim tilted his head. "Not Uncle Gabe?"

"He and his wife are good friends with Mum and Dad, but not that kind of friendship? And more after I was ten. Now he says I'm an adult, doing adult kinds of plots, I can call him by his name. Also, he doesn't really like titles. Calling him Council Member Edgarton is a way to get his back up."

The idea baffled Jim more than a bit, but he just nodded. "And what do I call him? Either of them. Lord Sisley's married?"

"Oh, yes. You can probably start with Penelope Edgarton. For Uncle Orion, try Lord Orion, and see what kind of face he makes. You'll like Aunt Hypatia, I bet. She's expecting, though, so not travelling much. She's a materia and sympathetic magic specialist. Not usually the one growing things, but interested in how they're grown and encouraged." Ursula leaned back, and Jim shifted to make that a more comfortable nestling.

This part, at least, he understood along with simply enjoying the feel of her against him. He was, at the moment, trying not to think too hard about a future in which he and Ursula might be considering children in a specific sort of way. The conversation reminded him, however, about what Paul had asked about the Council. "Ursula, love? Can I ask about your plans? Long-term?"

"Always. And I'll do my best to answer, if it's you

asking." That put him in a particularly small group, he suspected.

"First, I did like your parents. And I think they, it was all right?" That was the first thing to check.

"Mum wrote before I finished changing for supper, and Dad by the time I checked after getting here? They'd love more time to get to know you, when we can find one. A Saturday out there, or a Sunday. Dad's got the bohort in the afternoon, but we can figure something out. You made an excellent impression, anyway, and I don't think Dad was too intimidating?"

"Your dad was extremely intimidating, but I could tell he was trying not to be?" Jim considered that once he'd said it. "And I'd like to talk more to your mum about the apples and all. Time to go see the orchard and the beehives next time?"

"Mmm." Ursula made another contented sound. "That'd be grand, yes. More questions?" She was at least encouraging him.

It gave Jim the courage to ask the one that mattered nearly as much. "Is challenging for the Council part of your plans? In the future?" Jim got it all out in one go.

"You'd rather I didn't?" Ursula's head came up, but he could not make sense out of her tone of voice, what she thought of it.

Jim let out a huff of breath. "To be honest, I'm not sure I could deal with that. That, the range of people? Even if it maybe included Paul. I understand Paul, but there's only one of him."

Ursula pushed up on her elbow, suddenly very earnest. "Can we agree that if any future children can decide they want to make a Challenge, we'll fully support them? The, um, hypothetical ones that are actually part of my long-term plans if we can manage it. After a certain amount of enthusiastic practice, of course, and both of us finishing our apprenticeships and what have you?"

The earthy part of that was— well, to be honest, it was more than a bit distracting. Jim was caught for a moment about what their children might look like. Or more importantly, if they'd have Ursula's sparkling intelligence and speed of wit. And whatever Jim could offer there, which was something he'd have to poke at more. But he thought it through carefully, then nodded. "I can agree to that."

"Excellent. In that case, I, Ursula Alexandra Fortier, swear on the Silence and on my magic that I will not make a Challenge for the Council of Albion, choosing to turn my magic and my oaths and my love of the land to other purposes." He could feel how whatever fear she held cut across her, the brush of it from the deepest magic of the land. There was a slight hesitation at the end, as if she might say something else, before she met his eyes and stopped.

Jim sucked in a breath, then he swallowed. "You —you just did that?"

"I have been wanting a reason to make that oath for at least three years now. It does not suit any of my long-term plans at all. Uncle Alexander might scold me for not leaving a clause about you releasing me from the oath, or by your death. But no. I don't want that."

Jim hugged her tightly, pulling her close against him. "You didn't need to, like that."

"Did." She said it mostly into his shoulder. "Don't want anyone pushing me into it. You are an excellent reason not to."

"It is going to take me all our - long - lives together to get used to the speed at which you rearrange your plans, isn't it?" Jim asked, over-whelmed now.

"Very long lives, I hope." Ursula nuzzled at his shoulder. "You like a challenge, don't you? And it comes with some advantages. Even if, I admit, Uncle Garin is complicated."

Jim nodded. "Is he— I mean, you haven't told him about us."

"No. And that's going to take some thinking." Ursula said. "But one reason for that particular oath is it'll make me more steady. It's not all the oaths I want to make to you, or because of you, or with you. But it will do for a step toward them."

"Nope. Not at all used to the way you think," Jim said, letting his head fall back, then reaching to stuff the pillow at a better angle. "But you're sure about me. Does—" The thought suddenly grabbed him. He knew there were stories about that sort of thing. "Does your family have, um, obligations about purity or sex or any of that?"

"Dad's did. Mum's doesn't. And we're both clear on which set I'm choosing, aren't we?" That made it conspiratorial, a thing they'd done together, which they had. And he'd asked, he'd made sure to check. They'd both wanted the joyous, enchanting sex they'd had. And Jim certainly wanted more of that, and soon. Tonight, again, he hoped. "It's certainly not Uncle Garin's to decide." She wrinkled her nose.

"Besides. I think my grandparents enjoyed their time in bed— it's hard to tell entirely from the notes? But I'm certain that Great-Uncle Clovis had a mistress, and his father, and no, thank you."

"And your Dad won't be, um..."

"Dad was in the gossip columns all the time, about who he was sleeping with. Not all of them were true. Mum walked me through the lists a couple of years ago. Because most of them are still around and turn up at parties, you know? She didn't want me to be surprised by it, or by gossip. And some of it is very useful gossip to know about for other reasons. Anyway. If he's difficult, Mum will sort it. I'm sure of that. And probably also if Uncle Garin is difficult."

"If you say so." Jim was dubious about that entire chain of events. But it also wasn't something he could do much about, and Ursula did not sound worried. "So. What do we do now?"

"Tomorrow morning, I should talk to Uncle Alexander. Probably that means going and getting the case I keep at the Fox's Den in Trellech and changing into something clean and having a bath first. From there, I don't know. Talking to Uncle Garin, if he's stopped being stuck in the previous century again. Uncle Alexander should be able to tell me that."

Jim nodded. "You're named for him?"

Ursula chuckled. "Mum sprung it on him. He tries to forget it. Dad's family runs to Merovingian names, and Mum absolutely refused. Ursa Major's her favourite constellation, so Dad suggested Ursula. Which is a fine name, other than not having a lot of nicknames. I am, as you can see, quite able to pick and choose the family traditions that actually make sense, and ignore the ones that really don't."

The question of family names was not a worry that Jim had had before. He suspected he'd be adding a lot of that sort of thing to a mental list now. Instead of fretting over that, he bent to kiss Ursula for a moment, just enjoying it. When he pulled back, he asked. "Are you too sore for another round? Would it be too much, given your tomorrow?"

"More. Please." Her arms went around his shoulders. "I expect to be saying that to you regularly, so you're properly warned."

"You, what did you like so much?"

"Ah." She nuzzled at his shoulder while he worked on figuring out a different angle for another round. Curled up behind her, he thought, so they could at least begin by taking their time. He moved to make that easier, as she went on, "You said it. Having the same desire about the land and the magic. I find that—" Words failed her for a moment, and Jim had not thought that was a thing that happened for her often. "I want to lose myself in that, and find myself with you, as much as we can."

It was a challenge to live up to, but one that Jim himself found compelling. He let his hand slip around her, arm across her hip, fingers beginning to reach and explore. "I love it when you explain." Then he was burying his face against her hair, and not at all in the mood for more words right now.

CHAPTER 37
SEPTEMBER 19TH IN TRELLECH

Ursula knocked three times on the door of Uncle Alexander's townhome just as the bells finished striking eleven. She was as well-armoured as she could arrange given the circumstances. She thought both Uncle Orion and Uncle Claudio would approve of her strategy and sequencing in this case.

Earlier that morning, she had chivied Jim through the Arundel portal before Uncle Garin was likely to be about. She'd sorted a chance for him to wash at one of the inns, followed by a hearty breakfast at her favourite cafe near Club Row.

Then she'd left Jim to the main library while she'd thrown herself on the skills of various of the staff at the Fox's Den. The best day dress she kept there had been pressed and freshened while she had a thorough bath, a touch of perfume, and her hair put up properly. With half a dozen charms making sure it stayed there, of course. And then the proper hat, more a decoration than anything of utility, except that it had at least four more charms keeping it in place and angled just right.

Now, she looked every bit an adult, in control of herself and her future. The cobalt blue of the dress complemented her eyes and her hair, and it made the chalcedony pin stand out nicely. She had nothing other than her ordinary jewellery on her, and she hadn't thought it worth getting anything from the Scali vaults. Besides, that might be a tad too obvious, even for Uncle Garin. But her dress fitted her exquisitely, the shoes went with it and her handbag perfectly. The rest of her things were waiting for her to retrieve them at her convenience.

The door opened promptly. Just the amount of time it would take for Uncle Alexander to finish one of his sentences, turn, and walk down the hall to the front door. He, too, was in a particular set of clothing, the deep turquoise over a black fitted under robe, decidedly less of Albion than usual. She offered her best smile. "Thank you, Uncle Alexander, for making the arrangements."

"You know, I am sure, how much I love you." He accepted the kiss on his cheek with a slight smile. "When your parents asked me to be godfather, I did not see this coming."

"Didn't you? I did." Ursula heard him snort, but then he stepped back to lead the way into the library. She could feel the layers of the wards, too, which was a great deal of why she'd wanted to have this conversation here. First, she absolutely trusted that Uncle Alexander not only would but could keep her safe in all ways, whatever Uncle Garin might decide to do. And second, it was the most neutral territory she could arrange without it also being rather public.

Uncle Garin was standing near the fireplace when they entered, looking actually rather worn. Ursula did not think that last night's particular delights showed explicitly on her face, though she had, in fact, left the mark Jim had made last night on her shoulder. It was covered properly by her frock, though. She felt in excellent form, though.

"Sit, Garin. Ursula, your usual chair, here?" Ursula sat, because of course neither of them would if she didn't. There were times that their more formal manners could be a tad tedious. On the other hand, she could amuse herself with the idea of what would happen if she bobbed up and down for any reason at all. Or if she began pacing, or whatever else might amuse. Not that she would. This conversation called for calmness and steadiness.

Uncle Garin was staring at her. His first comment was not what Ursula expected, and not, she thought, what Uncle Garin had meant to say. "Have you been doing anything your father would object to?"

The answer to that was flippant, but actually quite easy. "Not unless he's far more of a hypocrite than I believe he is." It applied equally to having had sex and to having made the oath never to challenge for the Council. That was a tidy bit of truth-telling, honestly. Mistress Renata would be delighted. Also Uncle Alexander. Well, probably, given the oath in question.

There was utter silence for a long moment before Uncle Alexander said, "And have you been doing anything your mother would object to?" He, however, was smiling, which made her fairly sure that either Mum and Dad had filled him in about Jim, or he'd made a series of clever guesses. Possibly both.

"Oh, that's much easier. No." Ursula kept her hands folded properly in her lap. "Where shall we begin?"

"You were— where were you last night?" Uncle Garin was keeping at least some hold on his temper, though she thought he had not anticipated any part of this conversation nearly enough.

"Somewhere safe. With company." Ursula said. "Not Mum and Dad, but I'm sure one of you checked on that. This morning, anyway." She waited. She would not make the first move here. That was abominable strategy. Every single one of her non-Schola uncles and no few of her aunts would come down on that like a load of bricks. Also, it was no good way to go forward. She would wait. Mum had taught her that one even more than Dad.

It meant there was a lengthy and increasingly awkward silence. Well, awkward for Uncle Garin. Uncle Alexander looked placid, as if he were arranging little hieroglyphic figures into new arrangements in his head as a puzzle. Both of them took even breaths. Ursula kept her gaze open, including Uncle Garin but not directly meeting his eyes. Uncle Alexander had the same open gaze, though he was at least partially focusing on Ursula. He likely wouldn't tell her later what he was considering, but maybe he'd hint.

It took a good three minutes - more like three and a half, Ursula hadn't started counting immediately - before Uncle Garin said, carefully. "I apologise,

Ursula, for my assumptions. And for making you feel you had to leave the estate. Alexander was, he was..." His voice stalled. "May I ask how long you have been working on the idea of Paul Wicken making a Challenge?"

"Directly?" Ursula counted back mentally. "Twelve days. Though Mum got me thinking about it indirectly on the fourth." Then she squared her shoulders. "About the larger idea that we desperately need to talk more about the land magic with people who actually work the land? Since my second year." That was giving a fair bit away, but she'd already mentioned a society.

"Your society." Uncle Garin's voice was utterly flat now. "Will you share that with me?"

"I only told Mum and Dad this summer." Ursula countered with that. "And I haven't told Uncle Alexander either." She glanced over, taking just an instant. "Though I believe he's guessed."

Uncle Alexander snorted, a little more relaxed, but he just waved a hand. "It is your choice whether, when, and who you tell. We respect that. And I certainly understand why you have been judicious about the telling."

Ursula acknowledged that with a nod, watching Uncle Garin. He sighed, and then said, carefully. "If, at some point, you are willing to share that with me, I promise I will listen and set my assumptions aside." He seemed honestly in earnest, and he added a moment later. "I'll make oath on it, even. If you'd prefer not to trust my self-control."

That made it suddenly a different problem. She could ask for his oath. Uncle Alexander could certainly ensure it was properly made. But then it would be there, between them, that she didn't trust him to behave decently on his own. That was no good either. She took a breath, exhaled, and counted to seven, like Mistress Renata had taught her. As evenly as she could, she said, "I prefer it when you choose the decent thing yourself, in the moment. I trust we won't need to have this particular argument again."

"I hope not." That got a burst of something she'd never heard from him before, an honest frustration with himself. "You've my word I wish to avoid the same mistake in future. Or any related ones, Alexander. You needn't point it out. And I will certainly not interfere with Master Wicken's challenge, or whatever support you wish to give him." Uncle Garin was using Paul's proper form of address, the one he'd earned. That was a good sign. Then he took a breath. "What you said about Maman and Father?"

Ursula would not apologise for it, not unless it were actually necessary. It had not been the kindest conversation she could have had about it, but it had been truthful and honest. "Yes?"

"We should discuss that further. Not today, of course."

"I need to work out some of the rest of it. I'm right at the key part, it needs a few more hours of work. And," Ursula glanced over. "Uncle Alexander, some of it deals with you and with your mother and brother."

"I'm not at all surprised." He lifted two fingers. "There are many things I don't know about that time, but some I have guesses about. And a few points that Dagobert and Laudine shared later on." He then focused entirely on Garin. "Garin, they asked me for my hand in training you, in part to help ensure that what had occurred would not happen again. They wanted another pair of eyes, someone with established ethics and no cause to be loyal beyond reason. I am sorry I was not enough of that for you, but you are not your cousins or your uncle. I promise you that. You do not have their, their...." He paused, the way he got when he was searching through multiple languages.

"I meant what I said, Uncle Garin." Ursula cut in, to spare the pause. "You care about the land, the Council, the good of Albion. That is so obvious to me, in all you do, and especially what you're working on right now."

Uncle Alexander nodded as she finished speaking. "You have done many things well, Garin, and the recent alchemical work is only the last in a long line. I do not wish to talk about that time— it was deeply painful for me. But I would rather do that now than have it warp the family more."

"Also your family." Uncle Garin said it hesitantly. "Ursula and Leo."

"You too." Uncle Alexander's tone was suddenly firm. Not sharp like a blade, but like the earth becoming solid under the feet. "You too. You and Isembard. Thesan and Ursula and Leo. And may I live so long, whatever children they might have, as well. I want something better for them."

Ursula said primly. "I intend to finish my apprenticeship first. Though I might be persuaded otherwise." She said it mostly to make Uncle Garin splutter, which he did.

Then he eyed her warily. "Are there more surprises for me, then? Someone in particular?"

"I think, Uncle Garin, that this is also a topic for later. With Mum and Dad handy. They've met him." Just barely yesterday. Yesterday had about forty-eight hours in it, honestly.

Uncle Alexander chuckled. Uncle Garin let out a sigh, and said, "All right. I know Alexander wants a bit more of a word with you. I will be at home. Shall I write to Isembard and Thesan and see if they can get away tomorrow? Or else we'll be waiting another week. Would you be available, Alexander?"

"For this, yes." Uncle Alexander nodded. "Ursula?"

"I think I can arrange the rest of it, yes. I'll be home later today, Uncle Garin, but working on those notes for most of the night, I expect."

Uncle Garin stood, then he came over, hesitating in front of Ursula. She considered, then stood herself, to find him bending close. "I remember you saying I do not touch people." His voice was soft enough she thought Uncle Alexander would have to use a touch of magic to hear it. "May I?" She nodded once and felt him kiss her cheek and his hand on her arm.

The thing about Uncle Garin was that he could be delicate and gentle when he chose to be. That was how his alchemical skills worked, just the right amount at the perfect moment. He then took a step back, making a slight bow to Uncle Alexander before Uncle Alexander showed him out.

A minute later, Uncle Alexander came back, brushing his hands off. "I do appreciate the lack of destruction of my crockery. Though this is Ummi's third best set for a reason." There was a slight edge to his voice, mostly in the last sentence.

"I'm sorry, Uncle Alexander, to bring up such hard memories for you." Ursula was. If it were hard for Uncle Garin, it must be doubly so, at least, for Uncle Alexander, who'd lost both his brother and mother to death that year.

"It has been there lurking for near sixty years. Being able to talk about any of it, that might be something. I haven't, you know. Not with anyone, beyond the bare outline." That was interesting, that he'd not discussed it even with Dad or the Carillons. "Now. Shall I tell you what I see, or will you tell me?"

"I'm curious what's, erm. Is the word visible?" Ursula was still standing, and she turned to better face him.

"To those with the eyes to see, isn't that the proper ritual phrasing?" Uncle Alexander considered, then took an easy rest position, his hands out slightly at his sides, looking at her with that unfocused gaze. She held still. There was no reason to make this more difficult. And she owed Uncle Alexander a bit of something for being obliging this morning.

"An oath about the Council?" Uncle Alexander's eyebrow went up. "And, mm. A more personal decision?"

"I had a very pleasant evening last night after leaving Arundel, it turns out." She then let out a breath. "An oath never to challenge. No oath against being in the Keep, of course, or even in the spaces above, if it's ever relevant." If there was ever a case like Aunt Livia, who'd been brought up there after she died.

Ursula would be there in a second— less than that— if it were Uncle Alexander or Uncle Orion, if she could be of help. Though she hoped maybe that wouldn't come to pass, that both of them would die a long time from now, in their bed and in peace. Ideally long-retired from their Council work, even if the idea of Uncle Alexander retiring still seemed impossible.

He just nodded once. "And the Society of the White Horse, I gather." He didn't make it a question. Her eyes widened. "Oh, that's not visible the same way. That you'd pledged to a society, yes, but the oath is twined in with other things. I worked it out last night. Were you with Jim, then?"

Now Ursula could feel herself blushing. She nodded just once. "Did Mum and Dad tell you?"

"Oh, no. Lizzie had a guess last week. And Paul is married and seems on the conventional side. But it hit me, Wednesday, that he had experience with ritual, if not the Schola sort of training. And last night, I was certain, when Garin said you'd mentioned he was your society's choice. The way the three of you were. Even if you're younger, by a bit." Uncle Alexander let out a breath. "I'd like to know more, if I can. Especially if there's something that would be reassuring to Paul. I'd prefer it if you told him I'd worked it out."

"We talked about that in advance. I said I wouldn't tell you, or Uncle Garin, but that it might come up, and I wouldn't lie. I don't know what that means about tomorrow. But I want Jim there. Mum liked him, and Dad wasn't too intimidating."

"And how recent is that plot, then?" Uncle

Alexander settled in his chair, gesturing for her to do the same "And where is he? Worrying?"

"In the library. We came into town together. I said I'd meet him for lunch, maybe a late one, and we'd find somewhere good and quiet enough. I can take a few more minutes, though. I was expecting Uncle Garin to take more time being upset."

"Oh, Ursula." Uncle Alexander's voice went deathly quiet. "Garin was over-set last night. He wrote to me to ask for my help, and he's never done that, not in so many words." He held up his fingers. "You were right, to stand up for yourself, and to leave when you did. But he spent the night, I'm sure, and more time before dawn, questioning a number of his choices and foundational principles." His mouth twitched. "You are my godchild, and I am intensely proud of you for doing that without destroying him. I could not have done so, for all it's needed doing."

Now her voice was small, she could hear it. "I didn't want to hurt him. But I couldn't let him go on like he was. He's, he's more than that, better than that, and I want better for him."

Uncle Alexander reached over to pat her hand. "I know. So does he. And so does Isembard. I am not looking forward to tomorrow, but we'll manage. Especially if Thesan can lend a hand. Perhaps talk to your Jim, show him a little of the estate while the four of us talk through the family history, and then share what makes sense?"

Ursula nodded. They spent a few more minutes sketching out what that looked like. Uncle Alexander promised to write Mum and Dad with more of the background and what Uncle Garin had done last night. "And I'll be writing Mum too. Oh, Dad should have given her my present. She might be a little teary about it today. You remember she's been looking for Mistress Eridana's copy of Anselm's *Stellarum* for ages and ages? I found it in one of the rare book shops."

It had been supposed to come to Mum, way back when, and it had been carried off by someone who didn't appreciate astronomy at all. It had taken about half of Ursula's allowance for the quarter, and that was in some ways a ridiculous thing to spend it on. But Mum would treasure it, her students would benefit from seeing it, and it could then be passed along to other people who appreciated it.

Uncle Alexander let out a low whistle through his teeth. "Oh, yes. That would do it. And it's a beautiful volume if I remember right. I've seen other copies."

It was. It had been printed on a press, but with illuminated pages at the beginning of every chapter, and a number of charm illustrations. The pages were rich with lapis lazuli and gilt and deep red and who knew what else. "In a month or two, Mum might even let Geoffrey have a look." He had a particular fondness for early incunabula, the first printed books. Ursula stood. "I should get back to Jim. He'll be worried."

"Do. And please tell him I know. If that would not intimidate him entirely too much." That, she was sure, was teasing, so Ursula just bent to kiss his cheek, then let him walk her out. She felt him sealing the wards behind her as she made her way back to the library and Jim.

CHAPTER 38
LATER THAT MORNING AT THE
LIBRARY

J im was grateful that Ursula had presented him
with a plan for the library. More than just the
library, actually. Since they'd arrived in Trellech, she'd brought him to an inn, arranged for
him to wash while someone did a variety of charms
to tidy and press his clothing. He'd wanted to protest
that he knew how to do them himself, and Ursula
had just raised an eyebrow. Then they'd had breakfast, before Ursula had brought him to Trellech's
main library. He'd been once or twice before, but not
nearly often enough to feel like he knew where
anything was. It was much larger than Snap's library.

A library was not exactly his usual habitat, but it
was more comfortable than a city park, and far less
awkward than a cafe. The parks he'd seen in Trellech
were tiny, almost artificial. A library, at least all he
had to sort out was the table and not bothering
anyone else. Here, she'd brought him in and had a
conversation with the librarian on duty that implied
Ursula had known her for a bit. Jim had been shown

to a comfortable reading table, able to glance out and look at people walking up and down the shelving.

The librarian had encouraged him to read whatever drew his eye, just to put anything he removed from the shelf on the cart at the end of the row. She'd come back a few minutes later with the day's paper and a couple of magazines. The books shelved near him were in fact about horticulture, so once he'd worked through the parts of the paper he usually bothered with, and one of the magazines, he'd settled into a book about apples. It was one part a retelling of different varieties and their histories, and one part an analysis of the folklore around the traditions. The first part was excellent, and the second varied wildly between the reasonable and making Jim wonder if the man had ever actually been in an orchard.

Which meant it was, in fact, rather distracting. He'd been on edge when it turned eleven; Ursula had not come back before meeting her uncles. But then he was reading, and he'd lost track of time. It wasn't until he heard steps coming down the centre aisle, between the rows of shelving, that he looked up.

Whoever it was, she was gorgeous. She was lit from behind. Jim did not know much about frocks. Not beyond what Alice pined over in the magazines, at least. But he knew enough to know this was cut to the latest fashion, a tailored jacket or bodice flaring out to a broader skirt. Not excessively, but there was enough fabric in the skirt to shift as the woman walked, and she was completely confident. Then she came closer, and he realised, startled, that it was Ursula.

Not Ursula as he'd seen her before. Every time so

far, she'd been wearing clothing for the moment. Country clothing, not working overalls or whatever, but comfortable. This, well, he supposed maybe this was what someone like Ursula wore when she was being fancy. Pointed. Pointed and fancy? The small hat on her head matched the blue of her frock, but it was trimmed with little white - something - that brought attention to her face. And her face was glorious. He knew without her needing to say anything that she was delighted.

Now she held out her hands to him as he stood. "May I lure you away from the books for luncheon?" Then she tilted her head, and Jim knew, with just as much certainty, that she was contemplating a dozen more plans. "How public may I be about my attention to you?"

Jim swallowed hard. "Isn't the usual question how attentive I may be to you?" At least this morning's efforts meant he was clean and tidy enough. He presumed it was sufficient for whatever she had in mind. Saying it that way made Ursula's eyes light up further, a broad grin taking shape.

"In that case, may I take you to lunch at the Fox's Den? This will involve me saying hello to a great number of people on the way there and introducing you without actually explaining you to anyone." She tilted her head. "We could do Bourne's, I suppose. But the Fox's Den is probably more fun for purpose." Bourne's was one of the particularly posh clubs, though her house club was just as much so.

"Has anyone mentioned that you might have an odd idea of fun, sweet?" Jim managed the last endearment. While he was overwhelmed, and would be more underwater soon, he could tell he was giving her a tremendous gift. And since he couldn't shower her in goods and physical presents, well, this would have to do.

She beamed at him. "Fox's Den? Do say yes?"

"Yes." Jim glanced around, then moved to tidy up the books, putting them back on the cart as he'd been told, then looking up. "The paper?"

"Bring it with you, and we'll leave it at the front. Step one of my very new plan. It has - oh, I'm up to fifteen steps right now. We'll see how high the count goes." Then she waited for Jim to offer his arm, he had that much sense. At the front, she chattered, quietly, but engagingly, with the librarian about how lovely it was, and thank you for the paper, and how was her sister doing. Then Ursula took two steps back, brought the conversation to a close, and Jim took the hint and walked her out.

He wasn't sure exactly where they were going for a good couple of minutes, but Ursula was absolutely taking advantage of a pleasant day and the lunch hour. She stopped every third of a block to say hello to someone. Most of them were people she apparently knew via her parents. They ranged from so posh Jim was surprised they were using their own two feet to quite ordinary people who didn't seem intimidating at all. With each and every one of them, she made pleasant conversation. Jim noticed that she was just blithely saying, "This is Jim Pullan, of course." As if everyone ought to know who he was. Four stops in, and he realised she was dancing around anything delicate in her answers. She'd give some comment that said nothing meaningful about her uncle - any of her uncles - or what she was busy with.

By the time they'd arrived at a terribly imposing building of pale grey stone, she'd also acquired half a dozen invitations for social gatherings. She'd turned none of them down outright, just encouraging each person to send her a note in the journal or by post, and she'd have to check her diary. That had been well-received, even though with two of them, Jim was fairly sure there was an entirely coded social duel going on at the same time. Now, Ursula said, "I'm on step thirteen, for the record. This is the Fox House club."

"Won't they be, um. Busy?" Jim asked.

"Not for me." Ursula waited for half a second, and added, "Also, I made a reservation this morning. Just in case. I wasn't sure we'd want to use it."

Jim shook his head, then patted her hand on his arm. "Go ahead, then. Steps fourteen to— what are we up to?"

"Twenty-three. So far." Then she began walking, entirely confident he'd match her, and of course he did. The man at the front bowed, escorting them along a long hallway. It made the two of them exceedingly visible, especially since Ursula was waving at someone here, nodding at someone there, and people were looking back at her.

When they were finally at their destination— a small private room with windows overlooking a terraced courtyard— Jim made a point of pushing in Ursula's chair. They'd been trained in those sorts of manners at Snap, though not, Jim realised with a certain amount of horror, nearly enough of the ones involving cutlery. As he sat, he realised there were quite a few more forks in evidence than seemed necessary for any meal, especially one under rationing.

Ursula simply said, "The usual to start, please, while we have a look at the offerings today." With that, they were left alone, Jim blinking at her from his own chair. She took a breath, tapped her fingers together three times, just loud enough to be audible. Jim could feel a curtain of something, as if someone had dropped a cloak over his head. An invisible cloak, but the weight of it was definitely there. "That's the privacy charm, the one Dad prefers. We're quite private now. They'll let us know when they are ready to come in. Oh, and they'll expect you to order for me. I'll have the fish and wine sauce, please."

Jim blinked several times. "Isn't that rude? Me, um."

"In this case, I've just told you what I want to have. Which is how people should do it. And it's my club, so it will go on my tab, which is very handy at the moment, though not really the best solution long-term. Remind me we should talk about that at some point? After tomorrow. Are you available to come to Arundel tomorrow afternoon? By which I mean, oh, one or two? Mum won't want to be up much before eleven, and it's going to go much better if she's had something to eat before talking to Uncle Garin."

"I'd, um. I ought to go home tonight. Or explain something to Luke and Alice." Jim considered. "I can? Especially if I could leave a horse with you, is that a thing I could do? And bring something to change into?" Then he asked, more hesitantly. "Who?"

"Me. That's the easy part, yes?" It got him one of her dazzling smiles, which did make it easier, certainly. And at this point, he was curious about Arundel. "Mum. Dad. Not Leo. He's got pavo practice, and that would be strange, anyway. Uncle Alexander. Uncle Garin. I didn't tell him about you directly, but I made it clear that you existed, if you see the distinction."

"I'm not entirely sure I do. I'm also not at all sure about meeting Lord Fortier." Jim was about to say more. But at that point, Ursula lifted her fingers, and the sense of pressure shifted like someone parting a curtain. One of the waiters came back with something to drink, and an inquiry about whether they were ready to order.

Jim almost panicked, before Ursula said smoothly, "I was trying to convince Jim to try the fish. Do tell me it's just the thing today?" It involved a good two minutes of the freshness of the fish and the excellence of the preparation. At the end, Jim could say, "The fish and wine sauce, please, for both of us." There was an inquiry about wine to go with it, and Ursula nodded minutely when the house white was offered. Jim said what seemed to be the right words, and the man went away.

Jim stared off after him once the warding was back in place. "Is it always like that, when you eat out? Or, actually. When you're at home?"

"Small staff at the house proper, these days. I'll introduce you to Mrs Borrowsmith when I get a chance. She's the housekeeper, there's a cook, one maid who lives on the estate and two more who come in five days a week for the cleaning. And then the stables and gardens and mostly the home farm, but you'd know that side of it." Jim did know that bit, at least, from the shearing and the conversations over the summer. "Oh, and for the fish, you want the outermost fork and knife from this setting. There'll be a soup before, and a fruit plate after. Those are easier."

"I feel almost competent with fruit." Jim looked down, making sure he understood which of these utensils were the right ones. Then he looked up, blinking. "You're used to explaining it?"

"Mum had to learn a lot of the fussy things, not like Dad who grew up just doing them. It's a lot easier to explain if you had to learn it deliberately. So she invites students up for a couple of meals. Just with Dad or me or Leo or someone else who won't tease, so they can ask questions and get more comfortable. Like one of Leo's friends, he's in Fox House, but he grew up in the East End of London. Very not posh, though he's a quick study with silverware."

"Huh." Jim nodded, then he took a deeper breath. "So why am I coming to Arundel? How did things go with your uncle? Uncles."

"Uncle Alexander was wonderful. Uncle Garin was actually remarkably reasonable, and I'm trying to figure out how much to worry about that." Ursula straightened her shoulders. "I said I'd been looking at some of my grandmother's records. When we get back, we can double check with the stables about tomorrow. I'll see you off, and you can go talk to your family and sort things out. I'm going to be spending most of the night working through the rest of Grand-mère Laudine's journals, as far as I can get. We need to talk about this; there's a rot, at the heart of things. Uncle Garin's never talked about it. Uncle Alexander hasn't. He told me that earlier today. I'm sure Dad hasn't, and I don't think he knows even as much as Uncle Garin. So doing it with everyone there, and Mum to help you out and be sensible, seems the way to go."

"It's not that I wish to say anything against your family, Ursula," Jim said warily. "But this seems an awfully delicate sort of plan."

"Can't be helped." Ursula said. "And honestly, if you're willing, I'd rather have you be available for it. I expect it'll be me talking with Dad and Uncle Garin and Uncle Alexander first, but then you and Mum too. And Uncle Alexander and Dad will make sure Uncle Garin behaves."

"You're sure of that?" Jim asked. "And, um, can you define what behaves means in this? I've heard stories. Not sure how many of them are true."

"Well, I faced down Uncle Garin last night, and all the warding held, so that's one thing." Ursula said it firmly. Jim did not think that was the sort of sentence one should say with that tone of voice, but he was not remotely sure how to argue with it. Ursula must have seen something in his expression. "We can talk through the actual risks, if it helps. But it held. Remember that. And he promised to be on good behaviour. He might say things. I hope not. But he's saying them at a shape that he thinks is you, because he doesn't actually know you. That's the part that

Mum's fantastic at dealing with. She's who I've been learning it from. Mostly."

"And you think this is necessary. Now. Even with us new to each other." Ursula nodded once at each sentence.

After the last one, she said, much more softly, a kind of tenderness that Jim wanted to store up for dark and miserable nights for years to come. "We begin as we mean to go on, you and I. I'm right, aren't I, that we both want this? What we'll be working out is timing, and how to make sure you can establish yourself, and how many of my plots you're going to actively help with. And how many you'll blink at and leave me to do myself."

Jim couldn't help chuckling, because yes, that was an entirely accurate count. "It would help, sweet, if you told me about the plots before we were in the middle of them. Easier to make some choices." He gestured at the hallway they'd come down. "What was all that, then?"

"Oh, making it clear we're together, including half a dozen of the most active gossips. That I was with you, with all the little clues that indicate I've chosen to favour you. They don't know who you are, but they know what that looks like. Also that I've never shown the slightest hint about anyone else."

"Right. So, erm. Are we expecting more meals like this, somewhere fancy? I'm going to need to sort out different clothing." That was touchy. For one thing, it wasn't like he had much of a place to keep more than he had. And for another, that all cost money and ration coupons.

"It'll be easier to figure this out after tomorrow, I

expect," Ursula said, her voice thoughtful. "But we know a number of people who have suits we could have made over for you. Evening dress, two or three suits for somewhere more public. Gods know there's plenty in the attics, and Dad has an excellent tailor. Most of what I wear came out of Mum's closet or someone else's. We've just remade it."

"Not that, though?" Jim nodded at her frock. "I'm right that that's new, aren't I?" He was trying not to think of the sort of event that would require evening dress.

"One really excellent frock for the autumn," Ursula said. "This is its first outing. Isn't it lovely?"

"You do know exactly how gorgeous you are in it, don't you? Like something out of an epic tale, made modern." Jim fumbled over the words, but Ursula beamed at him. He then added, "You, um. You did all of that deliberately? That's why you're wearing it today?"

"Exactly. See, you pick up on my plots entirely fast enough. Are you sorted for the moment?"

Jim considered. "I— you need to finish the work on your notes. And I'm thinking it's proper you should tell your family before you tell me. It's about them, for one thing. If you're sure Lord Fortier won't take immediate offence at my showing up."

"No, he won't. We'll make sure of that." Ursula looked so resolute, and to be entirely fair to her, she had an excellent record of success with her plots so far, at least the ones Jim knew about.

"Tomorrow, then. Can you, erm." Jim tried to figure out a topic. "Will you tell me more about the club and who else we might run into? And then I can tell you about that ridiculous book about apples I was reading."

"That is entirely fair!" Ursula settled into explaining. She was really excellent at explaining when the situation allowed. Jim kept realising that she wasn't assuming what he did or didn't know. She'd add half a sentence, see how he reacted, and change course from there. It was like when she was plotting, just doing something different with the same skill. He'd be thinking about that one for ages.

CHAPTER 39
SEPTEMBER 20TH AT ARUNDEL

"Ursula, love." Mum hugged Ursula hard before stepping to the side and offering the same to Jim. Then she twisted to peer at Ursula. "How late were you up last night?"

"Four. I got a few hours this morning." It was after lunch. Ursula had hoped the hours hadn't shown that much. She'd dressed and used the cosmetic charms to hide the smudges under her eyes. She could sleep tonight. Probably. Dad came through the portal then, which at least gave her an excuse to not say more. Dad hugged her, then offered Jim his hand. "Mum, you really don't mind?"

"Giving Jim a tour of the estate? No. Besides, it's easier to start outside. The house is a bit much, all at once." Mum added cheerfully to Jim, "The first time we spent more than a day here, I kept worrying I'd turn around and my elbow would take out some irreplaceable heirloom. Outside's much easier on the nerves. I've my journal. We'll make a large circle, not too far to come back if you want us."

Dad just nodded once. "Alexander's here? Shall we?"

"Uncle Alexander got here half an hour ago. I just need to grab my notes." Dad glanced at Mum, and then set off, only barely waiting for Ursula to kiss Jim once on the cheek. Mum would take good care of him. More importantly, Mum was doing her utmost to be welcoming. And Mum had wanted to talk apples and bees with him.

Dad, on the other hand, was absolutely on edge. It was entirely understandable. Ursula was as well. Dad waited just long enough in the entry for Ursula to dash up to her rooms and grab the armful of notes. They were all ready. She'd laid them out once she woke up. Then they walked through the Great Hall, up the stairs at the far end. Outside the door, Dad glanced at her, saw her nod, and knocked three times. "Me and Ursula, Garin."

"Come." Uncle Garin's voice was brief. Once they came in, Ursula realised he'd rearranged the furniture, or someone had. There were two sofas facing each other, as well as two easy chairs. He'd pulled in the one from the gallery upstairs, she thought. She remembered something of that description on the inventory. Uncle Alexander had one of the individual chairs. Uncle Garin was standing in front of the other. "Ursula. Isembard. Have a seat, there's tea on the table. And if you've records, Ursula, the central table."

"Thank you, Uncle Garin." As she sat, she felt the warding slide into place, like a curtain. And not only Uncle Garin's, she'd expected that. But then, a second later, Uncle Alexander's and then Dad's. She could see the way the three of them arranged themselves, too. Uncle Alexander and Dad were like great towers of some castle keep, attentive and strong. Uncle Garin's was more like the land it stood on, a different kind of defence and foundation.

Her eyes widened a bit at that, and Dad leaned over. "We discussed it by journal. Here, these are what you want out?" She handed over the stack of her translations, as well as the relevant journal, bristling with bookmarks. Uncle Garin sat, a little scrape of the chair echoing as he pulled it closer. "Where do you think it best to begin?"

Ursula was so grateful for Dad being right there, and also for the way he was making space for her. It was a particular skill related to duelling, but also teaching. "Uncle Garin, Uncle Alexander, Dad. I worked out a lot more last night and this morning. I don't understand all of it yet, but I don't know. Ninety per cent, maybe, of what they were doing, but less of how. I think that's deliberate, though."

"Go on." Uncle Garin just nodded once.

Ursula began with all the things she'd done up to the last week or two. How she'd gone to Aunt Cammie when she realised the entries were coded. And then that she'd done research on some of the stones that Laudine had used for coded names and concepts. She touched on what Mum and Dad had told her about the events at Schola. Uncle Garin and Uncle Alexander knew most of that.

Next, Ursula passed around copies of the decoding she'd made. That brought her to the complicated bit. "It became clear, a few pages into this section, why there was this new dense section, and in 1894, five years after what she's writing about." Ursula's chin came up, and she looked directly at Uncle Garin now. "Exactly five years, in a particular case. Chrodechildis Fortier died on the summer solstice, 1894."

All three of them must have known the date. Dad, more intellectually. He'd only been four. But Uncle Garin would have been home from Schola after his first year, and Uncle Alexander had been done with his apprenticeship, three years from his challenge for the Council. He'd done the maths, Ursula saw that, but Uncle Garin and Dad hadn't.

Now Ursula went as gently as she could. "Five years. On the solstice in 1889, there were two deaths. I haven't gone as far into the newspapers as I want to, but they were the same night, I'm fairly sure. After the Council rites. Council Member Metaia Powell was killed. And Uncle Alexander's brother Philip died."

Uncle Alexander nodded once. He looked resolute and determined, but also ashen under the brown of his skin. "Ummi was furious. As you might expect. But deliberate about her actions, as she always was."

"And?" Uncle Garin asked it, where Ursula would never have dared.

"Ursula, go on with what you have found, and I will then tell you what's accurate, and what else I know that's relevant. Usual bounds." Uncle Alexander's voice was as pitch-perfect neutral as she'd ever heard him, clipped, utterly of Albion, and yet as distant as a far galaxy. It made Ursula hurt for him, but she went on, because he'd asked. Because of how he'd asked.

"In summary, what Laudine lays out was a plot by the central members of the family—Chrodechildis, Clovis, Childeric, Sigbert, and Dagobert— to work with the developments of electrical fields to create something that would form and hold a space outside of the Pact, magically. Where other enchantments could be made, bindings prohibited by the Pact and the oaths on the Silence. They never got it to work. Almost all the notes about what it was, even the hints of what it did, were destroyed."

"You're certain of that?" Uncle Garin broke in.

Before Ursula could say anything, Uncle Alexander said quietly. "Yes. I had some small part of it from Dagobert and Laudine, eventually. This morning, I confirmed the details with Cyrus. He had notes on Hereswith's records, the ones she kept as Council Head, not available to the rest of us." There was a tired pause in his voice, before he said, "Isembard, you never knew her, and Ursula, of course, you'd know her only from notes." He did not actually explain further, and the silence dragged on for a good half minute before Ursula cleared her throat and went on.

"Laudine did not know at the time what they were doing. And Dagobert was badly injured, that same solstice night in 1889, when he objected to some piece of it. She talks about that, in the part I decoded last night." Well, about two in the morning, it was why she'd pushed on until she had actually finished. "His mother and brother both cursed him at the same time. He dealt with the consequences for the rest of his life."

Her fingers twitched, because that had been a

particularly painful part to read. "She quotes some of what he described, how it was his vitality draining away, over and over. How they couldn't be near each other for long, because she would want to help him too much." Ursula did not look immediately at Dad, but she counted to ten, before she looked first at Uncle Garin, then across at Dad. Uncle Garin looked like stone. "She describes a set of linked talismans that allowed her to support him, deliberately. And she talks about how much they hated being apart."

Dad was blinking, as if gravity had somehow just reversed. "Those are— those are not the parents I knew."

"What made you think they didn't love each other, brother?" Uncle Garin's voice was low, a rumble, now. Dad, well, Dad looked like he desperately wanted Mum to explain things to him. Ursula felt that was entirely reasonable in the circumstances.

"I don't know, the fact they lived in entirely separate demesnes? They spent the night under the same roof, what, twice a month at best? We'd come out here for supper, and it would be - it would be..." Dad's voice trailed off, then he said, his voice cracking. "They didn't let anyone see. Even me."

"You were young, Isembard." Uncle Alexander cut in, perhaps before Uncle Garin could say something that would be a problem. "By the time you were old enough to pay attention, to understand what you were seeing, they had settled into a pattern. They did love each other, enough to take care of each other, even in extremis. I didn't know the extent of it when I came back from my Grand Tour, but over the years, especially after Lady Chrodechildis died, they told me a little more." Uncle Alexander turned his palms up. "I've not said this to anyone, ever, before. But Laudine was— she was extremely tired, at the end. All the time, a kind of desperate exhaustion, only she was far too fatigued to fight it. She said, a month or so before she died, that she could feel it lightening. As you were about to turn twenty-one, Isembard."

Ursula had found something about that. "There's a note, in her last journal, about feeling that she was permitted to set down what she'd been carrying for so long. I don't think she wanted to die. It wasn't seeking it out? But it was being released, in a way that she knew meant the end of her life. And she was sorry for that, Dad, but she was—" Ursula stopped and swallowed. "Look, you should read it sometime, in private, with Mum right there. I have a copy for you, and an interlined version, in case I missed something in the decoding."

Dad waved a hand, almost blindly, before pulling a handkerchief out of his pocket and blowing his nose. Uncle Alexander spoke into the quiet after. "Dagobert knew it would mean his death, in due course. But she'd left him enough of her vitality to draw it out, if he wanted, and he did his best. Over the years, he'd found that being on the demesne land, every day, his feet on the earth or on a horse, helped a great deal. He couldn't do his own alchemical work safely anymore, so he would bring in a recent apprentice for their help and to get them established. He trained Garin, of course, for the same reasons."

"You didn't talk about it with anyone, Uncle

Alexander?" That was something Ursula had been puzzling over.

"No. Who would I tell? There are a few people who know pieces of it, but they didn't want to be burdened with it. And it was— it was an old pain. But what they were doing, that I did not know. Or why people died, though I have ...."

"Laudine had guesses about that." This was the other terribly difficult bit, or at least the personal difficult bit. The whole question of what they'd been trying to do was an entirely different horror, utterly repellant to every one of Ursula's sensibilities and all of her training. "What do you know about the other deaths, Uncle Alexander? Childeric, your mother, Clovis, Maylis, Sigbert?" She asked it as clearly as she could, because perhaps, just perhaps, she might get an answer.

There was a faint twitch of his lips. "That was the question that Ummi went to great lengths to make sure no one would ask me. I'm as certain of it as I am of my own names. I don't know exactly what she did, but I know the heart of what she knew." Before Ursula had to figure out how to press the point, he went on.

"There is a rite— it is a reasonably standard part of our funerary service, on Ummi's side. It is a sort of debate between Isis and Set, a particularly opaque ritual form. She had me learn it, and be the spearpoint. The idea was to catch those who had guilt on their hands and their souls. I was certain then that those four were involved. But that rite did not tell us what they'd done, certainly not anything that could have been brought to the Guard. Not given that they were Fortiers, and the family was at its strength."

Uncle Alexander took a breath, but no one dreamed of interrupting. "I do not know for certain what she did with that knowledge, but I can guess. You can all guess. She brought their deaths. Not Childeric's. I do not think she could reach into the Challenge chamber." Uncle Alexander hesitated. "Probably not. Albion was never her native idiom, magically."

There was utter silence for a good minute before Uncle Garin spoke. "She died, though. Before all the others."

"I know that the more esoteric forms of ritual are not your preference, Garin, but there are certainly magical forms that can bring death. Especially if someone is willing to give their own life for it. They had killed her Horus, they had broken all trust she'd held with them." Uncle Alexander's mouth twitched. "You spotted something, Ursula, didn't you?"

"I asked Dad about it a couple of weeks ago, but I don't know the details. When she came here, with Philip, and you, you just weren't born yet. There were formal agreements with Vauquelin." He'd been Lord then, still firmly in his power, and unlike the later family, he had been a ritualist. "I've looked at the agreements, but I'm missing a nuance."

Uncle Alexander held out his hand, and Ursula rummaged quickly for that folder, putting it in his hands. She stood and went to pour a cup of tea, first for Dad, then for Uncle Garin. Finally, she poured for Uncle Alexander, then for herself, bringing them back to the side tables one by one. By the time she'd done that, Uncle Alexander had one piece of paper sitting out. "There were a series of oaths. I'd— I'd not looked at them since I went through Ummi's papers when I came back. They weren't relevant, not anymore. They were made with her, not with me. Dagobert and Laudine made it clear we would have a different sort of arrangement, too."

Then he tapped the pile. "Some of them bound her to the good of the family, but without specifying names. Some of them were specific to Vauquelin. Here, Ursula. Spot quiz. What does this one do— and what doesn't it do?" Uncle Alexander handed a piece of paper back to her, and Ursula stared at it, trying to get the thing to make sense.

Slowly, she thought she saw it. "How was this missed? The oath's to him and his household. When he died, it wasn't his household anymore. That's why — I think, it must be— Laudine was asking Dad about the warding, much later. How much of the protections were, um, anchored? I know it's not the right word here, Dad. Give me a moment." Ursula handed the sheet over to him as she spoke.

"Just so." Uncle Alexander sounded both exhausted and relieved. "It's not so much a matter now, I expect. But I am certain Ummi saw that loophole when the oaths were made. If no one redid them after Vauquelin's death, she had space to do what she thought was needed."

Uncle Garin swallowed. "She killed my family." It was like four great boulders falling from a height, but almost immediately he went on. "But they had— before."

"The story Dagobert told me was that Philip died

saving his life." Uncle Alexander's voice was again that painfully narrow neutral. "That is not wrong, really. Without Philip, I suspect Dagobert would have been dead that night. One way or another. I don't know much of what happened specifically. Dagobert was not there for whatever happened to Philip. They all left the Council rites earlier than expected. Philip went with them. We expected him to be back in the gatehouse within a couple of hours. And then he wasn't. He was found in his rooms in Trellech, where he had no reason to be."

"Laudine thought, it's in the last couple of pages of that section, that they must have threatened to make things horrible for you. Something of the kind." Ursula was watching Dad and Uncle Alexander in alternation now. "Could they have made him go back to Trellech without anyone noticing?"

"Perhaps. Someone took the ring from his hand, one of the tokens that held a key to his warding. Almost certainly that night. I know Clovis, Childeric, and Sigbert were all seen wearing it, before it came back to my possession." Uncle Alexander spread his hands. "I know, and I don't know, all at once, and it is an awful feeling."

"You've been alone with it." Ursula said, before Dad looked up at that comment. "Does it bother you, being tangled up with the family?" She couldn't imagine what her life would have been like if he hadn't been, but she had no idea how to say that in words.

"Ah. You, I chose. Leo, I chose. And Dagobert and Laudine asked for my help with Garin and Isembard. They did not compel, and they made it clear they'd understand if I declined. Only there, I admit, it was less of a pure choice. I had no other support in Albion. Vauquelin and Chrodechildis had arranged my apprenticeship, vouched for it. I had the money to pay for it. Ummi had been exquisitely careful about that sort of thing. But I would not have had the connections, not without Fortier help. I did not have many choices, not if I wanted to make my life in Albion. And I did. The land has had my heart for a long time. The hour of my birth, if not before."

Before he went on, Dad said, "You don't— it wasn't a burden asking you?"

"No." Uncle Alexander's voice was crystalline. "And it was not a burden to train you, or you, Garin. You both are blameless in whatever happened. The question, now, is how you go forward."

Uncle Garin cleared his throat. "That's what brought you to this, isn't it, Ursula? Figuring out what the land, particularly the estate, needs. I suppose you had best ask your mother and your young man to come up. If he's going to join the family eventually, he might as well understand what that means."

The framing of that was utterly not what Ursula had expected. Dad's mouth twitched. "We did quite a bit of writing last night. I'll go fetch Thesan and Jim, then." Before anyone could say anything, he stood, parting the warding and letting himself out through the door.

"Ursula," Uncle Garin's voice was softer now. "I am not, this is not a pleasant conversation. I am not happy. But I am, I think, relieved, that it is no longer hidden. And that, Alexander, you are not carrying what you knew all alone."

"A few others knew pieces of it. But there has been a great deal I could not talk about in total. And now, perhaps, a little more." Uncle Alexander stood. "Brandy, Garin? Ursula?" Ursula shook her head. She wanted her wits about her, but Uncle Garin nodded, and they busied themselves with those small things.

CHAPTER 40
THAT AFTERNOON

"This is the secondary poison garden." Jim nodded, a little cautiously, as Professor Wain led the way into another of the gardens. They had, at this point, been through two formal gardens - one in the English mode and one in French. There had been the rose garden, not at its peak given the season, though obviously thoughtfully tended. And there had been the first poison garden, quite large and worryingly near the house if there were any small children nearby. "You're wondering why there are two. There are actually three, but one is in the greenhouses, the former orangerie."

"Yes'm." Jim nodded.

"They're exceedingly traditional for alchemists, actually. And they're quite useful for some of the protections and wards. If you want a topic to discuss with either Garin or Isembard, they'd find that one quite agreeable. And Ursula's quite capable of explaining anything Garin glosses over, in that case."

Professor Wain offered it amiably. Then her head came up, suddenly. It was the kind of thing that made Jim startle, take two steps back, and instinctively duck.

She immediately said, "I beg pardon for startling you. Isembard's on his way out. We've charms on our watches that make it easier. No end of use when we're in different bits of Schola's keep." Jim nodded, taking a breath. He'd just got his heart to settle down when Professor Fortier came through the opening in the hedge, aiming right for his wife.

Professor Wain immediately opened her arms, and it was watching the hug that confused Jim even more. He'd thought posh people, these sorts of families, wouldn't show what they felt. Not that Ursula was shy about it, but this was— this was proper adults, with power and responsibility and faces they showed the world. But here was Professor Wain, supporting her husband, and he was soaking it up, explaining something into her ear, having to stop several times.

It made things awkward, though, as Professor Fortier kept on. There was quite a lot he needed to share, apparently. She nodded several times, then gestured at Jim. "Beg pardon, Jim." Professor Fortier turned to face him. "It's been a hard conversation. Several things were not at all what I expected. We'll be a while working it out. But Garin suggested you might join us. Rather, mmm. He said that if you're going to be interested in Ursula, best know what you're getting into. If that gives an idea."

"Sir," Jim said, settling into a formal stance. "If that's what Ursula prefers."

"The question at hand is what the estate needs, and I'm certain she thinks you have ideas and would like to hear them. Or at least, how you'd start out going about it. Shall we?" Jim tried to trail the two of them, but Professor Wain was having none of that, including him firmly in a comment here or there. The inside of the house would have had him stopping to gawk every two steps if it weren't for the fact they had somewhere to be. Part of it was that there was so much space, the rooms were enormous. But part of it was the way all of it was decorated and made and carved and specific. It wasn't just a wall, it was a wall with about six purposes, only one of which was holding up the roof. Professor Fortier led them up a set of stairs, then knocked twice before opening the door.

It opened onto a long room, with a group of chairs and sofas. Ursula was on one of them, and she beamed as she saw him. Her Uncle Alexander was standing by one chair, and her uncle by the other. Seeing Lord Fortier with Ursula's father made it clear exactly how closely they were related, not just in their appearance but how they moved the same way, looking over as Jim and Professor Wain came in.

It was like a herd turning to evaluate something new and decide if it were friend or foe. Not like sheep, sheep didn't quite move like that, they relied on the people and the dogs for more warning. More like horses, turning to shelter the weaker members of the herd, able to use teeth and sharp front hooves if needed.

Professor Fortier nodded once as they came closer. "Do sit with Ursula. Thesan, love, tea? Garin, this is Jim Pullan. Jim, my older brother, Garin, Lord Fortier. Do be clear how you'd like to be addressed, Garin, please, for everyone's nerves." Professor Fortier was trying to make it sound ordinary, as if he were introducing Jim to someone simple, and of course, it wasn't at all. "And for our parts, if you don't wish first names, we are often Professor Iz and Professor Thesan to students informally. Alexander, well." That at least got a nod and a murmur of agreement that it was his name.

Jim took a deep breath and went to offer his hand - or maybe a bow - to Lord Fortier. The man was tall, the same height as Professor Fortier. They both had an inch or three on Jim. "Sir."

"I think under the circumstances, we might begin with Lord Garin. I am interested to meet you, Mister Pullan. I gather you've not had a chance to apprentice yet." Then the hand was in his, sturdy. That much was something Jim understood, at least.

It might be taking everything Jim had not to turn and flee, but he was standing there, being properly polite. "Jim, please, Lord Garin, if you'd like." He got it out without stammering, and Ursula patted his arm. "May I— may I sit?" She tugged him down next to her, offered him a cup of tea— she'd had one waiting— and then there was silence.

Ursula apparently would not let that last for long. Jim felt the pressure of her fingers on his arm, as if she were counting to herself, ten taps, before she spoke. "The question at hand is what the land needs, and how it needs, what will nourish, not just maintain. Laudine's journals suggest several locations of note, and I'd like to propose a proper investigation of them, which will need specialists."

"Which spots, please?" Lord Garin spoke briskly, but Jim wasn't sure how to take the rest of his tone.

"The old mill, out on the river." Ursula added, for Jim's benefit, apparently, "Southwest from here, where the Arun curves directly south. The old barn, just inside the estate wards, a bit east of there. That's been in ruins since..."

"Since that year." Lord Garin's voice was more like stone now, something unreadable. Certainly to Jim. Though then Professor Iz leaned forward. "Did Maman comment about it?"

"That it was related. Earlier testing. I didn't work out all the details yet. Some of it is obscurely technical. Do you know anyone who's competent with electricity, Jim?"

"Dad does." Jim said it before he could think of being wary. "Sort of man who loves puttering about. He was on the railroad for decades. Of Albion, of course."

"That might do nicely." Ursula scribbled a note. From there, she talked about a dozen different pieces of it. Jim couldn't follow all the details— not that Ursula wasn't doing her best to explain it, but there was so much Jim didn't have context for. He paid attention to the way everyone else was reacting. There were other spots too that didn't seem to connect to anything directly, but Ursula had a map that laid them out.

All of them, her parents, her uncles, were focused on her. No one interrupted her, and when they had questions, they were, they were taking her seriously.

After maybe ten minutes of that, he'd had a chance to relax a little before she asked, "Jim, can we talk about different approaches for mitigating these sorts of problems? It's decades later, if they were going to heal fully on their own, they'd have done it."

"I know a fair bit of the theory, and some applications, but I'm not an expert. Sirs. Ma'am." Jim felt his heart in his throat again, but then Ursula was squeezing his forearm, and that helped.

Lord Garin shifted, just slightly, and no one else in the room spoke. Or moved, as far as Jim could tell, just waiting, like Jim was waiting. "Yesterday, I asked Ursula how long she'd been working on her plan for Master Wicken to challenge." He'd given Paul his proper title, the formality of it, and that nearly made Jim's jaw drop. "If Ursula asked for your thoughts, I suspect she has reason. I would be pleased to hear it, if you're willing."

Jim did not understand near any of the layers that were going on in this room, but he understood enough. Lord Garin was being careful to ask, not assume, and he was making that obvious. Jim didn't understand why, or why it mattered to anyone besides Ursula. He swallowed, then began as best he could. "I gather from conversations with Ursula that there's some overlap in how we name and describe things, but not as much as there might be." It was the Society of the White Horse that saved him, really. They talked about it, had phrases for it, far more than his actual classes had. And it gave him a framework for explaining it, because he'd had it explained to him, the same way, once he'd joined.

Once he'd got through a few of the basic phrases,

figuring out what they already knew, terms and concepts, he at least had a place to start. "There are a number of reasons farmers might rotate crops or live- stock— the balance and benefit of the soil, breaking chains of parasites. But one reason we do it, in Albion, is that it allows for a tuned approach to the land. This crop holds more water, it can rebalance an area that is dryer. This one responds better if there's a concern for flooding that year. This other one is protective, best for an area. Professor Thesan was showing me the poison gardens, sir, I gather that's something of the same theory?"

Jim was rewarded with a quick beaming smile of approval from both of Ursula's parents and Alexan- der, but Lord Garin nodded once, thoughtfully. "Not just crops, I assume. I've generally just approved whatever Lambert recommended. And that has not touched these areas."

"Begging your pardon, sir, but if he weren't aware of the older history, he might not have taken it into account. Magister Knox is exceedingly well- respected, and he manages substantial estates with great competence." This was where it got delicate. "But he left Snap in 1910. He's kept up with advances in the field since then, but it's been..." His voice failed him.

"I had not looked at it specifically." Professor Iz picked up a moment later. "But I'm guessing it's one of the fields where the deaths in the Great War had a disproportionate degree of damage in the following years. Both in the deaths out of season of experts, but also in the people who would have apprenticed to them."

"Yes, sir. It's part of why it's been hard to get apprenticeships now. Besides the more recent war, people coming home, and it being hard to find work." Jim hesitated, then added, "That's something I'd like to learn more about, and I've not had the opportunity. The ways to tend to specific points, with magic and with agriculture both."

"What is it you're doing with your time now?" Lord Garin's voice cut across that. "Don't you answer for him, Ursula." That part wasn't as sharp as it could have been. Ursula certainly didn't seem bruised by it. She snorted, but slipped her fingers into Jim's.

Jim took a long breath. "I was seriously ill— pneumonia— at the end of the war in Europe. A friend met an American nurse. I went with him to meet her family and see him married, and that was good for my lungs. I came back to Sussex in June. I've picked up work as I can, sheep shearing, helping my brother with the family farm. I'd like to apprentice, but I don't want to leave Sussex. West Sussex, preferably. There hasn't been a place that's come open near enough home. My parents are in Worthing now, and my middle brother."

"Ah, yes. Ursula asked about you, a while back, and about your family. Good knack for livestock, Lambert's spoken well of that, and Gerald, our livestock man." Lord Garin at least hadn't torn his background to shreds. Or at least Jim thought not. "Go on, about Lambert. What would you suggest looking at?"

"Besides the livestock and crop rotation, I wonder about orchards and beehives. They're often used to help with particular spots of concern. I was talking to the head gardener at Petworth House. He's extremely well-respected, but not magical. I was thinking about whether additional apple varieties might be of interest, but also useful for this. Ursula and I had talked a little about it, but it would need someone to look at the specific locations. And I know more beehives are a work in process."

"Huh." Lord Garin leaned back. "And you learned all of this at Snap?"

There it was, the sharp blade Jim had not seen coming fast enough to dodge. It wasn't quite like a bullet. This slid in and out before the shock of it hit. Beside him, Ursula straightened up. "Uncle Garin, honestly. You said you wouldn't press on that point. You do have manners."

Something in the way she said it made it possible for Jim to take a breath. A moment later, he heard Alexander start to chuckle. "You did promise, Garin." Then he focused on Jim, and that was uncomfortable in a different way. "I figured it out, to let you know that. But I won't press either of you to expand."

Jim glanced at Ursula, and he managed a little shrug. "What number of your plots are we on now? Go ahead, if it suits."

Ursula beamed, leaned to kiss him on the cheek, and then angled herself so her hip was pressed against his thigh, but turned her body to face Lord Garin. "In my second year, I was delighted to accept an invitation from the Society of the White Horse. As I said, I didn't tell Mum or Dad or Leo until this summer. Uncle Alexander just worked it out. I am pleased to be there, but I had always expected it would be a long-term plan. They have no reason to trust me, beyond my oaths, and they certainly haven't known what to do with some of my ideas about scope."

"That, Ursula, is because almost no one knows what to do with your ideas about scope." Professor Iz said it, but he was laughing. Laughing and watching his brother both.

Lord Garin was taking his time saying anything. "And?"

"And Jim as well, though obviously several years ahead. Jim has been very clear about making sure I understand more of the things that everyone who went to Snap already learned and helping me make more connections. I couldn't get away easily while I was in school. The Lammas rites, for example, or we've plans Monday night."

Her uncle held up his hands. "You needn't protest too much." Now he considered. "Why did you make that decision?"

"You know that's not fair. I can't make my arguments properly without talking about things I'm not supposed to know." Ursula sounded joyfully indignant, like her uncle had just walked into a particular conversational trap.

Her uncle honestly sighed, visibly. "Jim, I presume we may rely on your confidentiality?" Jim nodded, murmuring his agreement. "Go ahead, Ursula. It's not as if the rest of us don't have this bit."

Ursula went on, as if she'd never missed a step of the dance. "Jim, you know part of this. Dius Fidius invited me, and I turned them down."

"Like kicking a nest of hornets is how it was put to me," Jim said, because she was encouraging him in that. "We did our usual considerations, and you were rather more interesting than expected. And have continued to be."

It meant he was rewarded with another kiss on his cheek. "Uncle Alexander, Uncle Garin, and Dad are all members. The fifth years all turned up and were sure Dad had told me. I could just count who was out of the House, when I knew Dad and Uncle Alexander were also busy, at the right times of year. It wasn't even that hard. Most people do not have any sense of how to keep a secret."

Lord Garin sighed, rubbing his face with his hand. "And you turned Dius Fidius down why? It would have given you scope for making changes."

"It would not have given me any scope I did not already have. And it would not give me the tools, or at least connections with people who had the expertise needed, that I thought was needed. We were under rationing. It turned out we'd made it through the worst of the Blitz, but we didn't know what might come. That just meant needing more ways to help. Jim's made sure that's more secure, now for me. He knows far more people and their particular interests and talents."

Lord Garin turned to Jim now, unsettlingly focused. "And what does that mean? What does scope mean here? Do you, for example, intend to be able to keep Ursula in the manner suitable for her station?"

Somewhere, deep in him, Jim found the words. It still helped that Ursula was right there. She didn't say anything, didn't even really move, but he wasn't alone with the challenge. Never mind that they hadn't talked about it. "Sir, that's the wrong question. I want to do my part. But I'm clear that whatever I do, no matter how expert I am, it won't match what she brings to whomever she chooses to share her life with. It's not just the money or the estate, or the care of the land, which matters more to me. You know her, and what she's able to see, far better than I do yet. I can't hope to match that, but I can, I think, be a ladder she can use to see further and do more. And, well, sir, I can't possibly match her for grace or skill with words, certainly not for beauty. But I intend to keep on admiring all three and all her other virtues for as long as she'll permit. Along with lending a hand and my magic to every one of her plots she'll share."

The ladder was not a particularly good metaphor, but maybe that didn't matter. Something in it had startled Lord Garin, anyway. Ursula's fingers squeezed his, hard, and Jim just focused on breathing and not bolting for the door.

Finally, there was a slow, "Well said. If I arranged an interview with Lambert, would you consider that an insult?" Jim did not have standing to take insult at that kind of thing. Though if he'd been asked a few weeks ago, he'd have bristled.

Now, though, he took a breath, thinking about it. "Sir, he invited me to speak with him after I'd done some shearing on the estate. I hope I did well in the conversation, but he was honest that he didn't have a position, and didn't know if he would. It'd depend on other people, if there were injuries, that sort of thing. I'd very much like the chance to learn from him, and to work on an estate with this kind of history. Even the uncomfortable parts. I won't make promises I can't keep, but I'd give it my best. I prefer livestock, but managing an estate like this takes understanding all of it, how it fits together." Jim had said that part often enough, in other places, that at least he didn't tumble over his words.

"I'll speak to him on Monday, then. You've a journal?"

"Yes, sir." That part was easier to answer.

"Good. In that case, if you don't mind, I'd like to think about a few things. Perhaps we might come back to this in a few weeks, when Ursula's been able to finish all of her notes, and we can do our own individual evaluations? Your next planned Saturday, Thesan, Isembard?" There were general murmurs of agreement. "Perhaps you might take a walk around the gardens again, with the land in mind? And Ursula, you're of course welcome to invite people to your rooms for supper." Not, apparently, for more than supper. "Let Mrs Borrowsmith know. I'll give some thought to additional concerns."

"Of course, Uncle Garin." Now, Ursula finally let Jim's hand go, so she could stand, cross to her uncle, and kiss his cheek, entirely undaunted. "Mum, Dad, can you stay? Uncle Alexander?"

Alexander waved a hand. "I ought to get back to Ytene, there are—" He paused, and Jim couldn't quite figure out why. "I ought to arrange for a conversation or two there. Enjoy your supper. Ursula, I assume we're on for our usual."

That left everyone making suitable farewells, and Ursula eventually nudging Jim to walk with her down the stairs, out of the house. It wasn't until they were some twenty feet into the garden on that side that she turned and hugged him tightly. "All right?"

"Coping. Turns out to be less terrifying than fighting my way through France. Barely."

It got him a tighter hug, so that wasn't all bad. Then she turned, her arm through his, waiting for her parents to join them. She encouraged Jim to get a feel for the land as they walked, pointing out various smaller houses on the estate, the way they clustered.

Once they'd had a restorative walk around the grounds, Ursula steered them all back up into her rooms. It was the first time Jim had been up there, and he was not sure what to expect. What he found was something that felt like Ursula. It was all honey and lack of clutter, with swaths of vibrant colour against pale coloured walls.

She gestured them all into a sitting room, even if it was larger and more posh than any sitting room he'd ever been in. There was a fireplace, a sofa, four comfortable chairs, and a nook tucked into the wall. "Mum, Dad, put on the kettle?" Ursula offered. "Let me show Jim a few things."

Ursula took his hand, and Jim went where she led. First, she showed him the guest loo. That was vastly more posh than he was used to, with marble on the floor, done up in shades of blue and teal. They stopped in the door of her workroom, the floor a polished wood and the walls bare, except for one window.

Finally, she brought him back to the sitting room, and into the little nook. That turned out to be a circular tower. He'd seen them from outside, with a desk made for the curve set against the stone. Books and papers were across the desk, though in piles, but that wasn't what caught his attention.

As soon as he looked out the window, Jim's jaw dropped. "Ursula?" His voice cracked.

"Yes?"

"This is the view out your window." Jim swallowed. "I mean, obviously. Just. I dreamt of it."

Ursula squeezed his hand. "When?"

"Put a bit of yarrow under my pillow, um." He had to think about the date. "August. August seventeenth. Do you know that tradition?"

"That you dream of who you're meant to be with, a love charm. Not a compulsion, but a knowing." Ursula glanced at the window, then shifted to look up at him. "And you dreamt of this."

"When I told Paul about it later, what I said was it was nowhere I'd been, but it felt good to be there. Ancient and solid, like a good yew or oak. That I could feel the magic of it."

"That seems a fine omen." She did not move to kiss him; her parents were right there, over their shoulders. Perhaps Ursula was shy of that, too. Jim certainly was. But she reached to touch his cheek, brushing her thumb against the skin. "These are my rooms, as long as I want them. When we're at a place where you sharing them is the right thing, you can have the view and the magic and the knowing. Come visit, before then."

"Oh, I will." Jim swallowed. "Promise."

She nodded, one of her decisive and satisfied nods, and then tugged him back to sit down and talk to her parents about far less weighty topics.

CHAPTER 41
SEPTEMBER 23RD AT SNAP

"Here we go. There's more cider on the hearth, more stew on the stove, and, well, the bread's not what we wish it were, but we'll make do." Milly, as Mistress Pipp had insisted Ursula call her, settled down in what was clearly her chair and picked up her bowl. "My Alfred will be back once the students are in for the night, so we've two hours yet. And we expect the others around then."

Both of them were teachers here at Snap, but from what Ursula had been able to tell so far, a somewhat distinct set of patterns than Mum and Dad. They had this cottage, where they'd raised two now-grown children. It was the first time Ursula had been out at Snap, and she was taking in the differences between what she'd seen here and Schola.

For one thing, Snap wasn't a castle or a fortress. The portal was right at the edge of the school's buildings. As she'd walked along the road to the staff cottages with Jim and Paul, she'd spotted not only the barns and pastures and fields she expected, but also a number of buildings of various sizes. One larger one, amid the others, was apparently their gathering hall. It was used for meals, a regular country dance, and other such events.

The Pipps' cottage was a good size. Ursula was wondering if the size of the front room was deliberately big enough to have a dozen people in there without too much crowding. Right now, it only held five. There were a few more coming later in the evening for the actual equinox celebration part of the gathering. The hearth had a good fire in the fireplace, though they didn't really need the heat of it tonight. It made the scent from the mulled cider stronger, though, enveloping everything in a smell full of comfort, and a number of the spices meant for blessing and abundance.

Ursula was keeping quiet at the moment, and for excellent reason. First, she was a guest. Second, she didn't know nearly enough of Snap's customs. Third, she knew there were going to be questions coming, but she was trying not to anticipate them. And fourth, Jim deserved a chance to be relaxed with his friends. So did Paul, for that matter. Jim was also quiet, though Ursula was sure it was for different reasons. Paul had been quietly chatting away with Roger Hemming, the last of the current guests, as Milly got things set out.

Ursula had offered to help, but she'd been waved off, which left her thinking about the current state of things. Uncle Garin had been in his lab since Saturday evening, with periodic notes like messages sent out in bottles. Lambert had written Monday afternoon to let Ursula know he was working on several requests from Uncle Garin. And also that he'd approved additional funds to add to the library, and that Ursula could determine the titles. Ursula felt that her own knowledge was not entirely up to the task, so she was hoping she might have time to ask for advice tonight.

Or she had, but then being here, everything was about doing, or learning directly from others, not so much about books. Oh, there were books here. But where Mum and Dad had shelves in the sitting room running floor to ceiling along one wall, and piles on their desks, there were just four modest shelves here. That wasn't wrong. Ursula wasn't so foolish as to assume that. But it was an entirely different mode from the ones she knew.

Jim was right next to her, but he was also quiet. Now he'd seen her rooms, the way she lived, or was living, or whatever the correct verb tense was. Ursula was worried that that, of all things, had made him uncertain. They'd written back and forth a little on Sunday and that morning. But he'd been kept busy helping his brother. The conversation had mostly been pragmatic things like when he'd be at the portal to come to Snap, and a few little messages of affection. Now Ursula had her hand resting on his leg, lightly.

"Let's see. You've had a busy few days, I gather, Jim. And Paul, you'd wanted to talk about the various considerations for the Challenge. Roger is here as another set of ears and connections. Later, of course, we'll have another two dozen people here, the bonfire out back, for a celebration of the equinox. We can't manage the sort of feast we'd like, but we'll make do. Stewed apples for that, mostly, as well as the beer and cider." Then she shifted, looking at Ursula and Jim. "Where shall we begin?"

Ursula swallowed, glancing at Jim. "I defer to Paul and Jim, honestly. Though if I can help with information, I am glad to."

Paul hesitated, then he said, "I think part of what I'm trying to decide, and your uncle said to ask you, Ursula, is what people will assume. From how I arrive at the, um. What do you call it anyway?"

"Dinas Emrys or the Council Keep. Or the Keep. In those circles, everyone knows which one you mean." She considered, thinking what it would be like for someone who'd never seen it, and who'd also never had the experience of being at Schola to help. "Can I ask what it's like here, when things are formal?"

"We've the gathering hall. There's a stage, at one end, but we normally don't use that. The staff eat at different tables, with students rotating tables every month. Breakfast and luncheon, people have their usual places they prefer, and of course we have people in and out at different times because of their chores. We're formal at times, but not, mmm. Often." Milly laid it out evenly enough. "What I want to know, to put it bluntly, is how to support Paul in this."

That put a more useful label on it, and now Ursula leaned back slightly. "And?" She would provoke, because she could tell there was more there.

"And Jim." Milly nodded at him. "Paul and Jim are grown men. They know their own minds, certainly. You are sworn to the Society, or I'd be a great deal more concerned. But there are deep waters here, the sort that pull people in."

Ursula nodded, just once, and she felt Jim's hand shift onto her leg, not quite a warning, but reaching for something he couldn't articulate. "Of course you worry about your students. Mum and Dad do." She flicked her fingers. "I bet you don't have all the photos up in here, because you invite people over. And some of them, you might get a question that wouldn't suit that. Too near the quick."

Milly's mouth dropped open. Jim's fingers tapped Ursula's leg once, and then he said, amused. "All the photos are on the stairs and in the hall above. I've seen them once or twice, when I was asked to fetch something from the upstairs cupboards." He then added, "Ursula's parents have dozens of photos up in their sitting room."

"And more in their offices. The sitting room's the ones they're both close to." Ursula agreed. "Some of them are dead now. Too many of them. And I know they've both worried to bits about some of them."

"Have they worried about one of theirs about to go into a Challenge?" Milly asked.

"Oh, yes. Uncle Orion, coming up on two years ago, after Uncle Garin retired. Uncle Orion's father was on the Council, Matthias Sisley." Adding the last name might be informative. As Jim had reminded her, not everyone carried around that mental list at the top of their mind. "They were worried.." She considered how to put this fairly when Paul cleared his throat and she let him go on.

"Lord Sisley has been writing to me a little. He

challenged because his, can you explain the relation-ships, please, Ursula?" Jim cut off there.

"Uncle Claudio." Ursula said, picking up smoothly. "Claudio Warren. Son of Hesperidon and Silvia Warren. Magister Warren was head of the Council for thirty-seven years, and Magistra Warren has been since last year, when Cyrus Smythe-Clive retired."

"You don't call them uncle and aunt," Paul said, thoughtfully.

"Uncle Claudio is an uncle. His parents? His parents, well, his mother now, disapprove of a lot of things. I am exceedingly polite with her, and that mostly involves keeping my distance." Ursula shrugged. "Uncle Alexander— Milly, Alexander Landry is my godfather— and Uncle Orion and Gabe Edgarton are all inclined to prod her into keeping an open mind about some kinds of decisions. I don't know all the details, mind you, but I can see about, oh, half of them? And I have bits of several more angles from Uncle Claudio and Uncle Orion."

Jim spread his hands. "You see what a conversa-tion with Ursula is like, yes? There's a scope that takes a bit to get your head around. But she's thinking about generations of cross-breeding, just about ideas, magic, the land. Not actual livestock."

"And you, Ursula? Do you have inclinations that way?" Milly pressed. "And you were saying about Lord Sisley."

Ursula laughed, letting it show, before she leaned into Jim's neck and he patted her shoulder with his hand. The fun now was figuring out how to answer that. "Jim asked me about it. I've promised I won't. It would get in the way of most of my other plots. Honestly, I need my hands free for other things."

It made Milly's eyebrows go up delightfully. Roger tilted his head, tapping a flesh-and-blood finger on the wood of his other arm. "I keep telling people you are also like your Uncle Seth. He keeps quieter about it, but he's got a slew of plots, him and Golshan and Dilly, all three."

"I do like to learn from every single one of my elders with something to offer. Sir." Ursula gave the honorific properly. "I've learned a lot from Uncle Golshan about proper aim. And, mmm. How to determine how far I can annoy someone and benefit. Not that I'm perfect yet. I mis-stepped with Uncle Garin a couple of times recently."

Jim twisted and blinked at her. "Did you tell me that part?"

"If I'd done it better, he'd not have lost his temper as he did. He might still have lost his temper, but it was the quality of it." Ursula said, firmly. Then she looked down. "I came closer to hurting him than I wanted to. Uncle Alexander, too. The places I know are tender. Dad taught me better than that. What we're talking about matters, it's life and death and what sustains and can be sustained. But that's no reason to cause hurt that's not actually needed."

Milly nodded once, but she didn't say anything. It made Ursula feel she had to go on, the sort of knowledge she couldn't let herself ignore. Carefully, she said, "I've been thinking about the conversation on Saturday. Without getting into details, there was something there that could have poisoned everything, for decades. The shape of it, the shattering of it. And I couldn't let it do that. But if something had gone wrong, I would have made things much worse. It's one thing to have a problem you're ignoring. It's another to be actively refusing to think about it." Then she looked up and cleared her throat. "I believe the proper metaphor is pruning, isn't it? As opposed to a wasteful destruction."

Milly snorted. "That's one possible metaphor, yes."

Roger leaned forward, though. "So, what are your other plans? Paul Challenging for the Council, for example."

"If Paul is successful— I hope he will be, and I think his chances are good. Uncle Orion hasn't been talking about it in a particular way, and Uncle Alexander is being quietly gleeful." Ursula grinned and went on. "Anyway, that part is up to Paul, mostly, what he feels needs doing. The thing about the White Horse is that we have the foundation in listening to the land. I want to see what happens when the Council has more of that. I think it can only help. Especially right now."

She then considered. "I've been talking more with several people - Lords and their Heirs - about how to better support the land. I started with the easy people to talk to, for me, anyway. Lord Richard Edgarton and Gabe— on the Council, of course. There's Uncle Orion and his brother Achilles, his son's still too young to be Heir. Lord Geoffrey Carillon and Edmund. Edmund's only a few years older than I am, but he's been Heir since he was twelve. The next trick is going to be expanding that beyond people who were already inclined to listen to me. To do that,

I'm going to need a lot of different angles of possible conversation. But also results to draw on. Some of that I've ideas about. Some of it, I don't. And I expect it to take a while, years, maybe longer, as much as we desperately need the help now."

"What sort of things—" Roger hesitated and tried again. "You do not consider yourself an expert in all things, then?"

"Of course not. Most of the actual agriculture, for one. I've a general sense, enough to begin to ask sensible questions, now? Lambert's been giving me reading lists. But I grew up with experts around me. I'm not a master alchemist. That's Uncle Garin or Uncle Jehan. Or, to grant her due skill in her work, Silvia Warren. I'm still learning the intricacies of Incantation, but that's where I intend to focus. I'm not an expert at Astronomy, but I've certainly picked up a lot from Mum over the years. I can go ask her, or ask whoever is an expert, I know who they are. Same with warding. There are skills I don't have as much reach for— oh, talisman making, the long-term sorts of illusion work, while I know Healers, not as many. Things like that." Her mouth twitched up. "Of course, my year mates at Schola are still all apprenticing. Give us ten years, and I'll know people in dozens of places."

Beside her, Jim snorted. "And how many of them did we go by on Friday?"

"Oh, only a dozen or so. But they'll spread the gossip." She added to the rest of the room, "Jim and I had lunch at the Fox's Den, and, mmm, I made a point of introducing him without explaining at all. What everyone knows by now is that there is a man named Jim Pullan who absolutely had my full attention and who was permitted to escort me. That's not something I've allowed before. The length of a dance, an evening out, yes. Not more."

Roger shook his head. "That's not a field we know. But then, I suppose that's why we were— do we like encouraged as a word here?" That was more or less to Milly, who nodded. "Encouraged to invite you. We can work the land, tend it, patch as much damage as we can. But we can't do that part. Or, I suppose, do as much to influence what the Ministry decrees are. I suppose you hear more of that."

"From several directions," Ursula agreed. "Though that's an angle I'd like to aim towards. I don't need to work, in the sense of earning my keep with a job I go to routinely. But I think I'd like to go into consulting, a significant amount in the Ministry. Precisely to build those connections. I know people who can get me started, in due course. Several of Mum and Dad's favourites, for one, and Uncle Jehan gets taken seriously by all of Fox House since he started. The ones a decade older than I am, they're starting to get into positions with a little influence."

Jim leaned back against the sofa. "When you told me, Lammas eve, that you were expecting your plans to take decades, you weren't joking, were you?"

"No, but the 'get the White Horse folks to understand what I might be able to do and trust me enough to let me try' part is a good fifteen years ahead of schedule?" Ursula got it all out before her nerves shivered. Jim caught that and squeezed her against him, and she let out a more secure breath. She managed to go on more evenly. "I can see enough of it to want to make it better, and I know my history. It's going to take a while. People don't change their habits just because you ask nicely. Or even logically."

Milly snorted. "Ah, there're the words of someone who's grown up around a school." She nodded. "Right. We can think some more about that. Now, we should start getting the others turning up in a few minutes. More cider? And do you have questions about Snap, seeing as you're here?"

"I'm curious about how you rotate the different chores and assignments, actually," Ursula said promptly. "And what happens if someone's horrible at something? We had that problem when students started picking up more of the chores at the beginning of the war. Some people should not be let near chickens. Or asked to stack dishes."

That got off onto a combination of practical conversation— Ursula promised to see about Mum coming out for a visit sometime to talk about that sort of thing— and a few hilarious stories. As others joined them, the gathering spilled out to the bonfire in the garden at the back. Ursula could settle into listening a lot more than she spoke, comfortably leaning against Jim on the bale of straw they'd claimed.

CHAPTER 42
OCTOBER 14TH AT THE COUNCIL KEEP

J im glanced around again, unsure what to do. They'd been at the Council Keep for about two hours now, and the last of the challengers other than Paul had come out nearly thirty minutes ago. Ursula looked unworried, and several of the others had circulated to reassure Jim and Emma and Paul's parents that nothing was amiss.

The other challengers were talking quietly with their family members, but Paul's group was third down on the right, not able to hear much. And also not saying much. Except for Ursula, Jim thought all of them were worried about making it obvious how out of place they felt.

There was another group of people sitting behind them, and Ursula had pointed them out as others with an interest in the proceedings. That little knot of people included Magister Smyth-Clive, who'd retired as Head of the Council last year, and Magistra Teague, his partner. It was her former seat that was

the one in question. It made sense she'd want to
know who followed her.

Well, being Ursula, she had gone over to them
once the waiting had begun, bringing Jim with her.
Ursula had introduced him, mentioned her Uncle
Garin was coming around to the idea, and then
launched into a dozen questions about ongoing plots.
Only about four of them, if Jim were keeping count
accurately, at least that came up directly, and one of
those was about expanding the materia grown in
Arundel's gardens. Magistra Teague had quite a few
ideas about that, and she somehow made it easy for
Jim to venture his own thoughts. But then other
people had wanted to talk to them, and Jim and
Ursula had retreated to their designated seating.

There was a brief commotion up at the front, and
then there was Paul. He was looking sunnily
delighted with the world, the way he did when one of
the White Horse events came off right. He still looked
as tidy as he'd started, all clean clothes but nothing
fancy. But now he was carrying two baskets, one
hooked over each arm. The one on his right was over-
flowing with flowers, the other, Jim couldn't see
what was in it. Someone tried to stop him walking
straight back, toward their bit of seating, but Ursula's
Uncle Alexander stopped whoever it was.

Jim stood, uncertain, and Paul beamed at him,
handing him the basket that didn't have the flowers.
Inside were twigs. No. They were scions. A second later
Jim could feel the magic, preserving them safely til the
spring. There were more than a dozen, maybe more
than two dozen. He looked up again, to ask Paul about

them, but Paul had kept going, coming to stand in front of Magistra Teague. A small crowd gathered behind him - Alexander Landry, Silvia Warren, Gabe Edgarton, first and foremost. But none of them were trying to stop Paul or make him shut up or do what he was supposed to do.

Paul made a slight bow. "The Lady in there bid me bring these to you. She said you would know what to do with them." Then, as if he couldn't help himself, and surely, he couldn't, he added, "If you get extra seeds from these three, would you consider letting me have a go?"

Magistra Teague blinked at him, then looked down at the basket. "I - she - oh!" Her face was startled. There were something like tears in her eyes, the sort no one decent would ask about. Magister Smythe-Clive immediately had an arm around her, the sort of support and care that ordinary people did, and posh people so often didn't. Then she gathered herself. "Welcome to the Council, Master Wicken. May all that you touch flourish. I will take excellent care of these. And yes, if there are seeds to be had, you may have them." Then her eyes flicked to the basket Jim was holding. "May I ask about the other?"

"Apple scions, to graft in the spring, and some instructions on where." Paul's voice was steady and clear. "Thank you, magistra. Magister." He made another slight bow, then turned back to the Council members who were waiting. "I appreciate your patience." He didn't apologise for upsetting their apple carts, as it were. Ursula was grinning her head off, mind.

The rest of the formalities took a few minutes more,

enough time for there to be an official announcement of what everyone already knew. Paul was greeted by each member of the Council, then everyone else who wanted to pay their respects. Or, as seemed to be the case, to get a good look at him. Finally, he could come back, hug Emma, and swing her around. "We can go home now?"

"We can." Ursula, thankfully, took charge. Most of the other people there had filed out by that point. They stepped through the portal to Arundel to find a cart and driver waiting to take them back. Paul hesitated. "Mum, Dad, Emma, you go back by cart. I think I'd like to walk, clear my head. Jim, if you'd walk with me?"

Jim blinked, but then he got a look at Paul's face in the charmlights by the portal and nodded. "Of course, as you like. Here." He handed the basket of apple scions over, then turned to give Ursula a kiss and a hug, murmuring that he'd see about tea tomorrow, assuming nothing came up that took him elsewhere.

Paul was entirely quiet until they were a good mile from Arundel, as if he'd needed it well at his back. There was no one on the road, and of course no moonlight, it being the new moon. They had a charmlight flickering away like a candle in the lantern. That was enough to see by. Eventually, though, Paul glanced over. "You've got to have questions."

"Plenty." Jim said. "You're all right, first? You're, um. You're going to be doing the thing."

"I am," Paul considered, a good ten steps before he spoke again. "I see why Ursula thought I should.

She's right. Is she going to be unbearably smug that she's right?"

"Probably bearably smug," Jim said, thoughtfully. "I'll see what she says tomorrow. Let you know. I'm expecting to be working with Lambert all day." It had been a bit of a variety in the fortnight of the apprenticeship so far. They were still figuring each other out, and the Arundel estates had a bit of everything. Then he swallowed and asked the question he really wanted. "Anything you want to, can, share about what it was like?"

Paul paused for a moment, snorting. "That's why I asked you to walk with me. I can talk about here, I think. The spaces between. Arundel and home. Roads are liminal, aren't they? There's part of your answer. It's got me in this sort of mood." He took a breath, then started walking again. "There were fields in there, and cows and sheep, a lot of sheep. Orchards. Grain, waiting to be cut, and hedgerows. And there was a lady. The Lady, the land."

Jim wasn't sure what he could ask about that. "What was she like?"

"Apples. She was like apples. Variety, all sorts of different uses, no one thing, right? Some for eating and some for baking and some for cider, all the shades of reds and greens and golds. Like, mm. Rosmerta? Young and old, both, and an apron she had apples in. She asked me questions, and some of them I'm not talking about, even with you. Not now, anyway. Ask me in a few years, maybe. But there was one..."

"Yes?" Jim kept walking, keeping his eyes on the road, rather than risking falling on his face.

"She asked me how I came to be there. Which meant I had to attempt to explain Ursula. Have you attempted to explain Ursula? You must have."

"Badly." Jim agreed. "To my parents and to Luke and Alice. Er. What did you actually say?"

"That there was this woman. Not my wife. That made her laugh. Daughter of one of the Great Families." Paul snorted. "She asked which one. And I said Ursula Fortier. I didn't know if she'd know the name? Though, I suppose..."

"I think," Jim said, after a moment's hesitation, "That whatever the Lady might or might not know is not a topic we really want to get into here and now." It was an open road, and the land was stretching out around them. "But assuming that such a lady pays attention to any individual humans, more likely Ursula than some? Given her uncles and her aunt?"

"True." Paul shrugged. "She said— wait, you'd said something about Ursula's cousin? The one who died."

"Childeric Fortier. Her, um." Jim had to count. "Her grandfather's older brother's eldest son. Second cousin, once removed."

"The Lady did not like him one bit. Not that she said it, exactly. She implied a lot. Or it was in my head without there being words? I'd say it was very strange, but I've got, what, fifteen years of the White Horse behind me. It was clearer than a lot of that. There were words, for one thing, not just symbols."

Jim snorted softly at that. "Nice change." He offered it as gently as he could. "I've wondered a lot about Childeric. And about, about what it meant.

Ursula and I have talked a bit about the notes she has. I don't think her grandmother liked him much."

"What the Lady said was that she'd, she'd taken his measure. Found him wanting. That was the implied bit. She didn't actually say what she did. But he died, so I suppose that's the amount of detail we need. And that there was something about, I assume Alexander Landry had a mother? I think the Lady liked her, but that didn't make any sense. The thing in my head was knowing the proper measure of a horse's parents by seeing it." Paul gestured faintly with his hands.

"There are stories about that, too. She was Egyptian. She's buried at Arundel, and his brother, her older son. They both died around that same time. Why do you ask?"

"For one thing, I think the Lady knew his mother. But that doesn't make sense, does it?"

Jim felt, on the whole, that they had got into even deeper waters than he'd expected, and he was not at all sure about getting back to firmer footing. "She wasn't on the Council. Landry wasn't until well after she'd died. A little under seven years."

"But now he's the most senior of them." Paul walked on. "He's promised to explain things to me. Take the time to do it properly. And he's said that, well. He's not going to retire immediately. This year. But sometime, he'd like to. That they've been trying to do that, more than dying in harness. Which I gather has been sort of traditional."

"Hard to pass things along properly if you do," Jim said. "We got taught that. Over and over, for good reason." Then something in the phrasing caught his attention again. "Paul, if there were a lot of deaths in your herd, cows, sheep, I don't care which. Pigs. Chickens. Ducks. What would you think?"

"All at once or spread out? And different ages or same age?" Paul asked.

"Over six months or so. Different ages and generations."

"I'd think they were getting into something on the land. It wouldn't be sickness. That would go through them at the same time, or at least close together. Something contagious would. Same thing with fodder, you'd expect to see it in the same batch. Come on, Jim, that's first year husbandry."

"I'm thinking about that lecture, and then the practical, third year. And then fifth, actually sorting things out." There'd been a whole series of exercises, each of them tending a specific bit of the school's livestock. They'd wake up and find a note with some new information.

"Oh, that's right. You got thing after thing, didn't you? Lost sheep, signs of mange. What was it?"

"Patch of St John's Wort, and that doesn't show up for weeks." It had made it damnably hard to figure out the actual cause. "So what makes a delay?"

"Some slow thing that's a poison. Bad breeding, something that comes out a couple of generations in. " Then Paul stopped dead. "Sometimes something deliberate. Sabotage, jealousy, that kind of thing."

"Yeah." Jim swallowed. "Three of the Fortiers died, after Childeric. One more, her great-grand-mother, had an apoplexy. Certainly looks deliberate, doesn't it?"

They walked along in silence for a good twenty

feet, maybe a bit more. "Do you think Ursula knows more than she's saying about it?"

"Probably. But here, what good would it do? Everyone's dead, they've been dead for ages. Can't punish the dead, can you?"

"No." Paul hesitated. "But the living might want answers. That, though, is your problem. I need to figure out how to talk at least a dozen people who don't know me into apple grafts, and tending the apples."

"Tell me about that, then. Can I help with the rest of it?" Jim knew where he was with an apple scion and grafting.

CHAPTER 43
OCTOBER 20TH IN THE ARUNDEL CEMETERY

Ursula had a plan. Well, actually, she had a series of plans, of course, but it began with waiting for Uncle Alexander in the cemetery. She'd checked with Edmund about Uncle Alexander's schedule for the day— and one other thing— and Edmund had been willing enough to help her. Without even asking many questions, he must have had something else distracting him.

In due course, she saw Uncle Alexander appear, the mist made it hard for her to see him, but also hard for him to see her until he was close enough it'd be obvious if he turned.

Instead, he let out a small sound, not quite a sigh. "Ursula. What can I do for you?"

"May I help with the offerings today?" It did not fool him, of course. He'd have figured out there was more than that as soon as he saw her. For one thing, if it had just been that, she'd have checked with him in advance. Now, though, he just nodded. She'd been waiting to the far side of the two sandstone monuments, next to each other in the furthest corner of the cemetery, entirely unlike any of the other memorials.

Uncle Alexander undid his satchel, bringing out a small case, and setting out small clay items— loaves of bread, jars of wine or beer or something of the kind. Then he set out loaves of actual bread, minuscule bowls the size of a thimble that each received a splash of beer. Then he pulled out an apple and a pocket knife, leaving three slices on each tomb. "Before the war, I'd bring something of marzipan. Not traditional to the ancients, but they'd have appreciated the artistry of it." His voice was soft. "Have you learned the prayers?"

She knew a few of the phrases, but she shook her head. "Not properly. Will you teach me, sometime?" Ursula had never asked before, this was something he kept so private. But if she was going to be Lady of the land, here, she wanted to be able to tend the cemetery properly, as well as the living land. "So I can, if, if you can't."

"Ah, that's a kindness. Yes, I will. Edmund's been learning as well." Uncle Alexander let out a small sound, not quite relief, then he pulled his cloak off, spreading it out, to fold himself kneeling down, on a level with the tombs. He bent forward, lighting a small cone of incense with a flick of his fingers. It had fire hovering there long enough for it to begin to smoke on its own. Then he sat back on his heels, beginning a long string of prayers, all in the ancient Egyptian. Ursula let it flow over her, repeating a few of the key phrases over and over again. As she listened, two things struck her. Well, one she'd already been thinking about. The other was new.

It took a bit, and she'd expected that. Uncle Alexander came out here once a month, six days after the new moon, whenever he could. She'd been able to figure that out over the last fifteen months, especially once Uncle Garin and Dad had woven her more fully into the wards. He never stayed terribly long, an hour or so, and he almost never came by the house on those days. Now, she waited patiently, not only for him to be done, but for him to be ready for a conversation. That was an entirely different measure of time.

Eventually, though, he looked up. "Were you waiting here for a reason? Would you rather go inside?"

"Actually, no. It's an outdoors sort of question." Certainly, it was easier for her to feel what she was doing properly on the land.

"Ah, then have a seat. Beer? The rest of the apple?" Uncle Alexander set to work slicing it up without waiting for her answer, as Ursula settled on the other half of the cloak. "A question?"

"Questions." Ursula said, weighing which one to start with. Then, because she was staring at the stones, she started there. "Uncle Alexander, what was your mother's name? In Egyptian." The Roman letters just gave it as Henut, the name Ursula knew she'd used as a forename.

Uncle Alexander snorted. "Henut, as you know. It means lady. She went around her entire life here, making everyone call her lady. A different sort. Mistress, that's the other translation."

It made Ursula snort. "You knew. And your brother. No one else?"

423

"She did not make a point of socialising with the people who might have known," Uncle Alexander said.

"And the rest of her name?" Ursula gestured at the tombstone.

"Why?" Uncle Alexander parried it back. Then, to soften that a bit, he handed her half the apple slices. "For the record, I am exceedingly pleased with your friend Paul already. Not least because he is not at all bothered by Silvia. I'm looking forward to Wednesday's meeting and seeing what everyone else makes of him."

"Grand." It was, too. "Jim's had a couple of really good conversations with him, since." Then she gestured with her elbow. "The name, Uncle Alexander. You know I don't read the hieroglyphs properly, but even I can tell the difference between two birds and a, whatever those are." One was a bit like a mouth or eye, the other was a semicircle with a flat base.

"A mouth and a loaf." Uncle Alexander leaned back. "Why do you ask?"

"The first one, with the birds, is on the papers, the formal agreements, when she arrived. I double checked them this week. The other, that's there." She gestured at the tombstone. "They're different."

He let out a long sigh. "You're the first to notice, for the record. At least that I know of." He stared at them. "She was Henutsekhemu, mistress or lady of powers, that's what it means. That." He gestured at the inscription, "Is Henutsekheret. Lady who defeats or wins. Something of the kind."

Ursula stared at it. "I thought you said you didn't know what she'd done."

"I did. I do not know for certain. But I did know the range of my mother's skills, and the fury she had." He let that sink in before he went on. "Before I left, near her last instruction was not to be too clever for my own good. Prodding at the problem when I returned to Albion would not have changed who lived, and it would have risked my future. I set the mechanics of the thing aside." Uncle Alexander shook his head, still focused on the stones. "Ummi was not warm, Ursula. Not like your mother is. Not even so much as Laudine was, actually, to give you an idea of the gap. But she took care of us, as fiercely as she could, until she couldn't."

"And she was—" Ursula was feeling her way through this. "She wouldn't have cared about the fact that what they were doing was breaking the Pact, would she?"

"Did you find more of that? It's the sort of thing you should tell your father and Garin."

"I'm telling you first," Ursula said, swallowing hard, then pushing forward. "You know about lightning, Uncle Alexander."

She'd caught him out, enough he couldn't help but let it show, and Ursula had never managed it before. She'd probably never manage it again. "Lightning." He cleared his throat. "What makes you ask about lightning?"

"What is lightning to you, please?" Ursula spread her hands out, palms up. "It's a particular destruction, isn't it?"

"It is. A powerful one, fire from the storm. Uncontrolled. You know your Tarot decks as well as anything else. The lightning strikes the tower and destroys it, forcing one to rebuild again."

"And? Personally. Culturally, if that's the word I want." Ursula gestured at the tombstones again.

"You will persist in asking the troublesome questions. I have only myself to blame, don't I?" Uncle Alexander took a breath. "That sort of destruction is very much within Set's realm, yes. Where are you going with this?"

Ursula would not mention at the moment that Mum and Dad had also had a hand in the difficult question skills. Also various other people she knew. "I'm still working out the details. I said that three weeks ago. Translating someone's coded language about something she was being particularly obscure about does not go quickly. I had to sidetrack into books from the library, and honestly, they're not at all sufficient. But best I can tell, and she had most of it secondhand, didn't she, Laudine? They were making a device. To separate a space from being limited by the Pact. They hadn't. It wasn't successful. But that didn't mean it didn't do damage. That lightning-struck barn and the old mill. Maybe other places. What do we do about fixing that? It's not just the lightning, it's the magic, it's the ..." She grimaced, frustrated at her inability to put things into words.

"Two more things you should know." Uncle Alexander's voice was very soft now. "Childeric's body was dumped on the landing outside the challenge door, soaking wet. The thing they couldn't help but notice was a Lichtenberg figure up his chest. A sign of a lightning strike. There's no reason for it to

426

have been like that. Not unless somehow she knew, the Lady whose hands hold the magics of Albion. And had her opinions. Perhaps she couldn't touch him until he came within her particular bounds."

Ursula winced, sucking in a breath. "Oh. But he chose to, didn't he? Thinking he'd coast through it, like everything else. Like his blood or his parents or his wealth would save him."

"And none of that matters when it comes down to that kind of magic." Uncle Alexander closed his eyes. "Hereswith was sensible about it. Hesperidon, who followed her as head, was not so much. Silvia is being... more judicious."

He went on before Ursula had to prod him, and that made her wary and concerned. "As to the other, Hesperidon knew Philip must have been the one to kill Metaia Powell. Of all the mysteries of this thing, that's the one I wish I understood better. I had a bit of it from Laudine, and you've said that the family was terrified she'd bring everything down. That she'd found a thread of what they were trying, and someone panicked. Laudine suggested that they'd have made it clear they'd make my life miserable if Philip hadn't helped." He shook his head. "No answers, there, no certain ones, anyway. What was your question?"

"If we're going to improve the land, the places that the lightning burns still are, the scarring from it, how do we do that? How would we do that in your idiom?" Ursula said promptly. She both wanted the answer to this question, and she saw no point in making Uncle Alexander miserable for no benefit.

"Ah. That's an interesting question, isn't it? Your

friends who went to Snap have some ideas, I'm sure. Like Paul and those apple scions. He has told me what books to hunt up. I need a new set of shelves for the library, clearly." That aside made her feel a bit better. "But they're meant to anchor the land magic more, mmm. Organically than currently. Deliberately as well. You want something like that with those two spots. You have had the transformation of the lightning, but not what it is transformed into. A stalled process, you see?"

"Huh." Ursula could see it now as he talked about it that way. "Reseeding the space into something productive, then? Set destroys and— who is it here? — restores?"

"The death of Osiris becomes the seed for the future crop, but Horus is the one who makes it flourish. Do your research, and we'll get Geoffrey out here — carefully making sure Garin's busy elsewhere, if you can manage that— and see what he thinks. I'd still rather not test putting them in close quarters." There were different ancient— well, 1920s— reasons for that, and Ursula didn't blame Geoffrey at all for wariness.

"Uncle Garin was thinking about going to a conference in France, alchemists working on the same set of things. We might get Edmund and Geoffrey out while he's gone?" Ursula suggested.

"Also, you're looking forward to seeing Edmund flinch every time you call his father by his forename, aren't you?" Uncle Alexander didn't seem to mind the idea, either.

"A woman's got to have enough hobbies to keep her busy." Ursula said it teasingly, and she was rewarded with a proper smile. "What sort of planting are we thinking here, so I can talk to Jim and Lambert about options?"

"Grain, if you can. That's probably better by the barn. Perhaps it's time to tear the mill down, replant the banks with something. Wildflowers, even. Though if you can find something that ties into the agricultural cycle, all the better. Pigs. Pig grazing would do."

"Except for the fact we'd have pigs escaping down the river, and that makes the neighbours gossip," Ursula said. "I'll do some research. And get Jim to help." She leaned back on her hand. "Thank you, Uncle Alexander."

He stared off at the stones. "It's difficult. But it also feels, well. It feels like the seeds being planted finally, to talk about it at least. I had kept all of it tight to my chest for so long. On the whole, I'm glad you pressed the point of figuring out what Laudine had said." Then he shook his head. "How is Jim?"

"Settling in nicely. Uncle Garin's redoing one of the cottages for him. It should be ready by when we actually make the engagement public. I, mind, am looking forward to that, because we can actually have time together without going out to the Essex house or worrying about running into Uncle Garin. Jim says it puts him off his inclination."

"Jim seems brave and stalwart, but yes, I can imagine that might make it difficult for him to, mmm. Relax and focus in the appropriate ways. Here, shall we go see if Garin's around? I do actually have a question for him, an alchemical one."

"Of course." The incense had burned down,

entirely. It took them very little time to tidy up and for Uncle Alexander to slip his cloak back on before they walked back to the house. On the way back, Uncle Alexander told her more about some of the other parts of the estate, beyond what she'd learned from the records.

EPILOGUE
NOVEMBER 8TH AT ARUNDEL

J im glanced around and felt surprisingly good about the entire afternoon. That was absolutely not what he'd expected of a formal betrothal party. But here he was, with a moment to breathe between talking to people. Well, breathe and admire Ursula, who was wearing the stunning blue dress again.

His parents were there, chatting with Ursula's parents. It wasn't the first time they'd met. No one had wanted that. It had meant, however, that both sides had spent a bit of time coming up with conversational topics that would be enjoyable for everyone. Dad was asking Ursula's mum about the mead traditions, and how beer and cider fit into that. Mum had turned out to have seen Ursula's dad back when he had played bohort in the formal league, and had a number of questions about that.

Ursula's uncles— and aunts— were many, of course, but they were mostly keeping each other occupied. Her Uncles Seth and Golshan were engaged in an amiable conversation with Paul and Roger Hemming, with Ursula's Uncle Seth periodically demonstrating something on her Uncle Golshan's wheelchair, or gesturing by way of explanation.

Her Aunt Dilly was right in there, making sure that Emma and Hazel felt at home and comfortable. She did it with all the ease of a woman who'd had plenty of experience not only raising her own children but lending a hand with an extended family of all ages. Hazel had taken to her almost immediately, and that was a kindness Jim was going to remember for a long time to come.

There was a little knot of the Uncles associated with the Council— likely to gather up Paul, at some point, for all this was an entirely non-professional sort of gathering. They were chatting across the garden, at ease with each other, or at least mostly so.

Ursula's Uncle Garin was standing more stiffly than the others. But her Uncle Alexander was gesturing agreeably, and her Uncles Orion and Claudio were obviously playing up a particular shared joke. Egged on, Jim thought, though maybe that wasn't right, by Gabriel Edgarton. Claudio had been his apprentice as a Penelope until recently. That might explain a lot of it. Both the comfort and the fact it didn't make any sense to Jim.

They were all sort of gathered on the lawn, with charms to give some warmer spots. In the other corner, there were a good dozen people from Schola. Most of them, Jim didn't know yet, but Milly and Alfred were over there chattering away and making the most of it. Jim suspected that it'd gain Ursula's parents in a few minutes. There were several others from the White Horse, too, though all people that either Jim or Ursula might, at least plausibly, have known independently.

Beyond that, there were plenty of people Jim didn't know, or had only had pointed out briefly. Lord Sisley's wife, Hypatia, was very pregnant, so she wasn't there. There was a Cammie Gates-Clark, apparently a good friend of Hypatia's, or some sort of sister, and her husband. A fair number of people from around Ursula's year at Schola, just as many men as women. Several of the Wain cousins, all older and who looked enough alike it was going to take work to keep them straight.

A moment later, Ursula's shoulder bumped against his, amiably. "They're just setting up for the dancing. All the country dances, nothing fussy. I know you know them."

Jim put up his hands. "I enjoy dancing with you. I've known that since the first night we met properly." Then he glanced around precisely to make sure no aunts or uncles who might take offence were within earshot. "Vertically and horizontally, but we'll have to wait for the second."

It made Ursula laugh with delight, enough to draw a bit of attention, but not bring anyone over. "Oh, I'm looking forward to that. Doing the thing in your new home for however long."

That was taking some getting used to, though he'd moved in properly this week. Ursula's uncle had fitted up a guest house or cottage or whatever one called it. It was across two gardens, away from the main house and private enough that no one was going to have a look in the window. Also far enough that he didn't feel Ursula's uncle looming. Oh, he'd been up in her rooms regularly now, but he still couldn't bring himself to relax enough for anything in bed. Not yet.

When they'd wanted privacy the last six weeks and more comfort than the shepherd's hut, they'd taken the portal to Essex, the house that had come down her father's side. It was ridiculously large, larger than Arundel, actually, but there was no one there besides a small staff. That house had been given over to magical rehabilitation work during the war. It had held people who mostly needed quiet to recover as much as they were going to. While Ursula was at home there, she was the first to admit it wasn't actually home, not the way she needed. Her magic needed her to be on the demesne lands. And she wanted plenty of chances to see Jim, the sort of casual time together that didn't take a lot of planning.

The cottage that was now somehow Jim's was a lot more manageable in both size and shape. There were two bedrooms upstairs and a sitting room and kitchen downstairs. There was space for Paul to stay if he got back from some meeting too late to get home easily. Jim got most of his meals either with Lambert or with Ursula, unless she had somewhere to be. Or the weekly suppers with her uncle. He didn't want to interfere with that. He wouldn't dare, even if Lord Garin had been entirely civil so far. And to Paul, as well, once they'd met properly in person. Not that Ursula wasn't keeping a close eye on it.

But the cottage meant other things. He had a bed all his own, broad and long enough. His feet didn't stick off the end. There was plenty of bedding to nestle in as the days— and the nights— got colder. And starting tonight, there'd be Ursula there on the regular, at least a couple of nights a week, depending on their respective schedules. "You sure it's all right? There won't be a fuss?"

"Uncle Garin tried making a comment about it last week. Mum and Dad were here after you left for the night. I told you that, didn't I? Or, no, we got onto the sheep the next day, didn't we?" She shrugged. She'd had a dozen questions about what you bred sheep for specifically, and also about crop and field rotations and the different cycles of livestock. It had quickly devolved into the sort of thing that needed a few large pieces of paper, several charms, and about six colours of ink.

"And?" Jim did actually want the answer to this question, since it would determine just how energetic he was comfortable being about some things. Demonstrative, too.

"Mum pointed out that I was sensible, and I'd had all the proper education about things dealing with the bedroom. Then she went right on to add that if Uncle Garin wanted me to produce children, we might as well get plenty of practice in. Absolutely scandalised him, but he shut up about it. And then, was it Tuesday? It's been a rush. He made a point of saying that he appreciated not having it out in front of him. But also that he wouldn't pry about things unless there seemed to be a problem."

"Well, sweet. We'll just make sure there's no problem. I don't want him prying." Jim did venture to lean over and kiss her cheek before settling his arm around her waist.

"Fairly sure that if he thinks there's a problem, he'll delegate to Mum. Or Dad. Or possibly Uncle Alexander, but not for the bedroom sort of problem." As if naming him had drawn him out of the crowd, her godfather excused himself from his conversation and came their way. The red of his wine gleamed with the light behind it.

"A joyous engagement to you both. I must say, this is a far happier and more enjoyable gathering than the last two betrothals here." Alexander lifted his glass in a toast. "To all the blessings you both may hold, and the land under you."

Ursula waited until he'd drunk, and until she'd had a sip of her own glass, then stepped forward to kiss his cheek. "The others? Not Mum and Dad, I know they only did the fussy bits for their wedding."

"It put out Garin no end, but it's not as if anyone was going to argue that party planning was one of Livia's better skills. Garin and Livia were quite young and their parents planned most of it. Not like you, where you presented us with what you were doing, and we only had the choice to agree or get out of the way." He was teasing now, his eyes dancing. "Jim, that is a delight, before you wonder whether I'm saying six things at once."

"Uncle Alexander is, but in this case, they're all kind. Who was the one before?" Ursula counted back. "No. Wait. It must be Childeric's. I was looking at the records of that, all sorts of illusion and enchantment work. The bill for it was, well. Vastly more extravagant than this. Multiples of extravagance. Even leaving aside the food rationing, and that all the wine here came out of the cellars that Dagobert or his father put down."

Alexander nodded once. "It was a splendid evening, and week, in all the ways that are supposed to matter. And quite a few of the Council there, as well as the Great Families. Here, the balance is a great deal more varied. And not only is that a better party, I think, it promises a fair bit of cross-fertilisation. I heard your Mistress Pipp, Jim, having a grand argument with Helena about working up additional approaches to materia, to take advantage of plants we have in profusion."

"Aunt Helena in this case being Head of Schola," Ursula supplied, though Jim had almost placed the name by the time she said it. "She's been wanting to push that for years herself, actually. And Uncle Garin and I have plans for the greenhouses once we can get things established. A couple of the nearer fields, if we can get the magical flow behaving enough for the more delicate magical plants. There's a gardener, someone who consults, up in Norfolk, and Mistress Pipp was going to make sure we get a proper introduction next month. She's pretty sure he'll talk to me, and to Uncle Garin if I'm there."

Alexander snorted, amused. "There we are." Then there was more sound of music. "First dance. Your parents look ready for it, both of you. Why don't you make up a set with them, and start things off?" He reached out, taking Ursula's glass for her, and then Jim offered Ursula his arm.

"Shall we show them what we're like together?" Ursula didn't need to answer him in words. She just hooked her hand through his elbow. Then she set off, straight and tall and long-legged, to join their parents in the centre of the dancing space.

I<small>F</small> <small>YOU</small> <small>ENJOYED</small> *Grown Wise* and would like to read more of this series, please sign up for my mailing list to get all the latest news and fun extras.

Your reviews (on whatever review site you use) are much appreciated, too!

Read on for more historical details about this book.

AUTHOR'S NOTES

Thank you for joining me in the terrifying delight that is Ursula Fortier! (I also love Jim, but he's a lot less hectic.) As always, my thanks to Kiya Nicoll, my editor and other half of my brain, for various improvements to this.

Grown Wise is the first in a four book series of post-war (Second World War) romances set between 1947 and 1950. The other three books in the Liminal Mysteries series will focus on romances for Edmund Carillon (seen here), Rowena Edgarton, and Claudio Warren. While there's no overarching plot, the four books are about how to navigate the needs and wants of the land magic in the aftermath of the war, the Blitz, and the massive changes to agriculture in the late 1940s. My newsletter is the best place to find out all about what's coming next.

Grown Wise also picks up threads of the Mysterious Fields trilogy, which takes place in 1889 and 1890 (beginning with *Enchanted Net)*. When I wrote that trilogy, I knew there were parts of that story that

Thessaly and Vitus (the main characters) just would never see or know about. Certainly not then. Ursula was a chance to return to the consequences of the trilogy for the Fortier family, nearly 60 years later.

Ursula is absolutely the best of both her parents in several ways, and she was able to bring several tools to the problem that no one had previously tried. You can find Thesan and Isembard's romance in *Eclipse*, and various details relating to Garin can be found throughout various books. My authorial wiki (celialake.com/wiki) has more details about where to find stories dealing with specific characters (including Garin).

Onwards to the specific notes!

Rationing continued in Britain until 1954. In 1947, basically everything that had been rationed was still rationed. That included flour, dairy (butter, cream, milk), meat, eggs, clothing, sugar, tea - the list goes on and on. Meals in restaurants had some limits on what could be served, but did not draw on individual ration cards.

People with their own gardens or other access could supplement the ration cards. In Albion, estates with home farms (like Arundel) could also supplement their food from their farms, but contributed most of what they grew to Albion's institutions. Beekeeping for honey - as Ursula explores for multiple reasons - was actively encouraged.

There had been awful flooding in the spring of 1947, leading to the loss of a huge percentage of the grain crops. That's the big reason flour was so hard to come by. (It hadn't been rationed until 1946, after the war.)

The question of agriculture is a complicated one in this period. Britain was desperate - had been since the beginning of the war - to produce more food. A great deal of land had been turned over to agriculture (including cutting down forests and otherwise disrupting various habitats and growth). This is when we start to see the beginning of much more mechanisation in farming as well. The Agriculture Act discussed in the first chapter was intended to help stabilise food supplies and encouraging people to continue farming.

Wilding: The Return of Nature to a British Farm by Isabella Tree follows the work of the author and her husband to return their estate (in his family for some time) to older agricultural practices. Many of the things they do are in fact how Garin (and the staff at Arundel) are managing their estates, with less overt governmental interference. A fair bit of the Fortier-held lands are magically protected and hidden, though not all of them.

Chapter 3: Jim served in the 70th Infantry Brigade, and I am deeply grateful to a history site of the brigade that outlined exactly where they were when. I've kept Jim's experience in line with that. (Except for his illness at the end, which is his.)

One of the more interesting questions in the

research for this book involved figuring out whether the various West Sussex farms had electricity. There are still places in West Sussex where access to electricity is quite limited.

The Bignor Roman villa site, which Ursula mentions in passing (walking distance from Arundel), is still not on the electric mains. They don't have enough electricity access for heat and light to allow visitors in the winter. Anyway, I decided that doing the sheep shearing with magic was more fun.

The sheep shearing customs come out of *The Folklore of Sussex* by Jacqueline Simpson, including the customs about the drinks at the end. The various nicknames are my own invention.

Chapter 6: The article referenced here is a callback to an article that Thesan (Ursula's mother) published in 1924. She and Garin have a conversation about it in *Eclipse,* Thesan and Isembard's romance. He gets details about it wrong, without realising she's one of the authors.

The 1924 article is called "Esse quam videri: An evaluation of astronomical implications for Materia preparation". Garin titles his "Prodesse quam videri" with a different subtitle, as a nod of apology. Esse quam videri translates as "to be, rather than to seem" (it appears in various classical texts). "Prodesse quam videri" might be translated as to benefit or to accomplish rather than to seem.

Chapter 12: My research suggests that cask is preferable to barrel for beer in this period, but there's some variation and I had to pick something. (Keg is not widely in use yet.)

Chapter 20: Basically everything I know about knuckers came out of *The Folklore of Sussex*. There are also some excellent retellings and snippets online if you do some searches. The locations mentioned are accurate to the folklore.

Chapter 22: We were not getting out of this book without rather a lot more about apples. (For previous apples in particular, see *Mistress of Birds*.) Frederic Streeter is an actual historical figure with a fascinating background. Jim touches on this, but Streeter began as a gardener, working his way up to the head gardener. He became a radio presenter, first with a show about gardening, and then one of the leading voices encouraging people to grow vegetables and other foods during the Second World War. For much of his life, he was based at Petworth House, Sussex.

The Petworth Non Pareil is an apple variety developed at Petworth. It disappeared in the 1970s, and there are no currently known trees. (I managed to track down a reference to it in a town newsletter in the 90s, to get that date. Clearly some of the trees might survive on the warded Fortier estates.)

The National Fruit Trials had the goal of documenting varieties of fruit with an eye to improving the range of options, resistance to various problems, and use for different needs. They also help with identifying unknown varieties. These days, the relevant orchards are in Kent, but during the Second World War, they were in Surrey. Individuals would submit examples and scions (for grafting) or other options (for planting) depending on the kind of fruit.

Chapter 23: Harrow Hill's lore is as Ursula describes - in some sources it's mentioned as the last location of the Good Folk in England. There are ancient mines in the base of the hill.

The song Ursula picks to sign is "The Brisk Young Ploughboy", collected on page 10 of John Broadwood's "Songs of the Peasantry of the Weald of Sussex", and with various sources to listen to it. That book was published anonymously in 1843.

Chapter 35: The charm Ursula references is an ancient Anglo-Saxon charm in praise of the earth. It's known as the Æcerbot, and dates (in the written form) to the 10th or 11th century CE. It's part of a larger ritual for the good of the land.

Thank you again for coming along on this story! We'll have three more romances in the post-war years. The next, Apt To Be Suspicious features Edmund Carillon during his time at Oxford in 1947-1948.

If you want to know more about what's coming, the best way is to sign up for my mailing list. You can also find me other places online - check out my contact page (celialake.com/contact) for more details.

Happy reading!

Also by Celia Lake

VICTORIAN

Mysterious Fields trilogy

Enchanted Net

Silent Circuit

Elemental Truth

Charms of Albion - standalone

Pastiche

Sailor's Jewel

Four Walls and a Heart

1920S

Mysterious Charm

Outcrossing

Goblin Fruit

Magician's Hoard

Wards of the Roses

In The Cards

On The Bias

Seven Sisters

Mysterious Powers

Carry On

The Fossil Door

Eclipse

Fool's Gold

The Hare and the Oak

Point By Point

Mistress of Birds

Mysterious Arts

Bound for Perdition

Shoemaker's Wife

Perfect Accord

Facets of the Bench

Weaving Hope

1930S AND 1940S

Land Mysteries

Best Foot Forward

Nocturnal Quarry

Old As The Hills

Upon A Summer's Day

Illusion of a Boar

Three Graces

The Magic of Four

Liminal Mysteries

Grown Wise

OTHER STORIES

Complementary

Winter's Charms

Forged in Combat

Learn more about the world of Albion and future books at my website, celialake.com. Additional information linking characters, places, and timelines is available at my authorial wiki at bit.ly/celia-lake-wiki (or get there from my website under the menu that says "more information").

Sign up for my newsletter to be the first to hear about future books and learn about fascinating bits of research. Happy reading!

www.ingramcontent.com/pod-product-compliance
Lightning Source LLC
Chambersburg PA
CBHW030749030726
47497CB00001B/209